Also by Faye Delacour

THE LUCKY LADIES OF LONDON
The Lady He Lost
A Lady's Guide to London

A Most Worthy Husband

FAYE DELACOUR

sourcebooks
casablanca

Published by Sourcebooks Casablanca, an imprint of Sourcebooks
1935 Brookdale RD, Naperville, IL 60563-2773
(630) 961-3900
sourcebooks.com

Library of Congress Cataloging-in-Publication Data

Names: Delacour, Faye author
Title: A most worthy husband / Faye Delacour.
Description: Naperville, IL : Sourcebooks Casablanca, 2025. | Series: The
lucky ladies of london |
Identifiers: LCCN 2025024447 | trade paperback | epub
Subjects: LCGFT: Romance fiction | Novels | Fiction
Classification: LCC PR9199.4.D4463 M67 2025 | DDC 813/.6--dc23/eng/20250627
LC record available at https://lccn.loc.gov/2025024447

Printed and bound in the United States of America.
SB 10 9 8 7 6 5 4 3 2 1

To Minou,
who kept me company during many 3 a.m.
writing sessions by purring on my lap.

Though you cannot read this, you are the best of all cats.

One

London, 1843

ALTHOUGH NO ONE WOULD BELIEVE HER AT THIS POINT, THE truth was that Hannah Williams hadn't planned to ruin her life when she'd kissed a near-stranger in front of a room full of people that fateful Tuesday evening. On the contrary, it felt to her as though everyone else (more specifically, her mother) had been ruining her life for ages, and her actions were nothing but a necessary form of self-defense. Inevitable, really. If Mama didn't want her to run away in the middle of the evening to seek out compromising situations, she should stop bringing Hannah to terrible places and forcing her to meet terrible men!

The terrible place where they'd begun their evening just a few hours earlier was Mrs. Anwar's town house. It might not seem too bad from a distance—sitting just south of fashionable Berkeley Square and hiding behind a deceptively pristine plaster facade replete with Corinthian columns—but what made it so terrible was the fact that it was filled with *people*. And not the sort of people that one might enjoy spending time with, such as a small group of dear friends. No, this house was filled with strangers! Hundreds of them! Roughly a quarter of whom were eligible young men that Hannah might be expected to dance with.

If Dante had shown the slightest care for accuracy in drafting his *Inferno*, he would have included a crowded ballroom as one of the circles of hell. A step or two above the circle reserved for murderers, but certainly below the ones for such trivial problems as treachery or waste.

"Why is it considered a mark of success to stuff one's home so full that no one can move?" Hannah reflected, blowing away an ostrich plume rooted in a neighboring lady's hair, which had drooped to tickle her nose. "If I had my own house, I should be very glad to invite exactly five people over to see it, and no more."

"I believe they do it to provide us with an excuse to explore the gardens for some air," Hannah's friend, Annabelle Danby, mused aloud.

"Never! You *know* how dangerous gardens are." Set one foot onto the green at the same time a member of the opposite sex was present, and you were liable to find yourself engaged. Hannah's older brother, Eli, had learned that the hard way a few years ago. Though he'd managed to escape the worst of it, Hannah had never forgotten the lesson. Gardens and libraries and secluded nooks were strictly off-limits if she didn't want to find herself trapped.

Which she most certainly didn't. As far as she could tell, marriage only made people grow to detest one another.

"I was only joking," Annabelle replied, a touch defensively.

"Forgive me, but I cannot find any humor in such things. You know my mother would seize on any excuse to marry me off."

It made no difference to Mama who the man was, so long as there was one. In the four years since she'd come out, Hannah's life had been a dizzying carousel of introductions, each more repugnant than the last.

As if on cue, Mrs. Williams materialized from behind the lady with the ostrich feather. "There you are, poppet. I was wondering where you'd got to."

I was hiding from you. If there was one advantage to the size of the crowd—and only one—it was that Hannah had managed to tuck herself out of sight for a full half hour.

"Let me see your dance card. Who has engaged you this evening?" Without waiting for a response, Mama helped herself to a look at the little card secured to Hannah's wrist with a yellow ribbon. Her face fell as she took in the empty space beside each song. "Why, you've made no effort at all! We've *talked* about this."

This was not strictly true. A more accurate description would be to say that Mama had talked—primarily about the fact that Hannah was doomed to die a spinster, as if it were a fatal disease that progressed from untreated shyness—while Hannah let her eyes glaze over and imagined she was someplace else. In fact, that might be a good strategy now. She would try to remember her favorite walking path back home in Devonshire. The one that wound down to the little stream where she used to dip her feet in the summer.

"Fortunately for you," Mama continued, "I've found a lovely young gentleman who would be pleased to ask you for a dance. I know his mother, Mrs. Horvath, and we both agree you would suit. Come along. Let me introduce you."

Hannah tried to shoot a pleading look to Annabelle, but she was already being bodily shuffled away (quite a feat, given the crowded state of the room). Once they had jostled their way past several innocent bystanders, Hannah saw the object of their search, a skinny gentleman of about thirty years with a pinched face and a premature stoop to his shoulders.

"Mama," she whispered. "Stop it. I don't want to dance with Mr. Horvath."

"Then you should have found your own dance partners," Mama hissed back. "You cannot stand idly by and wait for the right man to appear. Every year that passes leaves you with fewer options. It's past time for you to show some initiative."

Though probably true, this was of no real consequence to Hannah. She looked forward to the day that everyone deemed her a hopeless spinster and left her in peace. The precise date of this happy event seemed to be forever shifting, as Mama vowed that each season would be her "last chance" every spring.

Hannah wasn't even sure how there could still be men left in England she hadn't already driven off. She'd never had a talent for making sparkling conversation. Nor was she especially pretty. She had an ordinary sort of face, with a nose that was a touch too pointed and plain brown hair that never held a curl for more than a minute before flopping limply on her too-long neck. With raw materials like these, it should have been easy to escape matrimony!

But though she spent most of these evenings hiding behind the nearest potted plant, Mama always managed to dredge up *someone*.

The three-thousand-pound dowry attached to Hannah's name probably had something to do with it. While not a vast fortune, it was enough to tempt the sad, faded bachelors who turned up at her morning calls.

I'm being sold off at a very depressing auction.

"Mr. Horvath, may I present my daughter, Miss Hannah Williams?" Mama said on cue. "She was just telling me how much she loved the grand march earlier."

A blatant lie. Hannah would never tempt fate by saying anything complimentary about the dancing at a ball.

"How do you do?" Mr. Horvath bowed deeply, wobbling a bit

on his way down. He smelled strongly of brandy. There was a very real possibility that Mama had gotten him drunk in order to secure his consent to this meeting. Her mood was more desperate this season than it had ever been before. It made Hannah uneasy. "Are you engaged for the next dance? It would be my"—he broke off to hiccup into his hand—"my pleasure."

"She is not," Mama answered for her, tugging Hannah's dance card off of her wrist and thrusting it at Mr. Horvath.

Should I argue? Hannah didn't like to make a spectacle of herself, but she'd had no choice but to overcome her reserve these past few seasons. She'd pretended to be a political radical when Mr. Brown came to call last month; then told Mr. Bailey that she'd taken a vow of chastity; and finally spilled her tea in Mr. Moore's lap. Her efforts had yielded resounding success: not one repeat caller in the lot!

But Mr. Horvath hadn't actually *done* anything to her yet, except smell of brandy, and Mama would hound her all night if she didn't dance a few sets. Perhaps it would be easier to get it over with and make an excuse to leave after.

Hannah allowed Mr. Horvath to lead her to the floor, executed the requisite curtsy, and linked her hand in his. It was a waltz, which meant they would have to talk the whole time. *Drat.* Of course Hannah wasn't lucky enough to get herself a country dance where they could change places too frequently for a real conversation.

"What part of the country are you from?" Mr. Horvath opened. A safe move, if uninspired.

"Devonshire," Hannah replied. *Where I would much rather be at present.* Not that she'd had any choice in the matter, with the way Mama had rushed her off without a moment's notice three weeks ago. "We're in town for the season to visit my brother and his wife. They've just had a baby."

"That's nice." Mr. Horvath looked bored. His eyes kept darting around the room to watch the other dancers. "Your parents must be thrilled to meet him."

"Her," Hannah corrected, though she didn't think Mr. Horvath was listening. Mama was thrilled to meet baby Gloria, at any rate. Papa must be thrilled too, even if he hadn't come along.

Hannah didn't want to correct Mr. Horvath's assumption that both her parents were in town. There was no reason to. After all, what business was it of his whether her parents travelled separately? It was perfectly normal for Papa to remain at home. He'd never liked London.

Although the row they'd had just before Mama had packed Hannah up and carried her off like an overburdened trunk hadn't felt quite as normal as the others. There had been an awful lot of "You've never understood me"s and "Oh, stop your wailing"s, which Hannah had tried not to hear from the safety of her bedroom with a pillow folded over her ears.

And then there was the fact that Mama kept changing the subject every time Hannah asked when they were going back home.

Never mind. Mr. Horvath certainly didn't need to know about any of that.

The conversation had lapsed into an awkward silence while Hannah had been ruminating on her worries, and she saw no reason to try to rescue it. Better not to give this man any false encouragement. Besides which, he'd already stumbled twice and would probably do better to concentrate on his steps. But Mr. Horvath seemed to feel the need to fill the silence with more noise, and stammered, "I b-believe I saw you speaking with Miss Annabelle Danby earlier?"

"Yes."

He brightened at this, finally focusing his gaze on Hannah instead of watching the other couples. "I say, do you know her sister, the elder Miss Danby? Such a stunning young woman."

"I do," Hannah replied slowly, wondering where this was leading.

"I don't suppose you might introduce us? I've been trying to manage it since last season, but it seems we're never at the same events. I would be so grateful."

"Are you…asking me to introduce you to another woman *while* we're still dancing?"

Hannah knew that her looks were underwhelming—and Della was, as Mr. Horvath had so eloquently put it, stunning—but this was really a bit much. Even if she had no interest in Mr. Horvath, if he was going to trap her in a dance, he might at least take the trouble to be polite.

"And why not?" Mr. Horvath grew indignant at the criticism in her tone. "We're all friends, aren't we?"

Praise heaven, the song was ending. Hannah gave a rushed curtsy, murmured, "Thank you for the dance, Mr. Horvath," and hurried from the floor before he could rise from his bow.

She'd been foolish to think she could flee so easily. Mama found her before she could even make it to the door. "Where are you going in such a rush? How did you like Mr. Horvath?"

"I didn't." Hannah saw no need to sugarcoat her words, though she kept her voice low. "Mama you *have* to stop foisting these men on me. None of them want to be with me. They only agree because you coax them into it, or because they hope to get at my dowry."

It wasn't the first time she'd tried to explain her objections, but Mama seemed determined not to hear her. Only last week, Hannah had been so incensed after Mr. Bailey's visit that she'd threatened to join a convent, but her mother had wryly observed that they "weren't Catholic" and that Hannah "wouldn't last a week." She hadn't even shed a tear at the prospect of losing her only daughter! It was very vexing, the way no one ever took her seriously.

"*Shhh.*" Mama's deep-set brown eyes widened in shock. "Don't say such a thing."

"It's true."

"Only because you won't make any effort! Of course I have to coax a little, when you hardly speak two words to anyone. If I didn't help you along, you'd never leave your room."

How unfair! She made Hannah sound like a recluse, when the truth was that there were plenty of things she might like to do if only Mama would allow it. "I would go to Bishop's if you let me," Hannah retorted.

"Absolutely not. It will ruin your reputation. No one will want to marry you if you're seen in a house of ruin."

This sounded like a winning prospect to Hannah. "If Jane can go to a gambling club, why can't I?"

"Because Jane is married, and your brother doesn't object." This subject was quickly making Mama lose her patience, if her tone was any indication. "Once you are married, you may do as your husband likes, but as long as you live under my roof, you will follow my rules. And I insist that you make an effort to be polite this evening and encourage a gentleman to dance. One to whom you give an honest chance before you dismiss him."

"But we don't live under your roof." The words were out before Hannah could stop them, though her face grew hot with embarrassment. She was tired of being put off. "When are we going home? Why didn't Papa come with us?"

Mama was so shocked by this that her mouth moved silently for several seconds. She suddenly looked her age, her brown hair shot with streaks of ashy gray and her eyes shadowed by dark circles.

"Never mind that," she finally snapped, looking around to make sure no one was listening to them. "Your place is to find your *own* home, as a wife and mother. Before you run out of time. London is the best place for you to meet someone."

"I want an answer," Hannah whispered. "Are you and Papa going to live apart forever? If I get married, would you go back home?"

Hannah wasn't prepared to make such a sacrifice, but she needed to know where they stood.

"Plenty of couples spend time apart, particularly once their children are grown." Mama's voice was carefully light, as though they were discussing a spot of rain and not the disintegration of her marriage. "And I expect that you might need my help to learn how to manage the household and raise your own children once they come along, if Eli and Jane don't need me here by then. Your grandmother Williams lived with us while she was still alive, and I was very grateful for her when you were small. You will be grateful for my help too, once you realize how much work it is."

So this was it. Mama really wasn't going back. Hannah had thought it would feel better to finally have some honesty between them, but it didn't. It felt much worse.

She knew her parents had their share of troubles, but so did most married couples. They were supposed to bear it privately, like normal people, not run away! What would everyone think when they learned of it? What was she supposed to tell her friends?

Hannah wanted to scream and cry and shatter a crystal glass on the floor, as if a tantrum might change Mama's mind. But she wasn't a child anymore. She had to act like a lady and pretend everything was fine.

Interpreting her silence as grudging acceptance, Mama kept on speaking. "Now, let's not have any more complaints. I'm going to the powder room for a minute, and when I get back, I expect to see you dancing with a gentleman. If you don't like the ones I've found, then pick one who pleases you better. If you would only smile and say a few kind words, I know any man here would be lucky to have you, poppet. All I want is to see you taken care of." Mama offered her a reassuring smile and left the room, giving Hannah a few blissful minutes alone with her thoughts.

She was absolutely *not* going to use this time to find a dance partner. If she'd been opposed to marriage before, it was unthinkable now that she knew Mama was planning to live with her as soon as she married to avoid going home. Hannah wasn't going to help her break their family into pieces.

She can't force me to marry. After all, Hannah had successfully avoided a marriage proposal for four seasons, and she was nearly halfway through her fifth. She was more than capable of escaping her suitors. The real problem was that Mama kept finding more of them. And London had a seemingly infinite supply.

What I really need to do is make myself so unmarriageable she'll have to give up.

The moment the thought popped into her head, Hannah recognized it for genius. How often had Mama scolded her for some faux pas or another that might spoil her for a match? Why, this was her chance! All she needed to do was slip away before Mama got back from the powder room and do something so shocking that it would ruin her chances for good.

If Mama saw that she couldn't use Hannah to hide from her own marriage, she would have to talk to Papa again and patch things up. After all, it had been *her* decision to run off to London, not his. Papa would take her back if Hannah could only get them talking again. He had to.

Then they could all go back to normal.

Hannah began to walk as if in a trance, letting her feet carry her away before she even knew her destination.

What can I do? Not the gardens. As scandalous as it might be to let herself be caught with some man, she would have to marry him, defeating the whole purpose of her plan. She might pretend to get drunk on too much punch or knock over some decoration and make a scene, but she wasn't sure that would be important enough to ruin her prospects. This had to be something big. Something no one could hesitate to cut her for.

Oh! But Mrs. Anwar's town house wasn't far from Jane's gambling club, was it? They'd dropped Eli off for the evening on the way here, and it had been only five or ten minutes by carriage. She could walk there!

Hadn't Mama always said that Hannah's reputation would be ruined if she set foot in the place? Perhaps it was time to put that to the test.

Heart racing, Hannah hurried her step toward the front door. She kept expecting someone to grab her by the wrist and shout, "Stop! Escaped daughter!" but no one even noticed her. There were unexpected benefits to being so forgettable.

When Hannah stepped out into the night air, a giddy peal of laughter bubbled up in her throat.

I've done it! She wanted to scream with glee. *I'm free.*

She could do anything she liked, at least until her mother caught up to her. At a ball the size of Mrs. Anwar's, it would take ages to realize that Hannah was actually missing, rather than hiding in a corner as she usually did.

This was her chance to seize control of her future. To ruin her marriage prospects forever and to fix her family. As long as she screwed her courage to the sticking place, no one could stop her.

"I'm sure Miss Danby will be here any minute," Eli Williams said with an apologetic smile.

"It's fine," Silas assured his friend. He was in no position to complain about tardiness. When he'd arrived in London a few days before, he'd had little more than the clothes on his back and a promissory note in his pocket—a remnant of the prize money he'd earned on the HMS *Echo* before his inglorious discharge.

That money was all he had left of a once-promising naval career. When it ran out, there would be nothing to follow. If Williams hadn't offered to set him up with work, he didn't know what he would have done.

All this explained how Silas found himself sitting in the least likely place he could have imagined: a fashionable little building on Piccadilly that proclaimed to offer the well-heeled ladies of London a place to gamble away their pin money. The cluttered office stood empty, save for him and Williams. They'd been supposed to meet the co-owner of the place, Miss Danby, at eight o'clock, but it seemed she couldn't be bothered to turn up when she'd promised.

Silas realized that he was bouncing his knee in his seat and focused on holding it still.

I should leave. This whole thing was a bad idea. He was bound to say the wrong thing or forget to bow deeply enough or some other damn nonsense the gentry all cared about so much, and then he would be turned away.

But if he left now, where would he go?

There was no place for him in the family business. His father had been more than clear about that. The only thing Silas knew was the navy, and they didn't want him anymore.

Rapid footsteps sounded in the hall outside before the door burst open to reveal a plump, pretty woman with medium brown hair and a round face. She stopped midstride when she spotted them, obviously surprised to find the room occupied.

Williams rose to his feet and Silas hurried to copy his example. His heart was already racing. It was always like this when he found himself under scrutiny. His brain seemed to freeze up and his tongue turned to lead. He hated being studied and ranked like an errant schoolboy. No matter what he did or said, they could always see right through him to spot the flaws beneath. It brought back too many memories.

"Miss Danby, may I present Mr. Silas Corbyn?" Williams said.

Silas bowed, trying not to rush through the motion despite the nervous energy that coursed through him. He wasn't sure what he'd been expecting, but Miss Danby wasn't it. He'd met the other co-owner, Williams's wife, when he called at their town house a few days prior. Though Mrs. Williams was young, she had a face that brooked no nonsense. He could easily picture her running a business, even if a gaming hell wasn't an ordinary choice for a wellborn lady. She'd seemed the sort of woman who had no trouble taking charge.

Miss Danby, in contrast, looked to be disorder personified. She was flushed as if she'd hurried in, her hat was askew, and she was carrying a notebook in her arms that looked ready to burst from all the scraps of paper tucked inside. When she dipped into a little curtsy to acknowledge their introduction, a note fluttered out and fell to the floor. She didn't seem to have noticed.

"I'm so sorry. Am I late?" she asked Williams as she rose. "I was held up meeting with some musicians to play here like we talked about. They're coming tonight, so we need to decide where we should put them." She finally turned to study Silas in earnest, running an appraising eye over his person. She didn't seem impressed by what she saw. But then, why should she be? He wasn't very impressive, with his hair that he hadn't had time to take to the barber since his return to England and a suit that was an ill-fitting hand-me-down from his father. It was obvious that he wasn't a member of her own class. Though the navy had been meant to transform him into a gentleman, he'd failed to last long enough to get the job done. He felt like a half-baked pie. "A pleasure to make your acquaintance, Mr. Corbyn. Please have a seat."

Silas moved to obey, placing his hands on his lap and making a conscious effort not to fidget. He would rather have been back at sea and in the midst of a heated battle than dealing with this. Trying to prove himself to some rich woman he didn't know so that he could work in a club that didn't interest him. The building looked like the setting for an afternoon tea party, from the damask wallpaper to the lace embellishments on the tablecloths he'd spotted on the way in.

He'd had real prospects, once. A respectable career that he was actually good at. Never mind that he'd never quite learned to hold his bloody tongue when he should; his superiors had been forced to respect his skill and quick instincts. How was he supposed to lower himself to working as a dealer for a bunch of pampered ladies with so much money they needed to create excuses to throw it away?

You can't go back, he reminded himself. *The navy is done. Stop thinking about it.*

"Shall we begin with you telling me how your naval service ended, exactly?" Miss Danby asked. "I don't wish to pry, but I need to know if you pose any risk to our reputation."

Hell. Not off to a good start, were they?

Williams shot him a warning look and answered for him. "He doesn't. It was all a misunderstanding. I can vouch for him."

He should be happy that his friend was trying to protect him, but it only made Silas feel small. He shouldn't *need* protecting. He'd done the right thing, no matter what anyone thought, yet he was supposed to sit here obediently and bite his tongue while everyone assumed the worst.

Miss Danby was staring at the little scar that curved over his chin, no doubt wondering if he'd gotten it from fighting. She clearly expected him to say something, but there was nothing he could say that would make her understand why a passed midshipman in line for promotion had sabotaged his career by attacking his commanding officer.

Why should it matter to her, anyway? She'd known his story before she agreed to meet with him. Surely there was no need to rehash it.

Silas raised an eyebrow in challenge. "You're a gaming hell. I wouldn't think you'd need to worry too much about a scandal."

Now they were both glaring at him. Well, it was true, wasn't it? Why should a gambling club need their dealers to be altar boys?

Williams jumped in to save him once more. "What Mr. Corbyn *means* to say is that he had a dispute with his commanding officer, but it wasn't due to any fault of his."

Williams had always been too noble.

"What sort of dispute?"

Silas couldn't take it anymore. Were they going to spend all day dancing around the truth to avoid upsetting Miss Danby? She obviously wasn't going to let the subject drop. Better to just get it over with.

"I broke his nose," he said flatly. "But he deserved it."

The room went dead silent except for the ticking of a mantel clock. Someone had obviously forgotten to wind it recently, for it was counting off the seconds at a far slower pace than usual. Or maybe that was only Silas's imagination.

Miss Danby had grown pale. She cleared her throat delicately, her voice coming out rushed and nervous when she spoke again. "Er... Where is your family from?"

Of course.

In her haste to escape the worst subject of conversation they could have chosen, Miss Danby had stumbled upon the second-worst one. Silas could almost have laughed. This meeting was going so badly that it seemed like fate.

"Don't have any family." Maybe that would put a stop to this line of questioning.

"Oh. You're an orphan? I'm so sorry."

"Not an orphan," Silas corrected. "Just no bloody family worth speaking of."

Beside him, his friend buried his face in his hands.

Miss Danby, seeing that she was quite alone now, made a valiant effort to keep up appearances. "Do you, er, have much experience at card play?"

If they'd started with this question, Silas might have had a hope of saying the right thing. After all, he knew all the rules to any games they might offer here and he was good with numbers. Those were the only skills he would need, weren't they? But it was far too late now. It had been too late from the moment she asked about his discharge.

"When we can manage to get a few minutes of rest from our duties, we often play cards at sea," Silas explained. "I'm sure I can handle this."

As he'd expected, this reassurance did nothing to salvage the conversation that was burning down around their ears.

Miss Danby gave a tight smile, speaking through clenched teeth. "Eli, might I have a private word?"

Time to put me out of my misery.

Silas rose to his feet and left them both with a curt nod. He shut the door behind him to silence their frantic whispering. He didn't blame Miss Danby for turning him out, but that didn't mean he wanted to overhear her reasons.

He would owe Williams an apology. After the man put in a good word for him, he'd gone and thrown it away. *Typical.* But what else could Silas have done? It was Williams's own damn fault for telling them about his discharge from the navy. He shouldn't have spread the tale if he didn't want them asking questions about it. And once they asked questions, what else could Silas say?

He'd punched his captain and he didn't regret it. The man was a bloody monster. The only thing Silas regretted was what the decision had cost him.

The door to the office opened again and Williams slipped out, shutting it behind him.

"What *happened* back there?" he hissed.

"I told you I wasn't good at small talk."

"You practically terrorized Miss Danby! Were you *trying* to muck it up?"

"Of course not."

Or maybe I was. Silas didn't know what he was doing anymore.

"She wouldn't stop asking about my discharge," he explained. "What was I supposed to say?"

"Anything but *that*." Williams passed a hand over his brow, looking tired. "Luckily for you, Miss Danby is exceptionally forgiving. She's agreed to give you a chance, but you have to promise not to act that way in front of the ladies, understand?"

Silas was too stunned to reply. He'd thought he was done. More than thought it—he'd *known* it without any doubt. Why should they want to give him a second chance?

Even his own family hadn't given him that.

"No cursing." Williams was still talking. "You aren't at sea anymore. Be polite and don't make any sharp remarks. Don't mention your service or your family or anything else that makes you angry. And most of all, smile more."

"Smile?" Silas echoed. He couldn't be serious.

"Yes. It puts people at ease. You scowl all the time and it isn't helping you."

Silas heaved an enormous sigh and forced his lips to turn upward. It felt like his face was wincing.

Williams recoiled. "That's *worse*," he said. "How is that worse?"

"So no smiling, then?"

"Let's just get you over to your table and I'll show you the ropes. I can't stay long, though. My mother is visiting and she's been suffering headaches lately. I promised to stop by the apothecary for her."

"I'm sorry," Silas replied automatically. "I hope it's nothing serious."

"No, no," Eli reassured him. "I think she's just overwrought. Things have been a bit difficult with my sister lately. But never mind that. I've put you at the vingt-et-un table just this way. You remember the rules, don't you? Tuesday nights usually aren't too busy, so you should have an easy start."

Silas trailed after his friend somewhat reluctantly. It still felt as though there must be some mistake, but the full implications of his turn of fortune were starting to sink in. He'd found work. He would be able to pay rent at the extremely dodgy boardinghouse where he'd taken rooms. (He was fairly sure the other occupants were lightskirts and thieves, but a bed was a bed.) Most importantly, he would have something to keep him occupied. To keep his thoughts fixed safely on wagers and sums instead of reliving every moment that had passed since the decision that had cost him his future. Something to keep him from thinking about what his life would be like if he hadn't set it all ablaze.

Shit. This means I'm going to have to talk to a bunch of highborn ladies all night.

Maybe he would have been better off if Miss Danby hadn't forgiven him.

Hannah arrived at Bishop's still riding high on her own triumph.

Though she'd been a little nervous walking alone at night, she'd made it here in one piece. All that remained was to go inside, soak up a healthy dose of scandal from the surrounding games of chance, and exit a ruined woman, safe from matchmaking forever.

Unfortunately, her name wasn't on the list.

"There's a list?" she complained to the doorman, exasperated. She'd walked all the way from Berkeley Square for this! In her dancing slippers! She couldn't turn back now.

"The club membership runs on subscription," the doorman explained.

Of course it did. This was just Hannah's luck. She would never get another chance like this, now that Mama would be on her guard. She had to find a way to talk herself through that door before her opportunity slipped away.

"Geórgios, you *know* me," she pleaded. "I'm family."

The doorman was an old friend of Eli's and had been given his present employment on the strength of their connection. Surely that should count for something?

Hannah put on her most pleading face. She was not above begging, if it came to that.

Geórgios rolled his enormous shoulders in a helpless shrug. "I'll ask Miss Danby."

Oh dear. Her plan had been to slip in unnoticed. What would she do if Della sent her packing?

But no, she was overreacting. Della had been nothing but friendly to her since she'd arrived in town. To be honest, she and Annabelle were the closest friends Hannah had now that Mama had dragged her away from everyone she knew. The only reason that Della hadn't already acquiesced to Hannah's (numerous) requests to attend Bishop's was because Jane had said no. And the only reason *Jane* had said no was because Mama forbid it, so there you go.

All I have to do is tell her they agreed.

She didn't like to lie, but what choice did she have? It would be just like her flight from Mrs. Anwar's rout—it looked impossible at first, but it was nothing once she actually mustered the courage to do it. Nothing at all.

Hannah wiped her sweating palms on her skirts as she waited for Geórgios to fetch his mistress. She was already facing the punishment of her life once she was caught. In for a penny, in for a pound.

Geórgios returned with Della a moment later. Before the other woman could say a word, Hannah blurted out, "Jane and Eli said that I could come and help you tonight so you wouldn't be all alone."

The fib must have been convincing, for Della immediately swept her into a hug.

"That's wonderful. You have no idea how happy I am to see you. I'm so glad Jane changed her mind!"

It was almost too easy. Hannah didn't care for the nagging feeling in the pit of her stomach, but it was too late for misgivings.

"Er, yes. Me too." It would be worth a little fib if she could make Mama give up her plans of matchmaking and take them back home. Just a few rounds of cards, a minor scandal, and this would all be over with. They might be packing their trunks by morning.

"Forgive me." Della seemed to realize that her embrace was too tight and released Hannah. She'd always been a tad excitable. "I'm just so glad you're here."

"What can I do?" While the offer to help had made a convenient excuse for her presence here, Hannah was happy to follow through with it. She wanted to see how everything worked! And besides, if setting foot inside the club was enough to make her unmarriageable, how much better would it be to take an active role in running the place? She wouldn't mind using her impending spinsterhood for something useful.

But Della exposed the flaw in her plans almost immediately. "Have you ever been in charge of instructing your housekeeper or your butler about the service of drinks and meals at home?"

"Mama handles all of that," Hannah was forced to admit. *Oh no.* Della was already frowning. She could practically see her chance slipping away from her. "B-But I could learn!"

Della mulled this over for a minute before she nodded.

"Keep an eye on how much the ladies are drinking and whether anyone appears to have overindulged, or whether anyone is hungry and hasn't been offered enough food. Check in on our cook and the wine cellar every so often to make sure we aren't running low on anything, and send our errand boy over to the greengrocer's if we need it. Oh! And your brother hired a new dealer, Mr. Cooper? No, Corbyn! That was it. He's a bit rough around the edges. Could you keep an eye out that he doesn't offend any of our members and fetch me straightaway if there's a problem? He's the tall, blond one with a scar on his chin. You can't miss him."

She was speaking so quickly that Hannah wasn't sure she'd understood half of this, but one part certainly made an impression.

Mr. Corbyn. I know him. That was the friend of Eli's who'd come by the house the other day. The extremely handsome one. She'd fled from the room to avoid giving Mama any ideas, but not before she'd had a good look.

Hannah wasn't sure she could face him again. Much as she hated talking to the thoroughly unattractive gentlemen that were trotted out for her, the attractive ones were far worse. Her tongue turned to pudding in her mouth. Only nonsense fell out, if words came to her at all.

It was all well and good for scaring suitors off, but it was also humiliating.

"Right." Hannah had to say something. "You can count on me."

Then she was inside and Della was gone.

It was dark in the club at this hour of the night, despite the gaslights that threw gold reflections onto everyone. The walls were decorated with various objects that caught the light: a large mirror here, a mounted clock there. Hannah recognized a painting that she'd gifted Della when she'd first arrived in London—a pretty landscape at sunset. It gave her a flush of pleasure to think that she'd already contributed something to the place.

She peered around as she inched her way forward, trying to take everything in. A quartet in the corner played a lively tune that was partly lost amid the bubbling of women's voices. There were more of them than she'd expected. Were *all* of these ladies ruined? When did the ruining start?

Maybe she needed to make her involvement known. It wouldn't serve much purpose to come all the way here if no one noticed her.

An extremely well-dressed lady glided by and Hannah squeaked out, "Excuse me," but her words were too quiet to reach the woman's ear. She was already gone, off to play at one of the tables with her friends.

If Hannah was going to have any hope of ruining herself, she would have to be more forceful.

She cleared her throat and tried again, selecting a patron at random.

"Excuse me." This time the words sounded more confident. "My name is Hannah Williams and I'm helping to manage the gambling club this evening. That's *Miss* Hannah Williams, by the way. I don't have a husband, but that didn't stop me from coming here. Is there, er, anything you need? Would you like something to eat?"

There! She'd done it. Exactly one other person knew that she'd immersed herself in a den of depravity, as Mama sometimes termed it. And this lady was only the first among many.

It turned out that the woman didn't need anything, but she lingered a moment to introduce herself before she went about her way. The ease of the exchange gave Hannah the courage to try again with other guests, and soon she'd amassed a dozen witnesses to her downfall. The only problem was that none of them reacted with anything more than a polite smile (and one request for a cucumber sandwich).

Cucumber sandwiches did *not* fit neatly into Hannah's idea of a life of ruin.

Why doesn't anyone seem scandalized by me?

She was young and unmarried, two qualities that Mama had assured her would mark her instantly as an interloper. But after a half hour spent circling the room, Hannah was beginning to suspect something was wrong.

There were plenty of unmarried ladies here. Why, the welldressed one who'd passed her earlier was none other than Lady Eleanor Grosvenor, daughter of the Marquess of Westminster. How could she be in attendance, if the place was so dangerous? Surely a marquess wouldn't let his own daughter be ruined!

But if she's not ruined, then how can I be?

Hannah's stomach sank so deep that it landed somewhere about her feet. So, this was *another* lie that Mama had fed her. The ladies who frequented Bishop's were no more a threat to her reputation than her own sister-in-law, and coming here wouldn't make one jot of difference to the future that had been planned out for her. It had all been for nothing!

Hannah could have screamed. She felt as if a steam locomotive were bearing down on her and all she could do was wait on the tracks. What was she supposed to do now?

She might try another location. Something that would be certain to condemn her to the ranks of hopelessly ruined women. A brothel, perhaps. Or a public house.

But it stood to reason that she might need to walk more than ten minutes to get there, and through a far more dangerous neighborhood. Hannah wasn't quite ready to risk her life to sabotage her mother. Not yet, at least.

Maybe I can still find a way to ruin myself right here at Bishop's.

What if she tried wagering a large sum? That might do more to shock people than fetching sandwiches.

Hannah scanned the room, trying to decide which of the tables looked the most risqué. She was familiar with the games one saw at house parties, of course, but she wasn't sure she knew the rules to everything on offer tonight. Which table should she choose?

Wait, she realized belatedly, *I don't need to know the rules. The point is to make a spectacle of myself.*

Once this obstacle was dispensed with, she recalled Mr. Corbyn was dealing at the table on the far edge of the room. She *had* promised Della she would keep an eye on him. If she made herself useful, she might feel a bit less guilty about the lie she'd told to get herself in the door.

Hannah observed him from a distance, trying to work up the nerve to go over.

He was ridiculously handsome. He looked just like a drawing of Poseidon she'd once seen in a book, except that the Greek god had been covered only by some strategically placed seafoam and Mr. Corbyn was fully clothed, thank goodness. But the features were the same. Perpetually windswept hair, piercing blue eyes, angled cheekbones, a slightly downturned nose, and an expression of fierce defiance. It was a very compelling face. Hannah had been so moved by the drawing that she'd kept that book hidden under her bed to look at from time to time when no one else was around.

Oh goodness, how embarrassing. Why did I think of that now?

If she kept staring this way, she would waste the rest of the evening. She had more important things to do than be dazzled by this man. Better to just force one foot in front of the other and put herself at his table before she could talk herself out of it.

She was doing this. Ruination was still possible.

Two

SILAS HAD MADE IT THROUGH A DOZEN ROUNDS OF VINGT-ET-UN without serious incident, unless one counted the flirtatious redhead who kept leaning forward to expose half her chest every time she asked him for a card. Miss Berry, she'd said her name was. It was obviously intentional.

Why won't she stop that?

If it had been a woman of lower birth, he would have understood the signal. A roll in the hay might be welcome, possibly for a price. But this woman was several steps above Silas on the social ladder, judging by her expensive silks and the pearl-encrusted pendant that hung from her neck. There was no chance that she planned to invite him back to her home when the night was done.

What was this, then, a sport? He'd attracted that sort of leering curiosity from upper-class ladies on occasion, and it never ended well.

Silas kept his attention on his deal, even to the point of appearing rude. It was better than inviting trouble.

He'd already turned up the second cards when a newcomer

appeared at the corner of his vision, inching forward so hesitantly it took him a minute to notice her.

"This round's just started, miss," he said. "Shall I deal you in on the next hand?"

"Thank you." Her voice was soft and smooth, like honey. Silas glanced up and realized that he'd seen her before.

"You're Eli Williams's sister, aren't you?"

"Oh." The young lady gave a little squeak. "Yes. I'm Miss Hannah Williams. I'm surprised you remember me."

"Of course I do. You're the spitting image of him."

Miss Williams hadn't said two words to Silas at the house before she fled, but it would have been hard not to notice the resemblance between the siblings. They were both tall and lanky, with the same dark-brown hair and eyes. She even had her brother's pointed nose. It wasn't exactly a pretty face on a woman, but she might have been called handsome.

The look she gave him just then could've curdled milk. Too late, Silas realized she might not have appreciated being compared to a gentleman.

"Damn it," he blurted without thinking. "Sorry. Uh...I didn't mean it as an insult. He's, um, very delicate-looking."

An obvious lie. Why was he still talking? Not two hours into his evening and he'd already offended a lady. Not just any lady, but Williams's sister. If Silas lost this job on the first night, he would never forgive himself.

"It's fine. Really." Miss Williams offered him a limp smile. It was obviously not fine.

"Can we return to the bidding, please?" Miss Berry interrupted, flashing a smile at Miss Williams that looked to be mostly canines. "I'll stand."

"I'm sorry," the young lady said, appearing to shrink into herself beneath the other woman's scorn. "I didn't mean to intrude."

"Nothing to apologize for," Silas assured her, before turning back to the players to take their bids. Miss Berry looked put out by his words, but he wasn't going to let her bully Miss Williams, who hadn't done anything wrong. If anything, it was his fault for making chit-chat. Weren't the help supposed to be invisible? And he was help now, not anyone who mattered to these people.

Best remember it.

Miss Berry lost her hand with a pout, and Silas added Miss Williams to the deal on the next round.

When the bid reached her, she announced in a breathless voice, "I'll raise *two hundred* pounds," immediately glancing to either side to see how her bid was received.

What the hell is she doing?

Did Miss Williams have something wrong with her? She hadn't struck him as a risk-taking sort, based on how she'd shrunk from Miss Berry's annoyance a moment ago.

"Sorry, miss," Silas replied. "We don't allow bids over ten on a single hand."

"Pardon?"

"Ten pounds is the most we allow," he repeated. Williams had been very clear about that. "Don't want anyone ruining their fortunes."

"But this is supposed to be a gaming hell!" She sounded indignant. "How is it gambling if you won't even let us decide what to wager?"

"Would you like to take it up with the owners?" Silas raised an eyebrow. He had no idea what Miss Williams was playing at, but he wasn't going to get caught in the middle. Let her quarrel with her own family if she took issue with the rules.

"No." Miss Williams seemed to deflate a little. After an awkward moment, she added, "Forgive me. I wasn't very polite with you just now. I spoke without thinking."

This surprised Silas nearly as much as the young lady's attempt to wager two hundred pounds had done. Why should anyone care if they were polite to *him*? In his experience, members of the upper classes rarely spared a thought for their inferiors.

"No harm done," he assured her. "I speak without thinking all the time."

Miss Williams laughed, and Silas liked her a little better. She might be reckless with her money, but at least she was kind. Out of all the women who'd passed his table this evening, she might be the only one to treat him like a person instead of an interesting decoration.

"Might we please keep the game moving?" Miss Berry didn't mask her annoyance with a smile this time.

Miss Williams squared her shoulders. "Very well then. I'll raise the stakes to ten pounds."

A number of the other ladies folded rather than matching such a sum. When the cards were all revealed, Miss Williams had conquered the others with a hand of nineteen.

"Congratulations, miss."

Miss Williams gave a muffled grunt of frustration. When Silas pushed the chips toward her, she looked absolutely furious. *Thinking of how much larger her win might have been if I hadn't refused her bid, no doubt.*

What must it be like to have so much money that you could afford to throw it away on a whim? Ten pounds would be the better part of a year's wages to his family, but for Miss Williams it was nothing but the sport of one evening.

They played another hand, and again Miss Williams bid the limit. Some of the other women grumbled as they bowed out, no doubt wondering how long this would go on. When Miss Williams won again with a hand of seventeen, two of them left the table in favor of other games.

"How does no one have a better hand?" she asked. "Seventeen isn't even that good!"

Miss Berry, who doggedly held her seat despite the recent loss of twenty pounds, spoke through clenched teeth. "There's no need to brag."

Is she bragging? Silas wasn't so sure. She seemed genuinely outraged by her victories, though he couldn't for the life of him understand why.

"Are you planning to bid the limit for all the hands, miss?" He posed the question as delicately as he could, remembering her brother's warning to be polite. If this kept up, she was going to drive his whole table away. Although Williams had told him that the club saw some high play among their wealthiest set, the women before him didn't seem to appreciate it. He would have liked to tell the chit to stop flaunting her money, but the memory of her earlier kindness made him hold fast to the remainder of his patience. "You might want to stop while you're ahead."

"Never mind." Miss Williams rose from her seat in a huff. "This is pointless. I must be cursed."

With that, she turned and walked away.

"Wait! You forgot your chips," Silas called after her. Between everyone she'd beaten, there was sixty pounds' worth on the table.

"Keep them." She barely slowed her stride. "They're no good to me."

What on earth is wrong with that woman?

What on earth is wrong with me?

It shouldn't have been hard to lose money. People did it all the time! That was precisely why gambling clubs weren't an acceptable place for a lady to pass the evening. If Hannah could only get herself in debt, she might diminish the only thing that was helping Mama attract suitors: her dowry. But it seemed that the fates wouldn't allow her a single victory tonight.

Hannah stomped to the kitchens, where she checked that Cook had everything in hand before helping herself to a sandwich and a glass of champagne. Mama never let her drink champagne at parties, but Mama wasn't here.

It was very fizzy. Hannah didn't like the way it tickled her nose, but she downed the glass with a little cough.

This was supposed to be the evening of her triumph! Nothing was working as it should. She needed to think of something quick, before Mama came to find her. By now, she must have realized that Hannah had given her the slip. With any luck, she would check Eli and Jane's town house before she thought to come here, and the trip back and forth across Mayfair would buy Hannah some time.

I can still manage to do something horrible. Should she start a fight, perhaps? She didn't like the idea of hurting anyone, but what if she just shouted a few insults? That might be enough.

Hannah brought a second champagne flute with her as she went back out to the main gaming rooms.

For courage.

There were only about seventy or eighty women in the club this evening, at a rough guess. Not enough to pack the rooms. But that might work to her advantage. If she made a big enough spectacle, it couldn't be lost in the din.

Her best bet was to harangue someone of some influence, who would be capable of starting an effective gossip campaign against her. Oh! Lady Eleanor would be a perfect target. But what was Hannah to say?

Your dress is unflattering. Your face is ugly and I don't like you. I heard that your mother was a dairy maid.

Everything she could think of was so *cruel*. What if she made Lady Eleanor cry? Hannah wouldn't want anyone to suffer just because she needed to cause a scandal.

"How are you doing?" Della was suddenly in front of her, cutting off her view of lady Eleanor's table. Her gaze fell upon Hannah's champagne flute. "Have you been drinking?"

"Only a little! I got so hot when I was in the kitchens checking on Cook."

Hannah braced herself for a lecture, as Mama would have given, but Della proved to be a more permissive companion. "It's all right. I saw you at Mr. Corbyn's table earlier. How is he with the guests?"

Oh goodness. Had Della noticed how much she'd stared at him?

"I see what you mean when you said he was rough," Hannah finally replied. "He swears like a sailor."

That was an exaggeration, but he *had* cursed when he'd apologized for comparing her to Eli. It wasn't often that anyone used foul language in her hearing.

"Were the ladies very offended?"

"Not really. I think that redhead has taken a fancy to him. The one in the green gown." Hannah flushed just thinking about it. The woman flirted so shamelessly. What would it be like to have that sort of confidence?

"Miss Berry," Della said, after a glance to Mr. Corbyn's table. "She'd best stay well enough away before she ruins her prospects."

"Why? He's very low-class, then?" She'd presumed as much from the fact that he was working as a dealer, but he'd seemed gentleman-like enough aside from the slight problem of his language.

"Not only that. He was dishonorably discharged for fighting with his superior. Your brother could probably tell you more about it than I could, but I certainly wouldn't be caught flirting with a man like that where everyone could see me."

I should have flirted with him! Hannah realized with a start.

Why on earth hadn't she thought of it sooner? It would have been perfect. But it was too late to go back, after the way she'd stormed off.

The truth was, Hannah could never have dared to flirt with someone like Mr. Corbyn. He was so handsome that half the ladies at his table were vying to catch his eye. Just look at that mouth. Though it was set in a severe line, his lips were too full to be anything but kissable, no matter how stern an expression he might wear. And that hair! It fell in golden waves that looked perpetually tousled. How did he do it? The most talented lady's maid in the world couldn't have produced such a masterpiece.

Hannah realized she was staring again, despite the fact that Della had probably been waiting for her to say something for a solid minute.

"Um...by the way, how is your book coming?" Hannah asked, fumbling for some topic of conversation to hide her obvious fixation on Mr. Corbyn. "Is the viscount being kind to you?"

The last time they'd seen one another, Della had told her about her plans to write a lady's guidebook to the sights of London. The Viscount Ashton was collaborating on the project with her, as he'd already written a similar book meant for gentlemen.

"*Very* kind," Della said in a telling voice. She even added a wink on the end, lest there be any confusion as to her meaning.

What?

Hannah's blood ran cold. She couldn't have heard right, wink or no. "What do you mean by that?"

She can't be involved with the man, can she?

Just the other day, Hannah had overheard Jane and Eli discussing their concerns that Della seemed overly attached to her new mentor. She'd presumed it was just Jane worrying too easily, but now the conversation took on a new significance.

Della's eyes grew wide, offering visible proof of her guilt. "Nothing. I only meant—"

"Are you and he...? But he's *married*, isn't he?"

"No. *No.* You don't understand. There's nothing between us. It's just a harmless flirtation."

A harmless flirtation? With a married man? How could Della say such a thing? She was just as bad as Mama, throwing away her marriage vows and driving a family apart to follow her own wishes.

"And he's been separated from his wife for years," Della continued, unaware that her every word was making things that much worse, "and she plans to divorce him before Parliament, so she wouldn't be hurt by it even if there were any connection between us, which there *isn't.*"

A divorce!

How could she bring herself to say that word without any shame? They were English, not French! People here weren't supposed to trade in their spouses the moment they grew bored.

Will Mama and Papa be next?

Hannah could just imagine it. All the ugly things they would say about each other in front of the whole world. Everybody looking on in scorn and pity. There would truly be no going back once they crossed that bridge.

"Not be hurt by it?" Hannah repeated, the words like angry bees stinging her tongue. "Not be *hurt* by it? You're carrying on with a *married man*, and you don't see anything wrong with that?"

It was so heartless! What if the Viscount Ashton and his wife could have reconciled and been a happy family again? Della was transforming their lapse in judgment into a permanent breach, and she didn't even see how horrid it was.

"Shhh. What are you saying? Hannah, calm down!"

"Don't tell me to calm down," Hannah snapped. "What a joke marriage is. Don't you care that you're driving a couple apart?"

"It isn't like that. Hannah, please—" Della reached for her hand, but she jerked back.

Hannah couldn't do this anymore. She couldn't pretend there was nothing wrong with the way everyone around her behaved. They all acted like it was perfectly normal to push Hannah toward marriage, while behind closed doors they cast off their vows the moment it suited them.

"Get away from me!"

Hannah ran from the room, heedless of her destination. She only knew that she couldn't be near other people right now. She couldn't go back to Mrs. Anwar's, nor did she relish the thought of returning to Jane's town house to face Mama. She didn't even have the money to hire a coach! She'd left everything she had on the card table when she stormed off without thinking.

Hannah pulled open the only door in the club she hadn't been through tonight to find a small office on the other side.

Thank God.

She slumped against the wall and let her tears overtake her. She'd thought Della was a good person. She'd seemed so worldly and independent with all her talk about the club and her book. Hannah had wanted to be just like her. How could she do something like this? Didn't anyone else care about the consequences of their actions?

Sometimes Hannah felt as if she were the only person in the whole world who took things to heart. After all, Mama and Papa didn't seem troubled by the fact that they were living apart. Even her brothers behaved as though it were perfectly normal. Hannah was the only one who understood that their whole world was falling down; the only one who couldn't bear to pretend that everything was fine.

She sobbed for a long while before she finally fished a handkerchief from her reticule and wiped her face. She probably looked a mess, but she didn't care anymore. She wasn't going back out there for anything. She would hide inside the office for the rest of the night, until she was strong enough to go back to Jane and Eli's home and face her punishment. Mama would shout and cry and tell her what a terrible mistake she'd made, no doubt. But at the end of it all, nothing would change. She would still be expected to make her morning calls tomorrow, just to find a man who would grow to hate her over the years or carry on with other women like they all did.

This was to be her life. There was no escape.

The sudden click of the latch was the only warning she had that someone was coming. Hannah gasped to find Mr. Corbyn before her, looking just as startled as she was.

Oh no, not him. Of all the people who might stumble upon her while she looked like a half-drowned rat, the dazzling Mr. Corbyn was the last one she would have chosen.

"You're not the old lady from earlier," he said, as if this was supposed to mean something.

"Um...no?"

He shook his head, apparently realizing he was talking nonsense. "Beg your pardon, Miss Williams. I was looking for someone else." He cast a glance around the room, then back to her. It was plain that he wondered what she was doing here, but didn't want to come out and ask. "Right. I'll leave you to your... Wait, have you been crying?"

Hannah wanted to sink into the floor and die. She tried to issue a persuasive "no," but her nose betrayed her with an involuntary sniffle. This was so humiliating.

"Did someone hurt you?" Mr. Corbyn's face darkened. Though Hannah knew the threat wasn't directed at her, she couldn't stop her heart from quailing. That wasn't the face of a man one should cross.

"No," she repeated. Though Mr. Corbyn didn't know her from

Adam, the look in his eyes told Hannah that he would have words (or possibly fists) for whomever he blamed for her tears.

He must feel an obligation to Eli. Even if it was only for her brother's sake, it felt good to know that someone was watching out for her.

It wasn't as though anyone else would.

"Then why are you in here crying alone?" he persisted. Those eyes were really too intense for comfort. A steel-blue that could have pierced her straight through.

"I just—" Hannah couldn't find an easy lie to save herself. Remembering her falling-out with Della, her lower lip began to tremble.

Oh no. She hated crying in front of other people. She was *not* going to cry in front of Mr. Corbyn. Hannah bit her lip to push the feeling back.

"It's a long story," she finally managed, once her voice was steady. "I'm sure you don't want to hear it."

He hesitated, as if he didn't rightly know what he wanted to hear, before he said, "You can tell me if you like."

The words were uttered in a tone she couldn't read. Was it reluctance, or a gruff sort of kindness? She didn't know Mr. Corbyn well enough to judge. But even if he did want to hear her story, he wasn't likely to understand how she felt. Her own family didn't even understand her.

"Hannah?" It was a woman's voice calling her name outside. Della's, she thought. This in itself wouldn't have been so bad (she had known they must face one another again eventually), except that it was immediately followed by another.

"Hannah, where are you?"

Mama. Was her time already up? She wasn't ready!

Hannah motioned frantically at Mr. Corbyn. "Close the door! Quick!"

Though he shot her a dubious look, he obeyed. "May I ask who you're hiding from?"

"My mother," she replied. "She'll have my hide if she catches me here."

"You aren't meant to be at the club tonight?" It was a little unexpected to see Mr. Corbyn caught off his guard. He looked so commanding, with that stern manner and the scar that snaked over his chin, as if he should be ready for any danger. But this had surprised him. "What were you doing at my table, then?"

"Playing cards."

"Don't joke. Is this some sort of adolescent rebellion? Is that why you were trying to throw away your money earlier? I still have your chips, by the way. I can't cash them out for myself or they'll think I'm stealing from the pot, so you'd best come back and get them."

"It's not an 'adolescent rebellion' because I'm not an adolescent," Hannah shot back. He was making her sound like a silly schoolgirl. "You don't understand the situation I'm in. My mother wants to marry me off to the first man who'll have me, and I *have* to stop her."

"Hmm." Mr. Corbyn shook his head, his judgment obvious. "So you're angry at your mum because she wants to find you some rich bloke to keep you comfortable for the rest of your life, and you've decided the best response is to sneak in here and leave sixty pounds on the table? That makes perfect sense."

I knew he wouldn't understand.

"Don't belittle me." Had she been intimidated by Mr. Corbyn's good looks before? His shine was quickly wearing off. She wasn't even sure he resembled Poseidon anymore. It had been ages since she'd looked at that drawing; her memory must have faded. "You have no idea what it's like to have your parents decide everything for you. To treat you like you aren't allowed to have an opinion on your *own life*."

"Actually, I do," he replied coldly. "You don't know anything about me."

"Oh." This gave Hannah pause, but she didn't have time to consider what he might mean. "Then you should be able to show me a little more understanding," she continued. "I'm going to have to share a life with this man, share children with him, share a—share a *bed* with him." She flushed at this, but no one else was here to hear them. She was too desperate to waste time on niceties. "I can't abide by it."

Mr. Corbyn assessed her with a cool glance. "Very well. You've made your point. But you can't hide forever."

"You could help me," Hannah said eagerly. The glimmer of sympathy in his eye wasn't much to bet her future on, but it might be enough. "Save me from her plans."

It was a reckless idea, and not one that she would have chosen for herself if she had a better option, but needs must.

"How do you expect me to do that? Shall I hoist you out the window? It's a drop to the ground and I don't want your brother after me when you break your ankle."

"*Hannah!*" The voices were much nearer now. They must be in the main game room just beyond the door. She didn't have much time before they found her.

And she was already alone in a closed room with a man Della had recently condemned for his reputation-ruining power. They were as good as halfway there, really. What was one more push?

"I want you to kiss me," she said in a rushed whisper.

"What?" Mr. Corbyn jerked back as if burned.

What a nice reaction for me. Very flattering.

"It doesn't have to be any more than that. I just need to borrow your lips for a few seconds until they come in and see us. A minute at the absolute most."

It was perfect. There was no possibility that her mother would force her to marry a disgraced midshipman with a dealer's income, which made him the ideal candidate to compromise her without any risk of being tied together forever. Mama would have no choice but to give up on her plans for the season and let Hannah go back home. Papa would welcome them with open arms, and this whole interlude would be like an unpleasant dream.

"Your brother will flay me alive!" Mr. Corbyn said sharply. "I need this job."

"How much is he paying you?"

"Pardon?"

"I'll give you the sixty pounds I won," Hannah offered. "All of it, just for one little kiss. Doesn't that sound like a generous bargain?"

Mr. Corbyn didn't have a quick response to that. His mouth hung open as he struggled to find words.

Footsteps sounded just outside the door. There was no time left for debate; they'd already been found out. If she didn't take her chance now, she would regret it forever.

"I'm terribly sorry!" Hannah cried. Then she launched herself at Mr. Corbyn and smashed their lips together in what she hoped resembled a passionate embrace.

Three

BLOODY HELL.

Silas should have pushed her away. Should have given her a good shove and jumped out the window the instant he was free. But of course he didn't, because he was too stunned to react.

He couldn't push a lady, could he?

And she'd offered him sixty pounds. That was more than he'd made in his wages from the thirteen years he'd served in the navy combined, if he excluded the prize money. A lot more.

While all these thoughts were whirling in Silas's head, Miss Williams was pressing her lips to his and gripping the back of his neck as tightly as if she were drowning. Rather more aggressive than he was used to, but it wasn't unpleasant. She smelled faintly of roses and tasted like champagne. Refined things. The taste of the life he'd been raised to aspire to.

She tasted good.

Despite himself, Silas began kissing her back. It was instinctive. He'd been too long without a woman, perhaps. His hand found the curve of her spine, pulling Miss Williams closer. She was nearly tall enough to be level with him, and it was nice not to have to hunch to reach her. He wasn't used to kissing someone who could match his own height. When she was pressed up against him like this, all he could think about was how well their bodies fit together, and how good it felt to have her so close.

Someone was screaming.

Shit. It was definitely too late to shove her and run.

A hundred voices clamored for attention at once:

"Get away from my daughter, you brute!"

"Hannah, what are you *doing*?"

Miss Williams was ripped from his arms and replaced with a red-faced woman who started beating him about the head. Not a fair trade.

"Ouch." Silas brought up his arms to shield his face. "Stop that."

"You monster! You've violated my Hannah."

"Your Hannah violated *me!*" he shot back, before he could think better of it. That might have been unfair. He *had* kissed her back.

The accusation certainly did nothing to calm Mrs. Williams, who screeched, "How *dare* you!" and thumped him across the shoulder with her reticule. It must have had lead weights in it, for it forced the breath from his lungs.

"Everyone out!" Miss Danby cried. "Give us some privacy, please."

This proved about as effective as one might expect, which was to say, not in the least. Silas managed a quick look around him, to find that every lady in the place was pressing past her neighbors to peer inside the office.

The only person who moved to obey was Mrs. Williams, who grabbed her daughter by the elbow and pulled her from the room. The young lady looked over her shoulder and caught his eye as she disappeared from sight, her lips forming words Silas couldn't make out in the din. She might have said "thank you", but he couldn't be sure.

Then all hell broke loose.

"What in God's name were you doing? How could you take advantage of an innocent girl? Have you no shame?" Miss Danby must not have expected answers to any of these questions, for she spoke so quickly there was no possibility of getting a word in. "Jane is going to kill me! How will I ever face her?"

"Who's Jane?" Silas ventured.

"*Mrs. Williams!*"

She must mean the younger Mrs. Williams, not the one who'd been knocking his brains round his skull.

"We'll never live this down." Miss Danby looked to be bordering on hysteria, though he knew better than to invoke that word at this juncture. "You need to leave," she continued, obviously struggling to hold back tears. "Don't ever come back here."

"Right." There could be no other outcome, after how they'd caught him. There was no point in trying to explain that Miss Williams had been the one to kiss him. He should never have let himself be caught alone with her in the first place.

Sacked after a single night's work. Was he cursed to ruin anything he touched?

Silas nodded curtly and walked to the door. The crowd parted before him like the Red Sea. It seemed that no one wanted to be tainted by close contact, though they were happy enough to whisper and gawk as he passed. He turned over his shoulder at the last minute, remembering the money he'd been promised. "Should I close up my table first? I left the chips there when you asked me to help search for that woman."

He wasn't sure if Miss Danby had found the errant gambler they'd been searching for when he found Miss Williams, but it hardly seemed to matter now.

"I'll get someone else to handle it," Miss Danby said tightly.

"The ones in the drawer on the left belong to Miss Williams. She left them behind after her play, but someone should return them—"

"Just *go!*"

Perfect. So much for his sixty pounds.

$$\mathcal{Jb}$$

Victory did not taste as sweet as Hannah had hoped.

It had been easy enough to endure the initial yelling and lamentation that awaited her back at the house. That part was actually reassuring in an odd sort of way, as it proved she'd finally succeeded in destroying everyone's ill-conceived plans for her future after all her false starts. The hard part came the next morning, when Hannah arose refreshed and content, to find that everyone was *still* in hysterics. (Although she hated it when men called ladies hysterical, she was allowed to use the term herself when it was appropriate, and it certainly fit here.)

Mama had been up sobbing all night, as Eli informed her. Hannah had taken breakfast in her room to avoid her family, but her brother had barged in on her despite the fact that she was still in her nightgown and wrapper.

"What on earth happened last night?" Eli asked. "She's in a terrible state, you know."

"She needn't be in any sort of state," Hannah replied. "She only needs to stop trying to marry me off when I've told her a thousand times no."

Her bacon and hot rolls filled the room with the most delicious scent, but the conversation was ruining her appetite.

"Did you know that she doesn't plan to go back home to Papa?" Hannah continued. "She wants to live with one of us forever. Did she tell you?"

"What does that have to do with anything?" Eli looked confused. "She's a grown woman. It's not for us to tell her whether to go back to Devonshire. The more pressing issue is why you decided to ruin your good name with a man who has no income to support you."

"You mean to say you've sacked Mr. Corbyn?" That made her feel a bit awful. But of course they would. In her rush to carry out her plan last night, Hannah hadn't had time to think about what would happen next. Still, the sixty pounds she'd promised should be more than enough to tide him over until he landed somewhere else. He would be all right.

Speaking of which, how was she going to get it to him? Where did he live?

"What did you think would happen?" Eli looked cross, which was such a rare occurrence that Hannah honestly couldn't recall the last time she'd seen it. He was normally mild-tempered. "We can't keep on a dealer who took advantage of a lady for the whole world to see."

"I'm sorry," she murmured.

"Not half as sorry as he's going to be."

"What does that mean?"

"That I'm going to find Mr. Corbyn and make him regret what he did."

"What?" Hannah's heart kicked into a panicked tempo. This wasn't supposed to happen. "But it was *my* fault. I kissed him."

She'd presumed that if she took the full blame upon herself, there would be no need for any of the theatrics of male pride. Dueling was for gentlemen anyway, and Mr. Corbyn was only a disgraced midshipman-turned-dealer. It wasn't fair for Eli to challenge him.

"He should have known better than to get himself in a room alone with you. A man doesn't do something like that unless he's up to no good."

"*You* found yourself alone with a lady!" Hannah pointed out.

"Twice! With two different ladies." What a selective memory her brother had.

"That was different."

"Different how?"

"I proposed both times, for a start." Eli glared at her furiously.

"Whereas Mr. Corbyn isn't in a position to propose to you."

"So it's acceptable to kiss a lady as long as you have a bit of money, is that it?"

"That's not what I said. But there are some lines you can't cross without a reckoning." On this ominous note, her brother turned and left the room.

"Wait!" Hannah scrambled to set her breakfast tray aside, push off her bedspread, and rush after him, heedless of her appearance. "Does that mean you know where he lives? *Where* are you going, exactly?"

But he didn't answer her, and the carriage left before Hannah could get herself properly dressed to follow him. Just her luck.

Though she wasn't truly frightened for Mr. Corbyn—Eli didn't have it in him to murder anybody, even if recent events had put him in a foul mood—Hannah did feel more than a little guilty for causing so much trouble. Any reckoning should be hers alone.

After that, the house seemed to become a spinning carousel of visitors and lamentations. First Della arrived, half-sobbing, and then Jane's cousin joined the call, sounding appropriately scandalized if a touch too curious. Hannah didn't have the courage to face either of them, but she eavesdropped shamelessly from her perch on the upper landing. From the snippets that wafted up to her, she gathered they were all very concerned about her future and couldn't imagine what had possessed her. Hannah was itching to know where her winnings from last night had got to, but it didn't seem like the best time to ask.

Why must everyone overreact so? After all, it wasn't as though she'd murdered someone! All she'd done was kiss a man. She hadn't even had time to properly enjoy it before it was over.

Not that she would have enjoyed it in other circumstances. Yes, the solid heat of Mr. Corbyn's body beneath her hands had been oddly satisfying, particularly when he'd slipped his hand down the small of her back. (She hadn't been expecting that part.) And yes, he'd tasted nice, and he smelled of fresh linen. And there had been a very intriguing shift in his reaction, when he moved from shock to, well, she wasn't exactly sure what had replaced the shock, but there had been a moment where he seemed to be doing something encouraging with his lips. She hadn't gotten the chance to find out what it was before she'd been wrenched away.

It was the only time she'd ever kissed a man. She would've liked a little more time to figure out what she was doing.

Never mind any of that. Hannah would be glad when all this fuss was over with and they sent her back to Devonshire. That was the point of the thing.

She waited upstairs for what felt like ages for both callers to leave. When the house returned to a peaceful silence, she tiptoed down to face her sister-in-law. There was no sense in postponing the inevitable, and she needed to find some way to reclaim her winnings if she was to pay Mr. Corbyn.

"Come in," Jane said, spying Hannah where she lingered in the doorway. She sounded exceptionally tired, but not as angry as Mama and Eli. "How are you?"

"I'm sorry about upsetting everyone," Hannah began. It couldn't hurt to open on a conciliatory note. "I hope it won't cause too much trouble."

"I just don't understand what possessed you to do such a thing. Did he frighten you? Put any sort of pressure on you?"

"No. It was my decision, I promise."

"But you don't even *know* the man."

In the chaos of her return to the town house last night, no one had been particularly interested in letting Hannah explain herself. Not that she'd thought far enough ahead to formulate a script.

Might they consider that she wasn't truly ruined if they knew it had been planned?

Safer to play the part of a fallen woman as best she could. "He's very handsome." This had the benefit of being true, at least. "I simply couldn't resist him when we found ourselves alone in the office. In fact, I–I *asked* him to meet me there." Though Hannah felt a bit nervous stretching the truth like this, it made for a very damning confession.

Jane certainly appeared horrified by it. "Don't you see how dangerous this is? Your entire future is ruined over one kiss. You can't believe it was worth it."

"It was." Hannah raised her chin proudly. This, too, was true. Despite the fuss everyone was making, she felt at peace for the first time in years. It had been so awful living in constant fear that the next caller would be the one that finally trapped her. At least now it was over. She'd taken the portrait they'd painted of her future and smashed it into kindling.

Jane sighed and rubbed her temples. "I won't try to lecture you. You and your mother will have to sort out what's next. But seeing as you caused a scandal at my club, I think it's only fair that you help make amends for the extra work this has caused us."

"I can help at your club?" Hannah perked up instantly. This was even better than she'd dreamed!

"Not when the guests are there. It's for the best if you aren't seen out and about for now, but we can always find work for you in the mornings before we open. Besides which, Eli and I are going to be taking most of the evening responsibilities over from Della for the next few days while she recovers from the shock, so you can also help your mother mind Gloria while we're out."

That wasn't so bad. Even if Hannah's niece was too young to do more than cry and soil herself, she was still more amusing than an evening being pushed toward an unwanted match. She was also quite adorable.

"I'll take excellent care of her," Hannah said warmly. Maybe if she was agreeable enough, they would forgive her sooner. "But speaking of the club, would you be able to tell me what happened to my winnings? Mama dragged me away so fast I didn't have time to collect them. They were at Mr. Corbyn's table."

A furrow appeared between Jane's eyebrows. "Della brought the money over, but I don't see how I can give it to you after this. You had no business placing such a high wager. We have a policy that family can't place bets, or people will suspect cheating when you win."

"But it's mine! You can't just take it. That's stealing."

"I'm not planning to keep it," Jane protested. "I'll give it to your mother. The two of you can discuss what to do with it."

How unfair! Hannah could endure everyone's condemnation, but she couldn't abide thievery. "I'm not a child!"

"I'm sorry, but you can't put me in the middle like this. We're all worried about you, Hannah. What were you planning to do with that kind of money, anyway?"

I'll pay Mr. Corbyn, that's what I'll do.

"I was only going to add it to my pin money." Lying was getting easier every time she did it. Hannah might have stopped to worry about that, if she didn't have more pressing concerns.

"No one needs sixty pounds of pin money."

Jane's expression said she would never relent, but Hannah had to get her hands on those funds. After she'd cost Mr. Corbyn his employment and caused Eli to go after him, the only proper thing to do was to pay him what she'd promised. Otherwise she would be no better than a thief herself.

Mama still hadn't emerged from her bedroom after her night of sobbing, which meant that Jane couldn't have turned over her winnings yet. If she didn't want to carry such a large sum on her person, it might still be somewhere in this room!

If only she would leave for a minute. Hannah sent a fervent prayer up to heaven. Couldn't she have one little bit of divine assistance in her efforts to destroy her reputation and spite her mother?

At that moment, Gloria began to wail, the sound as beautiful and welcome as birdsong.

Thank you.

"Oh dear. She's woken up again." Jane jumped to her feet without a second thought for Hannah. "We'll talk about this later."

"Of course."

What luck!

The moment she was gone, Hannah began rummaging through every hiding place she could find. It didn't take her five minutes to fall upon the little envelope tucked inside a drawer in the nearest end table. She opened it quickly to confirm it was all there. Sixty pounds. Things *were* turning in her favor.

Though her heart was hammering at the threat of discovery, Hannah didn't feel too bad about taking the funds. It was her own money, after all. Now all she needed to do was devise how she would get it to Mr. Corbyn.

"How could you take advantage of my sister?" Williams looked ready to punch Silas. It must be a stroke of good luck that he hadn't done so yet. He'd woken him bright and early from a poor night's sleep on a lumpy mattress by pounding on the front door of the board-inghouse where Silas had been staying. "I trusted you. I thought we were friends."

We were, until your sister set my life ablaze.

Williams was a good man, and they'd gotten along well when they'd served on the *Libertas* together, before that ship had wrecked and Silas was reassigned to the *Echo*. This was poor thanks for every-thing Williams had done to help him when he'd heard about Silas's discharge from the navy.

"I'm sorry," Silas said, meaning it.

"Sorry isn't going to un-destroy my sister's reputation."

No. It wouldn't.

A creak on the floorboard alerted the men that they had a spec-tator. It was Thomas, the welp who belonged to the woman renting the second floor. He was in the habit of slipping downstairs to visit old Mr. Kurtz and his son, the other renters who split the first floor with Silas. Though he'd only taken the room five days ago, Silas had already seen the boy skulking about a half-dozen times.

"Go back up to your mother," he scolded. "We're having a private conversation."

Thomas obeyed swiftly. He must have been frightened by the shouting, for he normally wasn't this obedient.

"You've got an illegitimate son here in town?" Williams exclaimed. "Just how many ladies do you have on your strings?"

"He's not mine. He belongs to the woman upstairs. His father died a few years back, I understand."

At least that was what the renter, Mrs. Taylor, had told him. Silas wasn't sure if the story was true or just a way to hide her indiscre-tions, for he heard a string of visitors going up and down the stairs most evenings. But it was none of his business how she paid the rent.

This seemed to mollify Williams somewhat, or else the sight of the little boy had simply reminded him that his shouting would attract attention he didn't want. He kept a more civil tone when he spoke again. "Why would you do it? After I recommended you to Miss Danby and gave you work. How could you hurt an innocent girl that way?"

Silas didn't want to insult Williams's sister, but this accusation was too much to endure. He'd never hurt a woman in his life.

"*She* kissed *me*," he said coldly. "I didn't pursue her."

"Hannah wouldn't do such a thing."

"Believe me or don't." Silas shrugged, with an indifference he didn't quite feel. "But I'm telling the truth."

Williams wrestled with this for a moment, his conflict written on his face. Finally, he retorted, "Even if she did kiss you—which I'm not saying is true—she's only a girl. You should have known better than to let her do such a thing. It was your responsibility to behave like a gentleman."

"But I'm not a gentleman, am I?" Silas couldn't keep the bitterness from his tone. "Anyway, she looked old enough to make up her own mind. How old is she?"

"One-and-twenty," Williams replied grudgingly. "But only just. And she's had a sheltered life. She's the baby of the family."

"Sounds to me like she wanted a bit of freedom. Maybe you shouldn't have tried so hard to keep her under glass."

Silas knew he wasn't helping matters, but he'd never been able to tolerate a dressing-down where it wasn't warranted. Everything he'd said was true. The chit had only kissed him because she felt trapped, not because he'd seduced her. Someone like him could never be a match for a gently bred lady.

"Don't presume to criticize my family." There was a warning note in his friend's voice. "You don't know what you're talking about."

Silas tipped his head in acknowledgment. "As I've said, I regret what happened and I didn't go looking for any of it. Tell me how I can make amends."

He would have accepted any punishment Williams doled out, if it would set things right. Even though he didn't believe for a minute that the man's sister was an innocent maiden, he still wished he hadn't been the instrument of her downfall.

But Williams wasn't charitable enough to grant him any sort of atonement. "There's nothing you can do. You've ruined her and she'll never be able to marry now."

At least Miss Williams would be happy with that outcome.

"Then why have you come here? To call me out?" One didn't pull a member of the working classes into a duel, but Williams might have judged it worth the breach to get his revenge. Silas wasn't sure what he would do in that case. He could hardly shoot his own friend.

"No." The swift reply let Silas breathe again. "I don't want to fight you, though you probably deserve it."

"What then?"

"To give you a piece of my mind, I suppose." Williams looked more than a little frustrated by the question, the dark lines of his brow coming together in a frown. "I could hardly let this pass without saying something. I've never had someone compromise my sister, all right? I don't quite know what I'm supposed to do about it."

"Right. Sorry."

They both stood there uneasily for a few seconds, before Williams seemed to decide he'd run out of insults and said awkwardly, "Well, that's that then. Don't ever go near Hannah again. Or I'll... Well, just don't do it, understood?"

His total inability to be menacing would have been comical, if only Silas could find the humor in the situation.

He was about to lose one of the only friends he had left. Not many people had stood by him after his discharge.

"You have my word."

"Humph." Williams's sullen grunt as he turned and left the boardinghouse made it abundantly clear how little Silas's word was worth.

Four

SILAS'S PROMISE PROVED JUST AS UNRELIABLE AS HIS FRIEND had suspected, for it so happened that he saw Miss Williams less than an hour later.

He'd barely had the time to shave and slice himself some day-old bread for his breakfast when she rapped on his door, bold as brass. She had the audacity to widen her rich brown eyes in surprise when she found him standing on the other side. As if *she* were startled to find him in his own home.

"Good morning," she said brightly.

"What the hell are you doing here?"

"May I come in? I'd rather not say where anyone might hear us."

Silas darted a glance to either side. Thomas hadn't dared to come back downstairs since he'd been scared off, and Mr. Kurtz must still be sleeping, so there was no one around to catch them.

But he'd promised Williams he would stay away from his sister, and here she was making a liar out of Silas before the day was out. This cursed woman couldn't seem to keep from landing him in trouble.

Deciding quickly, he took her by the wrist and pulled her inside, then slammed the door behind them. Better that the neighbors shouldn't see her.

Miss Williams gave a little shriek at this rough treatment and stumbled on the hem of her gown. Before he'd had time to think about it, Silas set a hand on her waist to steady her.

They both froze. It brought the memory of their kiss flooding back, as strong as if she were still pressing her champagne lips against his. Silas's heart was pounding a little faster as he released her and cleared his throat. What was wrong with him?

Miss Williams had turned a rather fetching shade of pink. "I brought you your money." She thrust a fat envelope in the direction of his chest. Then, as an afterthought, she added, "You should really curse less. It's very shocking to a lady."

"I'll be sure to keep that in mind if I should meet one." Although the insult escaped his lips before he'd had much time to think about it, his irritation lessened as he took the envelope and peered at the stack of notes inside. Was there really sixty pounds inside? That might not justify all the trouble she'd caused him, but it certainly lessened the sting.

"Excuse me!" Miss Williams's cheeks went from pink to mottled red. "You've no right to speak to me that way."

"And you'd no right to kiss me last night. You cost me my job and your brother's trust. Besides which, it's not very ladylike to pay me to compromise you and turn up at my home unchaperoned, now is it?"

"Well, no," she was forced to admit. "I suppose not. And I *am* sorry about all that. But it was for a good cause."

"Ruining your own life?" He raised an eyebrow. He didn't care what she did. Not really. But he couldn't entirely suppress a spark of curiosity. There'd been real desperation in her eyes in the minutes before her disastrous decision. And the way she'd spoken of her family... Well, Silas had meant it when he said he understood that part.

He might not know much about Miss Williams, but he understood the weight of her resentment. That restless burning that had her stalking her own downfall. If no one stopped this girl, she might come to real harm before she turned back.

"I call it an improvement," she retorted. "No one will marry me now, which is exactly what I wanted. Sixty pounds well spent, I say."

"Shh!" Silas darted forward to press his palm over Miss Williams's mouth, as if there were some way to seal the words back in before the other boarders heard her. They'd seemed to be a good enough sort, but poverty made people desperate. Did the chit want to get herself robbed?

Her eyes widened in shock. Silas almost pulled away, but stopped himself. Why should he take care to keep from frightening her when she'd used him without a second thought last night? *Someone* certainly needed to stop her from getting into any more trouble.

A little scare might do her some good.

⁂

Hannah's heart was pounding so hard she was sure Mr. Corbyn must hear it. Why did he keep *touching* her?

Yes, she had touched him first, if one counted yesterday. But that was then. This was now. She'd made an effort to be businesslike when she'd come over here.

The money would more than compensate for what she'd cost him, and then Hannah wouldn't have to worry about him anymore. Wouldn't have to think about him ever again, in fact.

But every time Mr. Corbyn put his hands on Hannah's person, the answering cry from her body made a liar of her. He leaned in deliberately close when he covered her mouth, flooding the air she breathed with his scent. Soap and clean linen, mixed with the background smells of the house—the smoky traces of tobacco and tallow candles.

"Don't talk about how much you gave me," he growled, his voice so low that she had to strain to hear it. Gentle as a storm in the air. Though he didn't touch her anywhere but her mouth, Hannah found herself unable to move a muscle. "There are other boarders here. You have no way of knowing if one of them might be willing to slit your throat for that sort of money."

He released her all at once. Hannah felt a little dizzy.

"You wouldn't let anyone slit my throat," she whispered, as much to reassure herself as for anything else. Surely this feeling was fear. That was why her hands shook and her heart raced.

But she didn't think Mr. Corbyn would let any harm come to her. Not after how he'd reacted when he'd stumbled upon her crying in the office. Despite his rough manners, there was kindness in him.

"You don't know that. You've only just met me." He was stubborn, but she wasn't fooled. The thought gave her the courage to press onward.

"Anyway, I *need* to talk about the money," she added in a whisper, dropping her gaze to the open button at the collar of his shirt. It was easier to talk to the man if she didn't look him in the eye. Like the sun, he was too dazzling for comfort. "I have to tell you something."

Mr. Corbyn scowled at her.

She would take that as permission to keep talking. It was the best she was liable to get. "I had to take a pound from what I owed you to bribe our coachman to take me to the same address he brought Eli this morning. I didn't know where you lived, you see, so it was the only way to get here."

She hadn't wanted to dip into the funds, but she'd turned all her pin money into chips at Bishop's last night and she couldn't very well ask her mother to give her more. The coachman had been quite reluctant until she'd plucked a note from the envelope for him.

"You *didn't* need to tell me that," Corbyn said curtly. "I don't care about your missing pound."

"But you might've thought that I was trying to cheat you!"

"You paid a man to kiss you in front of a room full of people and that's what you're worried about?"

His mouth was twisted in a crooked line, but his blue eyes were icy and aloof. If he found her amusing, it wasn't complimentary.

This was so mortifying—to be overcome by the looks of a man who saw her as a mere annoyance. Even if she were going to leave in just a moment, Hannah would have preferred to swirl in and out with a worldly, seductive air and leave him longing for another kiss.

Now you're being ridiculous, she scolded herself. *Once was enough. You have no reason to kiss him again.*

Except that Hannah found—to her horror—that she couldn't seem to stop thinking about it. She'd hardly had the time to appreciate their kiss the first time. It had been over before she'd even had a chance to figure out what she was doing. When he'd leaned in to whisper his warning in her ear a minute ago, she'd suffered the most terrible longing to try again.

He didn't even want to kiss you the first time, Hannah reminded herself firmly. She wasn't the sort of lady who could inspire a man to passion. She never had been.

"What will you do now?" she asked, trying to turn the subject away from her blunders.

"I'll start by getting you out of this house and back home to your brother, for one. Is your carriage waiting outside?"

It was, though Hannah was in no hurry to return to it. The only thing that awaited her at home was another scolding. "I meant for work. Perhaps I could help you find something, seeing as it's my fault you lost your post."

"I think I've had enough of your help." The words made Hannah wince. "If your brother learns you were here, he'll have my hide."

Eli again. What had he said to Mr. Corbyn? She wished they would all stop interfering in her life.

"He'll never learn of it," she promised. "The coachman has as much to lose as I do if anyone finds out he brought me here in exchange for a bribe. He'll tell them that he took me to call on some other ladies."

Hannah had thought herself quite clever for having planned it all out so thoroughly, but Mr. Corbyn merely grunted. Never mind. She didn't need his approval anyway. He was right; they were little more than strangers and she was making a fool of herself by lingering here.

She cast another glance about the boardinghouse, a sense of regret making her reluctant to say her goodbyes. The surroundings seemed too shabby for a man as beautiful as Mr. Corbyn. Grime and years of wear had turned the wood of the floorboards an ashy gray. They matched the soot-stained walls. A heavy set of footsteps marched up the stairs, sending an ominous creaking through the beams of the roof above their heads, followed by a rapping on the door from the floor above them and the sound of a man's voice.

How could Mr. Corbyn stand to hear every move his neighbors made? What had happened to drive him from his naval career and land him in such circumstances? It must have been a significant fall from what he'd hoped for. It would have driven Hannah mad to live in a place with so little privacy.

Mr. Corbyn cast a glance upward as the creaking shifted to a different part of the ceiling, perhaps thinking the same thing.

"You should go," he said, his voice clipped. "Now."

Hannah bristled at this. "You're very rude. You could at least say thank you for the money first."

"Thank you." He'd obviously only obliged the request in order to be rid of her. He wasn't even looking at Hannah as he barked out the words. His gaze was still fixed above his head, where the creaking had taken on an oddly rhythmic quality. Was someone up there using a rocking chair? "Now hurry, before you hear something you shouldn't."

"What does that mean?"

At that moment, the moaning began.

Oh. Hannah's eyes grew round as she understood. It wasn't a rocking chair.

Mr. Corbyn sighed, raking a hand through his hair and setting the burnished gold into messy waves. He didn't seem surprised. He'd been expecting this.

"Do they...do that every day?" she asked timidly. The lady seemed to be enjoying herself a great deal, particularly given that they'd scarcely been at this for a minute. Hannah wondered what the gentleman was doing to make her shriek that way.

Mr. Corbyn cast Hannah an incredulous look. "Do you really want me to answer that?"

"No," she squeaked. "Best not."

How could he listen to them without feeling embarrassed? Hannah wasn't sure where to look. But then, Mr. Corbyn probably had no trouble finding a woman to share his bed. That sort of thing must be so commonplace to him that he'd long since lost any sense of shame.

With a start, she realized he was staring at her. As if he'd been reading her thoughts with that penetrating stare of his. No, not penetrating. That was the *last* adjective she should be associating with Mr. Corbyn at a time like this. Nor should she be wondering if he knew how to make a woman scream that way.

Hannah tried to swallow, and found her throat had gone entirely dry.

"Well, I'll be off, then," she said tightly, before she could embarrass herself any further.

A prolonged groan several feet above her left ear said that the gentleman upstairs was likely off as well.

She couldn't bear to meet Mr. Corbyn's eye as she fumbled for the doorknob.

"Wait." His clipped baritone caught her on the landing like a fish on a hook.

"Y-yes?"

He looked at her for a long time. (Could she describe it as a *piercing* stare? No, that was just as bad. Why were all the descriptors for stares excessively sexual?)

"Take care not to make things worse for yourself, Miss Williams."

"Pardon?" She was so flustered, she could hardly follow what he was saying.

His eyes seemed almost softer, as if their icy blue had melted a touch. "I don't pretend to know what you're doing, but I've seen what it looks like when someone cares more for their own anger than for their safety. It doesn't end well."

Oh dear. His voice was so serious, it gave her a frisson. But who was he to give her advice? The only thing that linked them was the fact that he'd been in the right place at the right time to help her outwit her mother. A fortuitous coincidence, but nothing more.

"Thank you, Mr. Corbyn, but there's no cause for concern. I know exactly what I'm doing."

It was true. For the first time in ages, everything in her life was going to plan.

But when Hannah returned to the town house, still giddy with the thrill of her daring adventure to find Mr. Corbyn, she found that nothing was going to plan.

She'd managed her secret excursion in less than an hour and had been hoping that she might escape notice entirely. Instead, she found the whole household waiting for her.

Jane answered the door herself. Their maid, Molly, must be occupied, or else Jane had been on the lookout.

The latter possibility felt more likely as she pulled Hannah indoors and hissed, "Where have you been? Everyone's worried sick!"

Before she could answer, Hannah found herself shuffled toward the study, where her mother and Eli were conversing in low tones. They broke off as soon as they saw her.

Mama's face looked pale and thin, the shadows under her eyes more prominent than they'd been since they'd left Devonshire.

"Where on earth have you been?" Her voice didn't crack like a whip. It was barely the snap of a thin, dried-up branch.

Hannah squared her shoulders. Why should she feel guilty for leaving the house in the middle of the day? Nothing had *happened*. "I just went to pay a few morning calls."

To a man who makes me feel as though my entire body is on fire whenever I'm near him.

Oh dear. Where had that thought come from? It was probably because she knew there was no chance she would ever be forced to marry Mr. Corbyn; it made her mind feel safe to entertain lustful imaginings.

"Morning calls?" It was plain this explanation hadn't found any takers. Jane and Eli exchanged a speaking glance as Mama barreled on, her voice trembling with emotion. "Who would receive you after what you've done?"

That stung. Though Hannah knew people would react poorly to

her illicit kiss (in fact, she was counting on it), there was no need to behave as if she were a leper. Surely a few loyal friends would still admit her into their company.

"We know you took the money that Della brought over this morning," Eli added grimly.

Hannah whirled to Jane. "You told on me?"

"I was surprised when I found it gone. You can't expect me to lie to my own husband," she replied, her voice defensive. "Hannah, we're *worried* about you. You haven't been acting like yourself at all. Are you in some sort of trouble?"

Now they were worried. Too little, too late, as far as she was concerned.

"You have nothing to worry about," Hannah said brightly, pointedly ignoring the déjà vu this conjured, so soon after Mr. Corbyn's odd parting message. "I'm perfectly well."

Mama extended her hand, palm up. "Give me the money."

"I can't."

"*Enough*, Hannah."

"I don't have it anymore."

Hannah wasn't mean-spirited. She didn't enjoy causing her family grief. But she had to admit, there was a certain shameful thrill in knowing she'd kept one step ahead of them.

"Where is it? What have you done now?" Mama cried. "For goodness' sake, you're taking years off of my life! Don't you care how poorly this reflects on the whole family? When your father hears about this..."

"Oh, are you speaking to him again?"

Hannah couldn't say which of them made that little gasp. It was as if the entire room drew a collective breath at the same instant from their identical, gaping mouths. The silence that followed was far more oppressive.

It was Eli who finally broke it. He rose to his feet, linked his arm with Hannah's, and murmured, "Come upstairs."

She didn't protest. She had an uncomfortable fear that she'd gone too far, but how was she supposed to back down when everyone kept treating her like an escaped convict?

I can't back down. If I do, this will all have been for nothing.

Eli didn't say one word to her on the way up the stairs and down the hall to her bedroom, but the tension coming off his body was loud enough. Hannah was trembling by the time he put his hands on the knob, sure she was in for the worst dressing-down of her life.

But Eli only motioned her inside and stood in the doorframe. After a long sigh, he said, "You should cool off for a bit. Let's talk about this at supper."

"It's two o'clock," Hannah pointed out. "What am I supposed to do until then?"

"Sit quietly and give everyone time to recover. Preferably without running away again."

He shut the door without further discussion.

Five

HANNAH *DID* SIT QUIETLY.

For about three hours, in fact. She wrote some letters to her friends back in Devonshire (hinting at her imminent return without mentioning the reasons behind it) and then hunted for a book to pass the time. She found a forgotten copy of *Eugénie Grandet* on the dresser, which Mama had brought with them on the insistence that Hannah improve her French by reading the original rather than a translation. She'd tired of the effort after twenty pages or so, but perhaps the story of filial rebellion would hold more interest for her now than it had before.

She'd made it to the part where Eugénie and Charles pledge their eternal love despite the opposition of her cruel father when a soft rap at the door interrupted her.

A muffled voice slipped in from the other side. "Poppet? Could I talk to you?"

Hannah swallowed. Her mother's gentle query was far more intimidating than anger would have been. Hannah knew how to let her mind go blank and wait out a scolding, but she wasn't sure how to deal with sadness. It made her feel ashamed, even though they'd hardly left her a choice. Why couldn't Mama just let her become a spinster, or a lady entrepreneur like Jane? That was all she wanted! Then they would never need to quarrel.

Hannah rose to open the door, stepping back to let her mother inside. She looked better than she had this morning. She'd changed into her going-out clothes and there was a little more color in her cheeks, so she must have distracted herself with morning calls or perhaps a bit of the floral arrangement she'd taken up since they arrived in town. Not a hobby that Hannah would have chosen for herself, but it seemed to give Mama something to do besides obsess over matchmaking, so at least there was that.

"Come and sit with me." Mama motioned to the armchairs near the window and waited until Hannah got herself settled. "I know this season has put a great deal of pressure on you, what with it being your fifth time," she began, her brows pinched together in worry. "But I hope you know that I've only ever had your future at heart. I wanted to make sure you had a *good* match with someone you cared for, not be forced into accepting an offer you didn't want because there were no other options for you."

Is that what happened with you and Papa? Hannah kept the question tucked safely inside, though her eyes prickled.

"Now all my worst fears have come true," Mama continued gravely. As if they were talking about Hannah's physical death rather than her social one. "You won't have many choices after something like this. Soon everyone in town will hear about it."

"I know." Hannah tried to school her features into contrition and make her voice a little sad. She couldn't wear her relief too openly when Mama was taking it all so seriously. "I understand no gentleman will want me now. I won't have any choice but to go back home and retire to a life of spinsterhood."

She even added a little sigh here, to show how hard this would be. Was that going too far? Mama must know how eager she was to escape matchmaking—Hannah hadn't exactly been quiet about it— but she seemed willing enough to believe that last night's scandal had been an accident. After all, Hannah had never taken such liberties with a man before.

I might have done, if I'd had any idea what it would feel like.

"It's not as bad as that, poppet." Mama reached out to pat her hand. "I've found you a gentleman who's willing to overlook your indiscretion, though I expect we might have to find some way to bolster your dowry."

"Pardon?" She couldn't have heard right. This simply wasn't possible.

They were *done* with suitors. That was the whole point of Mr. Corbyn.

"Sir Richard Fielding," Mama continued blithely. "A *baronet*. He's a little older, to be sure, but he only has daughters from his first marriage so your son will be the one to inherit everything. He's perfect. He even has a country house in eastern Cornwall, so you'll be settled close to home. I knew you would like that part. It took me most of the morning to sort everything out. I hope you'll finally be happy with this one, because we don't have any other options left."

"Daughters?" Hannah echoed, trying to wrap her head around the words that kept flowing from her mother's mouth. She expected Hannah to become a stepmother? None of this made any sense. She'd *kissed* a man in front of a crowded room. And not just any man—one who'd been sacked from the navy in disgrace and didn't have manners enough to keep himself from swearing in mixed company. She was supposed to be ruined!

What's the point of judging ladies over every step we take if I can't even ruin myself properly when I want to? It shouldn't be this hard to get the job done! Was she going to have to *sleep* with Mr. Corbyn next?

The thought brought a nervous flutter to Hannah's heart, as a memory flashed unbidden in her mind's eye. The sight of his easy, bored manner as the couple upstairs had cried out with pleasure. It was nothing mysterious to him. Would she have to experience that before anyone would accept that she was a fallen woman?

No. There were limits to how far she would go.

Her mother was still talking. "I know it might be a bit intimidating to come into a family that was formed before you, but I met his children at tea just now and they're *lovely* girls. The eldest is already out, so you might not even have her at home much longer—"

"Already out?" Hannah interrupted, shocked from her indecent musings. "Just how old is this man?"

"Don't worry about that until you meet him. Age is far less important than kindness. And he's sure to treat you gently, with the way he dotes on his girls. That's what matters."

"No!" Hannah cried, abandoning any pretense of submission. "You can't mean it, Mama. I'm not marrying a stranger twice my age."

"That stranger is likely the only man who'll still have you, after what you've done." Her mother's voice rose an octave as they fell back to quarreling again. Why did it always turn out this way? If Mama would only *listen*, they might find some peace.

"Good! I don't want any man to have me. I want to be a spinster."

"And who will take care of you once your father and I are gone? Eli and Jane don't have the funds to support another mouth to feed, and it will take everything we have saved to buy a living for Jacob. You need a place of your own while you still have a chance to secure one."

"I could support myself just as Jane does if you would let me," Hannah said stubbornly. "I won't marry Sir Has-a-daughter-who's-already-out."

"You most certainly will." Mama's eyes were burning two holes directly through Hannah's forehead with the strength of their fury. "He is calling on us tomorrow at eleven, and you will receive him and *smile* when he speaks to you. This is your last chance, Hannah. I will not allow you to ruin things again."

"I'm in love with Mr. Corbyn," Hannah blurted out.

Where did that come from?

She hadn't planned the words, but she saw immediately that they were her only hope. Mama already refused to accept that Hannah might prefer to spend her life alone, but the story that she was in love—so deeply and thoroughly in love that she couldn't even look at another man—might prove more persuasive. After all, hadn't that been exactly what they'd all been pushing her toward for more than four years? Didn't they want her to lose her head?

Be careful what you wish for, Mama.

"That ruffian?" Mama drew back, affronted. "He took advantage of you! He's the reason your good name is ruined. I don't know what pretty words he said to trick you into it, but you mustn't believe him. A man like that is nothing but trouble."

"You're wrong about him. He might look a bit rough from a distance, but he's actually kindhearted and good. He was worried about me. He tried to help me when I needed it."

Hannah didn't have much time to plan. They were shooting accusations back and forth so fast that it was all she could do to keep up. Maybe that was why she found herself speaking something very near the truth, instead of another lie.

Mr. Corbyn *was* all those things. It wasn't fair for Mama to criticize him so harshly without even taking the time to know him.

"I worry about you," her mother cried, exasperated. "*I've* been the one helping you, though you never see it. All of us have been. You don't need to throw yourself after a common scoundrel to find love, Hannah. He'll never give it to you."

It shouldn't upset her if Mama spoke of Mr. Corbyn with such disdain in her voice, or if she called him a ruffian or a scoundrel. After all, he wasn't here to be hurt by it, so it was silly to be hurt on his behalf. It was *good* that Mama thought so little of him, for it was the only reason they weren't being marched to the altar together at the end of a rifle. Hannah wasn't sure why it troubled her.

I don't want love, she reminded herself fiercely. *I want a way out.*

She drew herself up tall in her armchair. "Either I marry Mr. Corbyn, or I marry no one," she announced, knowing full well the first option was impossible. "I won't have any man but him."

Check and mate. Let Mama try to bring her baronet to call now.

A note arrived for Silas bright and early the next morning.

I'm very sorry to trouble you, but I'm in a bit of a bind and it would be extraordinarily helpful if you could come by the house at <u>exactly</u> quarter past eleven in the morning and declare your undying love for me. Don't worry if they won't admit you, just be sure to yell loudly enough that we can hear you indoors. I'll leave a window open.

<u>I'll pay you double what I did last time!!</u>

—H. Williams

Bold of her to presume I can read.

Silas had been educated as well as means would allow, his father having put all his hopes of social advancement into his firstborn son, but not many men of his station in life were so fortunate. Miss

Williams couldn't have known. He wasn't sure if her thoughtless assumption that he was her mental equal was flattering or merely further proof of her naivete.

He glanced at the note again, then crumpled it up and tossed it in the rubbish bin. It might have been better if he *couldn't* read; it would have saved him from seeing such nonsense.

A hundred and twenty pounds to make an ass of himself. The sum was incredible enough to give him pause. If the woman was searching for ways to bankrupt herself, would it be so wrong to help her along? He could use the money.

Besides which, what if she truly needed his help? *A bit of a bind* could mean anything. She'd been so rash before; who knew what she might do if Silas ignored her plea.

But if he turned up on Miss Williams's doorstep, her brother would have little choice but to put a stop to the show. No. He wasn't getting involved in this. The girl had a good family that seemed to care about her, which was more than could be said for most. And Silas had his pride.

Anyway, there were less humiliating ways to earn a living. He was going to see about some of them right now, in fact. It was only seven o'clock, but this was the best time to make his way to the dockyards, before the day's work began. He set a hat upon his head and then he was off.

Of all the dockyards in town, St. Katherine's and the adjacent London Docks were the ones nearest his modest lodgings in Southwark. As he drew nearer to his destination, the neighboring alleys seemed to grow more cluttered, the buildings a little sadder and more crooked. There were common lodging houses by the dozens proclaiming low rates for the dockers and watermen who worked nearby. Silas might easily have been forced to sleep here, in a run-down doss-house with twelve men to a room, if it weren't for his prize money.

And Miss Williams's sixty pounds, he reminded himself. Despite his misgivings, he couldn't deny that the stack of banknotes she'd thrust in his hands yesterday bought him some comfort.

The shops had begun to take on a maritime character, and Silas assessed their potential as he walked. Here was a slopseller, the windows full of hammocks, flannel shirts, canvas trousers, and well-oiled sou'wester hats. Beyond that stood a tavern, and then a sack maker's.

None of them seemed particularly promising, until Silas came upon a window full of bright brass instruments—sextants and chronometers and a large mariner's compass. *This might do.* Navigation was one of the first things he'd learned as a cabin boy when his father had apprenticed him out to the navy. If he asked for work here, he would bring some skill with him.

The shop looked to be closed, but he could see movement inside. Silas raised his hand to knock on the door, but stalled in midair, unable to bring himself to do it.

Was he really going to beg for work in a shop?

He could just imagine what his father would say. Actually, there was no need to imagine. He'd already heard it when he'd arrived home after being discharged—the first time in thirteen years he'd set eyes on his parents. *Have you any idea how much I've sacrificed to give you the chance to raise yourself up? And this is how you repay me, by bringing shame on our family name!*

Silas sucked a breath in through clenched teeth. It didn't matter what his father would think; they weren't likely to see each other again. The old man had made that clear enough.

And why should Silas regret it? His parents were little more than strangers to him after so long at sea. He didn't need them now; he was able to make his way alone.

If only he could bring himself to knock on the door first.

Silas lowered his fist. It wasn't that he was still chasing his father's approval—God knew he'd never been able to earn that, even before things went bad—but the sinking feeling in his gut told him this really was a fool's errand. Even if Silas found work here, he would be nothing but a shopkeeper's assistant, counting coin and delivering parcels. Wouldn't it be smarter to find some enterprise he could make his own? His prize money and the winnings Miss Williams had given him weren't enough to live on forever, but they could serve as a modest investment.

Silas continued on to the docks, arriving at the main entrance just in time for the morning call on. A crowd of several hundred men had gathered in the square before the gates: young and old, English and foreign, all jostling one another for a place near the front. As the gates opened, the calling foremen made their appearance and read out the names of the men they needed.

Silas had to wait for the crowd to thin and the rejected men to slink back home before there was room to press on. A cool morning mist hung low in the air, chilling his bones.

He wasn't like these men. They were unskilled laborers with little choice than to break their backs unloading cargo for wages that would barely pay their rent. He knew how to navigate and handle rigging; how to splice ropes and mend sails; how to read and write; and how to do sums. He would find better options inside.

And if you don't, you still have time to declare your love for Miss Williams in exchange for a hundred and twenty pounds.

Where had that thought come from?

No matter how tempting, it was an absurd offer. He needed to find something *real*, not the fantasy she was living.

The dockyard itself was within a walled enclosure spanning some twenty acres, divided into Eastern and Western docks with distinct areas dedicated to various imports. The air grew pungent, the smells of the cargo layering over one another in waves—tallow, rum, tar, and burnt tobacco. (This last one was ever present, rising in great black plumes from the long chimney of the tobacco warehouse, where they burned the leaves that had been ruined by mold or rot.)

Imposing, yellow-gray brick buildings framed the quay in an orderly row that stood six stories high. Most of these were bonded warehouses to store the wealth of the empire's colonies—tobacco, sugar, tea, timber, ivory, and all other manner of goods. Silas didn't stop here to inquire about work. That sort of trade was an ugly business, and not one that he wanted to be a part of.

The bright, ringing sound of a hammer striking metal drew his attention to a middle-aged man on the quay, hammering iron hoops around a large oak cask. The wood staves that formed the rounded sides of the cask trembled slightly with every blow.

Silas's father was a cooper, though he worked for a brewery rather than a dockyard. Still, crafting kegs couldn't be that different from crafting barrels to hold whale oil or wine.

If only the old man had seen fit to teach me the trade.

He'd been adamant that Silas wouldn't need it. He would have been furious to see his son come back to this, despite all his efforts to claw their family up the social ladder.

Perhaps that, more than anything else, was what pushed Silas to approach the man.

"Good morning," he called.

The cooper acknowledged him with a nod, pausing to wipe the sweat from his brow and catch his breath. "You lookin' to buy?" He gave Silas a once-over, trying to assess what his role might be.

"No," he replied swiftly, before he could give rise to any false hopes. "I'm looking for work."

"Are you a cooper?"

"No, sir." He seemed to be good at causing disappointment. "But my father was. I grew up watching his craft."

A shameless exaggeration. Silas couldn't remember more than bits and pieces of his father's work—the sounds of beating metal and the scent of toasted wood mingling with the yeast of beer from the brewery. He'd done more growing up at sea than he had at home.

"It takes at least five years to be better than useless, an' most of my apprentices start young." The cooper raised up his hammer again, apparently deciding that he'd taken enough time from his work. When he spoke again, Silas had to strain to catch his words between his strikes on the iron hoop that banded the wooden staves together. "How old are you?"

"Four-and-twenty." An age by which he'd hoped to make lieutenant.

"Bit late to start on somethin' new."

Silas stiffened at the frank assessment. Did this man think he was clever to have noted the obvious? "Be that as it may, I need work."

"Why didn't your father take you on?"

"I don't see how that's any of your business," Silas said coolly. This was going about as well as his conversation with Miss Danby at the gambling club.

Steady, he reminded himself. *You can't afford to lose your temper.*

"Beg pardon," he forced himself to add through a stiff jaw. "I'd rather not get into it."

The cooper shrugged, though only with the shoulder that wasn't engaged in hammering. "I already have an apprentice." He glanced up at Silas, his gaze lingering on his arms. "I might find room for a strapping fellow like you, but only if I could be sure you'd stay on long enough to be worth my while. Plenty of folks say they want to learn the craft, but don't have the eye for it. I'll not waste my time if you lose heart after a year or two. What's your name?"

"Silas Corbyn."

"John Davies," the cooper replied without formality. "You have someone who can vouch for you? Someone who can prove you're a man to finish what he starts?"

"Uh..." He could hardly ask his former captain for a letter of recommendation after what happened. And all of his fellows in the navy either believed the lies Captain O'Brien had spun about Silas or were too afraid to speak out. *The only one who believed my side of the story was Williams, and I ruined that when I kissed his sister.* "I suppose I don't."

"Afraid I can't help you then. I'm sorry, but I won't take on a perfect stranger." Davies was kind enough to make his apology sound sincere, if not particularly impassioned.

Silas thanked the man and set back off, his step a good deal heavier than when he'd started.

Of course the cooper would want a recommendation. Any craftsman worth his salt knew that his knowledge was too valuable to give away to anyone who knocked on his door. Why hadn't he expected that?

Silas was startled from his troubles by the chiming of the hour a little further down the waterfront. Already nine o'clock. Not much time left now before the hour of his engagement with Miss Williams.

No. Not an engagement. I never agreed to it.

Still, she was likely expecting him to come. Was counting on it, perhaps. What was she doing now? And what was happening at exactly quarter past eleven that she needed him for?

Miss Williams's problems are none of my concern.

Whatever it was, she couldn't be in real danger. She had money and a family to protect her, which was more than he could say for himself. She didn't need saving. This wasn't like what happened with O'Brien.

Silas pushed his hair out of his eyes and tried to shake off the lingering doubt that clung to him.

He forced himself to wander a little further and knock on another door—the sailmaker this time, and after that the rope works—but their answers were the same. They already had apprentices, younger and more experienced than Silas. None of them were willing to take on a stranger without a friend to recommend him.

This is hopeless. He turned back down the same path he'd taken into the dockyards, eager to be gone. He should have known better than to think it would be so easy. When O'Brien had ruined his good name, it hadn't stopped with the court-martial. Even if Silas could find someone to vouch for his character, they would change their mind about him as soon as they learned about his past.

His own family didn't want him. How could he expect anyone else to?

𝒥𝒷~

When Silas returned to his shabby lodgings in Southwark, he was so distracted that he didn't notice the couple standing on his doorstep until he was nearly upon them.

He came up short, observing them silently. They had their backs to him and seemed to be debating whether to knock at his door.

"I'm sure this is the right one," the woman said. She had a mass of unruly blond curls and was dressed like a tradesman's wife. Something about her seemed vaguely familiar, but Silas couldn't have said what without seeing her face. The stocky young man at her side didn't trigger any memories.

"Can I help you?" They both turned at Silas's voice. Now that he had a good look at them, he was no closer to saying who these people might be. "Are you looking for Mr. Kurtz?"

The woman squinted at him intensely. "Silas?"

She had a face full of freckles and a snub nose that reminded him of his grandfather. "Marian?" he guessed. He hadn't seen his cousin since she was small, but the woman before him bore a certain resemblance to her. And he couldn't think who else might be looking for him.

"Oh good, it *is* you. This is the third place we tried." Marian's wide grin revealed crooked white teeth. "You might have written to say where you were staying, you know."

I didn't think anyone would care to find me.

The young man at her side hadn't spoken yet, but he was staring at Silas expectantly.

"Um...?"

"You can't be serious!" he exploded. "You recognize your cousin but not your own brother?"

Shit. Half of Silas's siblings had still been small children when he'd left home. The younger ones were perfect strangers, known only to him by the occasional mention in his mother's letters, not by their faces. "Paul?" he tried.

"*James!*"

"Sorry." Silas winced. James had only been five when he'd left, which would make him barely eighteen now. He'd grown up to be a strapping, broad-shouldered young man with a shock of sandy-brown hair and Silas's own sharp cheekbones. "What are you both doing in London?"

"Aren't you going to invite us in?" Marian scolded. "Where are your manners?"

Silas apologized again—hoping it would be the last time—and waved them into his lodgings, stopping by the kitchen to put a kettle on before he took a seat with them at the table.

"I can't believe you didn't recognize me," James was still muttering when he arrived at his chair.

"I haven't seen you in thirteen years," Silas pointed out.

"You might have done if you'd stuck around a bit longer when you came back! Imagine my surprise when I got home from the market to find that you'd been there and left again already. Mum was in a state."

"I wasn't welcome."

James shifted uncomfortably at the edge to his brother's tone. "Ah, that's just Pa being Pa. But I would've been glad to see you."

"You're seeing me now." Silas spread his hands to encompass his person and their surroundings.

"And we're very glad to do so," Marian cut in. "How are you, cousin?"

"Grand," he replied, trying to keep the bitterness from his tone.

"I'm so sorry about everything with the navy," Marian continued, her hazel eyes soft with sympathy. "Have you found other work?"

"I'm still weighing my options." He wasn't about to recount his disastrous efforts at the docks, nor his single night as a dealer at a ladies' gambling club.

"Wonderful!" James grinned, until Marian elbowed him sharply in the side.

"What James *meant* to say was that we have complete faith in you."

"But we do have an opportunity to discuss, seeing as you're not busy."

"James! Let us visit a minute before we get into all that. We haven't even had tea. Honestly."

The kettle was whistling by now, but Silas ignored it. "What sort of opportunity?" He studied the unlikely pair before him. They didn't look like businessmen. He hoped whatever "opportunity" they'd found was something more respectable than thieving. As the youngest of five sons, James might have reason to want to seek out his own fortune instead of trodding in the footsteps of everyone who came before him. But why should Marian want to get mixed up in whatever he had planned? And why should they involve *him*?

"Well, you know that Grandpa has been looking for someone to take over the brewery," Marian began, before interrupting herself. "Or maybe you don't. *Do* you know?"

"Mum wrote me."

"All right. So anyway, I offered to do it, since I've only been working there my *entire* life, but then Jack said he wanted it. So even though he knows absolutely *nothing* about the business and he's spent all these years training to be a cooper, now everyone's decided he should get the brewery instead."

"Typical," muttered James.

Silas had no idea whether it actually was typical or not. The petty rivalries of a family belonged to people who lived in, well, a *family*.

All he had was a collection of faded memories that abruptly ceased before he'd been old enough to appreciate their value.

"So I said to myself, I know everything there is to know about brewing beer. I grew up crawling through hops and I have connections to half the pubs in Staffordshire. Why shouldn't I start my own? All I need is someone to make the barrels—"

"That's me," James put in, quite unnecessarily.

"And an initial investment for the premises and to buy the hops." Marian smiled broadly as she finished her explanation.

Silas drew the obvious conclusion. "And I'm your investor? How could you know I have any money?"

Miss Williams may not have been discreet when she'd turned up with an envelope of banknotes for him yesterday, but he hardly thought the tale had reached Staffordshire.

Marian scrunched up her short nose. "Isn't that why Uncle John sent you to join the navy? I thought everyone got rich on prize money out there. Your kettle is boiling, by the way."

Silas grunted his acknowledgment and rose to prepare the tea in the next room. He could use a minute to collect his thoughts.

It felt like fate, the two of them showing up here right when he needed an opportunity. And he had fond memories of his grandfather's brewery; the smell of yeast thick in the air as he'd run around behind the barrels to jump out and scare his cousins. His imagination could easily paint an idyllic picture of the life he might have if he said yes—a business of his own to bring him a steady profit, surrounded by family. What would it be like to have that connection again? He might not know James very well, but they were still blood. And Marian had always been a dependable, hardworking girl. She'd never complained when she'd had to roll up her sleeves and help their grandfather with something.

But this was risky. They would want him to put in everything he had. If the business failed, he would have nothing left to fall back on.

He brought the tea out and sat back down, his voice carefully neutral as he spoke again. "How much are you asking for?"

"I think three hundred should do the trick."

Silas nearly choked on his first sip. "*Pounds?*"

"Well, I don't mean shillings!"

He rubbed a hand over his brow. "I don't know how much you think a midshipman earns, but you're sorely mistaken. Don't you have anyone else who can contribute? Is it just the two of you?"

"Three of us," James corrected. "Marian stole Jack's brewmaster because the fellow's sweet on her—"

"He is *not* sweet on me. Would you stop being so unprofessional? We're discussing business."

"But we don't know any more rich blokes to come up with the funds."

"*I'm* not a rich bloke," Silas reminded them. "Even if I were sure about this, I don't know where I can find us three hundred pounds. Could you do it on two? I might be able to come up with two."

If he took all his prize money, plus the sixty pounds from Miss Williams, plus the hundred and twenty she'd promised him to come back today, he was nearly there.

That was assuming that he could still make it to Mayfair in time. "What time is it?"

James pulled out a rather worn pocket watch. "Half ten."

"We need to keep this quick." It would take him several minutes to find a hansom cab, and there was no telling if the roads would be clogged. He might have already missed his chance.

"We came all the way to London to find you!" James protested, indignant.

"It isn't that I don't want to see you, but the only place I can think that I might be able to find that sort of money comes with a very precise time limit. Now, can you do it with two hundred or can't you?"

Marian shot a doubtful look at James. "I don't know," she replied, fishing a small, leather-bound notebook out of her things. "It's easier to start out small than it used to be since they lowered the price of a brewing license, but we'd still need money for supplies and workmen. And there aren't many buildings up for rent with the space we'd need. I'd want to stay near Burton, where I know all the suppliers and pub owners, but I wouldn't want to be so close to Jack that he thinks we're trying to run him out of business. That only leaves a few options. I drew up an estimate of the initial costs based on what Grandpa spends."

She pushed her notebook toward him, where a list of rents and potential expenses were neatly laid out.

"*Are* you trying to drive Jack out of business?" Silas asked absently, skimming through the numbers. It looked like Marian had done a thorough job of planning, at least. "You could set up shop somewhere else."

"Why should I have to run away when I haven't done anything wrong?" She scowled, which made her look more impish than threatening. "If you can't get us the money, do you have any friends who might want to invest? We'd rather keep it to family, but beggars can't be choosers."

"No." Most of his friends had disappeared when his fortunes had turned. He couldn't ask them for that kind of loan.

Marian slumped at this news, though it didn't stop her for long. "You could get two hundred, though?"

"Possibly. If I leave this instant." In his haste to make sure the opportunity didn't slip away, Silas scarcely had time to think about whether it was a good idea.

"Go, then!" James urged. His earlier pique at being abandoned had evaporated once he learned money was at stake. "We'll be here when you get back."

Marian wrinkled her nose as she looked around the room. "Actually, we'll leave you a note with the address where we're staying. We rented some rooms from a lovely woman not far from here. We're only a few streets down from the Anchor Brewery and we thought we might try to tour it tomorrow. Why don't you come and stay with us? It's much nicer than this—sorry—and we could plan our next steps together."

Silas was hardly listening. He was still dressed for the dockyards and needed to change his clothes before he could show himself in Mayfair. "Yes, yes." He waved her away quickly. "We'll sort it all out once I'm back."

He needed to hurry. He had a lady to help and a hundred and twenty pounds to make.

Six

"WHAT ARE YOUR ACCOMPLISHMENTS, MY DEAR GIRL?" SIR Richard smiled at her. He was a balding man with a large, white mustache stained with yellow along the bottom: the effects of too much tobacco.

He had been sitting in her tearoom for ten minutes already and there was still no sign of Mr. Corbyn. *What if he doesn't come?*

At this rate, Hannah was going to have to scare her suitor off herself. She'd been trying her best, but Mama was scarcely letting her get a word in.

True to form, she interjected, "My Hannah is perfectly fluent in French and Italian, she paints, *and* she plays the pianoforte."

Yes. An enormous amount of time and effort had been devoted to equipping Hannah with a list of skills to impress people at dinner parties.

"How lovely," Sir Richard replied, obviously pleased.

"But my true passion is taxidermy," Hannah said, seizing a pause in the conversation. At last! This was her chance to horrify their guests.

"Pardon?" Sir Richard didn't seem nearly as put out as she'd hoped. If anything, he was confused. He blinked his eyes in a grandfatherly sort of way.

He did most things in a grandfatherly sort of way, if Hannah was being honest.

It was his daughter, Miss Fielding, who wrinkled up her nose in disgust. "Do you mean to say you actually go about collecting fallen birds and things to stuff for dioramas?"

It wasn't entirely clear why Miss Fielding had accompanied her father. Perhaps their parents had expected the girls to form a fast friendship given there were only two years separating them, but if so, the hope was quickly proving misguided. Miss Fielding seemed nearly as underwhelmed by the potential match as Hannah herself.

"Yes," Hannah replied brightly, at the exact moment her mother said, "*No.*"

They exchanged a simmering glare.

"Hannah has such a delightful sense of humor," Mama continued. "Very refreshing. Wouldn't you agree, Sir Richard?"

She's ruining all my efforts to ruin things!

"Oh." His laugh was little more than a dry wheeze. "Yes. Er— most refreshing."

"Would you like to hear more of my jokes?" Hannah asked. "I know a number of amusing limericks."

"That won't be necessary. Thank you, poppet." Mama's smile was growing brittle. "Sir Richard, why don't you tell us about your home. You're situated near Liskeard, aren't you? It's such a lovely town. And so close to us in Devon!"

Hannah pretended not to see the hopeful look her mother threw her way.

"Oh yes." Sir Richard smiled. He had crow's feet around his eyes that grew more pronounced with every movement. "I remember when

Liskeard was nothing but a sleepy farming town. But since the copper mine, it's grown dreadfully busy. Such a commotion on market day…"

This last observation sounded rather like a complaint, but Mama clung defiantly to her optimism. "How wonderful. Industry breathing new life into the region! I'm sure there must be plenty of activities there to keep a young lady occupied."

She nudged Hannah gently in the side.

Across from them, Sir Richard seemed to be engaged in a similar battle of wills with his own daughter. "If you'd like to call on us in the country, I'm sure Mary would be happy to show you the town, wouldn't you, my dear?"

Miss Fielding looked as though she'd been asked to give a tour to soldiers invading her country. Hannah might actually have got on well with her, under different circumstances. They both understood the torment that could be wrought by deluded parents.

"That would be lovely," Mama replied on Hannah's behalf. "You're too kind."

Behind them, the lace curtains fluttered in the breeze like a flag of surrender. Hannah had taken care to crack the windows this morning, but there was *still* no sign of Mr. Corbyn. It was twenty past eleven. If she didn't sabotage this call soon, she might actually find herself engaged to an octogenarian before nuncheon.

I don't need Mr. Corbyn. I can make a fool of myself all on my own.

"I'm afraid it's impossible." Hannah raised her voice over her mother's desperate attempt to shush her. "You see, I expect to be married soon."

This didn't have the desired impact at all. Miss Fielding was the only one to furrow her brow in dismay, while Sir Richard gave another breathy chuckle.

"My, my, rather eager, aren't we? But I suppose it's only natural. All girls dream of becoming a wife…"

Oh no. He thinks I'm talking about him, Hannah realized. Of course he did. Hadn't the events of the past two days proven that she was cursed with a complete inability to escape unwanted suitors?

"To a dashing young midshipman I met recently," she added. "He swept me off my feet and I'm desperately in love with him."

Miss Fielding perked up at this. She looked happy for the first time all morning.

Best of all, this revelation finally provoked the desired reaction from Sir Richard.

His face grew red as he drew back, sputtering, "Why—I had no idea! I understood you to be an eligible young woman, Miss Williams. Your mother assured me that the recent rumors about you were nothing but idle talk."

"They are," Mama said quickly. "My daughter is *confused*, Sir Richard. You mustn't pay her any mind. She's an impressionable girl who fell prey to some sweet words, but I assure you that her virtue is perfectly untarnished. She only needs someone older and wiser to guide her."

"I'm in love," Hannah repeated, unable to keep the desperation from her voice. "I won't have anyone else."

If only Mr. Corbyn were here! They would never have ignored *him*, with his commanding presence and icy stare. Without his help, her mother was making Hannah sound delusional.

Silly as the hope might have been, deep down she'd thought he would come.

"You will cease this nonsense at once," Mama hissed in her ear. Her tone was clearly meant to escape notice, but their guests had likely heard it in the stillness of the room.

"It isn't nonsense. It's true," Hannah retorted. Unlike her mother, she didn't bother to keep her voice down.

Although Sir Richard looked as though his tea had curdled, he still hadn't put an end to the call. After a long-suffering sigh, he said, "If young Anna is to stay under *my* roof, there will be no more flights of fancy. But I expect a baby or two might be just the thing to keep her occupied. It would be so nice to finally have a son…"

Is he talking about me?

"My name is *Hannah*," she corrected. "With an H."

"Oh dear, what did I say?" Sir Richard seemed to come back to himself with a start. "Pardon me. My late wife was an Anna. It's only force of habit."

This can't be happening! Hannah shot an urgent glance to her mother, but her attention was fixed solely on their guests.

"We're grateful for your understanding and patience, Sir Richard."

Grateful! For the understanding of a man who couldn't even keep his wives straight?

Hannah would set her hair on fire before she accepted this. In fact, that might still be an option. There was a matchbook in the cabinet beside the candlesticks, wasn't there?

"Shall we come to the point of it?" Sir Richard asked, interrupting her frantic schemes. "It seems we're in agreement that your daughter needs a firm hand. It probably comes from letting her be exposed to the fast crowds of London without her father here to keep order."

Mama stiffened at this, but Sir Richard carried on as if he hadn't noticed.

"The best thing for her is to be married without delay and removed from any corrupting influences. If we have the first banns read this Sunday, I can have her safely to my country house before the month is out."

Hannah opened her mouth to shout her objections, but found a vanilla wafer stuffed rather violently between her lips before she knew what was happening. While she tried to keep from choking to death, Mama spoke over her. "Have a biscuit, darling. You were so excited that you scarcely ate a thing at breakfast."

I was not excited, Hannah wanted to protest. *I was planning my insurrection.*

But she couldn't talk until she chewed and swallowed, which was taking an inordinate amount of time. Why on earth had Cook made these things so dry? It was like having a mouthful of vanilla-flavored sand in her mouth.

"Why don't you and I settle the details later, Sir Richard?" Mama continued. "This was a marvelous introduction. I know Hannah was simply delighted to meet you, but these girls don't have the patience for a discussion of the marriage settlement. I can call on you tomorrow to work everything out between us."

"Won't her father handle that?" Sir Richard looked surprised.

"Er—he'll come to town to formalize matters with the solicitors presently, but rest assured that I speak with his full authority until then."

"Mmph!" Hannah pleaded. Would she manage to swallow before her wedding day? She held up a finger and scrambled for a mouthful of tea to wet her throat. "I didn't agree to—"

"We'll talk about this later, poppet."

"But I—"

"Have another biscuit."

Hannah was ready for her this time, jerking her face away an instant before the inevitable collision smeared powdered sugar down her cheek. "Would you *please* stop that? I don't want a biscuit!" *Wait a minute. That wasn't what I meant to say.* "And I don't want to be *married* either," she added. That was the crucial part.

"A little more gratitude would suit you well, young lady." Sir Richard wagged his finger in the direction of Hannah's nose. But it wasn't his dry, raspy voice that had captured her attention or made her sit bolt upright in her chair.

Had she only imagined it, or was there someone outside? For a second, she thought she'd heard her name.

That, or desperation has made me hallucinate. The last few days had certainly begun to feel like a fever dream.

Her mother was back to task. "I promise you, Sir Richard, she's really a very lovely girl. She only needs a little time to appreciate all the advantages of the match..."

There! Hannah rose from her seat and scampered to the window. There really *was* someone outside.

"Miss Williaaaaams." The voice was louder this time. She recognized that rich timbre and gruff tone. Hannah wasn't one to pay much mind to what a man's voice sounded like, but in her present circumstances she had to own that it was the most attractive sound she'd ever heard.

"I'm here!" she called back, throwing the curtains to one side so that everyone could see her knight in shining armor. She hadn't imagined him!

Mr. Corbyn was actually wearing a tweed morning coat, not armor, but his golden hair shone brightly in the sun, which was nearly as good. He looked heroic, at any rate. Particularly when Molly went outside a moment later to try to shoo him away with a parasol and Mr. Corbyn stood his ground in the face of this siege.

Despite the distraction, he seemed to spot Hannah's face in the window. He cupped his hands over his mouth and shouted, "I'm in love with you." After a pause, he added, "Undyingly."

Oh my.

Hannah had never received a declaration of love before. She'd expected it to sound a little more passionate, even if it was an act. But Mr. Corbyn had spoken in the sort of tone one might have used to say, "I'm going to the dentist to deal with this persistent toothache."

Still, he'd arrived in the nick of time and he'd remembered her name. Hannah couldn't afford to be choosy.

"What on earth...!" Mama reached her side, her face turning scarlet as she recognized the man she'd beaten with her reticule the other night. "*Him.*"

She grabbed the latch to the window and slammed it shut so quickly that Hannah worried that they might damage Eli and Jane's house. Then she tugged the curtains back into place with a rough jerk.

"Careful," Hannah admonished. "That's French lace."

Her mother turned to their guests. "Sir Richard, I can explain."

But it was too late. Mama's baronet and his daughter had already risen from their chairs to get a good look at the man professing his love on the front lawn. Judging by their thunderous expressions, they were none too impressed. Sir Richard carried himself with great restraint as he spoke. "I believe this call was a mistake, Mrs. Williams. We shall bid you good day."

"That man is nobody," Mama said quickly, rushing after her guests as they made toward the door. "I beg you to pay him no mind."

"He's my dearest love," Hannah called after them, a giggle of triumph bubbling up from her lungs. "We shall never break faith, though the world conspires to keep us apart!"

She needn't have bothered with this last part. Sir Richard and his daughter were already gone, hurrying from the room and down the approach to the house with a disdainful glance toward Mr. Corbyn, who was still dodging the maid's assault.

It worked! I'm safe!

There was no chance that Sir Richard would be back after this. He was brave enough to take on one headstrong girl, it seemed, but not her strapping young lover. And hadn't Mama said this was her *last* chance for a match?

Oh dear. Now Mama had gone outside to join in the fray. Hannah craned to see them through the window. Mr. Corbyn had managed to escape the maid and put the hedges between himself and his pursuers, but with a second person in the mix he wouldn't be able to evade them much longer. *I'd better go out and make sure they don't hurt him.*

It would be a poor reward to send the man home with a bloodied nose in exchange for saving her life.

෴

What the hell am I doing here?

Silas had asked himself this question a hundred times on the journey over to Mayfair, but it took on a new urgency as Mrs. Williams descended the front steps and stormed toward him. At least he didn't see a brick-stuffed reticule in her hands this time.

"What is the meaning of this?" the woman bellowed, red-faced. "Do you have any idea what you've done?"

Scared off a pair of callers, from the looks of things. The old man and the young lady who'd hurried past him with matching expressions of horror must have been the reason for Miss Williams's invitation, though Silas didn't care to guess why their presence should require his intervention.

"Er... Sorry to intrude," he tried. "I just came to speak to Miss Williams."

What was he supposed to do now? She hadn't provided him with a script for this part.

"You won't so much as *look* at Hannah again if I have anything to say about it!" Mrs. Williams made a lunge at him, but Silas stepped backwards and her elbow collided with the hedges in a cacophony of snapping branches.

"Mr. Corbyn!" Miss Williams chose that moment to emerge from the house and rush down the steps. "You *came*."

She didn't look like she was in any danger. A brilliant smile lit up her face as she approached, her dark eyes sparkling with joy. Her cheeks were pink with exertion as she hurried toward him.

Silas wasn't sure when he'd last met anyone so happy to see him. It was strangely gratifying after the abysmal failure of his morning, until a sudden "*Aha!*" and a vise grip on his forearm reminded him that he was still supposed to be dodging her mother and their maid. The pair had moved in to flank him from both sides while he'd been distracted.

"Don't hurt him!" Miss Williams cried, immediately stricken by his capture.

How embarrassing.

This had to be the most humiliating way he could have chosen to earn a bit of coin, but could he truly afford to complain? After his spectacular failure to find work at the docks this morning, he was forced to acknowledge the truth. There was no other way to come up with the money he needed for Marian and James's brewery.

"Go back inside, Hannah," her mother snapped. "I'll deal with this one."

Her tone heavily implied that Silas might soon find himself stuffed in a sack and thrown into the Thames, though he wasn't convinced these women could manage the job without reinforcements. That maid looked a bit frail. He could probably break free of their grasp with one swift twist, but he didn't want to hurt either of them.

"Your brother isn't at home, is he?" Silas asked Miss Williams, in what he hoped was a fearless tone.

"No. Why?"

At least there was one piece of good news. Though Silas might still have to search for new lodgings before Williams came back and learned of all this. Maybe he should take Marian and James up on their offer to stay with them.

"Stop talking to him!" Mrs. Williams scolded her daughter. "You've already spoiled your chance at a match with Sir Richard. I won't have you encouraging this ruffian."

"I can hear you, ma'am," Silas pointed out. It was bad enough that they insisted on hauling him up like a sack of coal. Did they need to speak about him as if he weren't there as well? And what was this about a match, anyway? "You can't mean to tell me you were really going to marry your daughter to that old codger."

The man who'd tottered down the walk was sixty if he was a day. What business did he have creeping around Miss Williams?

"Mind your tongue," her mother returned. "Sir Richard has more dignity in one finger than you have in your entire body."

This was difficult to argue with, given his present circumstances.

"You've no right to interfere with Hannah's prospects," Mrs. Williams continued. "If you truly cared for her, you'd have the decency to stand aside and let her find a man of her own class. Surely you must see that you could never hope to marry her."

Everyone paused to look at Silas here, as if awaiting his confirmation.

Who said anything about marriage? He wanted to retort. *I only met the girl two days ago.*

They shouldn't even need to hear him say it. It was obvious he couldn't match a gently bred lady like Miss Williams, who'd been raised with every refinement he lacked.

But Miss Williams was staring at Silas with a particular urgency, her dark eyes pleading. Clearly, she'd said something to make her mother believe that he had grander intentions than a stolen kiss at her brother's club. That was why she'd needed him to show up and profess his love.

Which he'd done. That was the real problem here: He kept agreeing to things he should have sense enough to steer clear of.

That had always been his problem.

Miss Williams must have grown tired of waiting on him, for she answered matter-of-factly, "We've made a vow in our hearts, even if you won't let us make one in a church. We'll never marry anyone else, no matter how long you keep us apart."

Oh. So that was her game, was it? He was her excuse to remain a spinster, even if they never saw each other again.

"Yes," he agreed. He'd already come this far. He didn't care to turn back without earning his pay, particularly when he had little hope of finding it elsewhere. "I'll, er, wait for you forever."

Miss Williams narrowed her eyes. Too much? It was no worse than all the rubbish she'd said. Besides, he'd never claimed to be an actor.

Her mother was equally unimpressed, judging from her expression.

"Is it money you're after?" Was the woman clairvoyant? Mrs. Williams abandoned her grip on Silas's forearm, confident that she'd found a better means to be rid of him. "I'll give you two pounds never to darken our door again."

"I'm not for sale," he replied, insulted.

Never mind that he was only here because Miss Williams had already bought him. That was different. He couldn't have explained exactly how, but it was. She didn't look at him with scorn, for a start.

"Then what *do* you want?" The gray-haired woman regarded him with a piercing stare.

My old life back. The answer sprang to his mind unbidden. But that wasn't something anyone could give him. Instead, Silas replied, "I...just want Miss Williams to be happy."

It wasn't a response he'd fully considered before speaking. It sounded far too sentimental. Not like him at all. But in a way, it was true.

If Miss Williams found what she was looking for, maybe she would stop asking him for help. More than that, maybe he would feel like he'd done something useful for once.

He might not be able to undo his discharge from the navy or find himself a new trade, but he could fix this young lady's problems before he went on his way.

"What's her favorite color?" Mrs. Williams snapped, crossing her arms over her chest.

"What?" *What has that to do with anything?*

"Her favorite food? What sort of music does she like to dance to?"

Silas didn't even have time to consider one question before Mrs. Williams volleyed a new one at him. He didn't have the faintest idea what to say, but they were all staring, even the maid. Miss Williams tried to signal him with a wiggle of her eyebrows. Was he supposed to know what that meant?

Maybe he could reason this out.

"Um...pink?" Women liked bright, flowery colors, didn't they? Miss Williams was frowning at his reply, but it was too late to stop now. "Cake? And...uh..." What did rich people even dance to these days? Dancing lessons hadn't been part of his education. "The waltz."

That was definitely the name of a dance that people did.

"Wrong on all three!" Mrs. Williams crowed in triumph. *Damn it.* He should have known better than to try. "You see? You don't know the first thing about my daughter. You can't possibly love her. I don't know what game you're playing, but I know when I'm being hoodwinked. Admit it."

"It's not a trick!" Miss Williams rushed to his defense. "I *do* love pink. And cake. Maybe you don't know me as well as you think, Mama. My tastes have changed since I was a little girl."

"And waltzing?" Her mother raised an eyebrow in challenge. "You hate dancing. I hear all about it anytime I try to take you anywhere."

"That one was a trick question! You didn't give Mr. Corbyn a real chance!"

"Enough." Mrs. Williams had raised her voice in her frustration, prompting more than one neighbor to peer out their windows at the spectacle. "You really expect me to believe that you're in love with this"—she wrinkled her nose in the direction of Silas, seeming to search for an alternative to the word *gentleman* before she settled on—"*individual?*"

"Yes," Miss Williams replied immediately. Silas was spared the need to feign agreement, as no one had asked him.

"And he's the reason you won't consider any other suitor?"

"Yes. Exactly," she said again. "I'm simply too much in love to give my heart to another man."

"I suppose this means you won't want to return to Devon." A self-satisfied smile melted the stern line of Mrs. Williams's mouth. "Seeing as how your beloved is here in town."

"Oh. Er—" Her daughter couldn't quite conceal her dismay at this turn. After a brief struggle, she squared her shoulders and bravely proclaimed, "Of course. Although I would have thought *you* would want to keep us apart, Mama. If you're letting me stay in London, does this mean you'll accept Mr. Corbyn as a suitor?"

Did they spend every day trying to outwit each other this way? It looked exhausting.

And Miss Williams might have *asked* him before she made plans to take this ruse any further. Just how long was he supposed to play along?

Thankfully, her mother didn't call this bluff. "No! He's entirely unsuitable and you know it."

"Then it seems we're at an impasse. You can bring as many men as you like to call; none of them could make me forget Mr. Corbyn."

"Fine." Mrs. Williams threw her hands in the air, finally at her wit's end. "I give up. You don't want to meet any of the gentlemen I worked so hard to find you? Don't meet them. You can pine away in your ivory tower. At least it will spare me the embarrassment of having to deal with your behavior at our morning calls."

A flash of relief crossed Miss Williams's face, though she concealed it quickly. It seemed she'd won.

Does that mean I've finished my part?

"I'll never forget you." She turned to Silas, dabbing at her eyes, which were perfectly dry. Yes, this act was reaching its logical conclusion. "I'll write to you every day."

"Uh, I'll write you too," Silas offered. It seemed the sort of thing he should say, though he hoped he wouldn't actually have to fulfill the promise.

"And I'll burn the letters," Mrs. Williams muttered angrily.

Seven

HANNAH SPENT THE NEXT MONTH CONFINED TO HER GUEST room in Jane and Eli's house, counting the petals on the floral motif on the wallpaper and generally trying not to expire from boredom. True to her word, Mama hadn't brought another gentleman caller to the house since the disastrous proposal from Sir Richard.

She also hadn't let Hannah entertain any of her friends, or attend any social events, or even leave the house except under the watch of immediate family. Annabelle Danby had tried to come and see her early in her imprisonment, followed by an inconsistent smattering of the other young debutantes she'd gotten to know since arriving in town, but Mama had turned them all away.

"You wanted to be ruined?" she'd asked Hannah with a cool glare. "Ruined girls aren't welcome in polite society. Respectable *married* women are welcome at any place you'd like to go, if you change your mind about Sir Richard."

"No, thank you." Hannah had pursed her lips and returned to counting petals.

She was allowed to emerge from her prison only to attend

Bishop's with Jane in the mornings, which proved far less exciting than Hannah might have hoped. She was given a long list of chores to accomplish to atone for her sins, and she was always whisked to safety before they opened their doors to guests in the evenings. She'd first been assigned to take an inventory of all the champagne in the cellar, then of all the preserves in the kitchens, and then finally, making sure none of the decks were missing a card.

Hannah was fairly certain that last one had no real purpose but to keep her occupied.

"How are you?" Jane asked over tea and currant buns, sometime toward the end of the fourth week, as they took a short break from their work. Hannah would say this much: Even if bishop's was nothing more than a variation on her prison cell, at least Jane brought treats.

"Fine," Hannah said. "Though I miss Mr. Corbyn dreadfully."

"Hmm." Jane took a bite of her bun, unwilling to comment on this.

Everyone seemed to harbor their doubts about the sincerity of Hannah's love affair—which was really quite rude of them, seeing as she'd gone to so much trouble to produce solid evidence—but they couldn't *prove* she was lying if she didn't admit it.

Though Jane didn't seem to be hunting for inconsistencies in her story as Mama did, one could never be too careful.

"Do you expect that your, uh, devotion to this gentleman will last much longer?" Jane asked delicately.

A trap! Hadn't she just been thinking she was safer here than at home? Jane might seem kind enough, but she'd already proven that she wouldn't keep secrets from Eli. And once Eli knew the truth, he couldn't be trusted not to share it with Mama.

I can't let my guard down with any of them.

"It will last for as long as I live," Hannah said tartly.

Jane's shoulders sank as she let out a long sigh. "All right, all right. I was only asking because my uncle Bertie has been wanting to come and visit, and I wondered how much longer the guest bedrooms would be occupied."

"You could turn us out if you like," Hannah suggested, trying not to sound too eager.

She'd expected that Mama would have admitted defeat and taken them back to Devonshire by now. After all, with her dreams of matchmaking up in smoke, there was nothing to keep them in London. But whenever Hannah tried to broach the subject, Mama stared her dead in the eye and asked, "Won't you miss your true love if we leave?" which made it utterly impossible to press the point any further.

Besides which, her mother seemed to be entrenching herself into Eli and Jane's life here in town. Della had reduced the amount of time she spent at Bishop's since that fateful kiss, meaning Jane and Eli spent more of their evenings there. Mama and Hannah generally watched Gloria now that they were no longer gallivanting across half the ballrooms of London in search of a suitor.

At this rate, it would take some external pressure to drive them from Jane's house.

But Jane retreated from the suggestion immediately. "Of course I wouldn't do that. You and your mother are welcome to stay for as long as you like. Please, forget I said anything."

"What if you gave your uncle Mama's room and put her in the nursery with Gloria? I'm sure she'd love to be closer to her grandchild."

Maybe the nighttime cries would finally do the trick.

"Don't be silly," Jane admonished. "Bertie can stay with Cecily. She has more room anyway. Really, I shouldn't even have brought it up."

Drat. But the nursery idea was rather inspired, if Hannah did say so herself. Was there some other way she could make the house intolerable for her mother? What if she filled her bed with fleas? No, that would be too disgusting. But Hannah resolved to think about it further. There must be something less drastic she could try.

Having run out of menial tasks to assign Hannah several days ago, Jane had recently begun teaching her how to look over the club's books and check that there were no errors in the calculations. Though it probably wasn't meant to be a reward, Hannah actually found the task far more satisfying than counting the inventory in the pantry. It felt important. It also gave her enormous insight into the inner workings of the club. She could see how much they spent on food and drink each month, how they split their profits or reinvested them, and how much they paid their employees.

Hannah's gaze lingered on this last item, tallying up the monthly amounts.

"The dealers only make fourteen pounds a year?" she asked, dismayed. How could anyone live on such a sum? She was sure Mama must spend nearly that much outfitting her in new gowns every season.

This did a good deal to explain the shabby state of Mr. Corbyn's lodgings. Hannah recalled the image with a trace of guilt.

"We're far more generous than they are at White's, I promise you," Jane said earnestly. "And given that we're only open in the evenings, many of the men find other work earlier in the day. It's a good way for most of them to supplement their incomes."

Had Mr. Corbyn needed that money? She hoped he'd found something else by now. She still hadn't contrived to get him the rest of his payment for sabotaging her engagement to Sir Richard. Even if she could find a way to get her hands on the funds, she was never alone long enough to find a way to bribe the coachman again, and

Mama was monitoring all her letters. Hannah was sure to find a chance eventually, but she wasn't optimistic that it would be soon. She hoped he wouldn't think that she'd forgotten him.

"Do you suppose there's any way you might hire Mr. Corbyn back?" It was probably hopeless, but she had to ask. "It was really my fault that he kissed me, and it's not as though he's likely to repeat the incident. There wouldn't be any harm in it."

Jane studied her carefully, her eyes kind but firm. "I'm sorry, Hannah, but we really can't allow him back after something like this. The ladies wouldn't trust that they're safe around him."

Not safe? Mr. Corbyn wasn't a danger to anyone, unless one counted the danger he occasionally posed to Hannah's thoughts. She returned glumly to the figures on the page, trying not to imagine his fate written among them.

Anyway, she didn't need to be poking around these records. Jane had only asked her to check over the tallies for the previous night's profits, not review their expenses. It was mostly Hannah's curiosity that had set her to snooping. That, and a desire to prove that she could be entrusted with a more important role than counting jam jars.

She finished reviewing Jane's calculations while her sister-in-law was still busy writing out the instructions she intended to give Cook for the coming week's menu. As usual, there were no mistakes in the careful sums. *So much for my chance to prove myself.* Jane never made an error.

With nothing else to do to pass the time until they returned to the house, Hannah returned to snooping, this time in the tallies for each of the game tables. She wanted to see where they made the greatest profit.

After a few minutes' study, she ventured a question. "Why do you offer baccarat and faro when they don't make you as much money as vingt-et-un or bridge?"

"Hmm?" Jane looked up from her notes. "Oh. Because even if they don't bring in as much, plenty of ladies like those and they're easy to learn. Running this place is as much about keeping everyone happy so that they'll want to come back as it is about earning the most profit."

"But you have three tables for baccarat when it's the least profitable. Couldn't you reduce it to two? If people had to wait a little to get a seat, they might try another game in the meantime and earn you more income."

Jane rose from her chair to peer over Hannah's shoulder at the figures on the page. "I suppose you might have a point," she admitted, sounding faintly surprised. "I'll talk it over with Della. I didn't realize you had an eye for business, Hannah. Thank you."

It was all she could do not to preen at this acknowledgment. Why couldn't Mama ever see that there were other options for her besides marriage, especially when they had a perfectly good example right here in their own family?

"I'm sure I could think of some other suggestions if you'd let me help out in the evenings," Hannah suggested.

Jane shot her a regretful look. "You must know it's impossible. It was all I could do to convince your mother that you'd be safe under my supervision here in the mornings. She'd never allow it after dark."

"You mean to say that you made Mama let me come?"

"I know it might not be the most exciting outing, but I could hardly leave you trapped at home all day long. You needed something to occupy you." Jane gave her an apologetic smile.

Maybe her sister-in-law *was* on her side. Hannah had thought the work was intended to be a form of penance, but this would explain why there were always delicious treats involved.

Regardless, it was better than counting the flower petals on her wallpaper.

Jane stopped in at the wine merchant's after they finished talking to make some changes to the club's order, so it was nearly three in the afternoon by the time they made it back to the town house.

"Where were you?" Her mother stood waiting for them at the door. "You normally don't stay past one. I was worried."

"I'm sorry," Jane said smoothly. "We lost track of time."

"Oh." Mrs. Williams blinked at this, her desire to keep watch over Hannah obviously warring with her desire not to offend her daughter-in-law while she was a guest in her home.

"I'll go check if Gloria is hungry," Jane excused herself.

"And I'd better go upstairs," Hannah tried. "I have a lot of, um, reading to do."

"Please wait a moment. I'd like for us to talk."

Ugh. This had better not be about Sir Richard again.

Hannah squared her shoulders and followed her mother into the receiving room, where there were biscuits and cold tea waiting. In fairness, it had likely been hot tea at the time they'd been expected home.

"I ate at Bishop's."

An awkward silence fell over the room. Hannah tried not to betray her impatience. She wasn't going to be the one to speak first.

Her mother didn't seem to be in any hurry either, for she turned her attention to the flower arrangement she had set up on the end table. She seemed to have been halfway finished when Hannah had arrived, for there were several fresh sprigs of lavender from the garden that she was tucking strategically around the peonies.

"Are you ready to reconsider Sir Richard yet?" her mother finally asked, without looking up from her hobby. "You could do far worse, you know."

How disappointingly predictable! And there could be little doubt to whom she was referring with that last comment.

"Have *you* reconsidered Mr. Corbyn yet?" Hannah shot back. Why must her mother be so unfair to the fellow? Even if he wasn't up to her standards, there was no need to speak about him with such disdain. He'd done nothing wrong except to take pity on Hannah when she was in need. "I've told you how I feel about him. Nothing you say can change my mind."

"I see that."

Hannah paused. *I must have misheard her.* They rarely agreed on anything. Was this another trick?

"I thought you would see reason after a few weeks of seclusion, but you're so stubborn." Mama set the last of her flowers in the vase and turned away from the arrangement without pausing to admire the final result.

"I find seclusion very peaceful. I would have made an excellent nun, you know." Hannah still remembered how Mama had scoffed at the idea with a touch of bitterness.

"Don't you miss your friends? Don't you want a place in society?" Her mother's eyes were clouded with what looked like genuine confusion. "You could have it all back if you marry respectably, but there won't be any hope of that if you continue on this way. I can't understand why you want to condemn yourself to such a life, poppet."

That was the whole problem. Mama had never understood. How was Hannah to explain what should be obvious?

Her mother had hated her marriage so much she'd run halfway across England to escape it, yet Hannah was meant to look forward to the same fate. How could anyone think that was a future to aspire to?

But she couldn't say any of that. She was meant to be in love with Mr. Corbyn.

Hannah pressed a hand to her breast and emitted a longing sigh, wondering what other signs of lovesickness she could display. "I have no choice. I must follow my heart."

Mama shook her head sadly at this, but only said, "Very well then. I give up."

"Pardon?" *Very well, what?* Were they finally going back to Devon? "Does this mean you've changed your mind?"

"I don't like it," her mother continued grimly, "but we can't go on like this. I won't oppose you anymore."

A little squeal escaped Hannah's mouth. *Finally!*

"Oh, thank you!" She leapt from her seat and threw her arms around her mother's neck, all their past quarrels forgotten. "You don't know how much this means to me. I'm sorry to have upset you, really I am. I just didn't see any other way—" Hannah stopped herself just in time. Better not to reveal her ruse and risk upsetting their newfound agreement. She composed herself and sat back down. "Never mind. It's all in the past now. Let's not think about unpleasant things any longer. Does Papa know?"

He would be happy to have them home again. He would have to be. Even if her parents fought sometimes, they must see that their vows should mean something—that they had a duty to try to work through their differences.

"No." Mama's face looked slightly ashen at this prospect. "And I can't think how we'll obtain his consent. A midshipman, of all things. *Former* midshipman, I should say. How do you expect him to support you without work?"

"Wait, what are you not opposing, exactly?" Even as the words left Hannah's mouth, she feared she knew the answer, but her mind still rebelled. It simply wasn't possible.

They were going back to Devonshire. That was all Mama had meant. It had to be.

"Why, your marriage to Mr. Corbyn," Mama replied. "Why, what did you think I meant?"

Hannah found herself completely incapable of forming a reply.

Eight

MARRIAGE.

To Mr. Corbyn.

Hannah tried to speak, but her lips had transformed into useless lumps of meat. Was this another trap? It *had* to be. But Mama seemed perfectly earnest, fixing Hannah with a raised finger and a warning look as she outlined her plans.

"I expect him to make certain assurances to secure your hand. He'll need to prove to me that he's really the gentleman you claim. I want to meet him *properly*, without any skulking about, and hear him explain how he intends to support a family when he's lost his livelihood."

"Um—"

"And *don't* tell me that he can go back to working at your brother's club, young lady. That might be all well and good until he gets back on his feet, but it's not a respectable profession."

"I wasn't going to say that."

Her mother's plans were so detailed, Hannah scarcely knew what to say. Mama didn't seem to want her input anyway.

"Do you think he might be persuaded to join the army? Even if he were only an ensign, people would think him perfectly respectable then. Only don't think for a minute that I'm giving up your dowry to buy the commission. We'll settle all your money on your children. He's not getting a penny."

Children.

Her children. With Mr. Corbyn. The same man she'd begged and cajoled into helping her, who'd likely never expected to see her again.

Hannah was so agitated by this prospect, she nearly confessed the whole plot to Mama right then and there—everything from the money she'd snuck to his lodgings in payment for his kiss to the note she'd sent to summon his help sabotaging her call with Sir Richard. This had gone too far. She couldn't keep up the act any longer.

Wait!

Hannah bit her lip, though her secrets were burning to escape.

Was this exactly what Mama had planned? She'd been suspicious of Mr. Corbyn from the start, quizzing him on her favorite things and such. Maybe she'd decided to call Hannah's bluff and was only waiting to see how long it would take her to crack.

And once I do, it will be straight back to Sir Richard with me. She had to hold strong, or all her hard work to escape the match would be undone in an instant.

"I–I thought you were determined to keep us apart." Best to test the waters first. She would see how her mother reacted if she played along. "What changed your mind?"

Mrs. Williams pressed her lips into a narrow line before replying. "If you're determined not to listen to me, I don't see what choice I have. I still think you'll regret the match, but I don't wish to keep you cloistered away forever. This might be your only chance to salvage what's left of your reputation."

She really seemed to mean it.

No matter what I do, I'm trapped. Hannah couldn't refuse Mr. Corbyn without exposing herself to an even worse fate. But if she agreed to the marriage, she would have to persuade Mr. Corbyn to play along until she could think of a way to escape with her freedom intact.

Hannah's heart began to race at the thought of presenting herself at his lodgings once more, this time to break the news that her mother wanted them to marry. *You were such a help pretending to be in love with me. Would you mind terribly if we pretended to be engaged too?* She couldn't possibly say such a thing to him. It was so embarrassing; she wanted to hide under her bed until sometime next year.

I have to make Mama abandon this idea of her own accord. But how?

Hannah spoke slowly, praying further inspiration would strike her soon. "What if Mr. Corbyn can't meet your expectations?"

That should be easy enough. It wasn't as though Mama even liked the fellow. All he had to do was swear too often or chew with his mouth open, and the whole business might be forgotten. It should come naturally to him. After all, he'd had trouble minding his language at the club during his astonishingly brief stint as a dealer.

"Do you doubt him? You've been very quick to argue his merits in the past."

Careful. Hannah pretended not to see the suspicious look her mother shot her way.

"Of course I don't doubt him. He's perfectly wonderful." She tried to keep her tone light. If a slight tremor crept in, hopefully Mama would take it for excitement rather than abject terror at her current predicament. "But you *do* seem to have set very high expectations, asking him to prove that he's a gentleman and to buy a commission and whatnot. I only hope you won't scare him away."

If Mr. Corbyn openly rejected her, she couldn't keep using their supposed romance as an excuse to refuse other suitors.

What he needed to do was *fail*. And not just a little bit. He needed to fail so spectacularly that Mama would have no choice but to back down.

How on earth am I going to pay him enough for all this?

Her winnings that first night at the gambling club had been a rare stroke of good fortune, but Hannah didn't often have ready access to that sort of money. If only there were some way she could get at her dowry. Three thousand pounds, just sitting there uselessly in a bank when she had real need of it.

"I'm going to need new clothes," she announced. That might serve. "If I'm to be a married woman soon, I need to look my best. And my trousseau doesn't have more than a few linens in it. Might I have some money to go to the shops?"

Even if it was only a few pounds, it would go to show Mr. Corbyn that she could be trusted to pay him eventually. She might find a way to send little bits each week until she'd fulfilled her debt.

"Your trousseau wouldn't be so empty if you'd been working on it like I asked you to instead of arguing that you didn't need it. Whatever happened to that tablecloth you were supposed to embroider last winter? Did you even finish it?"

"Let's not worry about the tablecloth now," Hannah pleaded. It was gathering dust in their country house, along with her hopes and dreams of freedom. "Might I please have a little money?"

"I can take you to the modiste tomorrow."

Drat. That was no good. She wouldn't have any chance to pocket the funds and slip away to Mr. Corbyn's house with her mother standing watch.

"Couldn't I please go with Miss Annabelle? You haven't let me see any of my friends in weeks."

"You can see your friends again once Mr. Corbyn has proven he's worthy of this family and made a formal offer for you in marriage.

Not a moment sooner." Mama frowned. "He can start by coming by the house for supper on Tuesday so that we can all meet him properly."

"*This* Tuesday?" Hannah squeaked. That left her no time to plan! How was she to instruct Mr. Corbyn on his spectacular failure? What if he succeeded instead?

Wait, that doesn't make any sense, she scolded herself. *It isn't as though he actually* wants *to marry me.* The greatest danger wasn't that he might persuade Mama that he could be a worthy groom; it was that he might grow tired of Hannah's continual demands and expose their whole subterfuge before she'd regained control of the situation.

If only she weren't so wretchedly dependent on him. It was her own fault for having kissed him in the office that night, but she'd never imagined how quickly that one little lie would spread. With every step, it only seemed to grow bigger, until it threatened to dictate all her actions.

"Your brother can extend the invitation." Mama finally turned back to her floral arrangement, apparently considering the matter settled. "Do you think I've added too much lavender? I don't want it to overpower the other elements."

How could she think about flowers at a time like this? Hannah drew a shaky breath.

There was no need to panic. She could still turn things to her favor. She would just have to find some way to get Eli to pass on a message to Mr. Corbyn along with his dinner invitation. Some signal that would convey her desperate need for assistance without revealing anything to her brother. After all, Mr. Corbyn had proven willing to help her so far. *Remarkably* willing, in fact. Hannah might not enjoy having to rely on him again, but it was the only way to keep one step ahead of her mother.

This new turn was merely a wrinkle in her plans, not a defeat. Everything was still well under control.

"I'd like us to go to the hops warehouse this week," Marian said over their supper of quail and fresh greens. "We can think about our choices, once we have the funds to buy. I think it makes the most sense to focus on pale ale. We can't afford the space to cellar much of the beer ourselves, so we'll turn a better profit if we can ship it to India or America and let it cellar on the voyage."

Silas was silent as he chewed his meal. Marian's cooking was a distinct improvement over the fare he'd been eating at the local public house before he'd moved his things over here. Though he wasn't sure he agreed with their decision to spend so much on rent, he had to admit that their lodgings were a vast improvement. And Marian seemed to think that she could make valuable connections in this neighborhood, which was known for its breweries. In the month since their arrival, they'd toured most of the larger breweries of London and invited more than one manager to dine with them. Silas was learning a great deal. He only hoped he would get the chance to use any of it.

"When are you getting your funds, though?" James watched him expectantly. "It's been a month and we still haven't seen a tuppence from that chit. Don't you think it's time to march over there and demand what she owes?"

"How exactly am I supposed to do that without letting her family know that the whole thing was a ploy?"

The way James carried on, one would think Miss Williams owed *him* the money.

"I don't see how that's your concern," James insisted. "You've given her more than enough time to pay."

Silas took another bite of his supper, mainly to avoid the need to reply.

Truth be told, he'd begun to share James's worries. Marian did too, though she was too good to say it directly. He could tell from the look in her eye whenever the subject came up. She'd harbored her doubts about the plan from the start, once Silas had explained what he'd done.

He'd expected Miss Williams to turn up on their doorstep any day, face flushed and nervous to intrude, just as she had been that first time. But in the weeks that followed his dramatic declaration on her lawn, Silas had received no word from her.

Maybe she doesn't know where I'm staying. He'd sent a note to her house when he'd moved lodgings, but her mother was almost certain to destroy it. And though he'd left instructions to the other residents to pass his new address along if any visitors came looking for him, he didn't think Miss Williams would have the nerve to ask them if she knocked at his door and someone else answered.

Nor did he like to imagine her wandering around his previous neighborhood, where anything might happen to her. He didn't trust that coachman of hers. What sort of man would bring a gently bred lady across the water for a bit of coin, anyway? It was reckless.

"Maybe we should see someone at the bank about getting a loan," Marian suggested hesitantly. "Even if Miss Williams pays you soon, it still won't be enough."

"No one will give us that kind of money without collateral." A disgraced, out-of-work midshipman, a woman, and an eighteen-year-old cooper. They weren't an impressive lot.

"Then we're back to searching for another investor."

"We must know *someone*." James groaned. "Think."

"You seemed to be getting friendly with the manager from Courage and Donaldson last week," Marian said to Silas. "Maybe he has some funds. Do you think he might prefer being the part owner of a small operation to being the manager of a large one?"

A sharp rap on the door interrupted them.

"I'll get it," Silas offered. There was always the small possibility that it would be Miss Williams, though he'd gotten his hopes up enough times by now that he didn't truly believe it anymore.

Marian and James are right. She isn't coming. He'd told himself that Miss Williams wasn't the sort to cheat him, with how worried she'd been about taking ten shillings for her coachman from the money for their kiss. But if she intended to come, she would have done it by now. She'd likely forgotten about him the minute he'd served his purpose. Why should she remember? He was nothing to her. Silas was so lost in thought that it took him a moment to realize that he'd opened the door and was standing face-to-face with a well-dressed gentleman.

It was Williams.

Silas tensed. He'd assumed that he was safe when no one had shown up to seek revenge after his little show on their front lawn, but he might have been too hasty.

Williams cleared his throat, looking just as awkward as he had the last time.

"How did you find my new address?"

"My mother intercepted your note to my sister."

"Right." That was much as he'd expected. "Should I...invite you in?" Silas studied his former friend for some sign of his intention.

"Please." Williams sounded slightly weary. As Silas stood aside, he stepped into the foyer. "This is a bit...odd. But apparently my mother has decided—" He broke off suddenly, his face darkening.

Silas turned to see what had caught his attention, to find Marian leaning her towheaded mop through the adjacent doorway, her eyes barely visible above the frame.

"Would you please give us a moment?"

"I'm sorry. I only wanted to see who it was." And then, in a stage whisper, she added, "You should ask *him*." With a pointed look to Williams's fine morning coat and the top hat he still held in his hands, she disappeared from sight.

"Ask me what?" Williams said coldly. It was evident that he'd drawn his own conclusions from what he'd just witnessed. No doubt he would go straight back to inform his family that he'd caught Silas red-handed with another woman.

Silas shouldn't care what any of them thought. His reputation was in tatters anyway; what did it matter if Miss Williams believed that he had a lover tucked away in town?

But he found himself making explanations, despite every intention not to. "That was my cousin, Miss Marian Brigham. She and my brother came to town, and I've been staying with them. And never mind what she wants me to ask you. It's only...sightseeing ideas."

Not the most convincing fib, but he could hardly confess the truth. He would sooner die than ask Williams for charity a second time.

"Oh. Well." This news seemed to calm his guest, though he still didn't look entirely at ease. He fussed with the brim of his hat for a moment, cleared his throat, then abruptly produced an envelope from his breast pocket.

Silas took it automatically, turning the fine white paper over in his hands without opening it.

"It's an invitation to supper," Williams explained. "My mother would like you to come by our house on Tuesday evening."

"She would?" Silas wasn't able to keep the skepticism from his tone. "I didn't think I was in her good graces."

What the hell can this be about?

"I suppose she's had a change of heart." Williams didn't sound particularly convinced either.

"And what does Miss Williams have to say about it?"

Williams winced, as if it were a great trial to answer this. "She asked me to tell you that her feelings for you remain unchanged, and that she looks forward to renewing your connection." His face transformed into a swift scowl at the end. "Which I trust will *not* include any more theatrics."

Silas stared at the crisp, white envelope in his hands.

Her feelings remain unchanged. Renewing our connection. Did that mean that she was prepared to pay him again if he performed on cue?

And if the going rate was sixty pounds for a kiss and double that for a declaration of love, might he not earn another hundred before the week was done?

Fighting not to betray any sign of his excitement, Silas opened the envelope and stared at the neat, ladylike cursive on the invitation inside.

It was full of all the sugary turns of phrase he'd been taught to employ to sound like a gentleman. *Mr. and Mrs. Eleazar Williams kindly request the pleasure of Mr. Corbyn's company at supper...etc., etc.*

The stationery smelled like potpourri and trouble.

And opportunity.

"Do you really believe that your mother will allow me to court your sister?" It was the only conceivable reason why the woman should invite him to dine. Silas didn't know what had provoked her sudden change of heart, but it didn't matter. What mattered was his chance to start a new life for himself. He might be able to get Marian and James everything they needed, and all for an evening or two of playacting.

"It would seem so." Williams's tone was guarded.

"And you?"

His former friend watched him from behind narrowed eyelids. "Do you really need me to say it? Whatever passed between you two, I expect you not to hurt her."

Hurt her? Silas had never wronged a woman in his life, though it might not look that way from where Williams stood. He would think Silas was toying with his sister if he came to supper without any intention of proposing—that he was behaving like a cad.

But Miss Williams *did* want him to come, if he'd understood her message correctly. She needed him, even if no one else did.

No, not no one. Marian and James needed him too. And he could solve all their problems by the same act.

"Please tell your family I'd be delighted," Silas said. He even managed a smile, if only because he was thinking of the difference this opportunity might make to his life. It felt almost like fate. At Williams's warning look, he added, "No theatrics."

He and Miss Williams had gone too far to worry about honesty now.

Nine

"DID YOU TRIM YOUR FINGERNAILS?"

"Of course I did." Silas's tone was clipped. "I'm not an unwashed bumpkin."

"And you've combed your hair?" Marian continued her inquisition, apparently unconvinced.

"Yes, yes."

Had he thought he would appreciate living with family? Marian's fussing had grown irritating as the hour of his supper with Miss Williams drew near.

"You should see about getting a new tailcoat." Marian adjusted Silas's white cravat and stood back to inspect the results. "This one is too snug in the shoulders for you."

She was right, but Silas wouldn't give her the satisfaction of admitting it.

"We don't have funds to waste on a tailor." He couldn't seem to stop his hands from fidgeting, his fingers alighting on anything within reach. "Anyway, this will all be over before he has time to sew me a coat."

It wasn't as though he'd had much need for black formal attire before now. Silas had worn his naval uniform to most of the dinner engagements in his previous life. But the prospect of sitting down to dine with the Williams family while they picked apart his every flaw made him wish he had something better in his closet.

What had he been thinking when he'd agreed to this? Mrs. Williams hated him. The only two times they'd met, she'd either been beating him with something or trying to manhandle him off her property. And Mrs. Eli Williams probably wasn't too happy about the scandal he'd caused at her card club. Her husband, the only person in the room whom he might once have counted a friend, was convinced Silas meant to take advantage of his little sister.

How was he supposed to win over these people?

"I don't think I can do this," Silas muttered. "I'm going to say something wrong."

"Of course you can do it." Marian brushed a stray hair from his lapels. "You're a hundred times more genteel than any of us. What were all those tutoring sessions for, if not this?"

Silas said nothing.

His father had believed that a good education would help his son impress the officers and mingle in the right circles. If courting a well-bred lady had ever been on the agenda, it must have been a far more distant goal, only possible once he'd made his fortune.

But you never made it that far, did you?

Never mind. He wasn't *really* courting Miss Williams. He was performing a chore for her—one that would benefit them both. That was all.

"You're sure this chit's finally going to pay you?" James asked, watching them both from the other side of the room, where he stood leaning against the doorframe.

"As sure as I can be without speaking to her."

"Sounds balmy, if you ask me." James frowned to himself. "Why would she *want* to be ruined?"

The story *did* sound a bit absurd when Silas laid it all out.

"That's her concern," he replied. He couldn't afford to start second-guessing his choice now, or he would never make it to dinner. "What matters is, she can help us get enough for your brewery. That's what you want, isn't it? Marian, help me with these cuff links, won't you?"

"But she still hasn't even paid what you're owed from the last time." James frowned to himself. "Wouldn't it be simpler just to marry her?"

Silas would have choked if his mouth weren't empty. "What the hell are you talking about?"

"Language," Marian chided as she fastened the cuffs on his left sleeve.

"If her family is as well-to-do as you say, she must have a dowry, yeah? And I reckon it's worth more than whatever she's giving you in bits and bobs for showing up to pretend you're in love and fool her mum, or whatnot." James shrugged. "So why not marry her? Then you get *all* the money and we can do whatever we want with it. Seems safer than waiting and hoping she pays."

"She doesn't want to get married," Silas explained. "That's the whole point of this."

"You sure the whole point isn't just that she's sweet on you and wants an excuse to keep you coming back?"

The look James shot his way rattled Silas's understanding of the situation.

Could Miss Williams have done all this to get his attention? It seemed a bizarre means to ensnare him. And her distress that first night in the club's office had been real enough. He didn't think her tears had been false.

James doesn't know what he's talking about.

He cast a glance at Marian, who seemed to sense his doubt. "Don't pay any mind to James," she assured him, echoing his thoughts. "He's always spotting attachments where there are none. Still..."

"Still?" Not a word he cared to hear at this juncture.

"It *is* a bit odd, her calling you back again and again this way." Marian raised her eyebrows in a knowing manner. "And you do seem to enjoy playing knight-errant to her, or you wouldn't keep answering."

"I'm not playing knight-errant!" Silas sputtered. What nonsense. They'd never even met Miss Williams, and they thought they knew everything about her. "I'm going for *your* sake," he reminded them. "Or would you rather I stayed home and missed our chance to get the funds we need?"

"Of course we wouldn't rather you stayed home," James replied easily. "I've just said I think you should marry her, haven't I? Why won't you consider it? Isn't she pretty?"

Silas recalled Miss Williams's face: the way her rich brown eyes sparkled with determination; her straight, dark brows; the heart-shaped lips that had surprised him with their eagerness when she'd kissed him; her nose that was a touch too long.

"She's...handsome enough," he concluded, feeling a bit uneasy at this realization. This whole thing would be a good deal less complicated if he didn't think about whether or not Miss Williams was attractive.

"Then stop stalling and go make us rich. It's not every day one of ours gets a chance to catch one of theirs."

"Are you going to be like this all the time?" Silas snapped, annoyed at his brother's meddling. His view of the evening had been much simpler before James started talking. "I'm starting to wish I'd stayed at the boardinghouse."

"You don't mean that," Marian said. "But James is right that you should be off." She gave him a final once-over and tucked a stray strand of hair behind his ear. "You have nothing to be nervous about. You look very dashing, no matter how the coat fits."

"I'm not nervous," he grumbled. Nor did he care if he looked dashing.

"Good." She smiled knowingly. "Because there's no need to be."

Silas snatched his hat and went out.

Williams had sent his carriage over to spare him the embarrassment of arriving by hackney, which was irritatingly thoughtful of him.

It made Silas feel that much worse about his deceit. But he wasn't truly doing anything wrong, was he? It was no more than Miss Williams had asked of him. And he wasn't toying with her heart; he was sure of it. Almost entirely. It was only James's baseless rambling that had put doubt in his head.

He had the entire ride to Mayfair to ruminate on the matter, so that by the time he arrived, Silas had nearly decided to ask the driver to turn around and take him back.

The white stucco facade of the town house looked too pristine for him, perched between its neighbors with its perfectly trimmed hedges and manicured lawn. Recalling how he'd spent his last visit to this place circling around those very hedges while the maid and Mrs. Williams tried to drive him from the property, Silas felt his face grow hot. He forced himself to march up the path and knock on the front door, pushing the memory down as deep as it would go.

Marian was right; he'd been trained for this. Even if it had never come naturally to him, he'd been taught what fork to use and how to sip his soup quietly and a hundred other tiny rules to keep from making a complete ass of himself in front of his betters.

He could do this. He could be what Miss Williams wanted him to be, if only for one night.

Williams and his wife were the first ones to greet Silas once he was shown into their receiving room by the same maid who'd tried to run him off. Despite their obvious reservations, the couple put on a good face, asking him a few polite questions about the weather and the ease of his journey over. (No one had the courage for more dangerous subjects, it would seem.) It was only when Miss Williams and her mother entered the room a moment later that things grew truly awkward.

"Good evening, Mr. Corbyn," Mrs. Williams greeted him. Her lips pinched shut as soon as the words were out, as if she'd smelled something unpleasant. When she looked him over, her eyes lingered at the seams on his shoulders where the fabric puckered.

So much for her change of heart.

"Good evening, Mrs. Williams." He focused on keeping his bow smooth and unhurried, despite the hot, prickling feeling inching up the back of his neck. She was looking at him like he was a street urchin who'd wandered in to beg for scraps. Silas clenched his teeth and forced some more platitudes out. "Thank you for the invitation."

He turned his attention to her daughter, eager to escape Mrs. Williams's scrutiny before he lost his temper and gave offense.

The young lady was dressed in a gold and emerald gown, with a matching gold ribbon woven into the elaborate braid that secured her dark-brown hair around her head like a crown. Everything about her was meant to look dazzling and expensive. Regal. When he'd first met Miss Williams, he might have judged her too self-conscious to live up to such a descriptor, but now Silas knew better. She had a streak of determination at her core, despite her shyness.

When their eyes met, she offered a tentative smile, blushed, and quickly looked away. Silas bowed and murmured a greeting to her in return, thinking about what James had said.

It was absurd to imagine he could ever be matched to someone like Miss Williams, trapped in so much finery that she shone like a jewel. But why did she blush? Maybe she really *was* taken with him, no matter how unlikely this pairing might be.

It was such an unexpected notion that he had trouble keeping his thoughts focused on what he was supposed to be doing.

"We're so happy you could join us," Miss Williams said. He'd forgotten how warm and reassuring her voice was—or perhaps it only seemed that way in comparison to the frosty temperature radiating from the rest of the room. Still, the sound did something to soothe the agitation that had plagued him all afternoon.

Silas realized he was staring, and quickly tore his gaze away.

Wait. No. He *should* stare. He was supposed to pretend to be in love with her, wasn't he? In fact, he should probably force himself to sigh a bit. Or compliment her. Or something.

"You, er, you look lovely this evening. That's a very pretty, uh, ribbon." Silas tried not to wince as he landed on the first object he spotted. He sounded like an idiot. But if Miss Williams thought his delivery was ham-fisted, she didn't give any sign. She merely thanked him in her gentle voice and took her place on the settee.

Mrs. Williams claimed the space beside her daughter, motioning Silas to the armchair facing them, no doubt eager to maintain a safe distance between the wolf and the lamb.

The interrogation began the moment he took his seat.

"So, Mr. Corbyn, what does your father do?" Mrs. Williams paused to take a sip of her tea. "I presume he must have some occupation. Is he in the navy as well?"

That didn't last long.

He'd hoped he would have more than a minute before he ruined things. He shot a glance to Miss Williams, who gave him a tentative smile of encouragement.

Did she believe his father was a gentleman? Would she be

disappointed to learn otherwise? He could hardly lie, with her brother sitting right there. He already knew Silas was a tradesman's son.

They'd likely all known the minute he'd walked into their house in an ill-fitting, hand-me-down coat.

He would stick to the truth then.

"No, ma'am." Silas kept his back straight and his voice firm. "He's a cooper. He works with my mother's father, who owns a brewery."

"I see." Mrs. Williams struggled to conceal her disappointment before she spoke again in a falsely bright tone. "No matter. It speaks very well of him that he wanted a better future for you. The navy is a very respectable path."

"Thank you, ma'am," Silas said tightly. This conversation was in danger of going the same way as his interview with Miss Danby, except that he didn't think he was liable to get a second chance this time.

Remember why you're doing this. You can get everything Marian and James need if you just hold your bloody tongue for a few hours.

By some act of grace, Mrs. Williams didn't ask for the details of his inglorious exit from the navy. Perhaps her son had slipped her a word of warning beforehand. Instead, she surprised him completely.

"Have you ever considered joining the army, now that you're, er, at liberty to do so?"

The army? Silas glanced toward Miss Williams once more. If only they could find some way to speak alone for a minute, he might know what script he was meant to follow. She'd left him fumbling in the dark. Again.

"I...hadn't really thought about it," he confessed.

Miss Williams's dark-brown eyes were boring holes into him, an urgent plea cloaked in total silence. What was that supposed to mean? Did she think he could read minds?

"Well, you *should* think about it." Mrs. Williams swelled up with enthusiasm at her own suggestion. "They couldn't keep you out on account of your leaving the navy, could they? They're entirely separate institutions, after all. I should think the only thing that matters is whether you can buy a commission." She coughed delicately, seeing Silas hesitate. "Perhaps your family could help you. It would be such a tremendous opportunity. A way to restore your reputation and advance in society."

Silas clenched his teeth. If his family could have afforded a military commission, they would have done that in the first place, instead of sending him to sea.

"Mama, I'm sure Mr. Corbyn has his own plans for his future," her daughter cut in smoothly. Perhaps she'd sensed the tension gathering on his side of the room. She didn't seem to like it when people were uncomfortable. "Eli told me that you have family visiting." She turned to Silas with a smile. "How are they enjoying London?"

"Please don't change the subject," Mrs. Williams scolded. "I want to hear what Mr. Corbyn has to say for himself. If he intends to marry you, he'll need a way to support you properly."

If he intends to marry you. The words shouldn't have made every muscle in Silas's body clench. After all, he'd known there could be no other reason to invite him for dinner. But it was one thing to suspect; quite another to hear it laid out in such plain terms.

Mrs. Williams was watching him expectantly. There was a right answer here and a wrong one. He was fairly certain which category his plans to found a brewery with a pair of rebellious youngsters fell into, which left him only one thing to say.

"I'll be sure to discuss the idea of a commission with my family. Thank you for the suggestion, Mrs. Williams."

His first outright lie of the evening. There was no way his father could come up with that sort of money, even if they'd still been on speaking terms. And if Silas managed to come out of this evening with some extra coin, he had no intention of throwing it after his old man's doomed fantasy of seeing him become a gentleman. He knew how that story ended.

Marian and James had a far more realistic opportunity. He would stick to his place from now on.

Mrs. Williams smiled, blithely ignorant of his deceit. He'd passed his first test.

But instead of looking pleased, her daughter bit her lip, her eyes flashing with...something.

What did I do wrong? Silas suppressed a surge of irritation. He'd come when he was summoned, put on an ill-fitting black tailcoat for her, and he'd told her mother exactly what she wanted to hear. What more could she possibly want, if none of that was enough to please her?

All Hannah wanted was for Mr. Corbyn to do or say something so offensive that her mother would declare the evening a failure and storm from the room. Was that really so much to ask?

He was ruining everything—precisely by *not* ruining things, that is.

Mr. Corbyn hadn't exactly been the most polished dealer at Jane's club. But he must be putting on his best effort tonight, for he managed to navigate the treacherous small talk before their meal without giving her mother any cause to eject him from the house.

And what was that business about joining the army? Pure nonsense! If only Hannah had been able to signal him somehow. But there had been no chance to get a word to Mr. Corbyn without Mama overhearing.

He even looked the part of a respectable dinner guest. Though his coat could do with some tailoring, he still looked very distinguished in his evening attire. If anything, the way the clothes hugged his muscular frame a bit too snugly made her acutely aware of what a striking figure he cut. His gorgeous hair was combed back in gentle waves that shone like brass in the gaslight. It really wasn't fair that a man should have hair like that.

Wait, what had she been thinking of a minute ago? Oh yes, how Mr. Corbyn was meant to be offending her mother instead of buttering her up.

Maybe he'll do better at the meal. All he needed to do was chew with his mouth open or knock over a wineglass, and the tide would turn against him. Really, he might accomplish his spectacular failure without any effort on Hannah's part. She was worrying over nothing.

She'd hoped to get a private word to Mr. Corbyn when the time came to go in to dine, but Mama wanted to be led in on Eli's arm, which left Mr. Corbyn to escort both Hannah and Jane to their seats.

Drat. It seemed there was always someone hovering at her shoulder. But at least she was seated beside her supposed suitor while they dined, instead of halfway across the room from him.

He pulled out her chair for her, his hand accidentally brushing her wrist as she stepped forward to take her assigned place. Hannah drew in a swift breath at the contact. With their gloves removed for the meal, the heat of his bare skin on hers had startled her.

She sat down, too flustered to thank him for his assistance.

Don't get distracted just because he has a pretty face. You need to be on your toes tonight.

"Where is your family from?" Mama resumed her inquiries the moment they were all seated and Molly brought out their first course, the consommé, and began to serve the sherry. It was strange to eat a meal served so informally with a guest in the house, but Jane and Eli didn't have the income to keep a full staff with a footman quite yet.

"Staffordshire, ma'am," Mr. Corbyn answered. "Burton upon Trent." That should be a point against him, seeing as how Mama was always saying that she wanted to find Hannah a husband close to home.

Then again, if Mama had gone all the way to London without Papa, there was no telling how far she might be willing to run.

"I *thought* I detected a northern accent. It's very faint, though."

"I left home young."

"How old were you?" Hannah asked. It wasn't only that she wanted the chance to wrest the conversation from her mother's grip; she was also curious to know more about Mr. Corbyn. For a man who'd become her partner in duplicity, she knew precious little about him.

"Eleven." He delivered this news as if it were perfectly ordinary, though Hannah couldn't receive it with quite the same composure.

"So young! How could your parents bear to let you leave home?"

Mr. Corbyn seemed as if he were about to shrug, but suppressed the gesture while it was still a mere twitch of his shoulder. He really *was* trying to be on his best behavior tonight.

"Most cabin boys start on at about that age," he replied lightly. "It's not that young."

If his naval service had been anything like her brother's, he probably hadn't had the chance to come back and see his family since then either. It struck her as terribly sad. At least Eli had been a young man when he'd joined the navy, but Mr. Corbyn had been nothing more than a child. At eleven, Hannah had still been ensconced in the safety of her schoolroom, under the watchful eye of her governess. She couldn't imagine being thrown into the dangers of a storm or battle at sea. He must have been so scared.

Perhaps his experiences were what had hardened him into his present, rather gruff exterior.

"The navy isn't really supposed to take them any younger than thirteen now," Eli added. "But exceptions are made. It helps young men get their six years of sea time faster so they can take the lieutenant's exam."

"Did you take the lieutenant's exam?" Hannah asked.

"Yes." Mr. Corbyn spoke without any emotion. "I passed, but there wasn't a vacancy for me. The wait can be long if you aren't well connected."

He'd been discharged before his chance had come. *How thoughtless of me.* Hannah should have realized he wouldn't want to talk about his service. She didn't dare another comment for the rest of the main course, afraid to put her foot in her mouth again.

When the meal was done, they all retired to the parlor together, their number being too small to support the division of the men from the ladies. Sensing her chance, Hannah contrived to place herself next to Mr. Corbyn on the settee. All she needed now was a distraction so that she might whisper in his ear.

"Won't you please play a song for us, Jane?" she asked hopefully. "Something lively, if you please."

By which I mean something loud.

Jane—who regularly neglected her practice in favor of such things as caring for her daughter or earning her livelihood—shot an indignant look in Hannah's direction. "Why don't *you* play, Hannah? You're much more talented than I am."

"I couldn't," she replied swiftly. "Nerves, you know."

Jane proved unable to find a polite way to refuse the request, rose from her seat, and marched stiffly to the instrument. Despite the occasional false note, she managed a passible rendition of a folk song by Haydn. More importantly, everyone in the room turned to listen.

"Stop trying to please my mother," Hannah whispered quickly, while the music hid her words.

"I thought that's what you wanted," Mr. Corbyn hissed back, leaning in a little closer as he spoke, the heat of his breath tickling her ear. Hannah's skin turned to gooseflesh at the sudden nearness of him. His familiar scent of freshly laundered sheets and something warmer. "Why did you call me here, if not to pretend to be your suitor?"

She'd forgotten how fierce he looked when he was cross. His blue eyes were so intense that she had trouble holding their gaze for more than an instant. Just as well. It was safer to keep her attention fixed ahead; she didn't want Mama to notice them whispering if she happened to look over.

"I need you to pretend to want to marry me, but *not* to win my mother over," she explained quickly. "She has to be the one to refuse the match. If I do it, she'll only try to pair me with someone worse."

Corbyn shot her a look.

"That came out wrong," Hannah amended. "You'd be a wonderful match for some other lady. I'm sure there must be plenty of women who'd *love* to—" *Oh dear.* She was babbling. And now her face was turning red. "Never mind that. Just act like you're in love with me, but then do something to make her hate you again. It shouldn't be hard. Just swear a bit or spill a drink on her and this can all be over with before the evening is out."

"So you want me to make a fool of myself."

Oh dear. This wasn't going well at all. Mr. Corbyn's jaw was tight and his eyes had taken on an icy chill. She hadn't meant to insult him. Surely he must be able to see that this was a matter of dire necessity, not a comment on his character.

"Of course not," she tried to reassure him. "I'm not asking you to look foolish, only..."

Rude? Low-class? Completely unacceptable as a husband? Nothing she might say sounded any better.

Corbyn seemed to realize that she was at a loss, for he cut her off without compunction. "I expect you're willing to pay?"

It sounded almost menacing when he said it in that low, even rumble.

But she didn't have time to fret over Mr. Corbyn's mood. Jane's song was ending, and their conversation was about to be cut short.

"Yes," she whispered. Then, in a louder tone, she issued a quick "Brava!" to her sister-in-law.

"That was lovely, Mrs. Williams." Mr. Corbyn's smile was tight. Without deigning to look at Hannah, he spoke in a low tone from the side of his mouth. "I want two hundred this time."

She swallowed.

"What are you two whispering about over there?" Hannah's mother had finally noticed their tête-à-tête, now that the music was no longer there to distract her.

"Nothing, Mama." Hannah tried to look innocent, though she suspected she wasn't doing a very good job of it. The truth was that her exchange with Mr. Corbyn had left her shaken. She was fairly certain she'd offended him with her clumsy instructions. Why had she worded it that way? If only there were some way to turn back time and do the whole thing over.

But of course there was no chance to explain herself, now that Mama had fixed her full attention on them again. Her gaffe with Mr. Corbyn had already done its damage. He thought that she looked down on him, and there was no way to persuade him otherwise.

"I don't want to see any more of that sort of behavior. It's time we had a frank talk about what I expect from you both if we are to proceed any further."

Jane cleared her throat. "If you'll excuse us, Mr. Corbyn, my husband and I need to step out for a moment. We left our daughter at my cousin's house for the evening so that she wouldn't interrupt our dinner, but we need to collect her before it gets too late. Please carry on without us. We'll be back in a quarter hour."

No doubt they had planned things this way to give them some privacy. Eli and Jane looked perfectly happy to escape the awkward conversation as they hurried from the room.

Hannah sat up stiffly in her chair, bracing for the lecture to come. She had the absurd desire to hold Mr. Corbyn's hand for strength, but caught herself before she could act on it.

Maybe you should act on it, a traitorous thought crept into her head. *After all, you're supposed to be pretending you're in love.*

She couldn't. He was cross with her and she simply wasn't brave enough. She would just have to ignore these troublesome impulses. Imagine what the weight of his hand in hers might feel like instead of reaching for it.

"Now." Mama's expression was stern as she looked from Hannah to her would-be suitor. "If you mean to marry my daughter, I expect you to do things *properly* this time. Half the ton heard about your...indiscretion"—her face soured on this word—"at my son's club."

"Jane's club," Hannah corrected softly.

Mama drew a swift breath at the interruption. "*As I was saying,* I expect you to repair the harm you've done to my daughter's reputation. You will announce your engagement. You will announce your intention to join the military. You will make an appearance at a few social events where you will be on your best behavior and impress upon everyone your good manners and fitness to participate in polite society, and you will do *nothing* else to cause a scandal." She paused for a moment, thinking. "We should perhaps make it appear that the engagement took place some time ago. People would be more forgiving of what they observed if they believed you were already promised to each other when it happened."

Mr. Corbyn spoke very carefully, lingering on each syllable. "You were beating me over the head with your reticule, madam."

"Well, I didn't *know* about the engagement yet, obviously," Mama replied. "It was a love match, concluded in secret, but I've come around to the idea now that I can see what a fine gentleman you are."

She was trying very hard not to grind her teeth, and it showed.

"What about Papa?" Hannah interjected. "Have you received any reply from him yet? Won't he want to come here and meet Mr. Corbyn for himself?"

It didn't feel right to agree to an engagement—even a fake one— without his blessing.

And if she could get her parents in a room together, why, they might find a way to make peace again! If Mama was too stubborn to return home, this was the only other way to repair the rift between them.

"He'll arrive in town presently." Her mother didn't seem to feel the need to elaborate any further.

It was perfect, now that Hannah thought about it. What was more likely to bring her parents together than the engagement of their only daughter? That was exactly the sort of thing that made people remember why they loved each other. Hannah would just have to slip word to Mr. Corbyn to put off his spectacular failure until *after* their reconciliation took place.

She could solve all her problems before the week was out! Papa would realize how much he'd missed them once they were together again. The plans for Hannah's wedding would remind them of their own vows. All she had to do was make it last long enough for her parents to come to their senses, and then things could finally go back to how they used to be, before it all fell apart.

"I'll put an announcement in the papers immediately," Mama continued. "We'll have the first banns read on Sunday. I shall ensure that you are both invited to a few events in the coming weeks, to launch you into society as a match. Mrs. Godfrey's wild rose party this Friday might do to start with. The hostess is a friend of mine, and I might be able to persuade her to help ensure you receive a warm welcome despite all the...unpleasantness earlier. It's an afternoon gathering, so it will be a bit less formal. Fewer chances of a mishap."

Hannah studied Mr. Corbyn as these plans were laid out. He was impossible to read, with the firm lines of his lips and brows held perfectly still. When he glanced in her direction, his eyes gave nothing away.

He might ruin all her plans if he wished. Expose her lies with a word and stride from the room, never to look back. If it had been a risk before, her clumsy instructions during Jane's song certainly hadn't helped.

He couldn't say no. Hannah needed him more than ever. If only she could make him understand how important this was.

When Mr. Corbyn finally answered, his voice had all the detached calm of a man discussing a business transaction, rather than his own engagement.

Which was fair enough, really.

"That sounds perfect. Thank you for all your careful planning. We're in your debt, Mrs. Williams."

Mama nodded, appeased by this praise, if not quite pleased. "She has a dowry, of course, but I trust you'll understand why we'll want to see those funds settled on your future children. We can draw up the marriage contract once my husband is in town."

"I'm afraid I can't agree to that."

What did he just say? Hannah whirled to stare at her almost-fiancé.

He was still using that eerily calm voice, though the words carried all the destructive power of a lit powder keg.

Her mother appeared equally stunned, struggling to summon the words to give Mr. Corbyn a proper dressing-down. Before she could begin, he spoke over her.

"If you expect me to buy myself a commission, I'll need some of your daughter's dowry to do it. I'll come up with as much as I can myself, but it would be impossible for me to shoulder the entire amount. We can settle everything that I don't need on our future children."

He didn't look at Hannah once during this whole speech, not even when he said the part about their children.

Why is he doing this?

Was it part of his plan to push her mother to refuse the match, as she'd urged? It must be. There was no other reason to make such a demand. He couldn't hope to touch her dowry unless he actually intended to marry her, and that was—

"Certainly not!" Mama recoiled, outraged. All the disdain she'd tried so hard to bottle up this evening was in danger of boiling over. "That money belongs to Hannah."

—*unthinkable*. It was unthinkable that Mr. Corbyn could marry her. This was all part of his plan to ruin things, and it looked to be working. If only she could have signaled him to wait a little longer, now that she knew her father would be coming to London. If they broke off their engagement too soon, he might cancel his trip. She had to do something before she lost her chance.

"Perhaps we should sleep on this," Hannah cut in swiftly, hoping Mr. Corbyn would follow her lead. "We should really wait until Papa is here before we make any important decisions."

"Those are my terms," Mr. Corbyn said coolly, as if she hadn't spoken. What had gotten into him? He wasn't acting like himself at all. At least, not like the self that she'd caught glimpses of in their prior encounters. *Maybe it wasn't the most brilliant idea to place my trust in a near stranger.* "I think you'll find them quite reasonable. I don't intend to take more than I need, and I'll treat your daughter well. Surely you can agree that it's a small sum to part with, if you truly want to see her settled as an officer's wife. The alternative would be far worse for all of us."

He let the implication hang in the air—that Hannah would be left without the fiction of a prior engagement to explain away their kiss at the club and salvage her reputation. That she would be left without anything at all.

What in God's name is he doing?

The rising sense of panic in Hannah's chest made her want to shout, but she hadn't the faintest idea what to say. Her instincts told her to protest; it didn't sound like he was trying to scare her mother off any longer. Quite the contrary, his game seemed to have shifted to one of persuasion.

She sucked in a long breath. *Mama won't agree. She'd sooner call off this engagement than let Mr. Corbyn get his hands on my funds.*

Indeed, she would likely do just that. Any minute now.

But even though her mother was obviously fuming—her brow drawn into a deep furrow and her nostrils flaring with each inhalation—she didn't unleash the tongue-lashing that Hannah expected. Instead, her struggle to master her emotions played out on her face for a long moment before she finally spoke through clenched teeth.

"Only enough to buy the commission. Not a penny more."

"Of course." Mr. Corbyn had agreed before Hannah could so much as blink.

It didn't make any sense! Why should he want to haggle over her dowry when they'd never agreed to marry? Could he really mean to use the money to join the army? He'd seemed surprised by the suggestion only a few hours before, but perhaps the chance to advance his station had proven too much to resist. There was no other reason for him to demand a portion of her funds.

They scarcely knew each other! He was far too gorgeous for her and she was far too gently bred for him. More importantly, this was *not* what they'd agreed to.

Hannah opened her mouth to protest, then closed it again.

How was she to stop this, except by confessing that everything she'd said and done in the past month had been one great lie? And then she would never get Papa here. She couldn't risk it.

While Hannah was still stewing, Jane and Eli returned home with Gloria and rejoined the group in the parlor. They were all obliged to rise to greet them, and in the commotion Hannah slipped beside Mr. Corbyn for a precious moment with no one watching.

"What are you doing?" she hissed in his ear.

"Don't worry," he shot back, his words so soft she had to strain to hear them. "If you pay me what we agreed, I'll do my part. This is just insurance in case things go the other way."

Hannah could scarcely speak, forcing the words out through numb lips. "What *other way*?"

That shouldn't even be a possibility! They wouldn't be talking about it if he hadn't raised the issue. But she'd forgotten to keep her voice down in her shock, causing everyone in the room to look.

"Is everything all right here?" Eli asked, his eyes guarded.

"Perfect." Corbyn had the nerve to smile, though the quirk of his lips didn't bring any warmth to his eyes. "We were just settling up the terms of our engagement."

Ten

"WHAT HAPPENED?"

"Are you engaged?"

"What did their house look like?"

The moment he walked in the door, Marian and James pounced on him with their questions like two excitable kittens sharing the same frayed string.

"Enough. Let me breathe first." Silas waved them away as he undid his cravat and shrugged out of his tailcoat, which had begun to feel confining about three hours ago.

Marian took the trappings of refinement from his hands to speed his progress, but made no move to take them to his bedroom.

"Could you please hang those up?"

"I'm not your maid." She snorted. "Stop trying to distract me and tell us what happened."

Silas *had* been trying to distract her, and suffered a pang of regret that it hadn't worked. He'd spent the entire journey home imagining how they might take the news that he was engaged—at least on paper, once the announcement ran. James was going to be insufferable.

A bare recitation of the facts was probably best, if there was no way around it. Silas resolved to lay out his situation in the briefest possible terms.

"She wants me to pretend to want to marry her and then behave so badly that her mother will have no choice but to press her to release me. I asked her for another two hundred pounds in exchange. Her mother's putting an announcement in the papers, and I'll need to attend a few society events to play my part."

He didn't mention the way he'd haggled for a portion of her dowry if the marriage went ahead. It wasn't that he was ashamed of his actions—really, it was nothing more than self-preservation, lest he find himself unable to escape the net Miss Williams had woven around them both—but there was simply no need to mention it. It wasn't likely to come to pass.

He was more than capable of mucking things up so badly that Mrs. Williams would reverse course and forbid their marriage. Hannah Williams must have sensed as much, or she would never have chosen him.

She knows I have some practice destroying my own life. Was that why she'd kissed him? Had she sensed his potential for wanton destruction even from their first acquaintance?

James whooped at this news, oblivious to his brother's darkening mood. "Two hundred pounds! Blimey. Do you think she'll really pay?"

If she doesn't, that's what the dowry is for. The thought brought him little comfort. Silas didn't want to know how far he was willing to go. With a minimal amount of effort on his part, the issue would never arise.

How hard could it be to make a fool of himself?

Marian observed him with more trepidation than James, her hazel eyes wary. "How do you feel about all this?"

"It's everything we wanted." Silas took his coat and cravat back from Marian, striding to his room to put them away. He'd said everything that mattered. There was no need to dwell on it.

But his cousin followed him, James trailing behind.

"Why does she want you to make her mother angry?" Marian pressed. "Couldn't she just jilt you herself?"

"She seems to think that if the decision comes from her mother, it will make it easier for her to avoid marriage altogether." Silas hung his coat in his wardrobe and brushed out the wrinkles.

"You sure she don't intend to keep you?" James caught up to them, his broad shoulders filling the doorframe.

"Her feelings aren't my concern," Silas said shortly, refusing to look at his brother's grinning face. That knowing tone was grating on him. "She's asked me to do a job, and I intend to do it. All that matters is the pay."

"But what about your reputation?" Marian had a furrow between her brows. "I'm not sure I like the idea of you behaving badly about town to try to goad some woman into forbidding your engagement."

"What reputation?" Silas couldn't keep the bitterness from his voice. He regretted the words almost immediately. He didn't want to invite a debate on whether or not his name was ruined beyond redemption, so he repeated the only essential point: "All that matters is the pay."

James seemed inclined to say more, but at Marian's sharp look, he shut his mouth again.

"We're grateful to you," Marian said. "Don't hesitate if you need our help with anything."

"There won't be anything to help with," Silas assured her. "It will be over and done within a week."

As it turned out, the molding of Mr. Corbyn into a proper gentleman was to be quite a drawn-out affair. Hannah had expected it to begin with their attendance at Mrs. Godfrey's wild rose party on Friday and end with the arrival of Papa in London the following week. Easy come, easy go.

As it turned out, her father wrote back to say that he had a fishing trip planned with the Lamburns this week and he didn't want to cancel, so he would come to London the week after. And Mama hadn't even told her! Hannah had to find his letter on the desk and read it for herself. It was really very difficult to plan a false engagement and lure her parents back together when no one saw fit to inform her of anything!

In keeping with this habit, Mama took it upon herself to outfit Mr. Corbyn in a new wardrobe without so much as a by-your-leave from anyone.

"I can't bring him to Mrs. Godfrey's in that ill-fitted suit," she announced, after ordering their driver to ready the carriage the morning after their supper. "He needs to look more presentable if we're to persuade the ton that this is a good match for you. I don't like the expense, but there's no help for it."

Hannah still couldn't decide if her mother was baiting her, or if all this was genuine. The references to money seemed designed to provoke a sense of guilt, and thus a confession.

I refuse to feel guilty for any of it. Hannah put on her best walking dress and a pair of matching gloves. *It isn't my fault Mama's decided to turn Mr. Corbyn into her idea of a perfect groom.*

They descended upon the unsuspecting man's doorstep, where Mama only paused long enough to wrinkle her nose at the country relatives who answered before ordering Mr. Corbyn into the carriage and on to a tailor's.

If he protested, it was more in the set of his mouth and shoulders than with any words. Whatever his true thoughts on this intrusion might be, Mr. Corbyn kept them to himself as he obeyed her mother's commands in stoic silence

Now he sees what I'm dealing with.

Hannah had never been inside a men's tailor's before. She tiptoed in with some hesitation, though Mama suffered no such qualms as she marched up to the gentleman at the counter.

"He'll need some black formal wear, a few trousers and waist-coats, and at least three morning coats. That should get him through the next two weeks." She turned abruptly to Mr. Corbyn after delivering these instructions, as if only just remembering that he was there. "Oh! Do you have a better top hat? Silk, I mean. Not that felted thing you wore at the house the other night."

Mr. Corbyn looked as though he were biting his tongue. Hard. "No, ma'am."

Mama frowned. "I suppose we'll have to go to the haberdasher's as well. This promises to be a long day."

"May I show you a few fabrics, madam?" The tailor motioned hastily to his apprentice, having quickly identified the paying customer in their number. "Blues and browns are very practical colors for a morning coat. There's a lovely check to this one that gives it some depth, do you see...?"

While Mama was thus occupied, Hannah inched closer to Mr. Corbyn.

"I'm sorry about all this fuss."

Her apology did nothing to soften the stern line of his jaw. Was he still angry with her for last night?

"Look on the bright side," she tried again. "You get a new wardrobe."

"That I'll never wear after this farce is over," he muttered under his breath. "It's wasteful."

All right. There was no point in trying to make peace with him this morning. Perhaps she would do better to stick to business.

"If you don't have any use for your new clothes, you could always sell them and take it from what I owe you. These are expensive fabrics."

He narrowed his icy blue eyes. "I'd rather have banknotes."

"Well so would I, but in case you haven't noticed, I'm not the one holding the purse strings." Hannah tipped her chin in the direction of her mother's back. "So if you want to be paid anytime soon, you're going to have to help me find excuses to get at those funds."

Mr. Corbyn looked as though he might have something more to say about this—and nothing complimentary, from the storm brewing in his eyes—but Hannah's mother called her over before he could share any unkind words.

"Which do you like best, poppet? The medium blue or the navy?"

"Oh. I—" Hannah edged forward. "Mr. Corbyn, wouldn't you like to choose?"

"Whatever you like best...*darling*." The endearment made Hannah's heart pound, no matter that he was being sarcastic. He'd drawn out the word in a slow, deliberate rumble. Like a rough hand sliding down the line of her spine.

Hannah shivered.

Fine. If he doesn't care, I will choose for him.

She glanced at the wools that had been set out for the morning coats. The muted navy was certainly more practical, but the other choice was a vivid cobalt that seemed to shine. She could picture it on Mr. Corbyn easily. It would suit his eyes.

"This one, please." She let her finger alight on the more striking fabric. After all, this was the only time she would ever walk into a gathering with such a beautiful man on her arm. Even if she wasn't really going to marry him, she might like to show him off. Just a little. "Do you think you could have it ready by Friday morning?"

Hannah picked out a few flashier silks for the waistcoats next—nothing garish, just enough to give him a pop of color beneath the more understated brown frock coat, and of course an ivory waistcoat for evening wear. Occasionally she held up a fabric against Mr. Corbyn, who by this time was being measured by the tailor's apprentice and looked thoroughly uncomfortable with the entire process.

"It's going to look lovely on you," Hannah assured him. She couldn't help but feel a bit sorry for him, stuck there awkwardly as everyone else fussed.

"I feel like I'm your doll," he muttered darkly. Hannah's mother was safely at the other end of the shop by this time, perusing ascots.

"Nonsense. You're just acquiring some valuables, that's all." She hadn't only chosen the fabrics that looked the prettiest—though that was certainly a factor. She'd also picked the ones that seemed expensive. Someone might be willing to pay for anything Mr. Corbyn was too stubborn to keep, though it would be a shame to see them go. He'd looked so handsome last night in his ill-fitting tailcoat that she could scarcely imagine what a properly tailored wardrobe would do for him. "By the way, I didn't get a chance to tell you last night, but I don't want you to spoil our engagement until after my father arrives in town."

Mr. Corbyn looked at her sharply. "How long will that be?"

She bristled at his tone. "He couldn't get away this week because he had plans, but he's supposed to set out from Devon next Wednesday, so I imagine he might reach town by the following Monday if the roads are good."

"What were his other plans?"

"A fishing trip with our neighbors," Hannah answered reluctantly. Why should this be any concern of Mr. Corbyn's?

"He couldn't cancel that for his daughter's engagement?"

"I wouldn't expect him to. Why should he have to rush?" What right did Mr. Corbyn have to judge her father? It didn't signify how quickly Papa came, so long as he got here. Mr. Corbyn was reading too much into this. "Anyway, I'm paying you enough that a few extra days shouldn't matter," she retorted, hoping this would put a stop to his questions.

It didn't.

"Why do you need me to keep up the act until your father arrives? I thought your mother was the one pushing you to marry."

"That's none of your concern," Hannah replied stiffly. If Corbyn made such a fuss about the timing of her father's visit, he wasn't likely to appreciate the merits of her plan to repair the breach between her parents. She didn't want to explain all that to him anyway. It was her problem to solve. "But I don't want him to cancel his trip, so please promise me you won't execute our plan until *after* he arrives. If you want your money, that is."

Mr. Corbyn let out his breath in a loud huff, evidently put out by this additional delay. "As you wish, my lady."

"I do wish you would stop that."

"Stop what?"

"Saying things that sound deferential or romantic in such a sarcastic tone." Hannah found it was hard to maintain eye contact with Mr. Corbyn while discussing this, so she addressed her comments to his Adam's apple instead. A far safer place to look. "You called me 'darling' earlier."

"You asked me to pretend to be in love with you," he pointed out. "I'm only trying to hold up my end. What is it you want from me, Miss Williams?"

"It's the sarcasm I don't like," Hannah tried to explain, feeling more flustered by the second. "If you keep speaking to me that way, people are going to notice that it's a hoax."

"Are you asking me to call you 'darling' like I mean it?" The movement of Mr. Corbyn's throat told Hannah that he'd swallowed. Of course, this made her look up, which was a terrible mistake.

He was staring right at her. That piercing blue that threatened to swallow her whole.

When he spoke again, his voice was scarcely above a whisper. So soft that it seemed to brush against the rise and fall of her nervous breath in a slow waltz. "Like this...*darling*?"

She never should have said anything. This was *far* worse than sarcasm. Even though she knew he was still mocking her, the gentle endearment brushed over her body like a caress. Hannah couldn't move a muscle, her heart pounding in her ears. How could he make her senses dance like puppets on his string when she knew it was all an act?

"We *must* do something about that hair."

"Oh!" Hannah nearly jumped out of her skin. How had Mama crept up on them so quickly? Had she overheard anything incriminating? She couldn't have, or she wouldn't be speaking with such a casual air.

"It's far too long. Once we've finished here, why don't you go to the barber while we get you a new top hat?"

"We're not cutting his hair!" Hannah protested, her voice shaking.

How could Mama suggest such a thing? It would be like chopping up the golden fleece to make a pair of socks. Sheer butchery.

"Of course we are. He needs to look like a gentleman, not a highwayman."

"He doesn't look like a highwayman. He looks perfect."

Oh no. Had she really just said that aloud? Mr. Corbyn's lip twitched, the only sign of amusement to break through his icy exterior since the morning started.

Hannah's face grew so hot, she was sure that she was about to combust. Mama fixed her with a long stare before she finally grumbled, "We'll see about a haircut later."

If Hannah was being tested, there was no doubt she'd performed convincingly just there.

A touch too convincingly for her own dignity, but never mind that. Maybe she could persuade Mr. Corbyn that she was only pretending to love his hair, the same way he was only pretending to love her.

Perhaps he had a point about how long it was taking her father to come to town. Every day that she passed with Mr. Corbyn made it more difficult to tell which of her feelings were part of their act and which were true. It was far safer to get this over with quickly, before it got too confusing.

Eleven

"STAND UP STRAIGHT," MRS. WILLIAMS HISSED, AS SILAS handed her down from the carriage before Mrs. Godfrey's house two days later. "No slouching."

"I wasn't slouching," he protested. "I was offering you my arm." It wasn't his fault the woman was seven inches shorter than him.

"A gentleman should be upright as a stone pillar, even when offering his arm."

It was all he could do not to snort. But gentlemen didn't do that either.

Silas kept himself stone-pillar straight as he accompanied the pair of ladies up the approach to the Godfreys' residence. Mrs. Williams was equally rigid, though her daughter was a good deal softer, both in her carriage and her manners.

Hannah Williams fit neatly against his side as she took his other arm. Her rosewater scent was so faint that Silas found himself tilting his head to catch it before he had the good sense to stop.

What are you doing?

Ever since James had put the notion in his head that Miss

Williams might really be fond of him, Silas had started to notice little details about the woman that he would have rather ignored. He had a heightened awareness of her presence, as if his senses had tuned themselves to her.

"You look very well in your new clothes," she offered. Silas was wearing the morning coat and trousers the tailor had sent over this morning, his errand boy no doubt wondering why such fine things were going to an address in Southwark with a trio of misfits inside. Putting on the new clothes hadn't made him feel any more prepared for this party, though he'd noticed the way Miss Williams's eyes had widened when their carriage arrived to collect him.

She liked what she saw.

There was that heightened awareness again. What did it matter if she liked the way he looked in his new clothes or blushed when he'd called her *darling* or anything else?

"Thank you." Silas didn't look at her as he spoke. The more he noticed about Miss Williams, the harder it was to focus on what he was supposed to do this afternoon. Make his introductions and make a good impression today, so that he could set it all ablaze tomorrow. Or whenever Mr. Williams arrived.

"Do you have word from your husband, madam?" he asked Mrs. Williams. "When do you expect that I might be able to ask for his blessing?"

The older woman stiffened at this question, though it should have been perfectly harmless.

"I don't have any reason to believe that his plans have changed, so we're still expecting him Monday after next. He would write to Eli if he'd been delayed. We'll host a dinner for you that evening so that you might...get acquainted."

There was something sinister in the way she paused. Or perhaps it was only Silas's instincts warning him off this whole scheme. It was one thing to continue the charade he'd already started with Miss Williams—after all, what was a little extra effort for two hundred pounds?—but it was quite another to invite the ire of the girl's father. He knew nothing about the man, nor how he might react if he sensed something was amiss.

"What is he like?" Silas asked.

"He's, um... Well, he likes to hunt and fish," Miss Williams offered brightly. "And he also likes..." She faltered here, searching for such a long time that they arrived at the entrance to the Godfreys' residence before she could finish her thought. In the hubbub of the ensuing introductions, the subject slipped away from them, and Silas didn't bring it up again. He hadn't failed to notice Mrs. Williams's silence, nor the tension that had radiated from her person when her husband was mentioned.

Is he cruel to them? Miss Williams seemed to be looking forward to his arrival, but plenty of men took their anger out on their wives instead of their children. Or the boys instead of the girls. Silas's own father had never given the strap to his sisters.

"Your bow to Mrs. Godfrey was entirely too shallow," Mrs. Williams hissed at his side, the moment their greetings were finished and they were led into the gardens to join the other guests. "Many a gentleman owes his ruin to a shabby bow."

Had he been worrying himself over this woman a moment ago? If anyone in the Williams family resembled Silas's father, it was *her,* not her absent husband. Always ready with a word of criticism to let him know where he'd fallen short. Even the subject matter of their complaints was the same! What to wear, what to say, how deep to bow. It reminded Silas of his last year at home, when his father had hired a tutor to instruct him in deportment, hopeful this would help ingratiate his son to the officers once he was a cabin boy.

He'd wanted regular updates on Silas's progress, growing

impatient whenever he forgot something. *Do you think I'm paying for my own amusement, boy?* he would bellow. *This is important. Best get it through that thick skull of yours if you ever want to make something of yourself.*

Except that he hadn't been satisfied with Silas's success either. Even once he'd begun to improve, Silas's father seemed just as angry. *Think you're too good for your own family?* he'd once snapped when Silas asked why they didn't have as many forks on their table as the place settings that Mr. Dupont had made him memorize.

Was this going to be the same way? Mrs. Williams harping at him if he failed, and her daughter harping at him if he succeeded?

Silas pushed the memory away. There was no use dwelling on the past. None of these people were ever going to see him again, once he got his money. He would go into business with Marian and James, where he belonged, and he would never repeat the mistake of reaching too high. He shouldn't care what anyone else thought of him.

The garden was an impressive size for a house in town, which was no doubt the reason their hosts had wanted to show it off. It was a large space that ran the length of five row houses in a shared courtyard, with several paved paths running around the border and crisscrossing through the middle. A large fountain dominated the center, while the various divisions created by the paths were devoted to different themes. There were rosebushes in one section, lavender in another, and shrubs that had been carved into the shapes of various animals guarding the entrance. On the sections holding nothing but trimmed lawn, someone had set up games of ninepin for the guests. Most of them were just arriving, but the event already had the makings of a large gathering. Perhaps forty or fifty people and quickly growing.

"Shall we explore the gardens?" Silas invited Miss Williams, hoping for a way to postpone the inevitable.

"That sounds lovely," she agreed. She looked about as daunted by the crowd as he was.

But her mother crushed their hopes immediately. "It's impolite to stick to the company of those you arrived with, without properly greeting the other guests. Come along. We're going to make the rounds. And remember to bow properly this time."

Silas found himself ushered toward a particularly large cluster of people on the lawn. Mrs. Williams used the walk down to whisper a last bit of advice into his ear, apparently convinced that he couldn't be trusted to do anything on his own. "You must take care to say a few witty things to everyone, but never to broach a subject that might divide the guests or give offense. If you cannot think of anything witty, it is better to hold your tongue than to say something foolish." Mrs. Williams gave Silas an appraising look that let him understand she considered the latter possibility a serious risk. "That's Mrs. Brandon up ahead, the one with the cleft lip. Only take care not to mention it."

"I had absolutely no intention of mentioning it." Silas spoke through gritted teeth. Did she imagine that anyone who hadn't gone to Eton had been raised by wolves?

"Mrs. Brandon, how *are* you?" Mrs. Williams's voice grew warm and sunny as she turned her attention to her friend. "Have you met my daughter's fiancé, Mr. Corbyn? Engaged *two months* ago, in fact. A love match. You can imagine my great surprise once I learned of their intentions. And joy, of course. Surprise and joy." She paused only long enough to draw breath. "Mr. Corbyn, this is Mrs. Brandon."

Was he supposed to smile, when Mrs. Williams had been insulting his intelligence only a few seconds before?

"A pleasure to meet you," he managed, with a bow that was *precisely* deep enough.

When he rose back up. Miss Williams squeezed his arm in reassurance.

The sudden pressure sent a jolt through his chest. He hadn't expected her to notice how difficult he found this. He'd never told her anything about his childhood, or about his father's hopes that he might one day find himself invited to exactly such a party as this.

She couldn't possibly know how Silas felt when he walked in here and realized that this was the closest he would ever come to achieving that dream. He'd worked so hard to earn each promotion, telling himself that even if it took him twice as long as the gentlemen's sons, in time he would accomplish what he was meant to. But in the end, the only way he could reach high society was to cheat his way in with a false engagement and a few borrowed clothes.

His supposed fiancée didn't know any of that. She wasn't trying to reassure him, she was probably only reminding him to give her arm back, now that he'd escorted her to the group.

Silas released her, embarrassed by his own assumptions. Why was he looking for understanding from Miss Williams when there was none? *Stop thinking of her that way. This is foolish.*

He was meant to say something witty now, but he couldn't think what. Silas looked to Miss Williams, hoping she might offer some help.

Her large, brown eyes grew wider as some inspiration struck. "Oh! I think I see my friend, Miss Annabelle. Please excuse me for a moment."

If he'd needed proof he was only imagining any support from Miss Williams's quarter, here it was. Without another glance, his fiancée turned heel and abandoned him.

$\mathcal{J}\!\!\mathit{h}$

Hannah didn't think she'd ever been happier to see another person in her life.

"Annabelle." The name escaped her lips as little more than a sigh of relief.

"Oh goodness, I thought you'd been locked in the tower," the other girl said with a questioning laugh. "Della told me that Jane told her that your mother wasn't letting you out."

Though Hannah had only known Annabelle Danby in passing before her arrival in London, they'd become fast friends. The Danby sisters had an almost heroic air to them. They seemed to do whatever they pleased, but their quick wit and warm manner made them welcome at every gathering. Hannah couldn't understand how they managed to get away with it all. She sometimes dreamed that if she could only get to know them a little better, she might learn their secret and become nearly as daring.

Or at least, she *had* thought that way. Until she'd learned what Della was up to.

"Um...how is your sister? I hope she's feeling well. Has she... Is she here with you?"

Hannah didn't look forward to their next meeting, after how they'd left things that night at the club.

"No. She had some sort of business to attend to." Annabelle's answer brought a wave of relief. And shortly after that, guilt.

"I hope you might tell her..." Hannah hesitated, struggling for the right words. "Please tell her I'm sorry for the trouble I caused before."

There. She might not be quite willing to forget that Della was involved with a married man, but Hannah *was* sorry for causing a fuss and upsetting everyone. In her haste to escape her mother, she'd failed to think about how much trouble her plans might cause.

"What happened?" Annabelle asked in a low tone. "Here, come over behind this elephant where no one will hear us."

"I think that's supposed to be a giraffe." Hannah studied the hedge for a moment. Its carver hadn't been as skilled as one might have liked.

"Never mind what it is. I want to hear your story."

I may as well start at the most important part. "I'm engaged."

"No, you aren't."

"Yes, I *am*."

"Really?" Annabelle's dismay was plain. "But I thought you refused to be married. You promised to be an old maid with me."

Though she was only nineteen, Miss Annabelle had made no secret of the fact that she intended never to marry, yet no one in her family seemed to mind—another curiosity Hannah couldn't explain. Their lives really were so different.

"You haven't even asked who my future husband shall be," Hannah scolded her friend. "It's Mr. Corbyn, the same fellow I kissed at Bishop's. So you can tell everyone we've been secretly engaged for months and they should all calm down a bit about what they saw."

Hopefully that would help smooth over the scandal and make amends to Della and Jane.

"*Have* you been engaged for months?" Annabelle had a narrow face, which always made her look more serious. To that image she now added a very judgmental tone. "I thought he'd only just arrived in town when you kissed him. Della said he'd been at sea before then."

"Must we debate the details? He was in London before his first night at Bishop's. I met him when he came to call on my brother. It was love at first sight. Anyway, the important thing is that we were engaged *before* we kissed."

Annabelle didn't seem to care about this critical piece of information in the least. Didn't she realize that it made all the difference if they wanted to counter the gossip for the sake of the club?

"I can't believe you would chain yourself to some *man*." Annabelle wrinkled her nose in disdain. "What if he's horrid?"

"He's not horrid at all. He's very kind. Have you met him?" Hannah slipped her gloved hand into that of her friend and tugged her gently out from behind the giraffe-elephant to observe Mr. Corbyn. He was still trapped with her mother, poor fellow. He looked so handsome today, the bright-blue morning coat bringing out the color of his eyes just as she'd known it would.

Would Annabelle believe that such a man could want to marry her? Hannah had been so excited to see him dressed up, but now she wondered if their pairing might look far-fetched by the light of day. The best she'd ever managed to attract in the past were the likes of Mr. Horvath or Sir Richard. Underwhelming, unwanted bachelors who'd only turned their sights to Hannah when no one prettier or richer would have them.

"He's over there, the one with blond hair."

Hannah studied Annabelle's face for the awe and wonder which would surely follow, but she took in Mr. Corbyn's good looks with no outward sign that they'd moved her. "How predictable," Annabelle finally said. "Are you going to move to the country and have babies now? I'm *very* disappointed in you."

"I doubt I'll move to the country," Hannah assured her. "He doesn't have any money. Mama wants him to buy a commission in the army."

"Oh, but that's perfect." Annabelle's sour expression vanished at this news. "Then you'll hardly need to see him."

I like seeing him, Hannah very nearly replied. She bit her lip before the words could escape. Why should she think such a thing? This was all an act, not a real courtship, and Mr. Corbyn seemed annoyed to be with her half the time.

But Hannah *did* like it when he was around. Despite his gruff exterior, she felt safer when he was nearby. Less alone.

She swallowed, suddenly flustered. "I suppose you're right," she replied, unsure what else to say.

She might have told Miss Annabelle the truth, but the risk that she might repeat the tale to her older sister was too great. If Della told Jane, she would tell Eli, and Eli would tell their mother.

Better to keep this conspiracy limited to herself and Mr. Corbyn. She didn't dare trust anyone else.

"Anyway, how are things at Bishop's?" Hannah asked, eager to turn the conversation away from her deceit now that she'd finished sharing the most critical information. "And your sister, how is her book coming along?"

"She's nearly finished," Annabelle replied. "Though the viscount had to step back from the project. You'll have seen the story in the papers, no doubt."

"Er—" In fact, Hannah hadn't been reading the papers lately. Mama had considered the news far too inflammatory for her delicate mind while she'd been shut away these past few weeks. Without any opportunity to speak to other people, she had no idea what was going on outside the walls of her guest bedroom.

"His wife is divorcing him," Annabelle confided, seeing her confusion. "They've gone through chancery court, and she's expected to bring a private bill to the House of Lords presently."

"My." Hannah swallowed. "That is shocking."

"He's all but retreated from society, from what I gather. We haven't seen him in weeks."

"But that must be for the best?"

Miss Annabelle made a noncommittal sound, her expression solemn. Surely she couldn't support her sister's connection to such a man?

This was the best outcome for Della.

"She's been spending less time at the club, and I understand Lady Kerr has taken on some of the extra evenings." Annabelle's youthful face transformed into something like a pout. "I don't see why *she* should be allowed to help. She doesn't have any particular genius, you must admit. I'm hoping I might convince Jane and my sister to let me join them instead."

"You?" Hannah blinked. "I didn't realize you liked cards."

"It's not about the cards," Annabelle explained patiently. "It's about the money. They bring in more profit every year, and I wouldn't mind having my own funds without having to ask my parents every time I want something."

Of course! That was how she would get the money to pay Mr. Corbyn. Hannah was already checking over the books for Jane. If she could prove to her sister-in-law that she was useful, she might find more work. Especially now that her engagement had made her respectable again.

Relatively speaking.

Hannah hazarded a glance to Mr. Corbyn. He didn't look to be enjoying himself much, but then, his smile was such a rare thing that it should come as no surprise if he didn't grace the wild rose party with its appearance. Maybe she should get back to him. After all, he *was* suffering through this event for her sake.

"I should return to the others, but please call on me soon. My mother should let me see you now." She didn't think she was quite brave enough to call on the Danby residence yet, even if Della *had* severed her ties to the viscount.

She took her leave from Annabelle and went back to Mr. Corbyn, but when she reached his side, he didn't even acknowledge her. Perhaps he was engrossed in his conversation with Mrs. Brandon.

"And then I told Lady Hawthorne, 'That's not a pudding, that's a custard!'"

No. The conversation couldn't be distracting him.

"How are you enjoying the party?" Hannah asked, trying to catch Mr. Corbyn's gaze.

"It's lovely," Mrs. Brandon replied for him. "And may I offer you my congratulations on your engagement, Miss Williams. I was *so* relieved when your mother told me the news."

"Er, yes," Hannah managed. "We're very happy."

She inched her elbow into Mr. Corbyn's side, hoping to prompt some display of affection. It was like nudging a brick wall. He couldn't have looked less happy if he were trying (which he very well might be).

"What was your engagement present?" Mrs. Brandon gave Hannah a quick once-over. "I don't see a ring. Did he give you a necklace?"

"Oh." *Why didn't I think of that?* She couldn't very well say that he hadn't bought one yet, if Mama was spreading the story that their engagement was already two months old. She should have thought to rescue some relic from her jewelry box that could pass as a love token.

"It's too fine to wear to an afternoon party," Mama cut in, with a speaking look to Mr. Corbyn, who was doing his best to pretend he couldn't see her.

Mrs. Brandon seemed to notice that something was amiss, for she watched Hannah's "fiancé" with a questioning air.

Hannah cleared her throat delicately. "Is anything wrong, m-my love?" She stumbled over the unfamiliar endearment. "You don't seem like your usual, sunny self."

He finally deigned to look her way, an unspoken challenge in his eye. "I'm sure I'm as sunny as ever, darling. How is Miss Annabelle doing?"

What had Miss Annabelle to do with anything? Was he put out that she'd gone off alone? It had only been for a few minutes; certainly nothing worth making a fuss over in front of the other guests.

"Quite well. She extends her congratulations." Annabelle would forgive the lie. Particularly once all of this was all over and she learned that Hannah wasn't really getting married.

The conversation lapsed into an awkward silence. Mr. Corbyn looked supremely uncomfortable. Though he was trying to stand at attention, his thumb was running over his index and middle fingers mechanically, in a repetitive motion he didn't seem to realize he was making. He must be more nervous than he let on.

It isn't easy to be the newest face at the party. Hannah still remembered how uneasy she'd felt in her debut season. And she had the advantage of extensive preparation, while Mr. Corbyn had been thrust into it with a week's notice. How did he feel about all this?

"Would you please take me to see the roses?" she asked, remembering his earlier attempt to avoid socializing. "I should love to go before the path gets too crowded."

For a moment, it looked like Mr. Corbyn might refuse, but then he extended his arm without a word and she slipped her hand through the opening to link their bodies once more.

"It was a pleasure to meet you, Mrs. Brandon," he said with a curt nod.

Mama must have felt that Mr. Corbyn had put in enough time to deserve a respite, for she let them go with a warning: "Don't be too long. I want to introduce you to a few more friends before we leave."

It was amazing what a difference the promise to marry had wrought. Only last week, Mama would have sooner died than let Hannah stroll through the hedges with a man.

Not that there was much risk to her reputation at a garden party in broad daylight.

"Is everything really all right?" she asked, once they were free from eavesdroppers. "You seem like something is troubling you."

"I'm fine." His voice was clipped. "This just isn't the sort of party I'm ordinarily invited to. That's all."

Even through the silk fabric of her gloves and the wool of Mr. Corbyn's sleeve, Hannah could feel the tension in his forearm. Like a spring coiled too tight.

"Are you angry with me for going off to see Miss Annabelle?" she guessed. "I'm sorry I left you alone, but I haven't been able to see anyone else in weeks."

"I'm not a child. I don't need you to keep me on leading strings."

"No," Hannah agreed, "but I suppose it wasn't very considerate of me not to help you through the introductions when it's my fault you're here. I'll stay with you from now on."

"If you like," Corbyn muttered. Though he tried to sound indifferent, Hannah thought he relaxed a bit.

She let their conversation lapse into silence, trying to read Mr. Corbyn's mood. He was a difficult man to know. It seemed everything that she'd learned about him thus far had been obtained in accidental snippets.

Still, even if he was mostly a mystery to her, Hannah had to admit that it was thrilling to walk around the garden party with the most handsome man here on her arm. Normally she spent her time relegated to the corners of these events, trying to avoid attention until she could escape back to her guest bedroom at Jane and Eli's house. This was the first time she could walk with her head held high—safe from her mother's machinations and happy in her present company.

"Do you want some refreshment?" She slowed their step as a waiter came by with a plate of almond biscuits and glasses of lemonade. The food was designed to be easy to eat with gloves on, and Hannah popped the tiny treat into her mouth in a single bite to avoid the risk of any crumbs. "Here. Go on."

She took a second one to offer Mr. Corbyn, who eyed the treat suspiciously.

When he didn't make any move to take it from her hand, she brought the biscuit to his lips.

The instant she did, Hannah recalled herself. What had possessed her to be so bold? She'd been so carried away by the thrill of appearing on the arm of Mr. Corbyn that she'd overstepped the limits of their arrangement.

Hannah froze, her gloved fingers a scant inch from Corbyn's lovely mouth. Could she still pull back or was it already too late? It would be so embarrassing if anyone saw him snub her publicly.

Mr. Corbyn must have been thinking the same thing, for he parted his lips and took the almond biscuit from her fingertips, barely touching them. The curve of his Adam's apple rose and fell as he swallowed.

"Thank you," Corbyn murmured, his voice devoid of any clue that might help her judge whether he had been annoyed by her display or whether he had already dismissed it as part of their act.

Hannah's hand was trembling as she brought it safely back to her side. She wished she could be half as indifferent. It seemed nothing moved Mr. Corbyn.

While they'd been distracted by the refreshments, they'd crept up on a trio of ladies just before them on the path to the roses, and now snatches of their conversation reached Hannah's ears.

"Discharged in disgrace, I heard. After a fight with his superior officer. I wouldn't let a man like that near *my* daughter."

"I'm not sure she had much choice in the matter. The genie's already been let out of his bottle, as I understand it."

Mr. Corbyn stiffened. He'd heard them too.

"Um, let's take this path, instead." Hannah steered them down a little fork to the right instead of continuing past the gossiping women. They walked until they were sheltered from view by a hedge wall that bordered this section of the garden. Mr. Corbyn released her arm as they stopped to rest. It was almost peaceful here, with the gentle breeze bringing the scent of the flowers to her nose. If only she could forget about all the people on the other side of the hedge. "I'm sorry about that," she said softly.

"Why are you apologizing to me?" Mr. Corbyn frowned. "You're the one I've ruined."

He said that as though he'd forgotten that she'd asked him to do the ruining.

"Yes, well, you wouldn't have to hear them talking about you that way if my mother hadn't insisted you come."

"I know what people say about me, whether I'm there to hear it or not." He almost looked indifferent. The matter-of-fact assessment and his expressionless face combined to form the image of a man who didn't care what anyone thought of him. That was certainly what he meant to convey.

But his thumb was still running over his fingers in that same nervous motion. Maybe some things did move him, after all.

Hannah reached for his hand before she could think better of it, the impulse born out of a sudden twinge of concern.

"What really happened?"

Mr. Corbyn jerked in surprise, though he didn't snatch his hand back. He was looking at Hannah as though he'd never seen her before.

"What do you mean, what happened? I punched my superior officer. There was an entire court-martial over it. There's no mystery here, Miss Williams."

"I don't believe that." Hannah wasn't sure when she'd come to doubt the story, exactly. It might well have been on that first night, when he'd found her crying and been kind to her. "It doesn't fit with your character."

"What do you know of my character?" His challenge didn't fool her. It felt as feigned as his indifference—a shell she might crack open with the right pressure. She was beginning to know him well enough to understand that.

"You might be a bit dour, but I don't believe you're violent. And you said you joined the navy when you were eleven. It doesn't make any sense that you could rise from cabin boy to midshipman without a blemish on your name and then one day suddenly attack your superior."

Mr. Corbyn said nothing to this, his silence the clearest confession she could ask for.

"I can't force you to tell me if you don't wish to speak of it," she conceded, "but I wanted you to know that I don't believe the rumors. In—in case that matters to you." She was starting to feel a bit self-conscious at his ongoing silence. Carrying on like this when he hadn't wanted to talk about it in the first place.

But to her great astonishment, Mr. Corbyn began to speak. Far from his usual brusque manner, his voice was uncharacteristically hesitant. "I did punch him," he began. "It was only that he deserved it. Which the navy wasn't much interested in hearing."

"What did he do to you?"

"To me?" Corbyn echoed. "Nothing worse than any captain. He was strict and would dole out punishments quickly, but I never gave him cause to whip me, so I had less to complain about than some." The muscles in his jaw tightened as if he were chewing on his words before he spat them out again. "One night at port he had too much to drink and decided he wanted the attention of a local girl who didn't much agree. I stepped in long enough for her to get away from him." His eyes filled with a dangerous mixture of fury and regret. "And that was the end of my naval career."

"But that's disgraceful!" Hannah gasped. "A captain shouldn't behave in such a manner. Wasn't there anyone who could tell the court-martial you weren't to blame? The tavern owner or another serviceman?"

"Those who'd seen what happened didn't want to bring trouble on their own heads. He was a gentleman. His word was worth more than mine."

"But it isn't fair!"

"Life often isn't."

Hannah fell silent. Her outrage sounded childish when compared to Mr. Corbyn's stoic acceptance.

"Maybe not," she admitted softly. "But just because that's the way things are doesn't make it any less horrid."

He was looking at her strangely. Again, Hannah had the impression that he was assessing her as if they'd never met before.

She was still clinging to his hand. She should have released him ages ago, but having failed to do so, she didn't know how to go about it now. Her hands kept gravitating toward him, it seemed. Like a magnet. It was extraordinarily disconcerting.

"Thank you for telling me," she said. Talking about himself didn't seem to be Mr. Corbyn's strong suit; she was grateful he hadn't brushed her questions aside. "I know it must not have been easy."

To Hannah's surprise, he laughed at this. A staccato bark that didn't seem to carry much humor.

"Why are you laughing?" She didn't understand. Had she done something wrong?

"Because it's absurd to hear you thank me. It should be the other way 'round." He squeezed her hand. So he *had* noticed that she'd been holding onto him this whole time. And now she'd missed her chance to slip free without giving the gesture more importance than she'd meant to. And *now* Mr. Corbyn was leaning forward as if he was about to whisper some secret in her ear, except that he didn't reach her ear at all, he imparted it directly on her mouth.

Oh.

Hannah couldn't move. Her whole body began trembling, though whether from shock or from force of emotion, she couldn't say. Regardless, Mr. Corbyn's response to this confusion was simply to keep on kissing her. He brought his other hand up to cup the back of her neck, drawing her firmly in.

She couldn't help but surrender.

This was nothing like the clumsy mashing of lips she'd inflicted on him at Bishop's. He was *doing things* with his tongue. Stroking her lower lip until she parted for him instinctively, and then he was inside her mouth, exploring her. It made Hannah fear her knees might give out, except that she couldn't afford to faint now because that would end the kiss. She didn't want it to end. A whimper escaped her, swallowed up by Mr. Corbyn. He seemed to swallow her better judgment in much the same manner. Any sense of where they were or why they shouldn't be doing this tumbled from her mind, leaving nothing behind but the most elemental urges.

Yes.

More.

Then it was over, leaving her gasping at the sudden sense of loss. She looked up at Mr. Corbyn, searching for words that wouldn't come. He looked nearly as surprised as she was, his face flushed, his breath coming in quick bursts. He dropped his gaze to her lips.

Do it again, she urged him silently. *Please.*

But before they could find out whether he'd understood her plea, a snapping twig alerted them someone else was approaching their alcove.

Hannah's reason came flooding back to her.

What am I doing? Mr. Corbyn had no business kissing her! She had no business letting him either. She should be ashamed of herself, behaving in such a manner when anyone might stumble upon them.

She'd acted out of necessity the first time, seizing her only chance to escape Mama's matchmaking. But that was done with. There was no reason for them to kiss again.

Hannah stepped back quickly, putting some distance between them. She was far too shaken to speak, but she tore her gaze away from his face. As long as she didn't look at him or touch him or stand too close to him, Mr. Corbyn couldn't muddle her thinking.

"There you are." It was her mother, looking a bit cross, though blissfully unaware of Hannah's turmoil. "I told you not to dillydally. There are at least a dozen more people you must meet and precious little time to do it."

It was probably the only time in her life that Hannah readily agreed.

Twelve

SILAS DIDN'T EVEN REMEMBER HOW THE REST OF THE AFTER-noon passed, except that he was fairly certain he hadn't managed to say anything witty enough to satisfy Mrs. Williams. No matter. There was no pleasing that woman.

It was her daughter who had him tied in knots.

What was he thinking? Why had he kissed her?

He had the entire carriage ride back to his lodgings to ponder these questions, staring at his "fiancée" for most of the way. His silent observation was probably making her uncomfortable, but Silas couldn't seem to turn away for more than a minute before he found himself drawn back to her face. What was it about her?

She wasn't a classic beauty. He hadn't been particularly struck by her looks upon their first meeting, but she'd seemed to grow prettier every time he saw her. Now her plain brown eyes had become warm and encouraging. Her nose was no longer too pointed; it was resolute. Her lips were... Well, the only thing her lips made him think of was the way they'd tasted when he'd kissed her. The tart hint of the lemonade mixed with the sweetness of her reaction.

He hadn't planned that. Miss Williams had drawn it out of him the same way she'd drawn out his story, listening with a patience his own father hadn't managed. She'd asked him what happened and she'd believed him.

Why?

That was what Silas couldn't understand. Why should she care about what happened, when he'd already been judged and condemned? It was too late to change anything. His fate shouldn't have mattered to her.

He was staring again.

Miss Williams's eyes darted up to meet his, caught him looking, then fled downward once more. They'd been playing this game for the past ten minutes.

"Your bow has improved." The grudging admission reminded Silas that Mrs. Williams was still in the carriage with them. He'd all but forgotten her. "But you need to work on your small talk."

"Not everyone is comfortable in a crowd, Mama."

There she went, defending him again. It wasn't that he needed her help to deal with her mother's criticism, but it gave him an odd feeling to know there was someone on his side. He'd never had that before. Silas had the unsettling suspicion that he could come to need it far too much, like a drunk who couldn't keep himself from the bottle. He'd only just tasted a hint of her kindness, and he already wanted more.

Don't get too used to it. It wasn't a good idea to come to depend on Miss Williams for anything other than the two hundred pounds she'd promised him. Three hundred and twenty, if he counted what she already owed from that day he'd scared off her suitor.

"The art of conversation is a skill one can learn, like anything else in life." Mrs. Williams turned to Silas, undeterred. "If you are at a loss, the safest course is to ask the other person some questions and feign a great interest in the answers, until eventually you stumble on an opportunity for a good discussion. What part of the country did he grow up in, how does he know the host, does he have any children, and so forth."

"Thank you, madam. I shall keep that in mind."

Miss Williams was struggling not to frown, though whether her displeasure was directed at her mother's patronizing advice or his chill tone, he couldn't tell. Honestly, she should be grateful that he'd managed to hold his temper this well. When it was finally time to sabotage their engagement, he would have a few words saved up for Mrs. Williams.

"You can practice at Mrs. Brandon's ball."

"What ball?" *What fresh hell is this?* "I thought the next event was to be the supper for your husband's arrival."

"It was," Mrs. Williams confirmed, "until Mrs. Brandon invited us to her ball next Thursday. This is a coup for all of us, Mr. Corbyn. I couldn't refuse."

"I don't dance."

"You *don't dance*?" She looked horror-struck.

This should have been obvious to everyone. Did they think the navy kept a dancing instructor on each ship to impart a little refinement to the men between their duties?

"I also don't dance," Miss Williams pointed out. "So I don't see how it will matter."

"*You* don't dance due to sheer obstinacy." Her mother looked at her through half-lowered lids. "Whereas I presume Mr. Corbyn means to tell us that due to some defect in his education, he does not know how."

Silas judged it better not to reply to this than to issue the retort that was on his tongue. He glanced out the window of the carriage. They hadn't even crossed the Thames yet.

"You will call on us tomorrow and we shall do our best to teach you," Mrs. Williams announced.

The words felt like a noose closing around his neck. "I'm otherwise engaged tomorrow," Silas tried. He had a very pressing obligation to do absolutely anything but this.

"Then you shall have to cancel your plans. What could be more important than your future bride?"

"Don't make *me* responsible for this," Miss Williams protested, an attractive flush coloring her cheeks. "I don't even want to attend this ball. Can't we send our regrets?"

"It would be the height of rudeness to cancel on less than a week's notice."

"Mama, she *invited* us on less than a week's notice. You can't think that she really minds whether we're there. She must have sent out her invitations a month ago."

"Which is why it's all the more important that we make an appearance!" Mrs. Williams scolded her daughter. "You were a social outcast only yesterday, but now that you are engaged, you're being given a second chance to prove there was an explanation for your behavior. It would be foolish to squander this."

Silas looked away. Once he found an excuse to disgrace himself and end their engagement, he didn't think her "second chance" would last too long.

It wasn't his concern. It was what she *wanted*. So why did he hesitate?

He didn't want this woman. He preferred a lover with a bit of experience, someone who knew what she liked and wouldn't expect more than he could give.

Hannah Williams was an innocent. She was naive. Her outrage at the story of his captain's misdeeds had been unfeigned, as if the prospect of someone in power using their position to do harm was entirely unknown to her. This must have been what her brother meant when he'd warned Silas that she lived a sheltered life.

It should have been irritating that another person could reach adulthood with so little understanding of human nature.

But that same innocence was what gave Miss Williams her unquestioning faith that Silas couldn't be guilty of what everyone said about him, for no better reason than that she liked him.

Another *why*. Plenty of women might turn their heads to watch him pass, but Silas wasn't sure that any of them had *liked* him. He'd never had much time to know a woman well, growing up on a ship. They were fairy-tale creatures that glided in and out of his life when he came to harbor. Half the time, Silas couldn't even speak their language. If one occasionally wanted to share his bed, it was only for an evening, and only because he had a striking face. They didn't know anything more about him.

He hadn't realized that he regretted that until Miss Williams asked him for his side of the story. Hadn't realized that he'd wanted someone to care about him.

I do want her. The knowledge cloaked Silas in something like dread.

What was he supposed to do with this feeling? He couldn't act on it; that much was clear. She'd chosen him for the sole reason that he was the most unsuitable man she could find. Though if the way she'd reacted to his kiss was any indication, her opinion of his social standing didn't keep her from wanting him in return. The way she'd trembled and then yielded to his kiss, her hands clutching at the lapels of his morning coat… It had been obvious what sort of power he held over her. If he put his mind to it, Silas had no doubt he could divest Miss Williams of her virtue before the week was out.

"Tomorrow then." Mrs. Williams seemed to have taken his prolonged silence for consent, rather than a very dangerous reflection on his ability to deflower her daughter. "Come by the house around three."

Dancing lessons. This was *not* the best way to deal with his inconvenient attraction to Miss Williams.

The dancing lessons were not only for Mr. Corbyn, as Hannah discovered the following afternoon. They were also for her.

"But I *know* how to dance!" Hannah protested when she was summoned to the dining room to find the table and chairs had all been moved to one side and her supposed fiancé was already waiting for her. "You don't need me for this."

Truth be told, she wasn't ready to face Mr. Corbyn again. She still wasn't sure why he'd kissed her. Until now, she'd always thought of herself as something of a nuisance in this man's life—she popped up and made unreasonable requests that he was only good enough to accept because he was in a state of financial desperation. The emotion that he provoked in her might be a confusing mix of guilt, gratitude, and attraction, but the only emotion that *she* provoked in *him* was supposed to be grudging pity.

Had it been a pity kiss? It certainly hadn't felt that way, but a lonely evening to ponder the question had left Hannah less sure of herself.

If Mr. Corbyn found her pretty (this was already a rather tenuous possibility, she was forced to acknowledge), then shouldn't he have given some sign before now? Paid her compliments, or sent her flowers with a coded message like the arrangements Mama was always working on? That's what men were *supposed* to do when they wanted to win a lady's heart.

Corbyn had been nothing but aloof with her. Kind, perhaps, but distinctly aloof. How could he have kissed her until she was desperate and eager to surrender to him? How could he have held her that way, as if he never intended to let go? Were men simply able to summon that kind of passion for any lady, or did it mean more? Perhaps he only enjoyed the sport.

But there had been a moment right before the kiss when something real had passed between them. Hannah didn't think she'd imagined that.

"Mr. Corbyn needs a partner," Mama admonished her. "Honestly, Hannah, if I didn't know better, I'd think you didn't *want* to spend time with your fiancé. But that's absurd, of course."

Hannah stiffened. "I'm very happy to spend time with Mr. Corbyn. I just don't dance very well, that's all."

She didn't care for how closely her mother was watching her as she hurried forward to take his outstretched hands. The moment they made contact, even through the shield of their gloves, Hannah found her pulse racing.

When she looked into Mr. Corbyn's cerulean eyes, he was as inscrutable as ever. Perhaps he wasn't even thinking about their kiss. It must not be any great event for him; he'd probably kissed plenty of girls. But Hannah had no prior experience to inure her to its appeal, and she found that the most terrible longing overtook her when she thought of it.

She hadn't been able to fall asleep last night until very late. She'd lain awake reliving that moment, desperate for some sort of release from the hold Corbyn had over her, until she'd finally run her hands over her body again and again while imagining it was him there.

This was *not* a good way to keep their arrangement uncomplicated.

"You don't need to know all of the dances," Mama began. "Mastery of a small number of basic steps will ensure that you are ready for any ball. We shall begin with the chassé, then move on to the allemande, the fleuret, the waltz traveling step, of course, the chassé setting step—"

"Pardon me," Mr. Corbyn cut in. "What exactly do you consider a *small* number of steps to be?"

"Do not interrupt." She flicked her fan through the air just before Mr. Corbyn's nose. "But to answer your question: about a dozen."

"A dozen isn't a small number." He sounded as if he were speaking through gritted teeth. *There. He's back to being annoyed.* It was a more familiar, far less confusing state of affairs. "It's a dozen."

"Which *is* small considering that it shall give you mastery over nearly every dance you are likely to encounter."

Hannah confided to Mr. Corbyn, "What my mother isn't telling you is that the steps aren't even the hard part. It's remembering what order they go in."

"May I leave?" he replied.

"No. You may *not*." Mama stomped her foot. "You are both so obstinate. I hate to imagine what your lovers' spats shall look like. Now, eyes on me. We begin the chassé with a temps levé."

"We begin what with a what?" Corbyn scowled at her in utter confusion.

"The temps levé is just a small hop. It's not complicated, I assure you."

"Why don't you just call it a small hop, then?"

His voice rose slightly with each question, and Mama raised hers even more in response, until she was practically shouting. "Because civilized Englishmen speak *French*, Mr. Corbyn. Have you really no education at all?"

Hannah stepped between them swiftly. "Why don't we break for refreshments?"

While the simmering hostility in the room boded well for the eventual demise of their engagement, she couldn't let it boil over quite yet. They still had to get Papa to town.

"We haven't even done the first step!" Mama pressed her hands to her brow. "You two shall be the death of me. We are not leaving this room until one of you can do a chassé."

Oh, very well. Hannah lifted her skirts ever so slightly to expose her ankles.

"Temps levé, one foot forward, close the step, leading foot forward again, now hop as your following foot closes and you're ready for the next temps levé." She demonstrated in time with her words, while Corbyn watched her feet doubtfully. When she'd finished, she turned back to her mother. "There. Now one of us has done a chassé."

"I meant the other one." Mama eyed Mr. Corbyn expectantly.

He emitted a strangled sigh. "Which foot am I supposed to lead with?"

"The right." Hannah executed the step for him again, this time a little more slowly. His eyes were fixed on her movements, which he reproduced clumsily a moment later.

"No, no, no," Mama scolded. "Don't look at your feet. Your back must be straight and your arms should be gracefully rounded."

"Couldn't I keep my back straight *after* I learn the step?" Corbyn executed the chassé a second time, this time keeping his back perfectly rigid. It would have been nearly passable if the expression on his face weren't so foreboding. No one wanted a dance partner who looked like he was about to choke down a spoonful of castor oil.

"I said *gracefully* rounded. Your elbows are pointing outward like a pigeon flapping."

"I think I've done just about all the chassé-ing I can manage this morning," Corbyn growled.

"A small break!" Hannah pleaded. "And we shall return refreshed. Mr. Corbyn, why don't you accompany me for a turn about the room?"

"So long as we're *walking*."

While her mother rang for the maid to bring in something to

drink, Hannah whispered to Corbyn quickly. "It's only dancing. Please endure it for an hour or two. I don't want you provoking my mother until *after* my father arrives in town, remember?"

"*She's* provoking *me*," he hissed. "She won't stop harping on every flaw."

"Imagine how I feel. At least you may return home when the lesson is done."

This silenced Mr. Corbyn, though Hannah regretted her hasty words a moment later. She shouldn't be speaking so freely about her family with an outsider. What was it about Mr. Corbyn that made her feel that she could confide in him? It must come from sharing a secret. Working together to fool her mother had given Hannah a false sense of intimacy, and now she kept forgetting herself.

She smoothed over her lapse in a calmer voice. "You were doing perfectly well. It would be easier for you if we could take our time instead of rushing through everything at once."

"You recall that we're attending a ball in less than a week?"

Goodness, is he actually worried about that?

"I don't expect you to dance with me. By the time we're finished here, Mama will see that it's hopeless." When Mr. Corbyn tensed, she quickly added, "I don't mean that as an insult. *No one* could learn how to dance in so little time. It simply isn't possible, but we're humoring her to keep the peace for a few more days, agreed?"

Oh dear. Hannah hadn't meant to offend him. Why must he take each task so seriously when they both knew it was an act?

"Not agreed." Corbyn narrowed his eyes. "What are we doing at a ball if we don't dance? Won't it make a poor impression before you're ready?"

"I don't mind," she assured him. "I never thought we would dance in the first place."

"Maybe I could learn one." Of all the things to fall from Mr.

Corbyn's mouth, this had to be the most unexpected. Perhaps even more than their kiss. After all, Hannah could understand why kissing felt good, while dancing had never brought her anything but frustration. Why on earth should he want to do it, except out of some perverse desire to prove that he could?

But Hannah wasn't going to be the one to tell him no. He got tetchy about that sort of thing.

She brought their walk about the room to a halt and motioned for Mr. Corbyn to stand facing her. Perhaps he would find it easier without her mother hovering over them. "Your arms should be like this." Hannah bent her elbows and wrists to the slightest degree with her hands in front of her body just below her hips, forming a gentle curve rather than a sharp angle. She held the pose patiently until he tried to imitate it. "No, hands closed. May I?"

She took Mr. Corbyn's wrists and turned his hands so that they faced sideways rather than palms down. Then she positioned his thumb atop his index finger. When she'd finished, she found him staring at her rather oddly. His eyes were far more intense at this distance.

Why can't I keep my hands off this man for more than a minute? No wonder he'd kissed her yesterday. He must have thought she was begging for it.

Hannah stepped back and pretended that she was calmly assessing his posture and not fleeing the sound of her own racing heart. She cleared her throat. "Good. Now just keep your upper body like that anytime you aren't extending your hand to a lady. And try to keep your toes pointed down and outward when you take a step."

"Should we try the one after the chassé?" His voice was far too determined for such a tedious chore, but Hannah couldn't argue. If Mr. Corbyn had his mind set to it, it would be pointless to protest. He really *was* just as stubborn as she was.

Hannah obliged by taking him through a simple waltz step and then the jeté (which Mr. Corbyn found more aggravating than the others at first, though he improved after a few tries). It was a bit amusing to have him copying her movements with such dedication. She wasn't used to people looking to her as an authority on anything; nor was she used to Mr. Corbyn playing the part of an attentive student. He was so much more experienced and worldly than she was. It gave Hannah a secret thrill to think that she might help *him* for a change.

She was so caught up in their efforts she didn't notice the time pass until the grandfather clock chimed the half hour. Where had Mama gone? Hannah looked around the room to find that her mother had been sitting on one of the dining chairs the whole time, watching their progress from over the top of a crystal sherry glass.

Hannah flushed. She'd let her guard down. Had she said or done anything that might not match the image of a devoted fiancée? She didn't think so, but she'd been so absorbed in their lesson that she hadn't been on her guard. She would have to be more careful.

"What do you think?" Hannah tried to keep her voice light.

"Better than when you started," Mama admitted after a long sip of her sherry. "I'm glad to see you're both taking this seriously."

Mr. Corbyn eyed the bottle and empty glasses the maid had left on the table. They were both a little flushed from their practice.

"May I offer you a glass, Mr. Corbyn?" Mama sounded reluctant, but there was no way she could fail to show hospitality to their guest. She poured out a miserly serving of sherry, which Mr. Corbyn downed with the enthusiasm of a man facing a firing squad.

"And me?" Hannah asked. It didn't hurt to try.

"You may drink sherry at four o'clock in the afternoon *after* you're married," Mama said flatly.

This is why I'm cursed to be the only clearheaded one in the group.

Hannah turned back to Mr. Corbyn. "We should start teaching you the formations for one dance before we run out of time."

He frowned. "We still have about nine more steps to learn, by my count."

"Yes, but we won't be able to teach you everything. To be honest, you can muddle your way through most of the footwork as long as you know where you're supposed to be standing and you get there in time. Dancing is mostly just walking nicely in time to the music."

"You cannot 'muddle your way' through good footwork," her mother protested. "Skill as a dancer is what separates a real gentleman from an oaf."

"I thought that a shallow bow was what separated a real gentleman from an oaf," Corbyn pointed out.

Her mother clearly didn't appreciate this remark, and Hannah judged it best to interrupt before a fresh quarrel could break out. "Mama, you have to admit that Mr. Corbyn is at a disadvantage. The other gentlemen have had years with their dancing masters where we have only five days. Our most realistic option is to pick the simplest dance to be called at the ball and ensure that he knows all the figures to it. So long as he keeps his position in time, no one will be staring at his feet to ensure his footwork is perfect."

Mama pinched her lips, but reluctantly agreed. "Very well, but we shall need to perfect *all* his steps before your wedding. This won't be your only ball, you know."

A trace of alarm flashed over Mr. Corbyn's face, but Hannah spoke before he could. "Of course."

It was no concern to anyone what she promised; they would end their engagement long before then.

Silas struggled to keep from protesting. It had taken his full resolve to learn the few steps they'd practiced this morning. How was he to keep track of even more? But Miss Williams didn't seem worried in the least.

Because her mother will have run me off by then, Silas reminded himself. Somehow, he couldn't seem to approach this charade with the same disregard as her. It felt wrong to keep making promises he didn't intend to keep.

Who is it you're worried about lying to? Surely not her mother.

"Let's begin with the First Set of quadrilles." Mrs. Williams strode to the dining table to fetch a dancing manual she'd set at the ready. "Now, there are several variations on this arrangement, but Thomas Wilson's version is likely to be the most useful to us. You may adapt it at the ball if you see they're following another."

Silas sincerely doubted his ability to tell one version of a quadrille from another.

Why did I agree to this? It had been a point of pride to tell Miss Williams that he could learn at least one dance by Thursday—to prove that he was capable of more than she assumed—but pride came before the fall.

In this case, the fall might be a very literal one, and was sure to take place publicly.

Mrs. Williams opened the manual to display the instructions she wanted. The lines on the page looked like an elegant pile of scribbles drawn by a five-year-old trying to fit every geometric shape they'd ever learned onto one page. As Silas took the booklet from her outstretched hands and flipped through the next pages, he saw that the First Set consisted of six distinct dances, each with its own steps.

Hell and damnation.

Mrs. Williams called out instructions as they began their practice, which helped a little, although her comments about the placement of the other dancers were rather distracting. "The head couples will dance for the first thirty-two bars. You'll likely be one of the side couples, so you can repeat everything they do afterward."

Miss Williams, standing opposite him patiently, seemed almost as lost as Silas. "This would be easier with music."

Her mother's emphatic "*one*-two-*three*-four" was more of a distraction than a help.

"We'll ask Jane to play for us next time," Mrs. Williams conceded. "She was engaged today. *Right* hand to the opposite lady here, Mr. Corbyn, then left hand back to your own partner."

"There *is* no opposite lady," he muttered as he passed an invisible phantom and extended his hand back to Miss Williams. She took it so tentatively that he could only conclude she'd lost all trust in him. She'd been behaving differently ever since that kiss. Where she used to let her hands linger on his body when she took his arm, now she pulled away quickly. As if she was afraid that Silas might pounce on her the instant she let her guard down.

The worst part was she might be right. When Hannah had taken his wrists into her hands to help position him earlier, Silas felt a jolt of...*something*. He'd grown uncomfortably aware of each touch, no matter how innocent.

It made it damnably difficult to focus on the steps.

When he accidentally turned left instead of right on the two-hand turn, Mrs. Williams decided she'd had enough. "*No*, Mr. Corbyn! It's always *clockwise*, remember?"

"No one in their right mind could remember all of this," he ground out.

"Why don't we finish with a waltz?" Miss Williams suggested. "It will be easier for him."

Silas bristled at the suggestion that he needed something *easier*, even if he was in no position to argue. Mrs. Williams seemed to recognize the urgency of their situation too.

"Very well." She was assessing him with something like despair. "You will only need the traveling step and the pivot for this. You stride forward for the first three beats, leading with your left. After that, Hannah will stride forward while you pivot—put your right foot back and then two small steps—until you've made a circle and you start again."

Miss Williams placed her hand upon Silas's shoulder, then clasped his left hand lightly in hers. He hesitated a moment, then set his right hand on the small of her back. They weren't exactly pressed together, but the distance between them was narrow enough that it felt decidedly more intimate.

He could see her pulse at the hollow of her throat. Imagine how soft her skin would be. Silas tried to focus on the steps instead of staring. Was that scent of roses from her soap, or did she put little flowers in her wardrobes? It was soothing. He fought the urge to pull her closer and inhale deeply.

Get ahold of yourself.

"*One*-two-three, *one*-two-three." Mrs. Williams clapped her hands on the first beat for emphasis, watching their footwork critically as Silas turned Miss Williams around the room in controlled circles.

This one was easier than the quadrille, for there was nothing much to remember. Once he got used to the rhythm, he managed it without stepping on her toes.

I will be able to dance with her.

The triumph was a small one, by any reasonable standard. He'd learned one dance, and the simplest one, at that. It was hardly exceptional. But Silas couldn't deny that it meant something to him.

He felt...happy.

The understanding nearly made him miss his step, but he caught himself in time. When was the last time he'd been happy? Months ago, certainly. Before he'd ruined his naval career. Before his father had cast him out like a criminal.

Somehow, being near Miss Williams made him forget all that for a while.

He studied her face as they continued to spin together. Her cheeks were flushed from exertion and her dark eyes sparkled. He wished he could kiss her again, if only they'd been alone. Last time hadn't been long enough.

Miss Williams looked at him with a touching blend of longing and trepidation. It felt good to have someone look at him that way.

Whatever their differences, she felt something for him. A physical attraction that came through in every touch. Silas might not be her equal in class, education, or good breeding, but he held that one advantage. As they fell into an easy rhythm, there was a sense of *rightness* to it he couldn't explain.

Silas let his eyes roam over her, imagining what it would be like if they were lovers instead of accomplices. Miss Williams might not have the confidence he was used to, but she had a rebellious spark. Enough fire to her that things might get interesting, once she learned what she was doing. And surrounding it all, there was a gentleness to her. A soothing quality that called to him.

But if he seduced this woman, there would be no going back. Silas would have to make their engagement a real one. They both knew that was impossible. Miss Williams didn't want a husband; she wanted an accomplice in deceit and perhaps as an occasional distraction. And her mother would never allow the match if she knew that Silas was secretly planning to use his three hundred pounds to fund a brewery instead of buying a commission.

"That's enough," Mrs. Williams said abruptly, startling Silas from his thoughts. "I think you've got it."

Without any music to guide them, they didn't stop at exactly the same moment. Miss Williams came to a halt one step before Silas, then wobbled uncertainly when he kept moving. He tightened his grip on her waist to steady her, his blood heating, before he released her and stepped back as he was meant to.

"Sorry," he murmured.

"It was my fault. I stopped too sharply." Miss Williams was looking at her feet, suddenly flustered. "You did very well."

Silas tried not to swell at this praise. He wasn't some foppish peacock, living for the moment a woman looked his way. It made no difference if he secured Miss Williams's good opinion before she paid him his due and flitted back out of his life. He would get his money either way.

This did little to explain why Silas accepted when Mrs. Williams pressed her copy of Wilson's dancing manual into his hands and instructed him to study as much as he could before the ball on Thursday. Nor could he account for the stubborn resolve that had him flipping through the pages on the carriage ride back to James and Marian's lodgings. It was probably impossible, but he wanted to learn it well enough to muddle through a few dances without making an ass of himself. If every other man in the ballroom could manage it, why shouldn't he?

It was the most useless sort of desire, but Silas couldn't seem to help himself. He was trapped in a cage of his own making. Even if Miss Williams was meant to be finished with him soon, he wanted to prove himself before the end. Starting with this ball.

Thirteen

Mrs. Brandon's ball was the first event of its kind that Hannah had attended without a knot of dread in her stomach. What a difference it made to know that she wouldn't have to fend off a single suitor tonight! She normally spent her time huddled up with Annabelle, or whichever friendly face she was fortunate enough to find, trying to avoid eye contact with eligible men until her mother pried her forcibly away and pressed her into the acquaintance of some third-rate fortune hunter.

But tonight would be different! With Mr. Corbyn there to protect her from any unwanted attention, Hannah would be free to enjoy herself however she wished, without any thought of matchmaking.

She wasn't even sure what she would do. This was the only time since her coming-out that she would spend an evening in mixed company without a defensive strategy. It was an entirely novel situation.

She dressed with particular care, fishing through her closet for something worthy of the occasion. Hannah normally didn't *want* to make herself look fetching, lest it help her mother's efforts, so she hadn't bothered to bring any of her favorite gowns with her from Devonshire. Now she rather regretted that decision.

I wish I'd known in advance that I'd be attending a ball with my unaccountably handsome pretend fiancé.

She solicited Jane's opinion, and together they finally settled on a teal blue silk that Hannah had considered a bit too plain for the occasion, but which Jane helped her elevate with a lace shawl and a series of hairpins that made it look as though she'd strung pearls through her braided bun.

"I wish you were coming," Hannah lamented. Much as she was looking forward to an evening of freedom, she wasn't entirely confident how she and Mr. Corbyn would be received at such a formal event. Some reinforcements might have been welcome.

"I'm needed at the club tonight." Jane offered her an apologetic smile. "Don't worry. I'm sure you'll do fine."

Just before she went down, Hannah remembered to put on her best necklace so that she could pretend it was an engagement present from Mr. Corbyn if Mrs. Brandon asked again.

There. Now she was ready. Hannah looked herself over one last time in the mirror, then wished she hadn't. Even done up to her best, she couldn't hope to match Mr. Corbyn. He had the sort of face that turned heads in a crowd, while hers faded into the shadows. Would people think them silly together?

Never mind that. Worrying won't change it.

Hannah forced herself to turn away and went downstairs to wait for their carriage to return. Mama had sent the coachman ahead to collect Mr. Corbyn while they finished dressing, seeing as he was in the opposite direction from Mrs. Brandon's Mayfair town house.

When he finally arrived, Hannah felt inexplicably nervous. It was too dark inside the coach at this hour to get a good look at Mr. Corbyn, but she imagined that she could feel his eyes on her as he murmured a polite "good evening." No one spoke much on the short ride over. There was tension in the air, though Hannah couldn't tell who was causing it. Surely this event was no more momentous than anything else they'd done?

Mama seemed to read her mind. "There is no greater test of a gentleman's mettle than a ball," she opined gravely.

Now Hannah was fairly certain most of the tension was coming from Mr. Corbyn's side of the carriage, if it hadn't been before.

"I'm sure everything will be fine." She repeated Jane's earlier prediction like a talisman. "What's the worst that could happen?"

No one seemed to find this statement as encouraging as Hannah had intended it. She winced. "Sorry. I didn't mean to tempt fate."

"That's all right," Mr. Corbyn murmured. "I speak without thinking all the time."

Hannah thought she could hear the smile in his voice as he echoed the declaration he'd made at their first meeting. It seemed so long ago now, but she hadn't forgotten. From the very beginning, he'd sent her his quiet reassurance. They were in this together.

Once they arrived, Mr. Corbyn got out first and handed Hannah down, his palm firm and warm even through the layer of his evening gloves. He set his free hand on her waist to steady her as she descended, though she hadn't stumbled. Surely she was imagining the way his fingertips lingered before he turned back to the coach to assist her mother. Reading meaning into commonplace gestures.

It was only once they reached the lanterns lining the approach to the Brandons' house that Hannah finally got a good look at Mr. Corbyn.

My goodness. It had been one thing to see him in the fine new clothes they'd had made for the garden party the other day, and quite another thing to see him in full evening dress. He wore the ivory waistcoat that Hannah had selected, with a matching bow tie framed between the smooth, black lapels of his tailcoat. This one fit him perfectly, skimming his muscular frame with an expert cut. He even had the new silk top hat that Mama had insisted on. Fortunately, he hadn't seen fit to follow her advice about the haircut. His golden waves were smoothed into place, tamed but unharmed.

"What is it?" Mr. Corbyn noticed her stare as he led them up the approach, but misinterpreted its cause. He slowed his stride. "Is something the matter?"

"No. You look perfect." Hannah was too dumbstruck to care whether she sounded foolish. She couldn't let him think there was anything wrong when he'd come here looking like that. "You were meant for these clothes."

Mr. Corbyn looked at her oddly before continuing up to the house. She wasn't sure whether her words had brought him the reassurance she'd intended. There was no time to think about it further, as Mama urged them on.

"Don't dally, we're delaying the queue."

Inside the house, a servant announced their entrance in a booming voice, causing a number of heads to turn their way. Mama ushered them over to pay their respects to their hostess directly. Though Hannah spotted some ladies murmuring behind the safety of their fans while she was trapped in polite conversation with Mrs. Brandon, her arrival had provoked less of a reaction than she'd feared. News of her engagement to Mr. Corbyn must have stolen most of the shine from the rumors.

Even so, Mr. Corbyn looked ill at ease with all the attention. Hannah recalled how wooden and standoffish he'd been at the outset of the garden party two days ago. These events took a toll on him, but he came because she needed him. Who else would have done this for her? Even if she was paying him for the service, Mr. Corbyn took his role far more seriously than she'd expected.

They spent the first hour being paraded around to Mama's friends like a shiny new bauble, and Hannah did her best to keep a smile on her face and steer the conversation in directions most likely to be easy for Mr. Corbyn to navigate. He played his part admirably, being perfectly charming to everyone. Well, perhaps *charming* wasn't the right word. He was a bit too reserved to make fast friends. But so long as they avoided the subject of his naval service, he gave no one cause for any offense, which was all she needed.

It was only once Mama had finally exhausted her supply of very dear friends and had progressed down the list to passing acquaintances that she finally saw fit to break for some refreshments, giving Hannah and Mr. Corbyn a much-needed moment alone.

"You're doing very well," Hannah encouraged him, sipping her punch and wincing at the taste. The Brandons had been far too generous with their rum this evening. She'd best watch herself, or she was liable to have a headache tomorrow. "Thank you for letting my mother introduce you to everyone she's ever met. I know these events can be a trial for you."

Mr. Corbyn stiffened. "I'm perfectly capable of making chitchat for a few hours."

Oh dear. Why did he always presume that she looked down on him, even when she was trying to be kind?

"I know that," she assured him. "I didn't mean to give insult."

This seemed to mollify him somewhat, though he still had a guarded look in his eye as he took a long swallow of his own drink.

"Mr. Corbyn, if we are going to spend the rest of the evening posing as an engaged couple, we may as well speak to one another openly."

"Very well." He waited.

"I really do have every confidence in you. But you can't deny that you become tense when we're forced to mingle in a crowd." As Mr. Corbyn didn't deny this observation when Hannah paused to draw breath, she felt bold enough to continue. "I understand it completely. I'm the same way. I only want to know if there's anything I could do to make it easier on you."

"It will be over soon enough," he replied simply, without acknowledging her offer. Was he counting the minutes until they could part ways? The possibility stung.

Just when she thought Mr. Corbyn must care about her, at least a little, he said something to make her wonder if she'd imagined everything.

"I tried not to leave you alone this time," Hannah pointed out, childishly wanting him to notice her efforts. "I hope that helped."

"You don't need to stay with me if you'd rather seek out your friends."

"I *want* to stay," she insisted. "You're doing me a favor. I want to return it in kind, if you would tell me how."

Mr. Corbyn finally seemed to realize that she wouldn't be deterred. He inhaled slowly and replied in a tight, even voice. "It isn't that I'm afraid of crowds. It's only that my father used to dream of the day I might find myself invited to a place like this. More than anything, he wanted to see me advance my station. It's difficult not to imagine what he might say if he could see me now."

"What do you think he *would* say?"

Hannah should have thought to ask Mr. Corbyn about his family sooner. It was a bit suspicious that she couldn't name most of the people who were supposed to become her in-laws shortly. Corbyn's family must be close if his brother and cousin had come all the way to town to see him, but Hannah hadn't forgotten his words to her on the night they'd met. That he understood what it was like to have a parent controlling his every move.

If Mr. Corbyn's father was as determined to advance his children's futures as Mama, perhaps they had a great deal in common.

His expression soured. "Nothing complimentary."

"You aren't on good terms, then?" she guessed.

"We aren't on any terms at all, is more like." Mr. Corbyn's face was grim as he explained. "I stopped being his son when I got myself discharged."

"I'm sure he doesn't think that," Hannah reassured him. Surely no one would cast off their own child. Mr. Corbyn must be overstating the breach.

"Those were his exact words." His voice was as cold and sharp as the glint of light off a razor's edge.

Oh.

Hannah had thought she understood what Mr. Corbyn was facing, but she didn't understand this at all. No matter that she and Mama might argue, Hannah couldn't imagine that she would ever be cut off. *And I've certainly done far worse than Mr. Corbyn has.*

He'd only been trying to help a woman in need. What kind of father would turn his child out for that? It was heartless.

"I wish you would say something." Mr. Corbyn sounded as if he were having second thoughts over his decision to share the story.

"I was just feeling embarrassed for all the times I've complained about my mother," Hannah admitted. "You must have thought I sounded like a spoiled child."

"I thought you had some fire in you. That's all."

Hannah smiled. She liked the sound of that. Most men took her for nothing but a dull, timid miss. Mr. Corbyn made her sound almost exciting. She was absurdly grateful to him for that, even if she hadn't already owed him more than she could repay.

"What if we forgot all about our parents this evening and simply enjoyed ourselves?" she suggested. After all, this might be the last time either of them were invited to such an event. Once she forced Mama to see reason and broke off her engagement, Hannah would return to the country and Mr. Corbyn would return to his own sphere of life. "Is there anything you've always wanted to do at a party?"

"I don't know. I've never been invited to a ball before."

"No, but you must have been to a country dance or a May Eve," Hannah encouraged him. "The same principles apply."

"I haven't been to many of those either," Mr. Corbyn confessed. He didn't sound embarrassed, exactly. Perhaps the right word was cautious. "I went to sea when I was eleven, remember?"

Hannah stopped to ponder this. She'd imagined that Mr. Corbyn was far more worldly and experienced than she was. And in some ways, he must be. He'd seen lands and peoples that she would never lay eyes on, learned lessons in hardship that she would never face. But his experience had come at the price of simple occasions she took for granted.

It filled her with an unexpected tenderness toward him.

"That's all the more reason to do whatever you want tonight." Hannah had planned to make the most of her evening, but now she found that she cared a great deal whether Mr. Corbyn enjoyed himself too. They could seize the moment together. Although it would be a good deal easier to accomplish if they left the area before Mama came back from the powder room to arrange any more introductions. "Go ahead. What would you like most? And remember, I've fled from a ball before, so I won't object if you want to go somewhere else."

Mr. Corbyn looked at her in surprise. "I thought you didn't want me to sabotage our engagement until your father arrives.

Though abducting you from a ball does seem an effective way to go about it."

"Drat, I suppose you're right. Something we can do here then," Hannah amended. "Only hurry, before Mama comes back and forces us to dance."

The musicians were tuning their instruments in the next room, the vibrato of a violin creeping out to reach her ears. If they lingered here too long they were liable to find themselves engaged for the next six sets.

She looked expectantly at Mr. Corbyn. There was the spark in his piercing blue eyes that told her he'd already seized on his idea, but he didn't share it with her.

"Well?" she prodded, shooting a nervous look over his shoulder. Her mother was already back! She'd just been waylaid by Mrs. Godfrey near a large potted fern. She might rejoin them any minute.

"I want to dance with you."

"What?" Hannah couldn't have heard him correctly. "But we don't have to. I don't even *want* to."

"I saw the program," Mr. Corbyn explained. "They're starting with the First Set. The same ones we learned the other day."

"Is 'learned' the right word?" Hannah asked delicately.

"I studied it some more back home."

Nothing seemed to deter Mr. Corbyn once he'd set his mind to something. If only he could have picked a better goal. "It's going to be exceedingly long and boring," Hannah warned him. The quadrilles were always the longest, with all their arrangements.

"There you are!" It was Mama, back to torment them before they could make their escape, just as Hannah had feared. "Why aren't you in the ballroom? They're about to begin!"

Mr. Corbyn observed them with a look of patient determination. "Your dance card, darling?"

Hannah knew when she was beaten. Or if she didn't, his endearments were always enough to make her flustered and forget her arguments.

She turned the card over to Mr. Corbyn, who wrote his name in the first space. The rest were blissfully empty, for her mother had been too focused on presenting their engagement to her friends to worry about any of that.

At least it's only one set.

They filed into the large ballroom to meet their fate.

With this many people in attendance, their hosts had arranged for several groups of eight to dance the quadrille in separate parts of the floor. Mr. Corbyn escorted Hannah to their place as one of the side couples in Mrs. Brandon's circle. The ballroom was full tonight. Hannah had danced the First Set so many times by now that she could probably do it in her sleep, albeit without much enthusiasm, but Mr. Corbyn had never done this before. She didn't think he'd take it well if he fell on his face in front of a crowd. Why should he want to risk it, when they might easily have escaped?

The first notes of "La Coquette" rang out, and the dancers all greeted each other with little curtsies and bows. It was only then that Hannah realized who stood across from her. The other side couple consisted of Sir Richard and a young lady she didn't recognize.

Oh goodness, how unlucky. He'd seen her, judging by the thin set of his mouth, but said nothing.

The head couples advanced to the center of the circle and withdrew again, beginning the dance. There was nothing for Hannah to do for the next twenty-four bars but stand awkwardly across from Sir Richard and watch the head couples chassé and set. Mr. Corbyn didn't seem to have noticed the source of her discomfort. His eyes were riveted to the head couple's movements, plainly trying to remind himself of all the steps before it was their turn.

Please don't let us stumble in front of Sir Richard. Hannah cast a silent prayer skyward until it was time to step forward.

Miraculously, Mr. Corbyn managed to execute the next few steps without error. Though his footwork was occasionally a bit shoddy or slower than his neighbors, he kept himself in the right position as they moved about the floor. When the dance had ended with a successful chassé croisé from all the couples, he shot Hannah an exuberant glance. She smiled encouragingly, afraid to offer any congratulations while they still had four more dances to get through.

But to her increasing astonishment, Mr. Corbyn performed the next two in the set, La Sybille and Jacintha, with the same methodical determination. He looked frequently to the other gentlemen to remind himself of the steps, and occasionally he hesitated, but he never faltered. Hannah could hardly believe her eyes.

By the time they reached Nannette, Mr. Corbyn had grown confident enough to tear his attention from the other dancers and make eye contact with her during the brief introduction to the song.

"How did you learn all this since yesterday?" she whispered.

"I told you, I practiced after with Marian."

Though he said no more than this, it was evident that Mr. Corbyn was pleased with himself. There was an energy in his gaze that she'd never seen before. Instead of nerves or frustration, it looked like triumph. There was something rather touching in the sight.

He must have done nothing else since our last meeting. Hannah could hardly comprehend the sheer scale of the effort involved. *She* had only taken dancing lessons because she'd been forced into it, but Mr. Corbyn had thrown himself into the task entirely of his own choosing, all to make this night a success.

For me.

Hannah wasn't sure when anyone had shown her such

consideration. Certainly none of the gentleman callers that Mama had dredged up from the rubbish piles of the season.

It made her feel a little sad that she would have to say goodbye to him soon. She was never going to meet someone who would show this much concern for her happiness again.

Because you promised him two hundred pounds, she reminded herself firmly. *For that price, of course he would take it seriously.*

But the explanation didn't seem as persuasive as it once had. Somewhere along the way, she and Mr. Corbyn had begun to blur the tidy lines they'd tried to draw around this arrangement, and now she wasn't sure how to put them back again.

Fourteen

He was actually doing it.

Silas's heart was hammering in his chest through the first four dances in the set as he waited for the moment he would trip and stumble. Though he nearly turned the wrong direction when it came time for all the gentlemen to step forward and pass around their partners to the right, he caught himself in the nick of time.

He was nearly there.

More gratifying than his success was the look Miss Williams had given him in between songs. (During the songs, he was too busy counting steps to look her way.) Her initial surprise had gradually been replaced by a joy that grew surer with every step. They had already reached the finale now. Just a few more minutes.

Silas stepped forward to cross the set, giving his right hand to the blond lady opposite as he took her former place beside her partner, a gentleman thrice her age, then crossed back, this time giving his left hand. There. Now he had nothing left to do except watch the other couples complete their turns and repeat the same steps a few times in between each pair. He'd done it.

When it came time for Hannah to step forward to meet her opposite, Silas was startled to realize the gentleman looked familiar. He hadn't had the luxury of studying the other dancers' faces while he'd been busy studying their feet, but now that his part was nearly finished, he could watch them at his leisure. Didn't he know this old fellow with the yellowing handlebar mustache? Silas didn't think he was imagining it. The fellow looked at Miss Williams as if he knew her, extending his hand with a reluctance that bordered on insult. She made no obvious reaction, but her face said everything. How had Silas failed to notice sooner?

Once Miss Williams was back at his side, he whispered, "Is that the same gentleman I saw leaving your house the other day?"

"Yes," she hissed back quickly. "Sir Richard." Then she linked her hand into his as they completed the set with a grand rond.

As all the dancers formed a circle for the last few bars, Silas made eye contact with Sir Richard. He hadn't gotten a good look at him the other time, but a closer inspection confirmed his first impression. The man was more fit to be a grandfather than a groom. How could Mrs. Williams have imagined that her vibrant, lively daughter belonged with *this*? It was disgusting!

When Silas had wondered what would push Hannah Williams to do something so drastic as hire a fiancé, he hadn't truly understood what she was facing. Or perhaps he had, and it was only that her hardship hadn't looked so serious compared to his. At least not when she'd still been a stranger to him, and one with enough food to eat and a roof over her head and fine clothes to wear.

It was different now that he knew Miss Williams had a gentle heart. Now that he'd kissed her and made her smile and warmed himself by the light of her attention. The idea of that old man putting his hands on Hannah filled Silas with such a visceral repulsion that it was all he could do not to breach the formation and grab Sir Richard by the collar.

The object of Silas's resentment began to grow pale beneath the sheen of sweat that dotted his brow. Silas must have allowed his anger to show too plainly. He tried to school his features into a more neutral expression by the time the last notes rang out and it was time to bow to Miss Williams, though it wasn't easy.

"Let's go," he murmured. "We've finished our dance." He needed to get out of here.

Mrs. Williams was waiting for them as soon as they withdrew from the floor, nearly as breathless as if she had been the one turning about to the music instead of her daughter. "That was *remarkably* competent, Mr. Corbyn. Truly."

Had she actually complimented him? "Remarkably competent" might not sound like high praise from anyone else, but from Mrs. Williams it was nothing short of a miracle.

"Wasn't he marvelous?" Miss Williams smiled. She was glowing from the exertion.

Silas should have been pleased to earn their approval—a minute ago, it was all he'd wanted—but the image of Sir Richard had spoiled his moment. Was he supposed to forget that she'd wanted that man for her daughter until Silas had chased him off? He wasn't sure that he could talk to Mrs. Williams without telling her exactly what he thought of her original choice of a husband for Hannah.

You aren't anyone's choice for a husband, he reminded himself. *You have no business getting jealous over a dried-up old codger.*

"Thank you." He forced the words out through stiff lips. "If you'll excuse me a moment, I'm going to find some refreshment."

He should have offered to fetch something for Miss Williams, but he didn't want a reason to come back here. He would do better to avoid her mother for the rest of the evening, lest he lose his self-control and say something he might regret before the proper time came.

Silas made his way to the balcony for some air to cool his head, pausing on the way to accept another glass of iced punch from a passing footman. He took a long swallow, followed by a long breath of the night air. The sound of footsteps alerted him that he wasn't alone. When he turned, he saw Miss Williams lingering in the doorway.

"You followed me."

"Of course I did. I thought we agreed to spend the evening doing what we liked together. Why did you rush off?"

"I wanted to clear my head." Noticing that Miss Williams had found her own glass of punch along the way, he warned, "Careful with that. It's strong."

"I know." She took a sip anyway. "I thought you'd be happy at how smoothly the dance went. Did I do something to upset you?"

"You?" he repeated. What had he done to make her think that? "No. Just the opposite. I was annoyed at seeing Sir Richard."

"But why? You don't even know each other. Did he say something to you?"

"He didn't need to. It's the *idea* of it. Him and you. It's..." Silas trailed off on a wince, aware that he was too angry about this. He swallowed the rest of his drink and set the empty glass down. "Why did your mother choose him, anyway?"

"He's a baronet."

"No better reason than that?"

"A rich baronet with no sons," Miss Williams amended, as if that changed everything. Perhaps it did. Women needed security, didn't they? A baronet with a bit of money was worth ten of Silas, at least in the eyes of Mrs. Williams. "And it was after our kiss, so I don't think Mama had many options left."

"You mean to say that if I hadn't ruined you, you might have done better."

"Mr. Corbyn. I think we both know that I ruined myself, and you were simply caught in the crossfire." Her lips were soft and plump as she brought them to the rim of her glass. Silas wasn't thinking of that first kiss any longer, the one that had ruined her. It was their other kiss that took hold of his impulses. The one that hadn't been for show. She'd made such an interesting little whimper toward the end. "The last thing I would want is for you to feel any sense of obligation over my decision. I was never going to make a good match, you know. That was half the problem."

"Why not?"

Miss Williams looked at him with suspicion, as if not quite sure whether he was mocking her. "Because I'm neither charming nor pretty enough to attract suitors on my own. I have nothing to offer but my dowry, which isn't large. The sort of men who are eager to settle for a girl with nothing to offer but a few thousand pounds are a wretched lot. They scarcely even bother to speak to you as if you're a person."

Miss Williams delivered this speech very matter-of-factly, but her voice wavered on that last part. She might want to appear indifferent, but the hurt was there for anyone to see.

For Silas to see, at least. He knew what it was like to feel second-rate. Growing up on the *Libertas*, then on the *Echo*, the distinction between the enlisted men and the gentlemen had been ever-present. No matter how hard he'd tried, there had been an unspoken understanding that separated them into those who mattered and those who didn't.

But no one should have made Miss Williams feel that way. She was thoughtful, and kind, and far stronger in spirit than she looked. She was one of the ones that mattered. Anyone could see that.

"'Charm' is just another word for a pleasing falsehood," he said firmly. "I've never seen the use for it."

"I've noticed that." A faint smile toyed with the corners of her lips.

"And as for pretty..." He drew near Miss Williams, until only the barest inch of space stood between them. Her smile faltered, replaced by that look she always gave him when he got too close. A painful cross between longing and doubt.

Silas couldn't help it. He wanted to scrub the doubt away and replace it with an emotion more to his liking. Passion, maybe. He pulled off his gloves and shoved them into his pocket so that he could run his bare thumb along Miss Williams's jaw and turn her chin up toward him. She shivered, her body confessing the power he held over her more clearly than her words ever could. "Don't underestimate yourself," he whispered, before he finally took what he'd been wanting for half the night.

Her lips were soft and yielding. There was no surprise in her reaction this time. She opened to him quickly, as if answering the question he wouldn't ask aloud. *Yes, I'm yours. Yes.*

It was a fantasy. Silas knew that. But she'd encouraged him to do what he wanted this evening, and what he wanted was to pretend they were real.

"I don't want to call you Miss Williams anymore." He breathed the words into her ear, marveling as she trembled against him. Did she have any idea how intoxicating her unpracticed responses were? "I want to call you Hannah. Invite me to."

As if they were true lovers, and not a hollow parody of it.

"Call me Hannah," she obliged. Her voice was little more than a whisper.

He decided to reward her by pouring every ounce of his attention into their kiss. Silas might not have any prior experience escorting a woman to a ball or dancing a quadrille, but he did know how to bring them pleasure. And it was evident that Hannah was eager for him, even more than she could admit. As he explored her mouth with his tongue, she began to make that whimpering sound again. It was a sound of frustration, of a need that could never be satisfied.

Silas began stroking her breast through the silk of her gown, running urgent circles over the nub of her nipple with his thumb, which only increased the noise she was making.

"What are you doing?" Hannah gasped. She was obviously trying to sound indignant, but couldn't manage to hide her excitement.

"Don't you like it?" Silas pressed a little harder, and her whole body shuddered in response.

"We're—we're at a ball," she managed weakly. "What if someone catches us?"

"Then they'll think you're my fiancée and I couldn't hold myself back until our wedding night," he growled. Silas could almost believe it was true. He felt like he'd been waiting for this for years, like he'd been promised to Hannah ages ago and was counting each day until he could call her his.

Hannah's breath was coming quickly, making her breasts swell above the confines of her corset with every inhalation. Silas couldn't tear himself from the sight. God, she was arousing. He bent his head to kiss the tender skin just above the neckline of her gown, wishing he could get her undressed.

Silas had been with more experienced women. With beautiful women. But he couldn't recall ever wanting someone the way he wanted Hannah. Every meeting added another layer to his interest, until it was nothing like the easy, uncomplicated feeling that he'd known as desire before this. Silas had thought that lust was supposed to be a whim, a passing impulse that struck if the right opportunity arose, but which could be dismissed just as easily.

He couldn't seem to dismiss what he felt for Hannah, no matter how he tried. He wanted to possess her. He wanted to show her that every other man she'd ever looked at was nothing, that *he* was the only one who could touch her this way. Not that wretched old man that her mother had tried to chain her to, not any of the pathetic

suitors who'd dared to hurt her with their misplaced disdain, whatever titles or fortunes they held out as compensation. Him.

"They'll think I've been wanting to do this for weeks," Silas continued roughly, his self-control slipping. "Every time you've touched
me, I've had to act the gentleman instead of pulling you into my
arms."

"You can't really mean that." Hannah pulled back from his atten-
tions, her cheeks flushed. There was that doubt again. "You wouldn't
even be here if I hadn't paid you to come. You didn't want me to kiss
you at Bishop's."

"I want you to kiss me now." Silas took her hand and placed it on
the evidence of his arousal, pressing her gloved palm against the head,
until the delicious pressure made him groan. "Can you doubt it?"

"Oh." Hannah's eyes widened in shock. She didn't seem to know
how to react to such an indecency. Silas let go of her wrist, realizing that he might have gone too far. He'd gotten carried away, and
he didn't want to scare her. But even once she was free, Hannah
didn't move a muscle. For what seemed like an eternity, her hand
rested lightly on his cock, while Silas grew increasingly sure that he
would combust any second. Then, very slowly, her fingers began a
shy exploration through the wool of his trousers, tracing the outline
of his arousal.

"Hannah, please," he gasped. He was in serious danger of spending himself. *Not here.* He wouldn't humiliate himself this way.
"Enough. You need to stop."

He pushed her hand away, struggling to get enough air into his lungs.

"Did I do something wrong? I thought you wanted me to."

Silas chuckled to himself. "Not wrong. Just not for the balcony at
a crowded ball."

"Oh." Hannah was staring at the bulge in his trousers with naked
curiosity. He couldn't help but imagine the things he could show her,

if only he could find some real privacy. She would be an eager pupil. Hell, if they had a more reliable barrier between them and the rest of the ballroom than the double doors a few feet away, Silas would have been all too happy to lift up her skirts and teach her how to beg for the release she obviously needed.

This woman was going to be the death of him.

"We should go back inside before anyone finds us." Silas forced the words out despite the desire that pulsed in his veins. It was the truth, even if it wasn't to his liking. "Or rather, *you* should go back inside while I cool down for a minute."

Hannah looked as conflicted as he was, but didn't protest. After a moment, she murmured, "Come and find me once you're ready."

She turned toward the doors, her silhouette framed in orange by the gaslight that shone out from the window.

"Wait."

Silas would have preferred to let her go without regret, but it was impossible. He hadn't had his fill yet. Nothing like it. Shamelessly, he slipped his hand along Hannah's back and tugged her close for one last kiss. Each time he did this, it felt like a promise. That Hannah was his, that he could make her feel something no one else could, that he'd proven himself worthy of a greater role than the one she'd assigned him. But as soon as he released her again, the feeling was gone, leaving him frustrated and uncertain.

Do you still want me to ruin our engagement?

Silas wanted to ask the question, but something held him back. Perhaps he sensed what her answer would be.

He knew he could make Hannah want his touch, but that wasn't the same thing as wanting a marriage. What would he do with a wife, anyway? He doubted very much that she would be thrilled to learn he intended to spend his life as a brewer, supplying beer to local public houses with Marian and James.

He would be taking Hannah away from all of this. She might want to escape her mother's plans to marry her off to the first man who offered, but she'd never expressed a desire to escape her place near the top of the social ladder.

She would have to be a fool to want that.

"I'll see you inside," Silas finished awkwardly, releasing her.

It was for Hannah to tell him if she'd changed her mind about breaking off their engagement. She was the one who'd hired him for exactly that purpose, after all. And she'd never been afraid to tell him what to do.

What they'd just shared was the result of pent-up desire and too much drink. It wasn't a promise of anything more. Silas couldn't let himself forget that.

Hannah wandered back through the crowded ballroom as if in a dream. A servant offered her a glass of punch, but she didn't think she could risk another while her head was swimming this badly. Who knew what might happen?

I can't believe he really did that. Hannah's whole body was humming, a restless vibration that settled over her skin. *I can't believe I didn't stop him.* She'd melted under Corbyn's touch. He could have undressed her right there on the balcony and Hannah would have happily agreed.

What's wrong with me?

How did Corbyn make her forget herself so completely? When Hannah had picked him as the means to escape her mother's plans, she'd been the one in control. She'd set the terms of their encounters and he'd grudgingly obeyed, predictable in his lackluster agreement.

There was nothing predictable about this. Nothing lackluster either.

Hannah shivered, drawing Jane's lace shawl tightly around her shoulders. It was warm inside the ballroom, but the heat of the crowd didn't seem to reach her. She couldn't shake the feeling that she'd crossed a breach tonight.

That had been far more than just a kiss. Not only in the intensity of the heat between them, but also in the consequences for their agreement.

She still needed Mr. Corbyn. Their engagement was the only thing bringing her father to town. Without it, Hannah had no hope of getting her parents in the same room to work out their differences.

Could she still rely on Mr. Corbyn? What if things soured between them, and he changed his mind about helping her?

What if things *didn't* sour between them, and she found herself in Corbyn's bed? Hannah's heart beat a little faster at the prospect.

She wasn't supposed to want that. Her mother had always said that only very wicked girls let a man steal their virtue; a proper lady would never let herself be used that way.

Hannah had always believed herself strong enough to resist seduction. On some level, she'd thought herself immune to it. But then, no one had ever wanted her before. Not the way Mr. Corbyn did. She should have been outraged at the way he'd touched her—at the way he'd invited her to touch *him*—but instead, she felt such a thrill, more intoxicating than any drink. The only thing that stopped Hannah from turning on her heels and racing back to Corbyn right now was the knowledge that there was no real privacy to shelter them.

Was there something wrong with her, or was Mama wrong about the way things were supposed to feel?

Hannah realized with a sinking feeling that the signs had been there for ages. From the very first moment she'd laid eyes on Mr. Corbyn, hadn't she been thinking of him in an indecent way? It had been getting worse in recent weeks, until the lightest touch was enough to obliterate her resolve. If there *was* something wrong with her, it wasn't going away.

Maybe she would have another glass of punch after all.

Hannah had just found the servant and was downing her drink with a grim sense of purpose when she spotted Annabelle Danby chatting with a pretty, dark-haired lady by the edges of the dance floor. When her friend noticed her, she bid farewell to the brunette and came over.

"Good evening," Hannah greeted her. "I'm so glad to see you here."

Annabelle was an adventurous girl. Maybe she had some experience in these matters, if Hannah could figure out how to ask her without causing any offense.

"I saw you dancing earlier, but you rushed off before I could ever say hello. I thought you didn't like dancing."

"I don't. Mama insisted." That wasn't strictly true, but Hannah didn't know how to tell her friend how hard Mr. Corbyn had worked to be able to join her on the floor for that one set. Nor could she explain the thrill she'd felt to see him so earnest and pleased with himself, his usual reticence abandoned. It hadn't been a chore to dance with him at all. It had been an unexpected delight.

Hannah looked down to her dance card, which was still tied to her wrist with a little green ribbon that matched the color scheme of the hostesses' decorations. She had always thought it silly when other girls saved their cards as a memento of every ball they attended, but she wasn't sure she had the heart to throw this one into the rubbish when the night was done. It was evidence of a perfect evening— one dance from Corbyn and no one else to trouble her.

She could easily get used to that.

"Annabelle, do you know anything about men?"

Her friend blinked at the abruptness of this question. "That depends. I do have a brother, if it helps. But you have twice as many brothers as I do so I imagine it might not."

"I mean…" Hannah leaned in and spoke in a conspiratorial whisper, careful to check that no one nearby was listening. "What to *do* with a man when you're alone and he wants to—"

"Lord, no," Annabelle interrupted. "You'll want to talk to Della about that sort of thing. She has a lovely book with all sorts of herbal remedies."

"Herbal remedies?" Hannah repeated. "I'm talking about kissing, not horticulture."

"No, no, they're for later. Never mind. I see that's not what you meant. Forget everything I just said."

That wouldn't be very difficult, as Hannah wasn't even certain she knew what they were talking about.

"I need advice, and I don't know where else to turn," she tried again. "What does it mean when he…"

Hannah was obliged to let her voice trail off here because she had no idea how to describe what she'd just experienced.

What does it mean when a man kisses you and touches you and makes your whole body feel like it's on fire and then puts your hand on his nether regions?

Hannah cleared her throat delicately. She couldn't ask about any of that. Though Annabelle seemed to be taking this subject in stride, her fervent denial made it plain that she had never experienced the shocking impulses that afflicted Hannah. What would she think if she knew?

Better to focus on another aspect of her problem. "If a man kisses you, does that mean he's in love with you?"

"If you kissed a man, does that mean you're in love with him?" Annabelle returned, one eyebrow cocked at a dubious angle.

"You're making me feel very stupid. I only meant... You know, is it easier for men to do those sorts of things even if they don't have a real attachment, or does it mean that their feelings are true?"

"Anyone can lie about their feelings."

"But how can I *know*?"

"I hope for your sake that we're talking about your fiancé." Annabelle assessed her critically. "In which case, I would imagine that his proposal is better proof of his feelings than a kiss. Anyone can press their lips together, but I wouldn't agree to spend my life with someone if I didn't love them."

Sensible words. Except Mr. Corbyn hadn't proposed. And Hannah had made it very clear that she didn't intend to spend their lives together. So where did that leave them?

"Never mind. Thank you." She would have to solve this herself. The whole knot was too complicated to undo without slicing it in two. Maybe it was safer not to try until after she'd accomplished what she needed to.

Mr. Corbyn had her so mixed up that she was in danger of losing sight of what really mattered. Her father would arrive in town any day now. Hannah had exactly one chance to show her parents that they'd made a mistake by separating and that they should devote themselves to repairing their marriage before it was too late. She couldn't let anything distract her from that.

Annabelle tipped her chin gently to the left, indicating something behind Hannah's shoulder. "I think he's looking for you now."

Hannah turned. Sure enough, Mr. Corbyn was standing on the edges of the crowd, his eyes roaming over the room.

Her breath caught in her throat. He looked sharp and alert, as if their encounter had infused him with a wild energy. The smooth waves of his hair were starting to escape the confines of the pomade that had tamed them at the outset of the evening, recapturing some of their former glory.

How could a man as beautiful as that really want her?

But when their eyes met across the ballroom floor, Hannah suffered a pang of longing so intense she was sure he must feel it too. Whatever this was, she wasn't imagining it.

That doesn't mean you can trust your future to it.

"I'll see you later." Hannah took her leave of Annabelle. She felt firmer after their conversation.

A kiss didn't mean love. Whatever she shared with Corbyn, it wasn't more important than her family. She had to focus on what mattered most now. There would be time enough to reason out what she and Corbyn meant to each other once her victory was secure.

Fifteen

HANNAH'S FATHER AND BROTHER ARRIVED ON MONDAY WITH-out any fanfare. They simply rapped on the door and let themselves in when the maid was slow to answer, so that Hannah came upon them in the hall without warning and cried out in surprise.

"Papa!" She launched herself into his arms, which only seemed to embarrass him.

"There's no need for a fuss," he said gruffly, brushing her hands from his morning coat. "It's only been a few weeks."

"Eight," Hannah corrected. "And we've missed you terribly. Mama and I both."

"Hmm." He didn't seem moved by this declaration, but then, Papa was never one to show his feelings. It didn't mean he didn't care.

By this point, Eli had heard the commotion and came down to greet their visitors. Gloria was tucked in the crook of his arm, sleeping soundly.

"Why isn't your nanny minding her?" Papa asked when he spotted them.

"We don't have a nanny," Eli reminded him.

"But where's your wife gone?"

"She needed to go to the club for an hour or two, but she'll be back presently." Seeing Papa scowl at the mention of bishop's (or possibly the fact that he was holding a baby), Eli changed the subject. "We weren't expecting you to arrive before four. I take it the roads were good?"

"Excellent." Jacob took the hint, turning their conversation away from any dangerous subjects. "Give us a proper look at her then." He craned his neck to peer at Gloria. "She favors Jane, I think. Fortunate thing. I was worried she might take after you."

Eli used his free hand to shove his brother lightly on the shoulder. "Come in. I'm not sure where the maid's got to, but we'll ring for some refreshments."

Why hadn't Mama come down yet? If Eli had heard them, surely she must have too.

It was just like her to sulk instead of greeting Papa properly! How was Hannah to ensure her parents reconciled if she couldn't even get them in the same room?

"Excuse me," Hannah said. "I'm just going to pop upstairs a moment."

She took the steps by twos and went straight to the guest room, only to find it empty. Not just empty of her mother's presence, but emptied of all its contents. Mama's powders and perfumes had been stripped from the vanity; the wardrobe stood ajar, one door still swaying slightly; and her most recent floral arrangement had disappeared from its place on the night table.

She's fled the house.

No. That was silly. She wouldn't pack up and leave when she believed Hannah was about to be married, would she? Why go to all the trouble of planning an engagement supper, then? She must still be here somewhere.

Hannah tried her own room next, where she found her mother and Molly (so that was where she'd got to!) trying to stuff far too many clothes into the wardrobe, crushing Hannah's new taffeta gown in the process.

"They won't all fit," she protested, rushing forward to save her dress before they damaged the beadwork on the bodice. "Why are you moving all your things in here?"

"Because Jacob and your father are taking the guest room and Mr. Bishop's old room. I'll have to stay with you until they return home."

"Why can't *they* share?"

"Men need more privacy than ladies," her mother said simply. Hannah might have suggested that her parents share, but she already knew what the response would be. Better not to press her luck this quickly.

"I think I hear them calling me downstairs, ma'am," the maid interjected. "By your leave."

"Yes, thank you, Molly."

"Where are you going to *sleep*?" Hannah asked warily, once the servant was gone.

"Where do you think? In the bed."

"But then where am *I* going to sleep?"

"There's room enough for two."

Hannah eyed the mattress with concern. If Mama had been suffocating her when they'd had their own space, how much worse would it be now? She was far too old for this! "I don't sleep well with another person. You're going to kick me and keep me up all night. Couldn't you stay in the nursery? Please?"

"Gloria would wake me up at all hours. Now don't be childish," her mother scolded. "It's only for a few nights."

A few nights? How was she supposed to engineer a reconciliation with so little time?

"Papa's not staying any longer? What about my wedding?"

"You'll have to ask him his plans. He hasn't informed me." It sounded as though Mama's patience for this conversation was nearing its end.

"Will you come down soon?" Hannah tried. "To greet him?"

"I have a lot of unpacking to do, and I still need to finish the centerpieces before supper. I'll see your father when we all go in to dine."

Hannah deflated a little. It shouldn't be this difficult to get them into a room together! Mama was being obstinate on purpose; she was sure of it.

I can't force her to come. I'll just have to work twice as hard this evening.

Hannah wandered away reluctantly, pondering her strategy. By the time she returned to the parlor, Papa and Jacob had installed themselves on the divan with Eli and were midway into a discussion of their recent fishing trip with their neighbors in Devon. Fishing and hunting were about the only things that Papa talked about with Hannah's brothers.

She settled into a nearby armchair and waited patiently for one of them to notice her. Eli was the first to oblige, turning the conversation her way as soon as their father paused for breath.

"Are you excited for tonight?"

It took Hannah a moment to realize that he was speaking of introducing Mr. Corbyn to the rest of the family, and not her secret plans to repair the rupture between their parents, where her thoughts had been occupied. In fact, she'd been trying very hard not to think of Corbyn at all since the night of the Brandons' ball. Anytime her mind wandered there, it grew heated and confused. It was bad enough that she kept reliving the aching pleasure of his touch in her dreams, waking with an empty feeling that nothing else could fill. She wouldn't let it cloud her reason in the day as well.

"Of course." She forced a smile. "I know you'll like Mr. Corbyn."

"Hmm." Papa frowned and took a bite of the bread and jam that Molly had brought out. "Your mother tells me you're quite taken with this gentleman."

She must not have told him about the scandal, or he wouldn't sound so unconcerned. Hannah cast a hesitant glance at Eli. He gave her a long look, but didn't say a word.

There was some loyalty among siblings, it seemed. Despite Eli's misgivings, he didn't seem eager to throw Hannah and his former friend to the wolves.

"Yes," Hannah replied. "We're very much in love."

"I'm happy you've finally decided to settle down." Papa underscored his point with a curt nod. "But a midshipman. Are you sure? You could do far better, poppet."

"Oh. Ah. He's not exactly a midshipman anymore." *Oh dear.* How to explain without turning her father against Mr. Corbyn? She didn't want the poor man walking into a trap tonight. "There was a bit of a misunderstanding. He's, er, expected to purchase a commission in the army presently. Mama could tell you more about it."

Let them have a reason to talk again. They could be united in their approval or their disapproval, for all she cared. The important thing was only that they spoke.

Regrettably, her father didn't take the hint. "I hope he's a respectful sort. Too many young men these days don't have any sense of duty."

"Would you like to take your things upstairs?" Hannah was struck by a flash of inspiration. "You must want to get settled in."

And if he ran into Mama and the two of them started speaking again, well, that would just be a happy accident.

But Eli immediately ruined everything. "I'll see to that. Here, take Gloria a moment, won't you?"

Before Hannah could object, the sleeping infant was unceremoniously dumped in her arms, and Eli disappeared in search of their luggage.

Drat!

"Shall we take a walk before supper?" Jacob suggested.

What was he doing? Couldn't any of them see what a tremendous opportunity this was? It had taken her weeks of planning and a fake engagement just to get their parents in the same house, and they couldn't even stop to appreciate the significance of this meeting before they went rushing off again!

Papa rose to his feet, apparently in agreement.

"But Papa, you hate London," Hannah reminded him. "You always say it's too crowded and full of miasma."

"Too true. But I could do with a chance to stretch my legs," Papa insisted. "That carriage was so cramped."

"Let's wait a moment for Eli to come back." Jacob offered Hannah a friendly smile, unaware that he was destroying all her best-laid plans. "You don't mind staying here with Gloria, do you?"

"I *do* mind," Hannah protested, indignant. "I had things to do before supper."

"Jane will be back in an hour or so," Jacob assured her. "You heard Eli."

"Don't you want to hold her, Papa?" If she could persuade him to stay here and mind the baby, Mama was sure to come downstairs at some point. And what could be a better reason to find harmony than the sight of their first grandchild? It would remind them of happier days together.

But Papa only scoffed. "I'm no good with babies. Don't know what to do with them at that age."

Fine. She was tired of being rebuffed at every turn. Let them go on their walk. She would concentrate on preparing for their evening meal, where she would redouble her efforts.

They would have no choice but to sit down to dine together, and Hannah would use every trick at her disposal to remind her parents why they loved each other. By the end of the evening, they would *have* to see the error of their ways. That, or Hannah would die trying.

It wasn't that Silas was nervous to meet Hannah's father. Not exactly. It was only that no one had told him what to expect. He'd never been in a situation like this before, needing to impress a lady's parents. What were they supposed to talk about?

Besides which, Silas hadn't forgotten that this was ostensibly his last service to Hannah. She'd asked him to keep up the act until Mr. Williams arrived in town, and now he was here.

Did she still mean it, after what they'd shared the other night? *Of course she still means it. Why wouldn't she?*

A few kisses under the moonlight didn't take their arrangement from a necessary trade to a love affair. If Hannah wanted him, she was no different from any of the other women he'd formed a brief connection with in his life. Drawn to a handsome face, but never expecting more.

She would have said something if it were otherwise. Smuggled him a secret note to call the whole plan off. She'd had three days since the Brandons' ball to contact him and she hadn't said a word, which meant he was still supposed to sabotage their engagement and set her free.

Silas rapped on the door and was greeted a moment later by the maid, who actually smiled at him this evening. Her disposition had gradually warmed over the past few weeks.

"Good evening, Molly." He gave her his hat and followed her into the drawing room where everyone sat waiting.

Silas greeted Hannah first, though she wasn't even looking at him by the time he'd finished his bow. That was odd. Normally he caught Hannah staring at him whenever they were together. But Silas had no time to reflect on it, as Mrs. Williams was already presenting him to the new arrivals.

Hannah's other brother, Jacob, looked much like Eli, save that his face was a bit broader and his hair a bit lighter. Their father was a beefy, imposing sort of man with deep lines on his brow that indicated that he'd frowned far more often than he'd smiled. He had a firm handshake and a critical eye.

Silas was introduced with a few pleasantries, though he couldn't shake the feeling that Mr. Williams was searching him for visible flaws. He was suddenly grateful for his new wardrobe. On the outside, at least, he could pass for a gentleman.

"So, what does your father do?" Mr. Williams asked gruffly the moment they all sat down. "Was he in the navy as well?"

"No, sir," Silas replied. "He's a cooper. He's in business with my mother's father, who owns a brewery."

This information clearly took Mr. Williams by surprise, though Silas had expected him to know it already. Why hadn't his wife informed him? Silas glanced at Mrs. Williams, but found her uncharacteristically silent, observing them at a distance from an easy chair.

She didn't seem quite herself. Normally she would have offered him some unwanted advice by now.

"A cooper," Mr. Williams repeated, rolling his mouth over the word as if it left a bad taste. "And Hannah tells me that you're considering the army next? Why should you change your career at your age?"

They really haven't told him anything.

If Silas revealed the truth now, it was sure to provoke the man. Was that what Hannah wanted?

No. Even if she still expected him to ruin their engagement tonight, surely she wouldn't ask Silas to use his disgrace from the navy as the source of the conflict. She knew how much it had hurt him.

Silas searched Hannah's face for a signal, but as before, she wasn't paying him any mind. She seemed to have eyes only for her father this evening.

Oddly enough, it was Mrs. Williams who came to his rescue. "It was my suggestion. The army is a more respectable profession, you know. Remember old Mrs. Peterson's eldest boy, who went off to be an ensign. He did very well for himself, you will recall."

"I suppose so." The concession seemed to be drawn from Mr. Williams against his will.

"He came home with enough money to buy that cottage for his mother."

Was Silas dreaming? Mrs. Williams was the last person he would have expected to help him. Perhaps it was only a coincidence. Whatever the reason, her comment had turned the conversation down another path, and now Mr. Williams and Jacob were debating whether the cottage in question had been a good purchase considering the shabby state of its roof. Silas was quite forgotten.

He owed Mrs. Williams a debt.

When they went in to dine, they found the table richly decorated with an elaborate centerpiece. Juniper branches formed a wreath around the base, while roses and hyacinth alternated to form a crown rising from below. A little spray of matching greenery had been set on each of their place settings.

"Did you make these, Hannah?" her father asked, picking up the tiny bundle from his plate and twirling one between his thumb and his index. It had a carnation in the middle, surrounded by a sprig of juniper to match the centerpiece on the table, all tied up with a little blue ribbon.

"No," she replied. "Mama did. Don't you think she's talented?" She was watching her father eagerly.

"Hmm." Somehow, this one empty syllable managed to convey his immediate disinterest. "What am I supposed to do with it while I'm eating?"

"You may put it in your lapel as a boutonniere, Mr. Williams," his wife suggested crisply. "Or you may give it to me if you don't want it."

Mr. Williams did neither, but simply cast the tiny arrangement upon a stretch of empty tablecloth before taking his seat without another word.

The temperature in the room must have dropped five degrees.

They hate each other, Silas finally understood. And not the routine annoyance that might build up between any couple if one caught them on a bad day. This was something deeper. The whole situation made a good deal more sense now—why Mrs. Williams and Hannah had come to town alone, why they had said so little about Mr. Williams whenever the subject came up. Silas wasn't sure what was behind it, but he didn't relish passing the rest of his evening walking the tightrope of their feud.

He examined his own boutonniere, which was complete with a little pin to ensure its safe anchorage, before he slipped it through the buttonhole in his evening coat as he'd been invited to do. He hadn't thought that Mrs. Williams would have gone to such trouble over this meeting, given how little she thought of Silas as a future son-in-law. But the boutonnieres must have taken considerable time to make.

"Thank you," he said, meaning it. "They're lovely."

There was a murmured agreement from her sons.

Mrs. Williams froze momentarily, as if surprised by his words. When she recovered herself, she offered him a tentative smile. "I'm glad you like them."

It might be the first time he'd received a sign of warmth from the

woman. Silas hardly dared to believe he'd seen it. But then, she'd
appreciated his dancing at the ball the other night too. Maybe he was
finally beginning to earn her approval.

Just in time to disappoint her. Was that regret he felt? No. Mrs.
Williams had hated him from their first meeting. Just because she'd
let her guard down once or twice didn't make them friends.

"So, where is your family from?" Mr. Williams fired the question
off sharply.

*Is he angry with me for complimenting his wife, or is that always his
tone?*

"Staffordshire, sir," Silas replied.

"I told you that in my last letter," Mrs. Williams murmured.

"No, you didn't."

Mrs. Williams bit her lip rather than arguing the point. She
looked like she'd tasted a lemon.

"Mr. Corbyn has a brother and cousin here in town," Hannah
volunteered. "They seem lovely."

"Are they in trade as well?" Mr. Williams looked suspicious, as
if the possibility betrayed some damning information about Silas.

"Yes." Better not to elaborate. Mr. Williams was no more likely
to approve of their plans to start a brewery than his wife would be.
It might be the only thing the pair would agree on, if their conduct
this evening was any indication.

"Hmm? Speak up. I can hardly hear you."

"Yes," Silas repeated, a good deal more sharply.

"I can't abide mumbling."

Silas flinched. He'd heard those words from the mouth of his
own father so many times that for an instant it felt like he was back
home, defending himself from an interrogation on his progress over
the dinner table. *Sit up straight, boy. Speak up. How do you expect
anyone to take you seriously if you skulk about like a thief?*

He hadn't even been mumbling; he was just thinking.

Silas tried to catch Hannah's eye. Surely she could see how uncomfortable her father was making everyone—not least of all himself. Why had she been so eager to wait until he came to town, anyway? She couldn't have expected this meeting to go well. The man was the type to never be satisfied. Silas knew his kind.

Did she want me to fail?

The notion crept into his mind like a spider, the brush of its arrival sending a shiver down his back.

Of course she wanted him to fail. That had always been their agreement. But Silas hadn't known that it would feel like this, with a demanding parent picking apart his every move. He wanted to signal Hannah somehow, to warn her this was a bad idea.

It all felt *wrong* suddenly. He didn't want to make an ass of himself in front of her family, not even for two hundred pounds. He wanted Hannah to take him aside and say the whole plan was off. That she'd changed her mind.

But she wasn't paying any attention to him. Her eyes were fixed on her father. "Papa, why don't you tell me what your wedding was like? All these plans for my wedding got me to thinking, I don't even know the story."

Across the table, her brothers exchanged a glance. It looked like Silas wasn't the only one who found this train of thought a bit odd.

"Oh." The question seemed to throw Mr. Williams off-balance as well. He coughed and took a long swallow of his wine. "It was so long ago, I hardly remember now. We were married in the parish church. I suppose your grandparents and your Aunt Catherine were there. It was just like any other wedding."

Hannah was obviously dissatisfied with this summary. "I'm sure Mama was a beautiful bride," she prompted.

No matter how ill-tempered he was, Mr. Williams didn't seem

prepared to contradict this openly. His response was a vague sound that could have been an assent or a harrumph.

Silas should have held his tongue, but he was feeling petty this evening. "I beg your pardon, sir, but what did you say? I think you were mumbling."

Hannah shot him a furious look, which he returned with equal vigor. Why was she acting this way? Why didn't she ever see fit to tell him her plans before he was in the middle of them?

The answer was obvious.

Because you aren't her equal; you're hired help. Silas had been so fixated on impressing Hannah that he'd forgotten what he was here for. Had he thought that learning to dance would turn him into a real suitor?

Mr. Williams opened his mouth—no doubt intending to issue a stern rebuke—but Eli Williams cut in before he could accomplish it.

"Has anyone been to Kew Gardens this season? I've heard the magnolias are in bloom." Silas was too irritable by this point to be able to appreciate the attempt to help. It was only Williams doing what he always did, rescuing Silas from his own missteps.

Hannah, for her part, didn't seem to appreciate the change in subject any more than he had. "What about after the wedding?" she persisted. Her gaze traveled between her parents, inviting her mother into the conversation. "What was it like in the first few years you were married?"

What on earth is she doing? The questions seemed designed to prompt some tender sentiments, but anyone could see that Mr. and Mrs. Williams had none. Did Hannah think that she could paper over the tension in the room with a few forced memories? It would have been better to stick to a neutral subject, as her brother had tried to do.

Mrs. Williams seemed to feel more obligation to keep up

appearances than her husband, for she was the first to reply. "I was very busy in those days learning to manage a household, just as you will be soon." Her strained smile encompassed both Hannah and Silas. The poor woman had no idea how wrong she was. "Your grandmother Williams was still alive then and lived with us, of course."

"Now *she* knew how to run a house," Mr. Williams smiled wistfully. "We had the most wonderful cook when my mother was alive. What was her name, now? Ah, I can't remember. She was a great, tall woman. Made the best fish soup you'd ever tasted."

He finished off the last spoonful of his own fish soup here, and motioned impatiently for the maid to take it away.

Even when he was thinking of something he liked, he managed to slip in an insult. Silas might almost have believed it to be unconscious, except that his barbs hit their targets too perfectly for it to be an accident. His own father had been the same. There was always some small complaint to be tossed out, whether it was aimed at his children or his wife. Each one was too insignificant on its own to warrant comment, but together they added up to an unending deluge.

I think I might hate this man nearly as much as his wife does.

"My mother passed in '17, and our cook the next winter"— Mr. Williams continued reminiscing as he cut into a lamb chop— "and we never had a cook like her again. Who was that first one you hired, Mrs. Williams? That skinny woman from the next village. Miss Young, was it? Didn't last a month. I felt ill after every meal. I can't imagine what you were thinking."

Silas clenched his hand around his fork until the metal bit into his palm. The desire to punch this man in the nose had grown overpowering.

"She was all I could find on such short notice." As she replied to her husband in a tired voice, Mrs. Williams was a far cry from the imposing matriarch who'd harped on Silas's manners these past few days. She seemed to have shrunk by half. "You will recall poor Cook passed very suddenly."

Mr. Williams frowned, as if to cast doubt on this explanation. "None of the cooks you hired after were much good. It takes a firm hand to run a house properly, I've always said. You simply didn't have the skill for it."

This provoked a very awkward, very tense silence.

"Sir." Eli Williams didn't look his father in the eye as he spoke, his discomfort plain. "Surely you don't mean that." His voice was calm, but carried a nervous edge—half-warning, half-pleading.

"Why don't we all go into the parlor before the dessert?" Jane suggested briskly, rising to her feet so that the gentlemen, her father-in-law included, would all be forced to rise as well. Nearly half their supper was still on their plates, but she must have judged the present mood to be more urgent than their meal. "I have a lovely new game I've been meaning to show you all."

"Not more gambling." Mr. Williams groaned. "You know how I feel about all that. I'll not have my Hannah placing any wagers, even if you two have taken up with that sort of thing."

At the words *you two*, he tipped his chin toward Jane, not Eli.

She bristled at his tone. "I was only going to suggest a *parlor* game, Mr. Williams."

"Oh." This mollified him somewhat. "Well, how was I to know?"

"You might try listening." Silas hadn't intended to speak. The voice that came out of him was sharp as a whip crack, so sudden that he almost thought the words came from someone else. "Maybe if you stopped criticizing everyone at this table, they'd be able to get a few words in."

It was the first time in Silas's life that he'd ever heard a collective gasp.

No one was quite so shocked as Mr. Williams, who gawked at

Silas for a very satisfying four seconds, his face turning purple before he found the wherewithal to respond. "How dare you speak to me that way! You are a guest in this house."

"So are you," Silas returned. "Though you don't seem overly concerned by that."

Mr. Williams hesitated for only a second before he sputtered, "You came here seeking *my* blessing." Of course he would scramble for a way to keep the upper hand. Men like him always needed some authority from which to punish others. But it didn't intimidate Silas the way it had when he was a small child, struggling to find the right words to prove himself to his father, too young to realize there were no right words. All he saw when he looked at Mr. Williams was a puffed-up old fraud.

Silas wrapped his tongue around each syllable with deliberate care. "That was before I realized you were an ass."

It was the second time in his life that he heard a collective gasp. Probably a sign he should stop talking, but Silas was too furious to heed it. The man badly needed a dressing-down. There was probably no one else in his life who would dare to speak the truth to his face.

"Mr. Corbyn!" It was Hannah's voice that cut through the others to reach his ear. "You will apologize to my father."

Her eyes, like her voice, were full of awful emotions: anger, shock, hurt, betrayal. She looked at Silas as though he'd hurled the insult at a different sort of man entirely—one who'd done nothing to deserve his scorn.

She looked as though he'd hurled the insult at her.

Silas ground his teeth, guilt warring with righteous fury. Some part of him had assumed that Hannah would be on his side, as she always was, no matter how unlikely.

He should have known better.

"I will not."

"You have no right to speak to him that way!"

"He earned every word of it." Had they been sitting at the same table? Couldn't she see what was right in front of her?

"Get out," Mr. Williams snarled. "I've never met a more ungrateful wretch in my life. You'll never marry my Hannah. You don't deserve her."

"I'm sure I don't," Silas snapped. "But people rarely get what they deserve in life. I daresay your wife doesn't deserve to be trapped with *you*."

Mr. Williams lurched toward him, fists half-raised, but his son got between them first.

"I'll see you out," Eli said, his firm grip on Silas's elbow leaving no room for dispute.

Silas went along willingly, ushered from the room before the row could turn dangerous. Though his heart was hammering, he felt an odd sense of calm. As if all his anger had frozen the minute Hannah demanded an apology.

This couldn't have been what she'd imagined when she'd asked him to behave so badly that she would have to release him.

Is it done, then? Have I broken our engagement?

Mr. Williams would never consent to the match now. And to think, Silas had been reluctant to sabotage their engagement. In the end, his temper had done the job for him.

Eli waited until they were in the foyer before he spoke. When he did, his voice was strained, but calmer than Silas had expected.

"I know my father isn't an easy man to get along with," he began. "I'm sorry you had to see that."

He had a gift for understatement, but never mind. At least he understood what had prompted Silas's outburst.

Unlike Hannah.

"I'm sorry I ruined the evening." The apology that had been impossible earlier found its way to Silas's lips five minutes too late.

Eli released a frustrated sigh. "You didn't ruin it. Or at least, not alone. But why couldn't you have just held your tongue? For Hannah's sake, if not for his."

It was a question Silas must have asked himself a hundred times since the navy threw him out. Why couldn't he just look the other way? Why did he have to speak up when it only brought him ruin, and probably made no lasting difference to anything? He'd saved one girl from O'Brien, but his former captain walked free, able to hurt whomever he wanted. He'd set down Mr. Williams, but the man would likely keep on bullying his family for the rest of his life.

It made no difference what Silas did.

"Let me ask you something. Has holding your tongue made things easier for all the people near your father, or only for him?"

Eli didn't seem to like this question much, but to his credit, he didn't try to argue the point.

"I held my tongue as long as I was able," Silas added. "Every man has his limit. Mine is just lower than yours on account of my lack of breeding."

"And Hannah?" Eli pressed. "Don't you care how she feels?"

Silas shifted his weight, suddenly uncomfortable.

"I thought you didn't like our engagement. You should be happy if your father runs me off."

"I didn't like the way it started, but I don't want to see you break her heart." Eli studied him with warm brown eyes, so like his sister's. "I considered you a friend before all of this happened. If you ever felt the same, then answer me honestly: Do you want to marry Hannah or don't you? If you truly love one another, maybe I can talk to my father. Find some way to repair the damage. But I need to know your intentions are genuine."

"I—"

The words wouldn't come, but the understanding hit Silas like a ton of bricks.

I do want to marry her. It was no doubt the most idiotic thing he'd ever wanted in his life. Hannah had told him from the start that this was a trick. That she'd only chosen Silas because he was too unsuitable to pose any real risk of trapping her in a marriage she didn't want.

But as he'd struggled and forced his way through the events of the past weeks, he'd found an unexpected thrill in every triumph. In every instance where he'd proven he could do more than anyone had expected. Not because he cared about impressing any of *them.* But because he'd needed to impress *her.*

He'd wanted Hannah to see him as more than the man who'd been driven from the navy in disgrace. To realize he was worthy of her admiration, not just for a stolen thrill, but for more.

A fantasy. No one had ever thought he was worth more. And if he'd come close to impressing her for a moment, he'd just dashed that hope against the rocks.

"Eli." Hannah's voice cut through the silence, echoing down the marble-tiled floor. She stood in the hall, looking more untouchable than he'd ever seen her. Anger had turned her gentle features hard and unyielding. "Give us a moment, please."

How could things have gone so wrong?

Hannah had been close, she just *knew* it. All she'd needed was to find the right words to make her parents remember the time when they'd still been happy together, and they would have begun to thaw. Until Corbyn had started yelling at her father and ruined the whole evening. All her hard work to bring them back together, gone in an instant!

He was supposed to be my ally! Hannah had entrusted him with so many secrets, she'd grown used to the idea that he would always be there when she needed him. What had happened? She scarcely recognized the man she'd seen tonight. Even if he grumbled about it, Corbyn had always treated her with kindness.

The dining room had been in such chaos afterward that no one had even noticed when Hannah slipped out.

"Answer me honestly." Eli's voice carried out to her as she tiptoed down the hallway that led to the foyer. "Do you want to marry Hannah or don't you? If you truly love one another, maybe I can talk to my father. Find some way to repair the damage. But I need to know your intentions are genuine."

She stood stock-still, her heart lurching.

"I—" It was Corbyn's voice, but no confession followed.

Why did he hesitate? Of course he didn't love her. And there was no need to keep pretending. Not after the way he'd spoken to her father.

She drew near enough to get a good look at Corbyn, his beautiful face stricken with a stronger emotion than she'd seen before. When had his eyes grown so vulnerable? He was supposed to be guarded and strong. Unyielding. He never showed his feelings so clearly.

For me, or for the lies he's told Eli?

It wasn't right that Corbyn should look that way. It wasn't right that he should kiss her and dance with her and make her feel things she wasn't supposed to, only to ruin the one thing she truly wanted.

Why had she put herself through all of this if Mama still wouldn't take them home? It couldn't have been for nothing.

I need to know your intentions are genuine, Eli had said. And

Corbyn still hadn't answered. Hannah couldn't decide which would be worse: if he scoffed at the idea, or if he confessed some deeper emotion. She darted forward, suddenly desperate to speak before he could.

"Eli. Give us a moment, please."

Both men started at the sound of her voice. It had come out louder than she'd intended. But after a hesitant glance between them, her brother padded from the room.

Hannah hardly knew how to begin. The snippet of conversation she'd overheard had turned her straightforward outrage into something more complicated.

"Did you do it on purpose?" she finally asked. "To ruin our engagement?" It was the most important question: Had this all been some misguided attempt to fulfill her instructions? If she was to blame for the row that had ruined her only chance to repair her family, she might never forgive herself.

Corbyn's face changed back again; he was once more the cool, stoic being that she'd first met. A flawless statue. It made her wonder if she'd only imagined the image before.

"Does it matter?" No trace of emotion reached his eyes. "You got what you wanted. Your parents will insist you call off our engagement."

No elaboration. Nothing more.

"It matters to *me*. You didn't need to say such horrible things to him! You ruined the entire evening."

"Your father ruined the evening. I only said what everyone else was thinking."

Hannah couldn't make her voice work properly after that. *He isn't even sorry!* How could he stand there and behave as though he'd done nothing wrong?

"Hannah." Corbyn's voice softened on her name. She couldn't

hear it without remembering how he'd asked permission to use it, and how readily she'd granted it. "I know you love him, but you must have heard the way he talks to your mother. The way he talks to everyone—"

"Stop it!" she interrupted. "You don't understand anything. We haven't seen him in months! This was supposed to be our reunion, and you spoiled it before they even had a chance to talk."

"He said plenty."

"Don't act as though you know him. You only just met him an hour ago."

"I didn't need an hour; I saw what he was within the first minute." Corbyn's words assaulted her ears with merciless precision. "Your mother must have been proud of the time she took with those decorations, and he tossed his aside for no good reason except to snub her in front of the whole room. He's a browbeater, Hannah. He enjoys making other people feel small."

"Because he was angry that my mother left him!" she burst out. Immediately, her face grew hot. She hadn't meant to speak the truth aloud, except that Corbyn had goaded her into it. Had the others heard them from the dining room? She couldn't let the admission stand alone, so she added in an urgent whisper, "Anyone would be angry if their wife did such a thing, but they could still have mended the damage if you'd only given them more time. He would have calmed down. I know it."

Corbyn didn't reply. He studied her for a long moment, while she grew uneasy under the weight of his gaze and the stretch of silence. Hannah wasn't sure what he was searching for, except that something in his face had softened.

When he finally spoke, his expression was very different than it had been a moment ago. "Do you really believe that?"

Was that pity she heard?

No. Corbyn had no business feeling sorry for her. She wasn't some misguided child, engaging in flights of fancy. Who was he to walk in here and judge her family?

He reached out a hand, but she pushed it away before it could come to rest on her cheek. "I'm not imagining things," she insisted. "I know my own parents better than you do."

Again, Corbyn said nothing. His censure hung in the air like a gathering rain cloud. Why wouldn't he say what he really thought, as he always did?

Why won't he stop looking at me that way?

Her eyes started to sting. Hannah blinked them quickly, determined not to break down.

"You have no right to act superior after the way you behaved in there." She threw out the accusation to protect herself, a shield against his silent judgment. "A *real* gentleman would have held his temper, even if someone at the table offended him."

Corbyn stiffened. "I'm sorry if I've embarrassed you." A bitter edge crept into his voice. "But you knew I wasn't a gentleman from the start, didn't you?"

"Yes." Hannah raised her chin, unflinching. "I did."

He twisted his lips into a shape that couldn't be called a smile. "Now you have your reason to release me. I'm sure even your mother can't believe there's any hope for me after that display. I've done everything you wanted."

Hannah couldn't bring herself to reply. He was right; it *was* what she'd wanted. But she felt too miserable to take any pleasure in her victory.

When she'd imagined the conclusion to their charade, it had always been a happy scene. After she'd secured her parents' reunion, Corbyn would do something carefully ridiculous, she would release him and pay him his money, and they would all go back to their old lives, a little better off than when they'd started. All the upheaval of her removal to London would be undone.

But when Hannah looked around her now, all she saw were ruins.

Corbyn was still watching her, as if waiting for something. *I have nothing left to give you*, she wanted to protest. *Nothing at all.*

When she still didn't speak, he bowed very slowly, held her gaze for one last moment, and marched from the house for good.

Sixteen

HANNAH AWOKE THE NEXT MORNING FEELING UTTERLY MISERable. She'd hardly slept a wink all night, though it was hard to say whether the blame lay with that utter disaster of a supper or her mother's ice-cold feet kicking her every time she'd almost drifted off. Then she'd woken so late on account of her poor sleep that she found the room empty and the sun streaming in through the windows when she called for her breakfast.

I'll have my bed back when Papa returns to Devonshire without us, Hannah thought grimly. Without her engagement to keep him in town, she didn't see how she could persuade him to stay.

Maybe he would take her with him. There was nothing left for Hannah in London now. Or more accurately, there had never been anything for her in London. It was only that sometime over the past few weeks with Mr. Corbyn, she'd grown too preoccupied with their scheme to remember that.

After he'd left last night, Hannah had calmly informed her family that her engagement was off. No one had protested. How could they, after the spectacle they had just witnessed? Though Jane and Eli had fussed over Hannah and seemed reluctant to leave her alone, she had assured them that she was perfectly fine, and only wanted to retire in peace. The only person she'd expected might have some words about it was Mama, but she'd been strangely silent for the rest of the evening, not even saying a word when she'd slipped into bed beside Hannah a little while later.

Whether Mama felt a certain righteousness at being proven right about Mr. Corbyn all along or whether she was disappointed to see Hannah relegated to perpetual spinsterhood, it was impossible to say.

Papa had posed no such puzzle to read. He'd gone to his bed still muttering indignant commentary on Mr. Corbyn's morals, parentage, and Mama's utter failure to find an appropriate match for their daughter despite the fact that it was her only real responsibility in life.

He's a browbeater, Hannah. He enjoys making other people feel small.

She wished she could shut the accusations out of her head, but they echoed again and again, complete with Mr. Corbyn's final look of pity as he'd left her in the entryway.

Why couldn't she stop seeing his face, and why did she feel so horrible?

Corbyn was wrong about them. He didn't know her family. Yes, Papa hadn't been at his best last night, but anyone would be short-tempered if their wife ran off. If Corbyn hadn't called attention to it and started a row, they might have patched things up.

Hannah found herself inexplicably close to tears, but shook the feeling off with a rough toss of her head. She couldn't afford to give in to self-pity. She had to figure out her next move.

Once she'd eaten and dressed, Hannah went to her father's room. She knocked, received a gruff, "What is it?" and tiptoed inside.

"Oh, it's you, poppet." Her father didn't smile exactly, but he didn't seem *dis*pleased to see her. That was a good start.

"I wondered if we could talk for a moment."

His eyes grew guarded. "There's nothing else to say about that ruffian. You were right to cast him off. Your mother should have known better than to allow you to form an attachment to someone like that. A midshipman! Honestly!"

"Not that," Hannah assured her father quickly, before he could work himself into more of a state. It wasn't yet ten in the morning. "I meant about what your plans are now. I hope you might stay in town a little longer. I'm sure that Eli and Jane would love to have you."

That might not be strictly true after how badly supper had gone, but there would be no chance to repair the damage if he left on a sour note. She had to convince him to fix things.

"Oh." Papa was visibly taken aback by this. "I might stay a day or two, but you know I can't abide the city. I don't know why your brother insists on living here year-round. The air isn't fit for anyone, least of all a baby. That girl will grow up with weak lungs, mark my word."

Hannah was used to Papa's little ruminations on whatever subject took his attention. It was just his way. They generally faded into the background of her notice—like the sound of carriages rolling past or crickets chirping or any other sound one heard so often that it ceased to be audible at all, but now Hannah couldn't seem to ignore them.

She kept imagining what Mr. Corbyn would think if he were here.

"Let's not talk about the air," Hannah pleaded. "I'm only trying to say that I want to see you."

Papa scoffed. "You've seen me now. I can stay out the day if you like, but I really must go back tomorrow. I have obligations waiting for me."

It was hard not to let her disappointment show. "Might I come back home with you, then?"

If he'd been surprised before, Papa grew downright

uncomfortable at this. "You know I love to see you, but Jacob and I had planned a foxhunt with the McAllisters before the season ends. You always say you don't like to watch those. And then it will be the spring planting. We'll be too busy to entertain you. Besides, it's not seemly for a young woman to be alone with a bunch of men. You'll be happier here, where your mother and Jane can keep you occupied and see about finding you a husband. That's women's business."

"Why can't Mama come home with me?" If Hannah couldn't persuade her mother to see reason, maybe Papa could help.

But he soured at this, suddenly irritated. "I never said she couldn't. She's the one who insisted on running off to town, saying she could find you a husband more easily here, and look how that turned out! I don't see why you couldn't just marry Mr. Keane's eldest boy, from over near Hemerdon. *He* never would have spoken back to his elders like that fellow you brought here last night."

"I don't *want* to marry George Keane." Hannah couldn't take any more matchmaking. It was even worse coming from her father because she hadn't been expecting it. Or maybe it was worse because she couldn't think of her pathetic string of suitors now without comparing them to Mr. Corbyn and feeling the sting of his sudden departure afresh. "I just want us to go back to the way things used to be. If you would talk to Mama, maybe you could—"

"Bah. It's too late for that. She's made her decision, and she's welcome to it. I'm not going to beg my wife to stay in her own house. If you want to try to talk some sense into her, you can go right ahead, but I have nothing to apologize for."

Hannah flinched away from the anger in his tone. *I didn't ask you to apologize.*

Now he was all worked up again. She hadn't made things any better by talking to Papa; she'd only made them a thousand times worse. She should have known better.

"I'm sorry," Hannah found herself mumbling automatically, though she didn't know what she'd done wrong. "I'm going to go downstairs. I'll see you in a little while."

She blinked back tears as she hurried away. Even Papa didn't want her back home. What had it all been for, then? She'd worked so hard, she'd convinced Mr. Corbyn to do so much for her, and she'd promised him an impossible sum that she still hadn't managed to pay, and for what?

Hannah paid no mind to where she was going, wanting only to put as much space as she could between herself and her father before she could do anything else to spoil things. When she rounded a corner, she nearly crashed into Eli and Jane.

"Careful," he admonished, then took in the distress on her face. "Are you all right? Is it about Mr. Corbyn?"

"It's not Mr. Corbyn, it's Papa." Hannah sniffled. She hated how utterly pathetic she sounded. "I want to go back to Devon but he says I have to stay with Mama, except she's not going back home, is she? Not ever."

Jane, who was holding her daughter in her arms, cast a worried look to Eli. "Would you like me to give you two a moment in private?"

"No need," Hannah answered for him. "Everybody knows. I'm just the only one who cares." Belatedly, she realized that there might be one other person in the house who cared, and lowered her voice. "Wait, where's Mama?"

"Out on a morning call," Eli assured her. "But why don't we all go into the study where we won't be disturbed?"

How can Mama be out on a call at a time like this?

Hannah followed them down the hall to a little green room filled with books and an oak table. Eli pulled out two chairs for the ladies, but Jane didn't take hers, instead kneeling down on a nearby patch of empty carpet where she could set Gloria on her belly to wiggle and grunt.

"I do care." Eli's voice was gentle. "I'm sure Jacob must too. But you can't say it was unexpected, Hannah. They've been unhappy for years. Just look at what happened last night."

"That was Mr. Corbyn's fault! If he hadn't made such a fuss over it—"

"It wasn't his fault," Eli said firmly. "Papa was rude to half the people at the table: Mr. Corbyn, Jane, and especially Mama. I should have put a stop to it myself before Mr. Corbyn had to say anything."

Hannah bit her lip. Coming from Eli, it was a damning condemnation. He'd always been the peacekeeper in the family, trying to distract their parents from their quarrels with some bit of news or a joke. She couldn't imagine him talking back to Papa as Mr. Corbyn had done.

"I don't want to interfere in your life if you're sure of your choice," her brother continued. "I expect you have enough of that from Mama. But if the only reason you rejected Corbyn last night is because of what he said at dinner, then I hope you'll think it over a bit longer. It's the sort of thing you should be sure about."

Hannah wasn't prepared for this. Was she really the only person who objected to Corbyn's behavior? Well, her and Papa, of course. And possibly Mama, who cared more for manners than for motives.

I'm turning into my parents. This realization was enough to make Hannah wish she could take back her harsh words to Mr. Corbyn last night, if she hadn't been halfway there already.

But what good did regret do? How could she be sorry for the loss of a connection that had never been real? She couldn't marry him, so their engagement was destined to end one way or another.

"I am sure," she promised Eli.

What Hannah regretted was only the way their rupture had come about. She'd hurt Corbyn when she'd agreed he wasn't a gentleman. And the worst part was, she'd *known* it would hurt him before she said it, but she'd blamed him for sabotaging all her weeks of planning and she'd let that frustration guide her.

He hadn't deserved that.

"It's only that I don't know what I'm supposed to do now," Hannah added quietly. She hadn't even paid Mr. Corbyn what she promised, unless one counted the value of the new clothes Mama had bought him, much as she hated to think of someone else wearing them. Those vivid blues had been meant for *his* eyes. "I don't want to marry anyone. I'd hoped once I broke off the engagement to Mr. Corbyn, Mama would have to let me go home, but Papa doesn't want me there without her, and I don't think she'll ever go back to Devon. She won't let me have my dowry, so I've nothing to live on. What's left for me now?"

A tear spilled down Hannah's cheek unbidden. Eli was right; things would never go back to the way they'd been. Even Corbyn had seen the truth after a single evening together: Nothing would make her parents love each other again.

Eli pulled her gently into his arms. One thing she would say about her oldest brother was that he was quite good at hugs. A moment later, Jane stood up to add her arms to the mix, and Hannah let herself be surrounded with love for a moment.

When it was over, Jane cleared her throat. "Maybe we should talk about the other thing." She was looking at her husband.

"What other thing?" Hannah asked.

"You go ahead." Eli nodded. "It was more your idea than mine."

Jane turned back to Hannah, who by this point was growing rather impatient. "After supper we got to talking about how you might need some other option, and I thought we might offer you work at the club, if you're interested."

"Me?" The sound that escaped Hannah's mouth was nothing but an incredulous squeak. She'd dreamed of this once, but it seemed so long ago.

"I know your mother doesn't like the thought of you being involved, but the truth is that we've been struggling to keep up since Gloria was born, and you did seem to have a knack for bookkeeping and some good ideas for the games. I would need to talk it over with Della first, but I—"

"Ma'am?" Molly stood in the doorway, a worried look on her face.

"We're a bit busy," Jane replied. "Is it an emergency?"

The maid didn't immediately answer, but looked gravely between her mistress and her master. In her hand, she held up a folded newspaper. "There's a story here about your friend. The washerwoman was talking about it. I think you'd best come and see for yourself."

Jane and Eli both hurried across the room and bent their heads over the page. Gloria was by this time entirely sick of being on her belly and had begun to fuss, so Hannah picked her up and bounced her a little until her cries subsided.

"Oh!" The cry that escaped Jane was one of pure terror.

"What is it?" Hannah asked, beginning to grow worried.

Neither of them answered her. Eli said to Jane, "You go. Take as long as you need," and his wife was out the door before anyone could so much as blink.

It was only once she'd gone that he thanked the maid and brought the paper over to Hannah, lifting the baby from her arms to let her read. The pages were opened to the legal section, and she had to skim several headlines about various court cases before she found one that read: *Lady Ashton's Divorce.*

Ashton. Wasn't that Della's viscount? Hannah read the story quickly, until she got to the part where a witness before Parliament named Della herself as Lord Ashton's suspected mistress!

"Good heavens!" She read it a second time, then set the paper quickly down, wishing she could unsee the story. "She'll be completely ruined."

And not kissed-a-midshipman-in-the-gambling-club kind of ruined that could be patched over with the story of a secret engagement. This was the sort of thing that got a woman cut from society. What would Della do now? And what about Annabelle? Being named in the papers this way would tarnish their whole family.

"It's a bad business." There was real worry in Eli's eyes. Though Della might be Jane's dearest friend, he clearly cared about her as well.

"What will this mean for the club?" Hannah felt gauche asking such a thing when Della's life might be over, but she couldn't help it. Jane and Della had founded the club together. If one of its owners was disgraced, was there a risk the club might fail? Jane and Eli depended on that money.

Eli seemed to be thinking the same thing, for his eyes darkened further. "We'll see what Jane says when she gets back."

"I can't believe you let her break off the engagement before she paid you! We're never going to see that money now. It was all for nothing." James was red in the face from shouting, which he'd been doing ever since Silas had given a summary explanation of their situation over breakfast. He looked a great deal like their father, suddenly.

"What was all for nothing?" Silas snapped. "All the time and effort I spent trying to impress Miss Williams and her mother, you mean? The thing that you had absolutely nothing to do with? Save your outrage. All you did was sit back and wait for me to make you rich."

"Which you didn't do! At least I bring something to this business. A brewery needs a cooper. What do you bring us, if you can't get the funds?"

"Careful," Silas growled. "If you think I won't hit you because you're younger, you'd best think again."

At Silas's threat, Marian positioned herself between the brothers. "Stop it, both of you. We'll talk about this later, once tempers have cooled."

But James ignored her. "There's not going to *be* a later for us if we can't get that money. We may as well go back home to Burton with our tails between our legs and beg Jack for work. Bloody hell. I can just imagine his face."

"At least you have a home to go back to," Silas shot off bitterly. He couldn't blame James and Marian for leaving, if that was what they decided to do. They'd already stayed in London far longer than they'd intended, waiting for Silas to get their investment. But he hadn't expected it to hurt this much.

Don't be such a fucking child. People leave. Especially once you stop being useful to them.

He should know that by now.

"Why didn't you marry her like I told you?" James threw up his hands in exasperation. "Then you'd have her dowry and we could do whatever we liked with it. If you'd just kept your mouth shut instead of insulting her father, we'd all be rich. Why couldn't you—"

"Because I'm an idiot!" Silas shouted. "Don't you think I know that? I don't know why I couldn't hold my bloody tongue, but I couldn't. It's done, James."

His blood was pounding in his ears. *Stupid, stupid, stupid.* He should have held onto Hannah until he'd gotten his money. For longer, even. But it was too late for regrets now. She would never forgive him.

He'd lost her for good, and he'd lost his future too.

"Come on." Marian grabbed James roughly by his collar and dragged him toward the door. Though he must have a solid two stone of muscle on her, Marian's confidence helped to balance the scales. "Out with you. Go for a walk and don't come back for an hour. I'll deal with this."

James might have mumbled a few more sullen protests on his way down the hall, but the slam of the door told Silas he'd been evicted from the lodgings. The room was deathly silent when Marian came back a moment later, her cheeks flushed. "Sorry about that."

Silas found himself staring at his feet. Without James there to yell at, all the anger fizzled out of him, leaving nothing but a hollow ache in its place.

"She might still pay me," he muttered. He'd kept up his end of the bargain, after all. But he would be damned if he was going to beg for it.

Let Hannah come to him, if she cared about her debt. Let her come and tell Silas why it was so easy to cast him aside.

She hadn't even hesitated.

"I'm less concerned with the money and more concerned about you," Marian said softly. "Are you all right?"

"Why wouldn't I be?" He looked up in surprise.

"You seemed to care for this girl," Marian said hesitantly. "I thought maybe—"

"I didn't. I cared about getting paid."

Marian didn't argue, but Silas didn't like the way she was staring at him. She couldn't have forgotten how many hours she'd spent acting as his dance partner when he'd been trying to learn the quadrille last week. He felt like such an idiot.

What had he expected—that Hannah might decide to keep him if he could master a few tricks, like a faithful dog? That her parents would welcome the chance to lower their standing by such an alliance if he could only bow deeply enough or use the right fork?

Laughable. And now he couldn't even take comfort in the brewery. James was right. He was as good as worthless if he couldn't get the rest of the funds.

"I know you did your best." Marian's smile was sad but kind.

"James knows it too, he's just a little hotheaded. Like you sometimes. But you both have good hearts."

"What about you? Are you going to go back home?"

Marian bit her lip. "It would be a shame to give up now. We've made so many connections to help us get started. Maybe there's some other way to get the funds. Or we could partner with an established brewery. Invest what you have to help someone expand their own business and bring us on to help."

"That wasn't what you wanted."

"Plans change. I wanted Grandpa to give me a chance to prove myself instead of turning the family business over to Jack, but I had to make another place for myself when he didn't agree. Maybe I can still do that, even if it wouldn't be my first choice. And that way you could come with us."

A sharp rap at the door interrupted them. James, no doubt, though it hadn't been an hour. Maybe his head had cooled as quickly as Silas's once there was no one to argue with.

"I'll go," Silas offered. He would try to make peace.

But it wasn't James at the door; it was the Williams's coachman. What was he doing here? Had he brought Hannah? More importantly, was she here to apologize or to deliver his money?

"Madame invites you to join her for a carriage ride, sir." The coachman motioned Silas outside and he followed quickly, pausing only long enough to shout a hasty warning to Marian that he would be back in a minute.

His heart was pounding. Hannah wouldn't have come all this way if she was still angry with him, surely. Which must mean she'd realized her mistake and wanted to make amends.

The coachman opened the door and Silas stepped inside, barely able to suppress a smile. He was going to remind Hannah exactly why they fit together so well. By the time he was done with her, she'd be moaning his name in between her apologies for treating him like a bit of rubbish she could cast off when she was—

"Good morning, Mr. Corbyn." Mrs. Williams sat on the seat opposite his, her gray-streaked hair pulled back into a severe bun, her dress buttoned up to her throat.

Not her!

Silas physically recoiled. He'd been three seconds away from kissing her, before he realized who it was.

Mrs. Williams raised an eyebrow at his reaction.

"You were expecting someone else?"

"Uh..." Probably safer not to answer that.

Silas glanced at the door, measuring his chances of ducking back out before the woman could speak again. They were slim, as the coachman had already shut the door and they were lurching down the street.

He squared his shoulders and prepared to face the firing squad.

"I trust you're well this morning?" she asked.

A trap. It must be a trap. There was no chance she'd come here to explain pleasantries.

"Well enough," he answered warily.

"Yes. I suppose it was a difficult evening for all of us." Mrs. Williams dropped her gaze to her lap.

What was going on? He'd thought she would have raked him over the coals by now for ruining her daughter's hopes at marriage, but Mrs. Williams couldn't even seem to look him in the eye.

"Are—are *you* well?" he asked. The question felt unnatural. Their roles would never have allowed it before. But something had changed between them. Where she might once have scolded him, Mrs. Williams had turned meek. Hesitant.

Sure enough, she sat mute for a long moment before she answered, "I don't suppose I am."

Silas had never been more lost in all his life.

A few days ago, he would have taken a certain satisfaction in anything that knocked Mrs. Williams down a peg. But seeing how she was treated by her own husband last night had sucked the wind from his sails. She looked so diminished that it was impossible to wish her any harm.

"I can't imagine what you must think of us." She addressed this misgiving to Silas's midsection rather than to his face. "We aren't normally like that, you know. At least—" She seemed to want to say more, but finally judged it unwise.

"I understand," he assured her. "I wouldn't judge you or your children by the conduct of anyone else."

"I hope you won't repeat the tale of what happened."

"Of course not." This seemed to reassure her. Was that why she'd come? To forestall any gossip about the state of her marriage?

"When I think of how I acted so superior to you when I can't even keep my own family in order..." Mrs. Williams finally found the courage to look him in the eye, though she was blushing furiously. "I'm ashamed of myself, Mr. Corbyn. I owe you an apology."

This must be a dream. The real Mrs. Williams would never apologize. She wrapped herself in rules like a suit of armor, shielded from any possible wrongdoing.

"Thank you." Silas spoke very slowly. Any minute now the other shoe was sure to drop.

"I want you to understand, I was only trying to protect my daughter. After the way you two met, I assumed the worst. I didn't want Hannah to make a mistake she might regret for the rest of her life."

The same mistake you did. Though Mrs. Williams left the words unspoken, the comparison was obvious.

She probably wasn't too far off the mark either. Though Silas would never treat Hannah the way her father did her mother, by any other standard he must be a poor match for the daughter of a gentleman. Even Hannah knew it, or else she would have stopped him from leaving last night.

Still, it was good of Mrs. Williams to see him off with kindness. He hadn't expected them to become friends before he reached the end of his time with this family. Well, not friends, exactly. More like acquaintances sharing a guarded truce. Whatever they were, it was a sharp improvement from the way they'd begun.

"I see things differently now," she continued. "You're the best match for Hannah."

"I under— Wait, beg pardon?"

Mrs. Williams kept right on speaking, heedless of his surprise. "At first I thought that this might be some ruse she'd concocted. It wouldn't be the first time she tried to lie her way out of a match. You should have heard the story she fed poor Mr. Brown about being a Chartist, when he was still trying to court her. But seeing the two of you together, especially after last night—"

"You...*approve* of the way I behaved last night?" He wasn't sure which surprised him more: the fact that Mrs. Williams had been onto their game from the start, or the fact that her mind had been changed by the very conflict that had ended things.

"Don't interrupt, please." Her scolding, while familiar, was gentler than before. "I understand you better. I know I can trust you to treat Hannah properly, if you were that upset at how Mr. Williams treated me. It showed me that you're a good man, Mr. Corbyn."

The acknowledgment was so unexpected that Silas was speechless.

"No one has ever stood up to him before," Mrs. Williams said softly. "No one has ever defended *me* either."

"My father was like your husband." Silas found the words slipping out of him without conscious intention. What was he doing, spilling his story to Mrs. Williams? This carriage ride felt like a strange dream. "*Is*, I should say. He's still alive, though I don't know that I'll ever see him again. He made it clear that I stopped being his son the day I got myself discharged."

Mrs. Williams looked at him with real regret. "I'm so sorry."

"I don't miss him," Silas lied. He wished it were true, which made it almost not a lie at all. "But I do miss my mother. She doesn't have the courage to go behind his back. If she were a little more like you, she might not have let him decide matters for the whole family."

"It took me twenty-seven years to stand on my own," Mrs. Williams acknowledged. "Maybe one day your mother will be able to do the same. But until then"—she reached across the carriage and took his hand into hers—"if you don't think it's too silly of me to say this, I'll be your family once you marry Hannah. I know we didn't get off to a good start, but I think I could do better now that I know what sort of man you really are."

It *should* have seemed silly. He was twenty-four, long past the age of needing a mother at all. But he found her little speech strangely touching.

Except for the part about Hannah marrying him.

"It's impossible now," Silas pointed out. "You heard your husband. He'll never consent to the match."

"No need to worry about that. I can deal with Mr. Williams."

"How?" He couldn't let Mrs. Williams suffer for this favor, if it would mean putting herself in his crosshairs.

"I have my ways," she replied. "Hannah's dowry is settled on her under the terms of my marriage contract, so he can't withhold it to punish her. And if it's an objection you're worried about, trust that I can apply a little pressure to prevent him from embarrassing you on the wedding day. There was a very shocking story in the papers just this morning about a viscountess who's divorcing her husband.

I might hint that I could do something similar if he proves too difficult. I won't really, of course, but Mr. Williams doesn't need to know that."

She said it so matter-of-factly, it made Silas reassess the assumptions he'd made last night. Mr. Williams might be a petty tyrant, but his wife wasn't broken.

But even her plotting wouldn't be enough. They hadn't addressed the most important thing.

"I'm grateful," he said, truly meaning it, "but Hannah won't have me now. She was insulted by my conduct last night. Nothing you do will change her mind."

"How can you say that?" Mrs. Williams puffed up to something like her former self. Indignation was a powerful restorative. "If she was determined to marry you despite all *my* protests, she won't be put off by a little scuffle with her father. You must have some faith, Mr. Corbyn. And besides that, you shall also have my help."

Silas couldn't stop himself; he began to laugh. What an absurd turn of fortune this was, to go from conspiring with Hannah to trick her mother, to conspiring with her mother to persuade Hannah.

"I don't think it will be so easy. She's headstrong."

"No more of this!" Mrs. Williams used her fan to swat at him lightly. "I won't hear any more complaints. I shall speak to Hannah today, and we shall keep to our original plans. You'll be married as soon as the last banns are read this Sunday."

But she doesn't want to marry me. She doesn't want to be married at all.

Hannah had never once expressed a change of heart. She might share an undeniable attraction to Silas, but if she'd wanted him for more than that, she would have come herself.

The sensible thing to do would be to refuse Mrs. Williams and send her on her way. Forget Hannah forever. Silas had learned by now not to reach above his station, no matter how tempting it had been to believe that he could fit into her world.

But he couldn't seem to do it. If there was a chance that Hannah could really be his, didn't Silas owe it to himself to try? He'd never met anyone like her before. He'd never known a woman who had such an exceptional mix of determination and gentleness, who'd seen him for who he was instead of who others had judged him to be. He wasn't ready to give up yet.

If he didn't try, Silas would always look back at this moment and wonder how things might have been different.

"All right." It wasn't as though anyone was *forcing* Hannah to marry him. She could say yes or no as she liked, but he wasn't slinking quietly off into the shadows. "Let's plan a wedding."

Seventeen

JANE ARRIVED BACK AT THE HOUSE BARELY THIRTY MINUTES after she'd left, Annabelle at her side.

"Oh!" Hannah gave a little cry of surprise as she embraced her friend. "Eli showed me the story. Are you all right?"

"As well as can be expected." Annabelle's eyes were red, though her voice held steady. "Della's decided to leave England until the story blows over. I don't know *how* she'll manage without me. You see what sort of trouble she got herself into when I was there to keep an eye on her, so you can just imagine how much worse it will be when she's free to run amok." She shook her head gravely.

"Well, she won't be alone." Jane sounded as worried as Annabelle, though she seemed to be trying to put on a brave face.

"What do you mean?" Hannah asked.

"Now that Viscount Ashton has his divorce, she intends to ask him to accompany her."

"But he's the reason that she's in this mess," Hannah protested, searching first Jane, then Annabelle for any sign of understanding.

Was she the only person who could see sense? "Hasn't she learned her lesson?"

It was Annabelle who answered. "I warned her something like this might happen." Her voice softened as she continued. "But the truth is, I really think he loves her. And he's good for her, in his way. They do seem to bring out the best in each other. If it weren't for the inconvenient fact of his prior marriage, they would have been a good match."

"That's a very important fact!"

"Yes." Annabelle sighed. "But he'd been separated from Lady Ashton for something like eight or nine years before he met Della, so it isn't as though she had anything to do with their rupture. If they've been unhappy for that long, I don't see why everyone makes such a fuss over divorce when there aren't any children to make inheritance a problem."

Annabelle said it so indifferently, as though the end of a marriage was no great tragedy simply because the couple in question had grown a little tired of one another.

"But what's the point of a marriage if the vows don't mean anything?" Hannah asked indignantly. It was a question she might have liked to ask Mama, if she dared. But it was far easier to say it to Annabelle.

"Are their vows so important that Lord and Lady Ashton should be miserable together for the rest of their lives instead of finding happiness with other people?" her friend retorted. "Plenty of couples make mistakes. I'm certainly not going to judge him if he'll be the one keeping Della safe. I'd rather they were off to the continent together than have her face the scandal alone."

Jane was nodding along silently.

Hannah wasn't sure what to say. She couldn't think of any persuasive argument why Lord Ashton should stay with his wife when she didn't know anything about either party, except that it made her feel very worried to think that every source of security she'd been told to aspire to in life was nothing but a piece of theater: a painted backdrop that could be torn down to reveal the emptiness behind. But she wasn't sure quite how to express this sort of existential dread without sounding hysterical.

"I'm glad to hear Della has a plan." Eli spoke up. "Is there anything else we can do for her?"

"Not at present." A deepening crease marred Jane's brow. "I gather she'll be leaving quite soon. We've agreed that Annabelle will exercise control over her share of the club while she's away. And we may need to buy her investment out." She exchanged a regretful look with Eli.

"Unless you like me so much that you decide to keep me on forever as a partner," Annabelle said, her voice bright despite the gravity of the subject. "Then I can buy Della out for you. I imagine she'll probably need the money once she spends all hers on something silly like new gowns in Paris."

"That's why we came back here." Jane turned to Hannah. "We need to plan out our next steps for Bishop's now that Della is retreating entirely from the business."

"I can still join you?" This was a bright spot in the morning, though she would have preferred it to come under better circumstances. "I wasn't sure what the scandal would mean for you."

"We'll have to inform our members that Della has withdrawn from her role in the club, effective immediately, but we won't give up." Jane's chin wavered, and Eli reached out to give her shoulder a comforting squeeze. "If you need an income to support yourself without a husband, we may as well help each other."

"Wait, you broke your engagement?" Annabelle whirled on Hannah. "Why didn't anyone tell me?"

"It was a busy morning!" Jane protested.

"Do you need me to be sad with you?" Annabelle looked her over apprehensively. "Or may I confess that I think spinsterhood is the only sensible option for an intelligent woman?" With a belated wince, she addressed Jane, who was frowning at her. "Sorry."

"I give you permission to be happy," Hannah assured her. "It was my decision."

This was perfectly true. If there was an odd little twinge in her heart when she thought of it, that only came from the abruptness of her rupture with Mr. Corbyn. Nothing more.

Jane was giving her a doubtful look, but thankfully didn't press the matter when they had business to discuss. "Cecily is already attending three nights a week, and we'll try to keep her on if she's still willing. Hannah, if you're interested in taking over the bookkeeping, it would leave me more time for other matters. If your mother will agree to keep watching Gloria in the evenings, I can attend more often until the crisis subsides. Annabelle, you can start coming in regularly on the evenings that Eli or I are there so that we can show you the ropes. How many days can you manage?"

They spent the next few minutes going over their schedules until they'd arrived at a plan for Della's absence, although they hadn't finished dividing all of the labor when a knock at the front door signaled that Hannah's mother had returned from her morning calls.

Oh no.

"How are we going to persuade her to agree to this?" Hannah wasn't sure whom she was asking. Herself, quite possibly, though she wouldn't have objected if Eli wanted to shoulder the burden.

But no one volunteered a plan before her mother walked into the room a moment later.

"Mama, we were just—"

Hannah's mouth stopped cooperating with her when she realized that Mr. Corbyn was with her, his lovely blue eyes somewhat guarded. Her heart lurched. What was he doing here?

Her mother looked equally surprised to find Annabelle in the room, though she recovered herself quicker. "Good morning, Miss Annabelle."

"Good morning." Annabelle eyed Mr. Corbyn with naked curiosity, but Jane nudged her gently toward the door.

"Why don't we give you a moment alone?"

Annabelle looked as though she might protest, her large brown eyes darting from Hannah to Corbyn, but she followed Jane and Eli reluctantly from the room.

Mama started in immediately. "Now, I don't know everything that was said last night after you left the dining room, nor do I need to know. All that matters is that you put the quarrel behind you and move forward with the wedding as planned. I shall talk to your father, so there's no need to worry about what he'll say."

"I beg your pardon?" How could Mama possibly still expect a wedding? There had once been a time when she would have deemed Mr. Corbyn unsuitable for parting his hair on the wrong side. An outburst such as the one last night should have damaged him beyond repair! "Papa will never agree to it now, and I'm not going to marry without his permission," Hannah insisted, seizing on the most obvious obstacle.

"I told you, I shall handle all that. Stop being so obstinate. Even when I agree to the man *you* picked, you still find reasons to quibble."

"Mrs. Williams," Corbyn interrupted gently. "Might Hannah and I have a moment to speak in private?"

"Of course you may, Mr. Corbyn." Mama was far warmer when she replied to him than she had been when speaking to Hannah. In fact, she was far warmer than she'd ever been in his presence. Had he bewitched her somehow? That seemed the only explanation for such a drastic change. "Is your father at home? I'll deal with him directly."

Hannah didn't dare to answer. She wasn't entirely confident that "deal with him" wasn't a euphemism for murder. But Mama didn't seem to need her confirmation, and she slipped from the room with quiet determination. What on earth was happening?

Once she'd left, Hannah turned to Mr. Corbyn. "What did you say to her? Why does she suddenly like you so much?"

"She appreciated my defending her yesterday."

"Of course she would." Hannah buried her face in her hands. That brought the total up to three people in this house who were on Mr. Corbyn's side—Jane, Eli, and her mother—while no one but Papa agreed with Hannah! She was rapidly being humbled for her actions.

"I'm sorry I lost my temper," Corbyn murmured, once it became apparent that Hannah was too lost to know what to say next. "I didn't care for the way your father was speaking to everyone, but I shouldn't have thrown fuel on the fire. He reminded me of the way my own father used to talk to me, and I wasn't thinking when I spoke. I should have known it would hurt you."

"No. I'm sorry," she confessed. "You're...not entirely wrong about him. I wish I hadn't been so unkind to you afterward."

They stood in silence for a moment, before Corbyn broke it abruptly. "I think we should get married."

"What?" Hannah wished the sound that had escaped her didn't sound quite so much like a squawking bird. She might have liked to be more graceful at this moment. "You don't have to do this to get the money I promised you. Jane's offered me a position in her club, and I'd like to accept if I can persuade my mother. It might take me some time to save up the funds, but I'll send you half my pay every month until the debt is clear."

Corbyn seemed to think about this for a moment. "I need the

money sooner than that," he said finally. "The reason Marian and James came to town was to ask me to invest in a brewery with them. Marian knows the trade from helping my grandfather, and James is a cooper. They have a brewmaster they can bring on as well. All they need are the funds for rent and supplies."

A brewery? "When did you decide all this? Why didn't you tell me?"

She knew it was silly, but Hannah felt a little hurt to learn that Corbyn had kept such a secret. She'd thought they'd come to know each other well these past few weeks. Why wouldn't he have told her his plans?

"You always said our arrangement was temporary." If Corbyn's words came out a little brusque, they were softened by what he said next. "And I suppose I didn't know if you might look down on me for it."

"I wouldn't," Hannah assured him. After all, she intended to work for her livelihood, if Jane could provide the opportunity. What was the difference? "But what about the army?"

"I never intended to go along with that. I just said what I thought your mother would want to hear, back when that's what you'd asked me to do." A shadow passed over Corbyn's face. "I haven't told her the truth yet. I don't know how she'll take it."

"How *she'll* take it?" Hannah echoed. "Why are you acting as though you and my mother are dear friends? She hated you until recently."

"I think we became friends this morning." Corbyn looked nearly as baffled by this development as Hannah. "She was actually quite kind. I wouldn't want to disappoint her now."

"She's spent the past four years trying to force me to marry the first man to learn my name!" Hannah protested. "In fact, several of them didn't *even* learn my name."

"So let's put a stop to it for good," Corbyn insisted. "Marry me."

"But I don't want to be married."

"Why not? I can understand why you wouldn't want to marry some decrepit old grandfather, but why not me? It would be in both our interests. I'd get the money I need for the brewery—no more and no less—while you have a permanent solution to your mother's matchmaking."

"Because it's..." Hannah hesitated. She'd never really had to explain herself before. Everyone dismissed her objections without listening to them, or else told her that she was sure to change her mind when she met the right man. "Well, it's all a lie, isn't it? People act like marriage is supposed to make a woman happy, but it doesn't do anything of the sort."

"We could be happy," Corbyn said. "You're an exceptional woman. I've enjoyed your company while we were pulling the wool over everyone's eyes. I expect I would only enjoy it more if we didn't have to worry about tricking anyone or proving ourselves all the time."

"Maybe for a time," Hannah conceded, "but attachments fade. I do appreciate the offer, Mr. Corbyn. Truly. But I can't accept."

Despite the veritable deluge of men who'd invaded her receiving room over the years, no one had ever proposed to Hannah before. She probably would have been horrified if they had. Most of the gentlemen hadn't even called a second time, with how hard she'd worked to put them off.

But Hannah found herself inexplicably touched by Mr. Corbyn's offer. If someone had asked her an hour ago whether she minded going through life without ever receiving a proposal of marriage, she would have issued a resounding no. Now that Mr. Corbyn stood before her, looking slightly nervous and tender despite himself, she realized that it wasn't true. She wanted someone to think that she was worthy of an offer. *An exceptional woman.* No one had ever said something like that to her.

If only she didn't have to disappoint him.

But Corbyn didn't look disappointed. He wore the look of a card player considering his next move, not one who'd been defeated. "You're afraid you might find yourself in the same situation as your mother," he finally said, his eyes inviting Hannah to deny it. She couldn't, of course. That was precisely what she was afraid of. And with good reason! "What if I could make sure that would never happen? Your mother talked about settling your dowry on future children. We could settle the money on you instead, free and clear. You pay me what we agreed for the brewery, but everything else is yours. You could use it to buy yourself a cottage somewhere, so that you'd always have a place of your own to go."

"You'd really let me do that?" It wasn't that Hannah was reconsidering her answer; it was only that Corbyn's suggestion surprised her so much that she had to make sure she'd understood him. Her dowry was the only reason her mother had been able to conjure up new suitors despite Hannah's lackluster looks and blatant opposition. She'd never imagined there could be a man willing to let it slip from his grasp.

Three hundred and twenty pounds was nothing in comparison to what he could have. If Corbyn didn't care about that, he must really have meant what he said earlier. He wanted *her.*

How had this happened?

"I'd let you do whatever you liked if it means we can come to an agreement," Corbyn said bluntly. "Name your terms."

"I don't—" He might just as well have asked her to organize a ball for two hundred people by tomorrow. Entirely in Latin. "I don't know that there's anything that could make me agree. Even if I had my own house to retreat to, it's the retreat itself that would bother me. What if we had children? I don't know if I could put them through that."

They were slipping into dangerous territory now. Far from couching her rejection in delicate terms, Hannah found that she was pouring out her darkest thoughts and fears. Their discussion had turned intimate.

Corbyn studied her carefully, catching each of her objections and tossing it back in the form of a new offer. "What if there were no children?"

"You don't want them?"

"Do you?"

Hannah was obliged to consider this before she could reply. It wasn't something she'd ever needed to think about except in the abstract, given that she'd known she wouldn't marry.

Gloria is rather sweet. Hannah could imagine herself with a child of her own to love, so long as the problem of the baby's father remained a vague, undefined figure. But Corbyn's offer to let her keep a cottage to maintain her independence would be completely meaningless if they had children.

She couldn't leave a baby behind. Nor could she take one with her, if it meant putting the child through the same thing she was living now.

"No. If I were to consider what you're proposing, I wouldn't want to risk a child. That way it wouldn't hurt anyone else if something went wrong."

She probably shouldn't have said *if*. She wasn't really considering this, was she?

"Then we won't have children," Corbyn said simply, as if it were that easy. Hannah was about to ask him how he planned to ensure this, but he explained himself before she had the chance. "We don't even need to live together if you don't want to. I'm going back to

Burton once Marian and James have the funds to set up. You could come with us, or you could stay here and help at Bishop's if that's what you want. But you'd be able to do so without a scandal over your name.

"If you marry me, you can still do everything you planned, except that you won't have to worry about being the woman who kissed someone in front of a room full of people and cast him off a few weeks later. You'll be a married woman. And your mother never brings home another suitor."

When he put it that way, it began to form a compelling case. Bishop's had suffered enough scandal. Wouldn't it be better to maintain a veneer of respectability if she wanted to work at the club? No one knew that Hannah had broken her engagement yet, except for family and Annabelle. She could still take it back.

What Corbyn was proposing wasn't even a real marriage. If they lived separately from the start, there was no risk of a broken heart or a family split apart. They would merely be two people helping each other along, as they had been since they'd met. Was that so wrong?

Taking her long silence for the indecision it was, Corbyn reached into his breast pocket and produced a small box. "I got this for you."

"Oh!" Hannah's gasp of pleasure wasn't exactly compatible with her view that this would only be a practical arrangement, but she couldn't help it. Inside the box was a round opal pendant strung from a gold chain. The stone's rich cream flashed with reflections of green and blue when she turned it in the light. "It's beautiful. But you didn't have to. I mean, you need the money for your brewery, and I haven't even paid you what I promised for everything you've done already."

"I wanted to do this properly." He looked a bit embarrassed as he explained himself. "We haven't been honest with everyone else, but we've always been honest with each other. If you'll have me, we wouldn't have to lie to anyone ever again." Corbyn's voice dropped to a whisper as he urged, "Try it on."

Hannah's fingers twitched as if to take it, but she held herself back. Was she really going to marry Mr. Corbyn? She'd never imagined herself in this position, but it didn't seem so unthinkable now as it had before. He was a good man. He meant what he'd said about protecting her independence, and they could ensure that the marriage settlement made it binding.

If I say no, I might never see him again. The possibility made her heart ache. Hannah had grown used to having Corbyn around. She liked the way she felt when he was near, the sense that she could rely on him, and the way he'd opened up to her, even when she suspected it didn't come easily to him. It was nice to have an ally.

Moreover, if Hannah refused his offer, she would be forcing him to wait months or years for the money that he needed to start his brewery. Even if he hadn't shared his hopes with her, they must be important to him. This was his future livelihood. After all Mr. Corbyn had done for her, she didn't feel right paying her debt in bits and pieces from whatever she might hope to make at Jane's club. Not when she had the funds sitting in her dowry going unused, and she might get at them easily with an arrangement that could bring them both independence. Three thousand pounds wasn't much to start a family on, but if they didn't have children and they were both investing something into profitable businesses, they could live quite well on it.

Oh goodness. I'm actually going to agree.

Hannah nodded. Her fingers were shaking too badly to get the pendant free of its box, but Corbyn took it for her, brushing her hair off her neck as he moved behind her to do up the clasp. "Thank you," he whispered. "I promise not to hurt you, Hannah."

Hannah's hand flew to the stone of its own accord. It was cool and heavy at her throat. She felt like a child playing dress up in her mother's jewelry, imitating a role she'd seen someone else perform countless times before her. But this was real.

Her heart skipped into a frantic pace, and Hannah had the sudden urge to turn and run back upstairs to her room, where she would be safe from this terrifying feeling. She could still tear the pendant off her neck and tell Corbyn she'd changed her mind. It wasn't too late. But then he bent his head to kiss the side of her neck, and the heat of his mouth made her shudder. As if he'd sensed her fears, Corbyn wrapped his hand around her waist and pulled her against his body, anchoring her in place as his lips wandered downward.

Stay, he seemed to be saying, overruling her nervous energy with desire.

Yes. A tiny whimper caught in Hannah's throat. Even if her mind balked at this prospect like a skittish horse, her body was quick to betray her. He'd always been able to summon that reaction. Hannah twisted to face Corbyn so that they could kiss properly. With his hands sliding over her body, she couldn't remember any of the objections that had seemed so important before.

Corbyn was prepared to give her everything she wanted. Independence. Access to her dowry. A home of her own. So long as she kept her wits about her, it could be the answer to her problems.

They'd done very well with a pretend engagement. Why not a pretend marriage?

Eighteen

THE MATTER OF THE MARRIAGE SETTLEMENT WAS RESOLVED A
few days later at the offices of Mr. Williams's solicitor. He was a tiny
man with wire spectacles by the name of Mr. Filby, who wasted the
first ten minutes of their meeting questioning the makeup of the
group that came before him.

"There's really no need for Miss and Mrs. Williams to be here,"
he explained patiently. "I can arrange everything the gentlemen
require."

"Mrs. Williams most certainly does need to be here," said Mrs.
Williams herself, with a menacing glare that encompassed both her
husband and the solicitor. The former only sat sullenly in his chair,
while the latter blushed and tidied some papers to avoid her gaze.

"And I'd prefer that Miss Williams hear the terms of her settlement for herself," Silas added.

"Yes, well, if you're sure…" Mr. Filby cleared his throat. "What
about your father, Mr. Corbyn? Mr. Williams informed me that you
don't have your own solicitor, but surely your family must want to—"

"He won't be leaving me any property," Silas interrupted. "My only possession of any value is the prize money I earned during my naval service, so I don't see why he should be needed."

"But your inheritance," Mr. Filby protested. "It really is necessary to establish the intentions of both fathers of the parties to the marriage settlement, or it leaves the door open to a dispute between the heirs once someone passes on."

"I've been disinherited. Pretend he's dead if you like."

Poor Mr. Filby looked overset by this frank pronouncement, but unlike Silas, he was too well bred to give free rein to his reactions with anything so gauche as words. Only his eyes betrayed his shock.

"L-let's get straight to business, shall we?" He fussed with the same papers that he'd just tidied.

Mr. Williams was curiously silent as his solicitor took them through the essentials. Whatever his wife had done to bring him into line seemed to be working, even if his beefy fists were clenched in a silent struggle. As Mrs. Williams had promised, the amount of Hannah's dowry was provided for in her own settlement, so there could be no dispute about it. Silas informed the solicitor that he wanted the full amount reserved for Hannah's sole use, although this provoked some debate from her mother about whether the funds should instead be settled on their future children.

"Miss Williams might wish to buy some property with the funds," Silas explained, half to her mother and half to Mr. Filby. "We'll need to keep the money accessible."

"You understand it would be your property, Mr. Corbyn." Mr. Filby forgot his timidity as he launched into an explanation. "Legally speaking, you become one person upon your marriage, and you would exercise Miss Williams's rights for her."

Silas wished there were some way to get the man to stop talking. He glanced at Hannah, trying to gauge whether this would be the thing that sent her racing out the door, but she kept her gaze fixed on her hands. She'd been difficult to read since his proposal.

She'd barely agreed to marry him as it was. If Mr. Filby began undoing all the promises Silas had made to secure her consent, who knew what she might do?

"There must be some way to arrange it." Silas fixed Mr. Filby with a stern look. "Isn't that the point of settlements? Why can't you provide that the property would be for her sole use as well?"

"I suppose." The little man polished his glasses on his shirt sleeve. "It would certainly be far simpler if she were bringing the property with her into the marriage instead of planning for a hypothetical, but we could make a provision in the settlement that any property purchased with the funds from her dowry must also be for Miss Williams's sole use during her lifetime."

"Do that, then," Silas ordered. Honestly, why did this have to be complicated?

"But what about your commission, Mr. Corbyn?" Mrs. Williams chimed in. "I thought you needed some of the funds to purchase it. We wouldn't want the settlement to interfere with your plans." It was the last thing Silas wanted to think about now.

Mr. Williams couldn't contain himself any longer. "It's not enough that you're giving this man our daughter without giving him our money as well? Why can't he buy his own commission?"

Don't react. Silas wasn't going to start a row in the solicitor's office. He wasn't. But he could practically feel Hannah slipping away with every new obstacle.

"Mr. Corbyn only needs three hundred pounds," Hannah explained calmly, though she'd tensed at her father's tone. "It's not much in the grand scheme of things."

"Not much? You'd think you were marrying a duke, the way you're prepared to throw away money."

Now Mrs. Williams joined the fray. "They're not throwing it away; they're making provisions for Mr. Corbyn's future. You should be happy you'll have a son-in-law in the army."

Silas winced. How was she going to react once she realized that he had no intention of buying a commission? He hadn't had a chance to discuss the timing of this revelation with Hannah before her mother had come back into the room the other day. Silas wanted to be done with lies, but if he said something now, it was sure to spark another argument.

Silas was suddenly more than a little angry at the pair of them. If they'd been able to control their quarreling, he might not have needed to offer Hannah her own cottage or to live separately or to never have children in order to persuade her that marriage wasn't a trap. She might have trusted Silas to care for her. Might have wanted it.

More than any dowry, the inheritance the Williamses had passed down to their daughter was the terror of their mistakes.

If it makes her feel safe, it's a small price to pay, Silas told himself. He didn't mind what Hannah did with her own money. If a cottage would give her the security she needed to marry him, then let her have her cottage. It didn't mean she had to live there.

There was real passion between them. In time, Hannah might learn to see their alliance as a gift, instead of a mutual necessity. He just needed a chance to prove that she could trust him.

So for once in his life, Silas held his tongue long enough to get what he wanted. He let Mr. and Mrs. Williams bicker their way through the next hour of the meeting until the question of pin money and jointure and all the rest was settled, and Mr. Filby released them with an exhausted farewell.

"Are you all right?" he murmured to Hannah on their way out. Her parents were heading safely to their separate carriages, her father having brought his own from Devon.

Hannah had been quiet through most of the meeting, particularly when her parents had argued. There was a tension in her shoulders that he would have liked to brush away, had they been alone.

"They're always like that," she whispered without meeting his eye. "I don't know why I thought I could change things. It was stupid of me."

"It's not stupid," he assured her. "It's natural to want harmony, but you don't have the power to decide your parents' lives. Only your own."

When Hannah looked up at him, the sadness on her face seemed to spring from deep within. It wasn't the sort of emotion one could erase. He couldn't tell if she truly understood him.

"Does it bother you that your family won't be here for the wedding?" she asked delicately. "Did you write to them?"

"I wrote my mother, but I doubt she'll ever see it. My father will likely take the letter when it arrives, and she won't go behind his back." It pained Silas, but he suspected that it was easier for him to let go of hope for change than it was for Hannah. Perhaps it came from having spent so much time apart from them. He'd learned from a young age that he could manage on his own. "I'm grateful to have Marian and James with me. That's more than I expected, and they're good people."

Hannah nodded gravely. "I'm glad too. I hope that you'll be very happy with them once I can give you the funds to start your brewery."

"You could be happy with us too." Silas almost didn't say the words. It was a delicate balance, trying to coax Hannah to let go of her fears without pushing her too far. But now that he'd risked it, he had to press on. "I know that you probably didn't imagine yourself married to a man in trade, but there's good profit to be made in Burton. If things go well, we could be living quite comfortably in a few years. You'd get on well with Marian, I think. You both have an independent spirit."

Hannah looked flustered. "I thought we agreed—"

"We did," he assured her quickly. "I won't force you into anything. I just want you to know that you'd be welcome, if you wanted to join us."

It was too soon. He shouldn't have pressed his luck. Hannah's father was calling her impatiently from his carriage, waiting to depart.

"I'll see you in a few days." Silas pressed a chaste kiss to her forehead and took his leave.

The third and final banns were read on Sunday, and Hannah married Mr. Corbyn the following Wednesday.

She wore a white silk gown with lace flounces, and Molly wove a crown of flowers to set above the pins that held her veil in place. It felt like a dream.

But not the kind of dream one waited their whole life to see come true. It mostly felt unreal, as if she might put her hand out to turn a doorknob and have it dissolve into thin air or step forward to fall into an endless hole.

Even Mama was acting strangely, sniffing and dabbing at her eyes as they made ready to leave for the church.

"The wedding hasn't even started yet," Hannah complained. "You're not supposed to cry until we say our vows."

"I was so worried you would never reach this day." Mama was tearing up again. Her handkerchief had seen more use this morning than it had in its entire existence. "I know you think I was too hard on you, but all I ever wanted was to see you happy, poppet. I knew the right man was out there for you somewhere, if only you let yourself believe it."

How could her mother want to see her married this badly when she knew firsthand that their vows didn't mean anything? It didn't make any sense. Hannah might find herself abandoned or miserable within a few years, just like her parents.

But you don't have to worry about that, she reminded herself. Mr. Corbyn had offered terms that would keep her independent. Safe. If Hannah was never a true wife to him, she would never risk her heart. The thought made her feel a little better.

"We should go," Hannah said. She didn't like to see Mama making such a fuss. "Are Jane and Eli ready?"

"Wait. There are some things I should tell you, now that you're going to be a married woman."

"What sort of things?"

"About your wedding night, I mean." Mama spoke rather quickly, as if rushing to get it over with.

Oh no. Hannah hadn't been expecting this, though she supposed she probably should have.

"Once you and Mr. Corbyn are married," her mother continued, staring pointedly at a spot on the wall somewhere past Hannah's left shoulder, "he will want to visit your bed. Probably quite often at first, but don't worry, it will be less frequent as time goes on. It will hurt less if you try to think of something else until it's over. You'll need to let him do what he likes to you if you want to have a child."

"Mama, I know where babies come from!" Hannah blushed furiously.

"Oh. Well, good." Her mother smoothed the wrinkles from her skirt. "Do you...er, have any questions about all that?"

Hannah's most pressing question was: *How do I escape this conversation before I die of embarrassment?*

But wait. If she didn't say anything, whom else could she ask? Now that she thought of it, Mr. Corbyn hadn't actually promised that he wouldn't visit her bed. He'd said no children, but there were other ways to avoid children, weren't there? She wished she'd thought to clarify all of this before her wedding day. These were very important details!

"Is there some way to make sure I don't have a child?"

"Oh." In her surprise, Mama accidentally made eye contact. "Well, if you rinse yourself out with vinegar afterward, that should help. Or if you find that your courses don't come when they should, you might ask the apothecary for some pennyroyal. But you won't need to worry about that until later, poppet. You must want one or two first?"

Oh! Was *that* what Annabelle had meant about herbal remedies? Her cryptic hints suddenly made sense. Good. Hannah could ask her for advice later.

"I don't think so," Hannah replied.

Mama looked crestfallen, but added hopefully, "You might change your mind, as you did about marriage. Give it some time."

They went downstairs together to find the others waiting. Though Papa had grumbled about the match all week and threatened to ride back to Devon a half-dozen times, he was still here for her wedding day. No matter how he might complain, he did care about her. That brought Hannah comfort.

At least until he whispered, "It's not too late to change your mind," when he handed her into the carriage.

Hannah landed on the seat with a thud. Of course it was too late. Mr. Corbyn would already be at the church waiting for them by now. Mama had planned a wedding breakfast for all their friends at Jane's town house afterward, and she'd stayed up half the night arranging the decorations. How could Hannah possibly change her mind?

She and Mr. Corbyn had an understanding. Never mind that the terms were less certain than she might have liked. Whatever her doubts about marriage, Hannah didn't doubt that he would keep his word. This was still the best way to secure her independence.

She murmured some platitudes to her father as the carriage rolled away, and soon they arrived at the church. They were a small party. Hannah's parents, Jane, Eli, and Annabelle—who, as her closest unmarried friend in town, had kindly agreed to be her bridesmaid despite her low opinion of weddings in general. Corbyn's younger brother stood as his groomsman, while his cousin sat with the guests.

The walk from the vestry to the altar seemed to take a year, as if time had slowed in accordance with Hannah's trepidation. Though her father made no further attempt to dissuade her from her choice, his disapproval settled into his bones as he led her down the aisle, as palpable as a brick wall between them. It was a relief when he finally deposited her beside Mr. Corbyn at the altar.

Her groom had worn the blue coat that Hannah liked best, with light gray trousers and a white silk waistcoat. He looked exceptionally handsome, though this was hardly anything new. It was his eyes that were different this morning. They radiated steady reassurance that helped her to forget the awkwardness of her father's sour mood. Something passed between them, some unspoken sentiment that eased Hannah's fears. He looked at her as though she were just as beautiful as he was. Had there really been a time when she'd found Corbyn cold? Blue seemed the warmest color in the world.

Hannah drew a deep breath. She could do this.

The priest began his "Dearly beloved..." innocently enough, but his speech took a more solemn turn when he reached the part about matrimony being an honorable estate, not to be entered into unadvisedly or lightly, but reverently, considering the causes for which is was ordained: the procreation of children and the mutual society and comfort of the husband and wife.

Must he include all of that? It wasn't really any of the priest's business if Hannah lived with her husband or not, so long as she wasn't entertaining other lovers! But the solemnity of the occasion made her feel less certain of her intentions. It was one thing to lie to her mother in the office of a gambling club or Jane's dining room. It was quite another to lie in a solemn vow before the church altar with everyone she cared about looking on.

When they reached the part inviting anyone in the crowd to speak if they knew of an impediment to the marriage, Hannah held her breath. She could practically feel her father's thoughts churning above their heads like a storm cloud. But he held his tongue, and the priest continued on.

"Silas Francis Corbyn, wilt thou have this woman to thy wedded wife, to live together after God's ordinance in the holy estate of matrimony? Wilt thou love her, comfort her, honor, and keep her in sickness and in health; and, forsaking all other, keep thee only unto her, so long as ye both shall live?"

Corbyn's vow was as firm and steady as his eyes. "I will."

He really means it. She'd seen Corbyn lie for her before, though he'd never been particularly good at it. He hadn't meant it when he'd declared his love on Jane's front lawn, nor when he'd promised Mama he would court her like a proper gentleman that night at supper. But no one could deny the conviction in his voice now.

The promise was impossible. To forsake all others for as long as they lived? Even if Hannah decided to live on her own and never see him again? The promise was far too great to equal the three hundred pounds she'd promised him—it encompassed an entire lifetime.

The priest seemed to see right through Hannah as he continued, "Hannah Elizabeth Williams, wilt thou have this man to thy wedded husband, to live together after God's ordinance in the holy estate of matrimony? Wilt thou obey him, and serve him, love, honor and keep him in sickness and in health; and, forsaking all other, keep thee only unto him, so long as ye both shall live?"

You've come this far. Don't back down now.

"I will." Hannah hoped she didn't sound as uncertain as she felt. She'd never been particularly good at obeying and serving, but if she found any meaning in the words, it was in the part to keep only unto him. From their first meeting, Corbyn had shown her an understanding and kindness that she'd never found in another man. If she'd never met him, there would have been no one else for her. He was an exception.

They finished their vows, and Corbyn placed the wedding band upon Hannah's finger, holding her hands steady when they trembled. Though his kiss before the assembled guests was chaste and proper, it summoned a wave of emotion from her heart.

After the priest had prayed over them, Hannah and Corbyn returned to the vestry to sign the certificate with her parents and their witnesses. As she wrote her maiden name for the last time, Hannah was struck by the finality of the act.

There was no going back now. Her course was set.

Nineteen

Mrs. Williams and Jane had prepared everything required for a wedding breakfast the night before, and they received about twenty people at the town house, mostly friends of Mrs. Williams. Silas had met enough of them during his feigned courtship that he didn't feel entirely out of place.

As Silas and Hannah weren't departing on a honeymoon, they dispensed with the usual custom of seeing the newlyweds off shortly after the cake was cut. Instead, Mr. Williams was the first to leave, pleading the need to begin the long voyage back to Devon before the day got too late. Jacob shook Silas's hand and offered his congratulations before he left, though his father couldn't bring himself to do the same. No matter. It was such a relief to be rid of the man that Silas wasn't even annoyed by the snub.

He might have to see Mr. Williams every so often for Hannah's sake, but if the man spent most of his life two hundred miles from this marriage, it would be the perfect distance.

Everyone at the breakfast was a little lighter without him, particularly Mrs. Williams, who smiled and laughed far more than Silas had ever seen her do before.

"Should we warn her that I'm not buying a commission?" he murmured to Hannah during a brief lull in the activity.

She observed her mother for a moment. "Let her enjoy the day. She's been waiting for this for twenty-one years. I'll tell her later."

Once they'd passed about two hours receiving their guests, Hannah began to show signs of fatigue and Silas offered to take her back to his lodgings. She'd probably had enough of crowds to last her until next year.

Mrs. Williams said her farewells with tears in her eyes. "Are you sure you wouldn't rather I came with you, poppet? What if you need my help?"

"No, no, we've been over this," Hannah insisted. "Jane and Eli need you far more than I do to watch Gloria in the evenings. And I'm only across the Thames, not the Atlantic."

"You'll visit often, though?"

"I promise." Though Hannah squirmed in her mother's embrace, her own eyes looked a little bright.

"You'll take care of her for me, Mr. Corbyn." Mrs. Williams dabbed at her tears with a handkerchief.

Silas assured her that he would, then ushered Hannah to their carriage. She collapsed gratefully against the seat, soaking up the silence. It looked like she could use the rest. Silas didn't like to disturb her, so he observed Hannah quietly for a moment from his side of the carriage as they began the ride home.

She'd leaned her head back against the leather seat and closed her eyes, her veil trailing behind her like a pillow. She looked lovely. Silas felt a possessive sort of pleasure to see the opal necklace he'd given her resting just below the hollow of her throat, where her heartbeat pulsed gently. They were finally alone. He wanted to put his mouth there, but judged it wiser to be patient. He had all the time in the world now.

My wife.

He'd never given much thought to the possibility of marriage before he'd met Hannah. After all, what use was a wife before one had a fortune to support her? But the risk that she might have refused him had shaken Silas to his core. It still did. There had been a moment in the church just before the priest called for objections when he'd honestly wondered if something might still happen to snatch her away. If someone might realize that he wasn't fit to stand beside a woman this fine.

But they didn't. She's mine now.

Silas had no sooner thought the words than he began to question them. They were married in name, but Hannah's vow meant little if she'd only given it on the understanding that she would stay behind when he went to Burton.

I'm hers then, he amended. If she held herself back, he would give enough for both of them until she decided she was better off with Silas than without him. He could show Hannah the advantages to being his wife.

A footman had already brought over most of her things while they were at breakfast, so that they found a small tower of chests and trunks in the entrance when they arrived. James and Marian must have let the servants into the apartments. Silas thought he'd noticed his brother slip away early from the breakfast, though neither of them were here now.

"Where has your family gone?" Hannah echoed his thoughts.

"I'm not sure. Probably they wanted to give us a little time alone to get settled in."

Hannah looked at him with mild alarm. Was she worried for the wedding night? Recalling how instinctively she'd reacted to his touch, Silas suspected things would be easy enough between them in bed. He'd been imagining it rather vividly since that evening on the balcony. She wanted him, whether she was bold enough to admit it or not. But that didn't mean that he could afford to proceed too rashly. It was important not to scare her off.

Hannah took a few light steps down the hall, then stopped to peer at her surroundings. She looked too elegant for this place in her lace dress and veil. The house was tidy and respectable enough for something this side of the water, but it wasn't Mayfair. "Where will I be sleeping?" she asked timidly.

"My bedroom is the last one on the right."

"Yes, but where is my bedroom?"

Oh.

They stared at each other for a long minute before Silas replied, "There are only two bedrooms. I was sharing with James until today, but he's moved his things to the sitting room now that you're here. Marian has the other."

Hannah's eyes widened, though she didn't speak.

She probably didn't know any married couples who shared a room. Her parents couldn't stand to be near each other, and most of her circle must be so wealthy that they had no need to squeeze together like sardines.

Idiot. You should have realized a woman of her class wouldn't expect to share.

"It won't be forever," he said quickly. "We can rent a larger house in Burton."

"But I won't be going," Hannah reminded him. "I want to stay in London and work at Jane's club."

"I know. I only meant—" Silas wasn't sure how to finish his thought. What had he meant? That he hoped Hannah would change her mind and stay by his side? If he pressed her, she might feel like he was going back on his word. The choice needed to be hers. "Would you like me to bring your things in?" he offered.

"Thank you, Mr. Corbyn."

"You're not going to call me that even now that we're married, are you?" Silas paused halfway through the act of removing his jacket.

"It's your name. What else should I call you?"

"Silas, of course. Or simply Corbyn, if you must, but not 'mister.' At least not when we're alone."

Silas bent to lift the first trunk. Hannah followed him into their bedroom, where he set it down near the wardrobe with a heavy thud. There were more gowns inside than they had room for, most of them far too fine for this part of town, which mostly belonged to publicans, brewers, and tradesmen. He left Hannah to arrange things to her satisfaction while he brought in the rest. It became clear after about a quarter hour that most of her things were going to have to remain packed away, but she organized the essentials in the space that he'd cleared for her.

"Would you like to rest a while?" Silas offered as she neared the end of her task. "You seemed tired after the breakfast."

Hannah cast a longing look toward the bed, then back to Silas, her face growing pink. "I–I don't…"

"I wouldn't expect anything you aren't ready for," he assured her, remembering her look of panic earlier. "You can just sleep for an hour or two if that's what you'd like."

But she only pressed her lips together and wrung her hands.

"What is it? What's wrong?"

Hannah replied in a whisper, though there was no one around to overhear them. "I can't get undressed."

"I beg your pardon?" Silas asked. "I can leave the room if you want privacy." Though he would have far rather stayed, they might not have reached such intimate terms yet.

"No, I mean I *can't* get undressed. I've always had a lady's maid, but I was sharing one with my mother while we were traveling and

I didn't think to ask you to hire someone for me here, with how quickly we decided to be married. All the buttons are at the back, and then after that there are my stays, and I can't..." Her voice trailed off helplessly.

Silas fought with all his might not to smile. She was distressed, and it would be rude to find any pleasure in this. Even if the problem had a very obvious, very gratifying solution.

He put on his most serious face as he offered, "Shall I help you?"

The noise Hannah made was an incoherent sort of nonword, but Silas could only take it for an assent. What other choice did she have? It was either this or wait for Marian to get back and ask her for help, however long that might be. Though Silas was determined to be respectful, he wasn't so gallant that he would suggest that possibility if she hadn't asked for it.

He circled Hannah as cautiously as if he were trying not to spook a skittish animal, coming to stop behind her back. She removed the crown of pink carnations from her hair and undid the hairpins herself so that she could remove her veil, which she folded neatly away into one of her trunks. Her dark hair hung loose down her back by the time she'd finished. Silas's breath hitched in his chest.

There was something so unguarded about the sight of Hannah this way that he almost couldn't bring himself to touch her, even as he ached to do so. He wanted to unwrap all her trappings and ribbons like the most long-awaited present, but he also wanted to make this moment last as long as possible. It was a tantalizing problem.

Silas finally settled on moving very slowly, which seemed to be the safest option given that he was already growing far too aroused at the sight before him. He began by stroking a hand through Hannah's hair, memorizing the softness of it between his fingers as he brushed the strands carefully over her left shoulder to expose the buttons on her gown.

There was a great number of them. Little silk-covered nubs that slipped and eluded his grasp, clearly made for a lady's hands.

I will not be bested by buttons.

Silas applied himself with methodical determination, working his way down the row as each one yielded a little more of Hannah's body to his sight. He counted thirty before he reached the small of her back, that enticing curve that seemed to be begging for his palm. He didn't let himself give in to the impulse. It was strangely satisfying to know that he could push himself to the edge of temptation without losing his self-control.

Silas wouldn't touch Hannah unless she asked him to.

"Can you step out of the gown now?" His voice came out hoarse.

"I think so." Why were they speaking so quietly when they were alone? It made the exchange feel like a secret. But this was his wife. There was no reason to be ashamed of undressing her.

Silas tugged one shoulder, easing the white silk down Hannah's arm until she was halfway out, then repeated the motion on the other side. Once her arms were free, he helped her pull the wedding dress over her head and put it carefully away. They stood facing each other when they'd finished, equally unsure how to proceed. It was strange. Silas had been with women before, but he'd never attended to one with such drawn-out care. It felt unexpectedly new.

"The petticoats next," Hannah whispered. "And then I should be able to do the camisole myself."

He saw to the ties at the back of the petticoats—all four of them—which were stiff and cumbersome to peel away. Once they were gone, Hannah lost the dramatic bell-shaped silhouette she'd worn all day and began to resemble a natural woman. He couldn't help but stare, longing to run his hands around the curves of her hips. So this was what she looked like without her armor.

When Hannah reached for the buttons to the camisole, Silas entreated, "Let me."

She swallowed, the movement of her throat the only sign that she'd heard him. There was no reason for him to do this part. The camisole that covered her corset did up in the front and was one of the few things Hannah could reach without assistance. But Silas had started this task and he intended to finish it. The hum of excitement in his chest grew stronger with every layer, calling him onward.

Hannah must have noticed what she was doing to him. He could hardly hide it. But if it bothered her, surely she would have told Silas to stop. Instead, she watched him cautiously, some message passing between them without the need for speech. A question asked and answered.

Without breaking his gaze, Hannah lowered her hands, leaving the buttons of her camisole untouched.

Yes.

Silas drew up to his wife until they were bare inches apart, looking her in the eye for a long moment before he let his gaze skim deliberately down her throat, over the swell of her breasts, to where the camisole fastened over her corset. He undid the buttons very slowly, taking care not to touch any part of Hannah that wasn't strictly necessary. It was enough to have this and no more.

She brought her hands up to pull the camisole away herself, trembling slightly as she did. Was it nervousness or desire? Silas wished she would tell him plainly how much he might dare.

"I can't do the stays." She turned her back to him once more, and he undid the laces to her corset with hands that had begun to tremble. God, she was perfect. He inhaled deeply, as if her rosewater might fill the hole yawning inside him. When they'd managed to maneuver the rigid whalebone off her, Hannah was at last down to nothing but her shift and stockings. "Thank you."

She made no move to step away, and neither did Silas. They stood frozen there for a long moment.

Finally, he ventured, "Would you let me do the rest?"

Hannah's eyes widened. "I–I don't need help for this part."

"I know."

She glanced downward toward the evidence of his arousal. "Do you expect me to—to fulfill my wifely duties?"

His lips twitched. What an unappealing way to word it. "I told you, I won't ask you for anything you aren't prepared to give. If you want me to leave you in peace to rest, say the word and I'll go. Only say it soon, please." He wasn't sure how much longer his restraint would hold.

"I want—" Hannah broke off, though whether she was unwilling to tell him or didn't rightly know what she wanted was hard to tell. "May I be honest with you?"

"Please."

"When you're very near me this way, I find it hard to think clearly. I sometimes think I might want you to touch me the way you did before, but I'm also worried it might hurt, and most of all, that I might get in a family way. You promised we wouldn't have children."

"Ah." It was all Silas could do not to give in to his desire right then. But she wanted reassurance first. He needed to stay steady. Just a little longer. "There can be some pain the first time I'm inside you, but there's no need for that tonight. If I don't go inside you at all, it's impossible to get with child." Much as he might have liked to bed Hannah, it was plain she wasn't ready. Better to take the time he needed to earn her trust than to lose it forever.

"You don't mind?" Hannah eyed him with suspicion.

"I understood you had reservations when you agreed to marry me. I wouldn't hold them against you now." Silas paused, letting her see that he meant it. "Would you trust me enough to let me touch you? It won't hurt. In fact, there are plenty of things we could do without any risk of a child."

"If you're very sure you can avoid any accidents." There was a trace of a question in Hannah's voice, reminding him to be careful with her. "Then yes."

The relief that flooded Silas was far too deep for such a small word. *Yes.* He bent his head to kiss her neck as he fumbled for the buttons on the bodice of her shift, his restraint crumbling away in bits and pieces. *Yes, yes, yes.*

He would make this perfect for Hannah. He had to.

Hannah let Corbyn lead her to the bed. He did everything so slowly that it was almost hypnotic, just as it had been when he'd undressed her earlier. His methodical, steady command of her desires was exactly what she wanted now.

Hannah had only the vaguest notion of what she was supposed to do, gleaned from the knowing whispers of married friends who'd deemed it improper to give her enough detail to be actually useful. She rather wished that someone had told her how she was supposed to touch a man or what she should expect once they had their clothes off. But Corbyn's methodical attention reassured her. He could take the lead, and she would gladly follow.

As much as she'd been nervous at first, she trusted him. He'd seen her through so much already; he wouldn't break his word.

Corbyn slid the hem of her shift up her legs, his fingertips grazing her body as he went. He'd been so gentlemanly in the earlier stages of her déshabillement that she found herself nearly ready to beg for his touch. She squirmed against him, longing for more, but he took his time tugging her shift over her head and moving down to her drawers, which he tugged open in a controlled but insistent motion. Once Hannah was naked except for her stockings, he laid her down upon the coverlet and climbed atop the bed after her.

Hannah should have felt embarrassed to let a man see her this way. Even her own husband. But the look of pure desire darkening Corbyn's eyes had her riveted in place. He ran his hands up her calf, beginning at the ankle and inching his way higher, until he found the ribbon that tied her stocking in place and pulled it free. He peeled the fabric away from her skin so gingerly that Hannah shivered. The whole time he'd been undressing her, she'd kept wondering when he would put his hands on her bare skin. She'd leaned toward him several times on pure instinct, but he'd always held back. Now that his hands were finally upon her, Hannah understood why. It was electric.

She might not want to risk getting in a family way, but she most definitely wanted this, the thrill he was always able to summon from her body when he was near. Corbyn was devouring her with his eyes, and then, very soon after, devouring her with his hands and mouth as well, running his hands up her hips, over her belly, and coming to rest on her breasts, where he caressed her nipple the same way he had on the balcony at the Brandons' ball.

Hannah gasped at the sudden heat that flooded her. She wanted to pleasure him too. She'd spent her entire life in ignorance, believing she would never experience anything like this.

"Should I undress you too?"

"No." He tugged the buttons to his waistcoat open in a hurried motion and was out of the garment a moment later. "I used up most of my patience earlier. Besides, I'm not used to a valet."

It didn't take long. For all that Corbyn had been slow and gentle in undressing her, he was rough and impatient with himself, pulling the clothes off so quickly that she worried for their integrity. Once they were both naked, he lay down on top of her, supporting most of his weight on his elbows. Only then did he kiss her on the mouth. His tongue pressed into her insistently, taking his pleasure.

Hannah whimpered, overwhelmed by sensations. His body was coarser than hers, and the feeling of his chest pressed against her was so unfamiliar that it drove her to distraction. His cock was hard against her thigh. Was she supposed to be able to fit all of that inside of her?

No, she reminded herself. *He promised we wouldn't.*

But when he kissed her that way and pressed his body against hers, Hannah found that she wished he would. Her resolve had been so much stronger when they were fully dressed. No matter what her mind knew was best for her, her body seemed to have an entirely different idea.

Corbyn leaned partly onto his side in order to slip a hand in between their tangle of bodies and pressed it gently against her sex.

"Oh!" Her cry of surprise made him hesitate, which hadn't been her intent at all. "Don't stop," she pleaded.

"Tell me if it's too much for you," he murmured, his voice little more than a rumbling breeze against her neck. Then he slipped his fingers inside of her.

She froze at the unfamiliar sensation, at once too much and not enough. Corbyn's fingers were rough and callused where she was most sensitive, but she found that only heightened her excitement. He moved gently but firmly, coaxing a wave of pleasure through her body.

"You're so wet," he groaned.

Hannah blushed. The embarrassment she'd escaped thus far had finally caught up with her. "Is that unseemly?"

"It's good," he assured her. "You have no idea what you're doing to me."

I should have some idea, she thought indignantly. *I am your wife, after all.*

She wished she'd been able to learn more about this. Remembering the way Corbyn had placed her hand on his arousal the other night on the balcony, Hannah wondered if she shouldn't touch him as well. If it felt this good for her, it stood to reason that it might also feel good for him, didn't it? She slid her hand down beside his and reached until she brushed the tip of his member, which sent a very gratifying shudder through Corbyn's body. Yes, he certainly seemed to like that.

Hannah took him in her grip and explored the shape, marveling at the feel of him. Considering how hard it felt, his skin was quite soft. And he was wet too, beading with liquid at the tip that slicked the way for her hand. She hadn't expected that.

"Please." The plea that escaped Corbyn's mouth was something entirely new. His voice had grown thick and heavy, as if he were a little drunk. What a thrill it was to think that she had done that to him!

"What should I do?" Hannah wanted to push him further, to give him what he obviously needed, but she felt clumsy and unsure of herself.

"Faster," he urged. "Like this." Corbyn wrapped his hand around hers and began to stroke together, guiding her to a brisk pace. His breath picked up speed as well, coming in halting gasps as she moved. He seemed to be very excited now.

Once Hannah had got the hang of it, he released her hand and returned to pleasuring her, but this time his movements had lost some of their careful precision. He seemed scarcely able to control himself as he slid his fingers back into her, driving an aching pressure against the source of her desire. Hannah didn't mind the change. Anything Corbyn had lost in caution was more than made up for in his eagerness. There was something unbearably arousing in knowing that he was just as lost in his pleasure as she was. That she had the proof of his desire gripped in her palm, entirely at her disposal. Hannah understood then that he was very close, and that he was trying his utmost to bring her with him.

He was succeeding.

Hannah lost track of herself as her climax overtook her. She heard a cry and recognized her own voice, though she hadn't intended to make it. A moment later, Corbyn's answering gasp and a liquid heat on her belly told her that she'd succeeded too. He collapsed beside her, and for several minutes neither of them did anything but catch their breath. Hannah didn't think she had the power to move yet. She was still trying to wrap her mind around what had just happened. It was very different from her own explorations.

Corbyn was the first to rise, and he fetched a cloth to clean themselves with. When he'd finished, he bent to kiss her again, moving with such deliberate care that Hannah marveled at his self-possession. She still felt as if she were underwater, her limbs too warm and heavy to obey her commands at a normal speed. She opened to him, letting Corbyn explore her mouth for as long as he desired. He was really very good at this, though she supposed she didn't have any basis for comparison. But surely men couldn't all kiss this way, or no one would do anything else! No, he must have a talent for it. She was persuaded.

Corbyn inched his kiss down her neck, finally bringing his face to her breast and teasing her nipple with his tongue.

"What are you doing?" Hannah shivered as an echo of her climax crept through her body. "I thought you'd finished."

"But you haven't."

"Yes, I have," she protested weakly. It was very hard to think clearly when he kept doing that.

"No," he insisted. "You've only just started." The promise in

Corbyn's voice nearly undid her. He increased the pace of his atten-
tions until Hannah squirmed beneath him, her whole body growing hot. Though she'd been thoroughly satisfied only a few minutes
before, Corbyn was coaxing her back to restlessness.

He trailed his mouth down her body, kissing his way over her
until he settled between her legs, where he drew back to look at
her sex.

It was all Hannah could do to watch as her husband bowed his
head and kissed her there, without a trace of shame.

She wanted to ask what he could mean by such a thing, but she
found that her throat was paralyzed. The only sound that escaped
her was a desperate whimper. It felt even better than what he'd done
with his fingers. Her self-control was drowning in a warm, rocking
current, powerless to fight the sensations Corbyn had summoned
from her. Before Hannah knew what she was doing, she arched her
hips toward the pressure of his tongue, moaning as he licked and
teased her toward the edge once more.

How was he so good at this?

"Please," she pleaded. "There."

He made a little sound of satisfaction in response, his lips humming against her. Hannah was growing quite desperate now. She
reached her hand down to grasp Corbyn's shoulder. She felt increasingly untethered, as if she might drift away without him. Corbyn
might have sensed it too, for he gripped her hips as he pressed deeper,
steadying her against the onslaught on her senses.

Hannah cried out. Her pleasure was different this time—a deeper
release that left her feeling raw and shaken. It was all she could do
to remember her own name afterward. Everything else had been
washed away.

She'd been so overpowered that she didn't notice Corbyn move
until he was already beside her. He nudged Hannah gently onto her

side (she was so limp with exhaustion that she was as easily manip-
ulated as a rag doll), and tucked himself into the space behind her
back, surrounding her with his body.

"Sleep for a while," he whispered into her temple. "You must be
tired."

Hannah wanted to thank him, but she couldn't even summon
the words before she drifted away, her thoughts fragmenting into
disjointed snippets.

Twenty

SILAS AWOKE BEFORE HANNAH THE NEXT MORNING. IN THE first minutes before he'd fully shaken off his dreams, he'd been surprised to find another person in bed with him, pressed neatly against his side. Then he remembered.

It was real. She was his wife now.

Should I bring her breakfast? Don't wealthy ladies usually take their breakfast in bed? He'd taken a light meal yesterday evening after their lovemaking, but Hannah had slept soundly through the rest of the night. She would be hungry when she awoke.

Silas crept out from the covers and dressed himself as quietly as he could manage, turning to check that Hannah still slept before he left the room. She looked peaceful.

Once Silas reached the kitchen and began fumbling for the kettle, James lumbered up from the pile of blankets he'd set out for himself in the next room.

"Sorry," Silas murmured. "I tried to be quiet. Did you sleep all right?"

"As well as could be expected," his brother replied without much enthusiasm. "I'll be glad to have my own bed again. How soon can we go to Burton?"

Silas spilled some water when he moved the kettle too suddenly, uttering a curse under his breath. "There's no rush. Marian said this place was paid up until the end of the month."

"I'm not sleeping two more weeks on the floor," James protested.

"Shh. Hannah's still sleeping."

James obliged him by whispering when he replied. "Walker wrote Marian that he'd spoken to the owner of a good place near the wharf. The sooner we get there, the sooner we can set up shop."

"When did this happen?" He'd known the brewmaster that James and Marian had left behind when they came to London had been looking into some premises for them, but his cousin hadn't mentioned they'd already settled on one.

I thought I had more time.

"A few days ago."

"And you didn't tell me?"

"Marian said she didn't want you to feel more obliged to get the money than you already did."

"That's right," Marian piped in from the doorway to her bedroom. She was dressed for the day, but her bleary eyes said that she wasn't quite awake yet. "And I won't hear any complaints about it. You took care of what you had to, and I've been taking care of what I had to. The last thing you needed was something else to worry about the day before your wedding."

"You should have told me," Silas muttered.

"What difference does it make?" James screwed up his face in confusion. "We're telling you now."

"I'm not ready to leave London yet. I need a little more time to—" He broke off awkwardly, reluctant to confess the truth of his situation. It was no secret that he and Hannah had married for mutual

convenience, but he hadn't gone into the full extent of it. In all honesty, he hadn't wanted to think of it more than he had to.

"To what?" James pressed.

He might as well tell them. He had to explain why he couldn't
pack up and leave town at the drop of a hat. "To persuade Hannah
to come with us."

Marian came into the kitchen, her worry plain on her face. "You
haven't told her we're setting up the brewery in Burton?"

"No, she knows that," Silas amended. "But she wants to stay in
London and work at her sister-in-law's club while we go on without
her."

"What's wrong with that?" James frowned. "So long as she keeps
to her end and gives you the money she promised, let her stay where
she likes. We'll be too busy for you to have time for a wife, anyway.
This way we can focus on the business."

"I don't want her to stay behind. I want her to live with me," Silas
confessed. He felt a little childish saying the words out loud. James
was right—they would have their hands full in the first few years. It
would make sense to leave Hannah behind until they were established, especially if that was what she truly wanted.

But what *Silas* wanted was Hannah. By his side each day and
in his bed each night. He wanted her gentle way of listening and
her determined spirit. He wanted months and years to explore each
other the way they had last night. Not memories to look back on
when they'd grown apart, too afraid to admit there was a real attachment between them.

He knew Hannah wanted that too. At least on some level. She was
just too frightened by what had happened to her parents to admit it.

"You want to stay behind in London? But what about the brewery?" James plainly hadn't understood anything.

"No. I still want to start a brewery with you." They were counting on him. And after so many years relying only on himself, Silas couldn't give up the chance to be near family again. But Hannah was his family too now, as much as Marian and James. He couldn't leave her behind. If he did, what if she realized she didn't need him anymore? "I need a little more time, that's all. If I can win her trust, I know I could persuade her to come with us. Give me a few weeks. The rent's already paid for that long."

It was Marian he needed to convince, more than James. She'd always been the guiding mind behind their plans. But she didn't seem to be listening to him. She was looking past his shoulder, her eyes widening slightly at what she saw.

Silas turned. Hannah had come out into the hallway, dressed in a heavy wrapper and breakfast cap to preserve her modesty. She had clearly heard everything.

She looked at Silas for a long moment, then turned and went back into their bedroom without saying a word. *Damn it. What have I done?* He hurried after her.

"Hannah, that wasn't what it sounded like."

She was sorting through her clothes when he walked in, her back turned to him. She didn't stop to look when he spoke, but continued to set out her corset and a green silk gown upon the bed. He wished she would say something.

"Do you think Marian would mind helping me into my corset? I can't go out unless I'm properly dressed, and I can't do it myself."

"Hannah."

She finally turned away from the gown she'd set out. When she turned to him, there was muted hurt in her dark eyes. "I thought we had an understanding."

"We did. We still do. I'm not forcing you into anything."

"No. You just wanted to win my trust so that you could persuade me to give up on my plans."

Silas winced. He would have worded things differently if he'd known she was listening. "You're making it sound like I tried to trick you, but it wasn't that. I wouldn't take advantage."

"But you hoped I would change my mind, even though I'd told you what I wanted."

"Is that so wrong?" he challenged. "I want to live under the same roof as my wife, that's all."

"Then why not tell me how you felt? Why pretend that I could buy a property and live separately if you never meant it?"

"Because I knew you would never have me otherwise. You were so worried about turning out like your parents that you needed some reassurance, so I gave it to you." This was ridiculous. Was she angry at him for admiring her? "Nothing has changed," he tried to explain. "You can still stay in London if you want to. I just...hope you'll reconsider."

"Why?" She shook her head. "You have everything you need now. I know there's a certain connection between us, but there's no need to let that dictate the rest of our lives. I want my independence. I told Jane I'd help at her club and that's what I intend to do, while you want to start your brewery. It makes perfect sense for us to part ways."

"A certain connection?" he echoed, trying not to be insulted and failing. "Hannah, I love you."

The words hung in the air for several minutes.

I shouldn't have said that. Silas had never made such a declaration before, but he was fairly sure it wasn't supposed to take this long for a woman to say it back, if she were going to. Hannah didn't look overjoyed or even flattered. She didn't smile. If anything, she looked more than a little worried, as if he'd revealed that he owed a large debt or suffered from some serious affliction.

"I should go call on my mother," she finally murmured. "I need to tell her the truth about your plans for the army before you go to Burton, and it will be worse if I put it off."

"Let me speak to her. I can fight my own battles."

"No. It will be better coming from me."

"At least have some breakfast first. You haven't eaten."

"I can eat something there."

She was running away, but Silas didn't know how to keep her here. Anytime he tried to cling to Hannah, she fought that much harder to slip from his grasp. How was he supposed to make her want something that didn't come from her own heart?

Perhaps there was no solution. She was too determined to escape the prison that had trapped her parents to imagine another possibility, and Silas wouldn't become her jailer. If Hannah's feelings for him were as strong as his own, he wouldn't need to persuade her. She would have wanted to stay.

Silas wasn't about to beg. There was nothing he could do but let her go.

Hannah scarcely knew how she reached Jane and Eli's town house. She felt as though she were floating somewhere outside of herself.

He loves me.

How could Corbyn love her? She wasn't the sort of woman who inspired love or passion; she was perfectly forgettable. Four years' worth of suitors hadn't seen anything to love about her—not that she'd given them much encouragement, Hannah had to admit. But all the same, there must have been at least fifty of them, if she counted every hapless fool her mother had pressed into a dance with her. Not one had grown besotted. Surely that said something about Hannah's charms (or lack thereof).

If Corbyn had been born a little richer or with a family pedigree, he might have had any lady he chose. He was handsome and ambitious and showed kindness to a woman in need. His strength was tempered by a keen sense of justice—a rare combination.

It was one thing for a man like that to desire her. But love, when he might instead have his freedom? Hannah couldn't understand it.

It was too early for a morning call, and everyone was still at breakfast in their rooms when she arrived at the town house.

"Please don't disturb everyone on my account, Molly," she instructed the maid at the door. "I'm only here to see my mother for a few minutes."

"She hasn't yet come down, ma'am."

That's right. Hannah was a ma'am now, not a miss. It felt strange.

"I'll see her in her room. I'm sure she won't mind." Hannah had walked the path to the guest bedrooms a hundred times since they'd arrived in London. She still felt like a guest, not a visitor. "And could you please bring me up something to eat?"

Mama still had her hair tied in curls beneath her breakfast cap. When she saw Hannah, she sat up straight in her bed, nearly upsetting the tray of food. "What are you doing here? Has something happened?"

"I'm perfectly well," Hannah assured her. "I just wanted to talk to you."

"You should be with Mr. Corbyn now," her mother scolded. "You're newlyweds. Did you have a quarrel already?"

"No!" Having one's husband confess his love certainly didn't qualify as a quarrel, even if it had put Hannah all of a dither. "I need to tell you something, that's all."

Molly came in with some hot rolls and marmalade for Hannah, who took a few bites and waited for the servant to leave the room before she continued. "He isn't going to buy a commission. He never was. He only went along with your suggestion because I asked him to try to impress you."

Mama's eyes betrayed her shock first, while her mouth took a little longer to catch up. "Not buy a commission? But he must! You agreed to marry an officer, poppet, not a nobody."

"He isn't a nobody," Hannah protested. "Don't talk about him that way."

Mama's tone softened slightly. "I've come to like Mr. Corbyn. Truly. But he has an obligation to provide you with the best life he's able, and a commission in the army is the only thing that would restore some respectability to his reputation. Unless he plans to use the money to buy a living instead? Does he wish to join the Church?" Her face fell a moment later. "No, I don't suppose his education would allow it."

"He's going to Burton upon Trent to start a brewery with his family," Hannah explained.

"A brewery? Oh, poppet, really, you must make him see reason. Tell him that he owes it to you to find a respectable station. Or if you won't tell him, then I will."

"You will do no such thing." The image of Mama descending on their lodgings in Southwark to complain in front of Corbyn's brother and cousin filled Hannah with dread. "The matter is already settled; I agreed to it before we married. I only came to tell you so that you wouldn't be surprised."

Mama looked hurt. "Why would you keep something like that from me?"

"Because I knew you wouldn't approve." Oh dear. Now she was sounding like Corbyn had this morning. "You can be very hard to please, you know. But none of the respectable men that you wanted me to marry cared one whit for me! Mr. Corbyn may not be wealthy or well-to-do, but he—"

He loves me. Hannah stopped before she said the words aloud.

Mama didn't seem to have noticed the abrupt end to her speech.

"But Staffordshire is so *far*. You always said you wanted to stay close to home. Somewhere in the south."

"I will be in the south," Hannah said numbly. "I've decided to stay in London and help at Jane's club while he goes north with his family."

She was hardly listening to her own words. Corbyn really loved her. The when and why of it didn't matter if the feelings were true. And she'd been cross with him simply because he hadn't wanted to be separated.

"Why should you want to do that? You're his wife. Your place is by his side." If Mama had been angered by the revelation that her new son-in-law would never be an officer, this new information seemed only to have perplexed her.

Of all people!

"There's nothing strange about it. You don't live with Papa," Hannah pointed out.

"Poppet…" Mama drew a shaky breath. "That's entirely different. You and Mr. Corbyn will fare better than your father and I."

"How do you know that?" How could anyone know that? No one expected when they exchanged their vows that they would be miserable together, but it happened all the same, and then where would Hannah be?

Mama's voice had grown far softer than it had been a minute ago. She spoke each word as if taking care that it should reach Hannah's ears gently. "Because Mr. Corbyn is a different sort of man than your father. He loves you, and you love him."

"Didn't you love Papa once?"

Mama dropped her gaze, nudging her food absently around her plate. "You know I don't like to talk about this sort of thing with you children, but if you insist on asking, then I suppose I thought I did. People grow apart sometimes. I didn't know him very well when

I accepted his offer, and our differences became more noticeable with time."

"What if I don't know Mr. Corbyn very well yet either?" Hannah insisted. "What if we grow apart? How can you expect me to trust my future to a man who might come to dislike me in a few years?"

Mama was silent for a long time. Her dark-brown eyes were pleading. "Hannah, I wish I knew how to reassure you. I tried to keep the peace with your father for a long time before I removed to town, but I simply couldn't manage it anymore. That doesn't mean that *your* marriage can't be a happy one. Is this why you tried so hard to discourage all your suitors? Because of your father and me?"

Hannah didn't reply. It would only hurt Mama if she agreed, and besides, Hannah could recognize now that she might have been a bit too hard on her for leaving Papa. He'd done his part to drive her away. Hannah had been too hurt and angry to see it at the time, but her father's behavior at supper showed how little he valued his marriage.

"There must be a reason that you said yes to Mr. Corbyn, when you were never tempted by anyone else," Mama continued. "You chose him as your husband. You can just as easily choose to try your best to be happy together, if both of you are willing to make an effort to be kind. Has he been kind to you?"

Hannah thought about how Corbyn had agreed not to have children when she'd expressed her fears; how he had devoted their wedding night to her pleasure without demanding anything in return; and how he'd insisted that the solicitor draft a settlement that provided any property bought with her dowry would be for her sole use.

"Yes."

Mama smiled, relief taking some of the tension from her shoulders. "Well then. You must resolve to be kind to him as well. That's all anyone can do."

Hannah wasn't sure she'd been kind this morning. All Corbyn wanted was to live with her, and she'd panicked at the suggestion.

"You make it sound easy, but if it were truly that easy, everyone would have a happy marriage."

"I think it must be easy when you're a kind person to start with, which you are, and when your husband is willing to be kind to you in return, which Mr. Corbyn is. So you're lucky. Now go back home to your husband."

"You're not angry he's going to be a brewery owner instead of an officer?"

"Of course I am." Mama clucked her tongue. "But you've never listened to me about anything before, so I suppose I can hardly expect you to start now. You're a married woman. You and your husband will have to decide for yourselves what's best."

Well. This day is full of surprises.

Hannah popped the last bite of her hot roll into her mouth and set the tray on an end table.

"Thank you, Mama." She leaned over to wrap her arms around her mother's neck and pull her into a quick hug.

"You're welcome." Mama looked a bit flustered—it had been ages since Hannah had last hugged her, and she probably didn't quite know what to do—but she seemed pleased all the same. "Remember how grateful you are when it's time for you to come all the way to London from Burton upon Trent for a visit!"

Hannah took her leave and hurried back to the lodgings in Southwark, feeling quite awful about how she'd left. She shouldn't have rushed off that way. All Corbyn had done was treat her well, and here she couldn't even let herself trust that he meant it. She'd probably hurt him, though he didn't deserve to be punished for her parents' mistakes.

When Hannah came into the kitchen, she found all three of them in the middle of a conversation that broke off when they saw her. She blushed, feeling very foolish for her behavior earlier with everyone watching her.

Corbyn was the first to break the silence. "Is your mother well?"

"Yes." At least she had some good news to share. "She's not happy to learn about the brewery, but she seems to understand. I think you shouldn't have to hear mention of the subject more than once or twice in your life."

Hannah smiled tentatively, but no one chuckled. Perhaps it was premature to try and lighten the mood before she'd addressed Corbyn's concerns.

"Might I speak to you for a moment?" she asked.

He murmured his assent and led the way to his bedroom—their bedroom, she reminded herself. He looked so solemn that Hannah realized that he must think she was planning to pack up her things and leave this instant. Could she blame him, after how she'd reacted?

But before she could open her mouth to set things right, Corbyn began to speak. "I had something I wanted to tell you too."

"No, let me go first, please," she insisted. God forbid it should be plans to separate their households immediately. "I'm sorry I reacted badly this morning. I shouldn't have run off like that. I was frightened."

Corbyn blinked. He clearly hadn't expected this.

"The truth is I—" Hannah swallowed. Why did it have to be so hard for her? Corbyn seemed able to do it easily enough. "I love you too." As she forced the words out, Hannah found herself tearing up. She blinked furiously, trying not to turn into an embarrassing mess before she could finish what she needed to say. "You've been good to me, even before we knew each other. You made me feel like I mattered when no one else would. You've never given me a reason to distrust you, and if I did it anyway, it was only because it's hard for me to believe that I could really have a happy marriage with a good man. I spent a very long time struggling to escape a bad match, and I wasn't used to hoping for better." There. Now Corbyn knew how much he meant to her. *Oh, wait! I missed the most important thing!* "And I'll come to Burton with you if you still want me to," she blurted out.

But Corbyn made a regretful half grimace with his lips. "Actually—"

"I was scarcely gone an hour!" she protested. "You can't have given up on me that quickly!"

"No." He chuckled. "I was going to say that I talked it over with Marian, and we're considering setting up our brewery in London instead of going back to Burton. We've been making connections with a number of the local brewery managers and publicans these past few weeks, so it isn't as though we'd be starting with nothing. The primary reason Marian intended to go back was to show my grandfather and my brother that she was capable of beating them at their own game, which I pointed out wasn't the soundest basis for a business." Corbyn offered Hannah a sheepish smile. "And this way you could still work at the club as you'd planned. I thought you might feel better about living together if you didn't have to give up your independence entirely."

If Hannah had been fighting back her emotions before, this was enough to tip the scales in their favor. She had no choice but to dab at her eyes before her cheeks grew wet. "You'd really do that for me? I don't want to disrupt your plans."

"I told you, we've been making connections in town this whole time. There's no real disadvantage to it. Frankly, I'd rather stay here than go back to Burton, where I'd be sure to cross paths with my father. It was only a matter of convincing Marian, which wasn't too difficult considering that London offers the largest market."

Hannah threw her arms around Corbyn's neck, holding him tight. She could hear the satisfaction in his voice as he continued, "We can still see about getting you property of your own somewhere if you want. You might rent it out, and that way you'd have another source of income as well as a place of your own if you ever wanted it."

"We can talk about that later." She wanted a little time to examine her own emotions once her head stopped spinning. There were practical benefits to Corbyn's suggestion, but most of all, Hannah appreciated that he was thinking about her. There might not be any way to guarantee the future, but Mama was right—she'd chosen Corbyn as her husband for a reason. If she had a chance at happiness with any man, it could only be him. "For right now, let's enjoy being newlyweds."

Acknowledgments

Thank you so much for reading this book, whether you bought a copy or borrowed it through your local library. It's very difficult for new writers to break into publishing, particularly in the historical romance subgenre, and I'm aware of how privileged I've been to have published this series. I appreciate everyone who picked up a copy or shared a word of encouragement.

I am perpetually grateful for the support and patience of my husband and children, who have had to put up with my benign neglect while on deadline to make this book happen. I look forward to spending some time with them again!

Thank you to my agent, Rebecca Strauss, and to everyone at Sourcebooks Casablanca for your work to bring this story to life: Deb Werksman, Jocelyn Travis, Sarah Brody, Annabelle Harsch, Jessica Thelander, Jackie Cummings, Emma Grant, Pamela Jaffee, and Diana Schmidt. I also consider myself very fortunate to have received thoughtful copyediting from Diane Dannenfeldt and proofreading from Carolyn Lesnick, as well as the most gorgeous cover from Alan Ayers.

I hope you've enjoyed reading about the Lucky Ladies of London and that you continue to support historical romance authors by reading, sharing, and leaving reviews.

About the Author

Faye Delacour was raised in the Canadian prairies before deciding that she needed a challenge and should move to a place where everybody spoke French. She now lives and works in Montreal with her partner and children, a reformed street cat, and an Australian shepherd, who hasn't yet accepted that he can't herd the cat.

Faye writes historical romance featuring strong, feminist heroines and enthusiastic consent.

Website: fayedelacour.com
Instagram: @fayedelacour